THE GREGORY'S GABRIELLA

by

Len Alberstadt

PUBLISHED BY WESTVIEW, INC.
P.O. Box 210183
Nashville, Tennessee 37221
www.publishedbywestview.com

ISBN 978-1-935271-54-3

First edition, June 2010

Printed in the United States of America on acid free paper.

To my wife and children,
may they always be close

V

FOREWORD

This fictional story was inspired by a woman named Edith
Stein. She was a German Jewess born in 1891. She was an
intelligent and inquisitive young woman who studied at several
universities where her primary interest was philosophy. After
deep contemplation and after reading St. Teresa of Avila's book,
The Life, she was moved to forego her Jewish religion and
convert to Catholicism. Her subsequent study of other Catholic
theologians, especially Thomas Aquinas and Cardinal Newman,
she made the decision to become a nun and in 1933 she joined
the Carmelite order in Köln (Cologne), Germany, taking the
name *Teresa Benedicta of the Cross*.

In Germany Adolph Hitler had just become the new
Chancellor and he wasted little time taking control of all the
levers of power. New, onerous policies regarding the status of
Jews in Germany suddenly became part of the fabric of the
German state. Krystallnacht (Crystal Night), November 9 and
10, 1938 was the watershed event as members of the Nazi Party
lashed out against Jews, smashing and burning thousands of
their businesses and demolishing nearly 200 synagogues across
the country. When it was over ninety one Jews had been killed.

Although by that time Edith had been a Carmelite nun for five years she was still in some danger. Certain aspects of German policy still considered her a Jew. Because of this her Carmelite superiors felt she had to seek better protection, so, they transferred her out of Germany to a convent in the Netherlands. Shortly thereafter, in 1942, the Germans occupied Holland and the Dutch Jews began being arrested and sent out of the country. Catholic Bishops in Holland spoke out publically against this policy. In retaliation for this public condemnation, angry Nazi officials ordered the arrests of all of Holland's Jews who had converted to Catholicism, including Edith, and sent to extermination camps. Edith ended up at Auschwitz where she was gassed shortly after arriving. Her body was buried in a mass grave.

In 1998 she was canonized by Pope John Paul II.

NOTE TO THE READER

The reader will encounter two references in the story to a city located in western Germany. The Germans refer to it as *Köln*, the French, British, and Americans refer to it as *Cologne*. In an effort to maintain a semblance of accuracy I have used both connotations depending on the context. If it is mentioned as the Germans see it, it is referred to as *Köln*, if as seen by the French, British, or Americans, it is *Cologne*.

1

AUGUST 1929
HUMBOLDT UNIVERSITY
BERLIN, GERMANY

Herwald Burkitz closed the door behind him and put down his suitcase against the wall and looked around the dormitory room with its shiny, dark-stained wooden floor on which was a small decorative rug. The room had two beds, two dresser drawers, two desks, and one closet. He walked over to the single window and peered out. From here he could see a large portion of the campus grounds, the walkways and the gardens.

The door behind him opened. He turned around. He saw a tall, slender young man wearing thin-rimmed glasses. He had a high forehead. He bowed slightly at the waist as he greeted Burkitz.

"I'm Klaus Fuchs," he said, and put out his hand.

Burkitz took it. "Herwald Burkitz," he said. "I guess we're roommates."

"May I have this bed?" Fuchs asked.

"Please," Burkitz replied. "This room is a good fit for work I think."

Fuchs swung his suitcase onto the bed. "Have you been to this conference camp before?" Fuchs asked. "I don't remember seeing you last year."

"This is my first."

"Last year was my first," Fuchs said.

"Exciting, isn't it?" Burkitz said.

Fuchs grunted. "I hope Herr Dr. Otto Kessler has thrown off his grotesque political views."

Burkitz frowned. "Kessler the mathematician?"

"The fascist," Fuchs scoffed.

"I am not into such things," Burkitz said. "All I care about is learning more about the new workings of things atomic."

Fuchs threw open his suitcase and began unpacking. "Of course, but all science is done under some political agenda, some social structure. To me it makes a difference. I want my work to benefit decent people, not just the oppressors."

Burkitz thought about that. "This new science will help everyone. It is so beautiful. Have you read Dirac's papers?"

"Elegant work," Fuchs replied. "The English have some good people."

"So do the Germans," Burkitz said.

Fuchs gave Burkitz a questioning look. "What's your family like?" he asked. "Where are you from?"

"Bremen. My father died two years ago. My mother has a small jewelry store there. I have a younger sister, Anna."

"My father is a Lutheran minister," Fuchs told him. "He preaches the holiness of sharing and taking care of oppressed peoples."

"He sounds like a good man."

Fuchs pouted. "Some believe he is too generous and too soft for this new age. They may be right."

Burkitz looked puzzled. "New age?"

Fuchs laughed but it sounded like a disparaging laugh. "Germany's new age. Our country is struggling, haven't you heard? Reparations! The French want their pound of flesh, and they're getting it. It's humiliating."

"We'll get through it. Our leaders will not let us down."

Fuchs laughed a little derisively. "You are naive if you think so, I have to tell you."

"I only want to do science," Burkitz replied. "I can't worry about the other."

"What do you think of the Russians?" Fuchs asked, seeming to change the subject. It caught Burkitz off guard. He hadn't really thought much about the Russians, or their revolution.

Burkitz blinked. "People say they are peasants."

"I think you have no sympathy," Fuchs said, smiling.

"People say they are not like us."

"How so?"

"Where are their scientists? I know of few good ones."

Fuchs closed the drawer to the dresser he had been arranging some of his clothes. He grinned. "Maybe that's why we should help them advance into this new age."

"You feel strongly about this, don't you?"

Fuchs hunched his shoulders. "They could be a force to be reckoned with some day. Stronger than Germany maybe. We should be their friends."

Burkitz frowned, puzzled that Fuchs could think that way. "Russia is in utter turmoil. There is so much killing."

"That will end soon. It has to," Fuchs said. Then added, "It could happen here. The killing."

"Impossible. Germans are too civilized," Burkitz replied.

"One might think. But then again ..."

Later Burkitz finished unpacking. The last thing he did was hang his one jacket in the closet beside his two pair of pants. Fuchs had finished unpacking moments earlier and had departed, saying he had to meet a few friends he had not seen since last year's conference. Burkitz was alone. He went to the window again and looked out. He thought of his good fortune.

The official German committee responsible for organizing this annual summer session in scientific inquiry for teenagers in their final two years of high school had awarded Herwald Burkitz a small financial prize for the paper he had written describing his ideas about the new quantum theory in physics and how it might be applied to the understanding of the nucleus of the atom. He was proud of the effort and that paper, along with his school record; it had earned him an invitation to this conference, at little expense to him.

Ever since he had learned about the marvelous things being uncovered about the behavior of the atom by such intellectuals as Niels Bohr, Werner Heisenberg, Max Born, and Paul Dirac, he had done little else but to think about finding a way to make himself a working part of this growing cadre of thinkers who had begun flooding the literature with their strange and wonderful ideas about nature's deepest secrets. For him, it had been the most recent papers by Paul Dirac that had really gotten him excited and made him begin to think that he, too, might actually make such contributions in this field. Dirac's insights seemed to present a simple and logical description of this whole new field of atomic physics and had made things so much clearer for him. It had been Dirac's papers that had gotten him thinking of how they could be extended. He had wondered whether he was being too presumptuous in believing he, a mere teenager, could really do it. It was his fondest hope to do something similar to what these men had done for this developing science, and make his mark, and begin preparing himself for an exciting life as a scientist. For the past year he had thought of little else and now he was about to take his first serious steps and try to gain an entrance into this fascinating new world of theories, calculations and experiments. But he was smart enough to realize that there was no guarantee he would be successful. The subject matter was torturously difficult and the individuals involved were geniuses indeed. Did he have the courage to considered himself one of these geniuses, he wondered? Was he really as good as he had heard some of his teachers saying he was?

The following evening after a long day of listening to lectures, Burkitz was at his desk. He was going through a formula that one of the lecturers had presented. Fuchs came into the room. His anger showed immediately.

"Kessler is worse that last year. The man has hardened. If there are many like him, Germany will have problems."

Burkitz looked up. "Are there more like him?" he asked.

Fuchs grimaced. "I fear there must be. Somewhere festering inside Germany, waiting to explode and do us all great harm."

"Why are you so pessimistic?"

Fuchs then grinned. "You should pay more attention to things, Herwald."

Burkitz went back to the formula, feeling a little irritated at Fuchs's comment. What did Fuchs think that he was too stupid to be aware of what was happening around him?

"What are you working on?" Fuchs asked, coming closer and peering over Burkitz's shoulder.

"Electron spin."

"Dirac has solved that," Fuchs laughed.

"Only to a point," Burkitz replied. "I think."

"I'd like to see what you come up with; if you actually do come up with something. Can you really improve on Dirac?"

Burkitz laughed. "It's a puzzle I like to amuse myself with."

Burkitz worked late into the night while Fuchs slept soundly on the other side of the room. In spite of his late night toiling over his calculations he was up before Fuchs and ready to head to the first morning lecture and discussion.

"You'll be late," he said to Fuchs who had the covers over his head, appearing that he would never get up. He gave a grunt to Burkitz, then mumbled, "I can't take any more of Kessler."

Burkitz left.

Later that morning Fuchs got out of bed, weary even after all the sleep. Bleary-eyed he went over to the desk and the papers that Burkitz had been working on. He began to follow the calculations; soon he sat down and made a more careful run over the material. Suddenly he became wide awake. The equations looked beautiful; they hung together in amazing coordination, if he was understanding them correctly.

"God almighty!" he said out loud to the empty room.

For the next hour he studied Burkitz's calculations, amazed at the intricacy and the brilliance. With the realization that was growing inside him he began to feel a sense of jealousy. Or was it anger? Almost without thinking he began to copy what he had before him. When he had finished he put the papers into his notebook. As he did, he knew exactly what he would do with them.

The previous year, Klaus Fuchs had met a young German science student just a few years older than himself and had been in communication with him several times since. His name was Rudolph Peierls, and he was presently working under the direction of Werner Heisenberg and Wolfgang Pauli in Zurich. Fuchs and Peierls had discussed certain aspects of the very things Burkitz was fussing over in his formulations. It seemed that today, fate had stepped in. Peierls would be present downstairs that very afternoon. Fuchs wanted to show him the formulation that Burkitz had worked up.

It was early evening when Fuchs got to see Peierls. They went and sat on one the benches just outside the building where most of the lectures were held. Peierls adjusted his glasses as he read the equations Fuchs had presented him.

Finally, Peierls looked at Fuchs. "I think I should show this to Heisenberg when I get back to Zurich. It looks too good, my friend."

"No, no," Fuchs protested. "I want to work on it some more. I'm still not sure," Fuchs replied.

Peierls handed the papers back to Fuchs. "As you wish, but I believe you may be on to something."

Fuchs looked off into the distance. "I'm not sure," he said again.

Peierls studied Fuchs. "How are your politics? You still carry your worries and hopes for the downtrodden? Have you lost any of your fondness for the Russians and their revolution?"

"As I recall, you once had similar feelings for the human condition," Fuchs chastised Peierls.

"I've learned that the best way to help is through our science. I'll help through my science. You should think of doing the same."

Fuchs grinned politely. "Sounds like good advice. Maybe that's the way I'll do it."

2

SPRING 1932
GOTTINGEN UNIVERSITY
GOTTINGEN, GERMANY

Nearly three years had passed since Herwald Burkitz had met Klaus Fuchs. For Herwald they had passed all too quickly, but they had been good years. His life had been nearly perfect. His school work had been well received, and he had been told by his teachers that his future in mathematics and quantum physics would be a bright one. There was even playful talk of a Nobel Prize. His work during the previous three years had been exemplary and, because of that, he had been awarded a scholarship to attend the University of Gottingen.

Unlike his other school, Gottingen was a far bigger place with more demands and more competition. From the very first day he set foot on the universty's grounds he felt a heart-swelling pride. He was one of the elites, at least that's what he had been told. To Herwald's way of thinking, everyone here was an elite.

By now he had grown accustomed to his new surroundings and was not fazed in the least by the increased rigor of the work. He relished it. Each day he gained confidence, both academically and socially. He had made friends and his classes were to his liking. He could not be happier. After today there would be only one more week before the end of the term, and he was looking forward to it. It would give him a chance to get back home to Bremen and see his mother and little sister, Anna.

On this sunny, warm day, stretched out on the campus lawn, he waited for the two people he enjoyed being with more than any other at the university. Fritz Eichenstat and Gabriella Sommers were a few years older than he and, as he saw them, far more educated and sophisticated in the matters of the world. He enjoyed listening to them debate issues. In almost every case those debates ended in total exasperation for each of them. Even so, each would laugh and go their separate ways, until their next encounter which would predictably end with the same good-natured disagreement. The last time that Herwald was been with them they had enthusiastically talked about visiting various countries during the coming summer; France, England, even America. Both Fritz and Gabriella wanted to see as much of the world as they could. This urge to travel was one thing that set the two of them apart from Herwald, whose main interest was mathematics and physics. Although he knew better, he had managed to convince himself that he could do acceptable work right there in Germany. After all, Germany was the center of action in the things Herwald was doing. Why leave? He had no need to travel. Many of the important physicists in other parts of Europe and America came to Germany to work and learn of

German progress; it was not the other way around. Sure, Herwald knew, being able to travel to visit physicists working in other universities and laboratories outside of Germany could be important; but not being able to do so did not prevent him from making his contributions. He could still read the literature to see what the others were doing. But the true reason was money. Herwald had little; his family had little. There was no money to travel. Not so for Gabriella Sommers and Fritz Eichenstat. What few Reichsmarks Herwald Burkitz possessed had to be spent frugally. His mother's jewelry shop in Bremen was making a profit, but only enough to meet routine family expenses.

Gabriella Sommers was a gifted woman, including her ability to speak French and English. Her family had instilled in her a desire to learn, and in doing that they had created a child who read much of the time. She branched out and began reading works in French and English. This reading led to her desire to want to learn of American culture. She learned things about American culture and its unique way it cast the English language when spoken. She was amused by this and collected idioms and foreign sayings. But in language she was no match for Fritz Eichenstat. He knew enough to converse in four languages, French, Spanish, Italian, and English. English was his speciality. It was the one he studied and read the most. He liked English novels. He spoke often of several American authors whom he had read: Melville, Poe, Mark Twain. He had recently read something by a new American writer named Hemingway who had just published a novel about the Great War, *A Farewell to Arms*. Just last week he had told the story to Herwald and Gabriella. This talent for languages came from Fritz's father who, as a successful businessman, had traveled to other countries to secure contracts and he knew the importance of being able to understand agreements and negotiations. On several occasions he had been asked to mediate official negotiations on Germany's behalf.

Languages aside, there was never a meeting of the three of them when some discussion would not break out over some idea or proposal, and almost always it would sink into argument. Most of it was good-natured fun. Often they would speak of their ambitions and dreams, and what each one of them imagined they might accomplish in life. It was all so stimulating to Herwald, and soul-healing comradery. Herwald relished it all so, and he was certain as he could be that Gabriella and Fritz thoroughly loved the combat.

What Herwald appreciated more than anything was that each of them was studying different subjects. He was head over heels devoted to mathematics and the new quantum mechanics; Fritz was pursuing degrees in European history but was reading on his own in archeology and was always fussing that there were no professors on staff who specialized in that subject. Gabriella was the philosopher, always speaking of the beauty and purity of the human spirit and the private joys of the inner self. Herwald felt that her contemplative temperament was more in tune with his own. Fritz seemed to be the kind of person who would charge off like the traditional knights of old, battling some evil enemy. Herwald and Gabriella seemed more inclined to dwell on abstract ideas and were satisfied to use thought processes that formulated themselves intangibly. It was the one thing about Gabriella that drove Fritz crazy. In spite of it Herwald could see that Fritz held a great affection for her and, he guessed, would do just about anything for her. He also guessed that Fritz loved her.

For Herwald, Gottingen was the only university for him. It was known for its mathematic prowess throughout Germany and the world. He kept telling himself that fate had sent him here, or, as he sometimes thought, possibly just luck. He took delight in thinking of the geniuses who had studied and taught here, men such as Max Born and James Franck who were presently teaching at the university. Some who were once here were legendary! Nobel laureats-Max Plank, and Werner Heisenberg; there were so many others. Herwald was drowning in his good fortune to be so close to where such people had studied and walked across the campus as he, himself, now did every day. As he reclined in the soft grass he closed his eyes and thanked God for such a blessing, and as he did a large smile broke across his face.

"You are obviously well-pleased with yourself, Herwald," the female voice said from above him.

His eyes popped open just as Gabriella tossed a book down on the grass at her feet and sank down beside him.

"It's just great to be alive," he said, admiring her near perfect body and radiant smile. It was no wonder that Fritz paid so much attention to her and spent anxious hours watching after her. While Herwald knew that Gabriella thought of herself as a free spirit, making herself completely open and accessible to the world, Fritz saw her as his very special lady who was formulating herself in a world in which Fritz, himself was at the center. Even Herwald could tell that this was not nearly so true a picture. Gabriella was too deep a person, he thought, to be attached so tightly to anyone to the near exclusion of all others. She loved people too much, Herwald knew.

"You are a dear soul, Herwald. So untouched by certain things," she laughed. "Your mathematics have kept you far too isolated." She laughed. "How many times have I said that to you?"

He knew what she meant. Klaus Fuchs had said almost the same thing when they had met that day at Humboldt University. It was true. He did tend to blur over the world of people who seemed to be forever pushing and shoving against one another-the politics of the times; this faction fighting that faction. In his opinion it was all so mercurial. He liked things to be concrete, fixed, and well-defined; well marked off. Mathematics gave him that feeling. But the world that was now evolving around him was eroding his life's anchors and putting too many things in motion.

"Here comes trouble," Gabriella said with a huge grin, shading her eyes.

The tall, distinguished young man came across the grass toward them.

"You two look contented," he said, dropping his body beside Gabriella and spreading it out beside her. His leg brushed against the book she had by her side. He picked it up and looked at the title.

"St. Augustine," he read out loud. "You have descended into religion again, Gabriella?" He then peered at her with a disapproving look. "It will get you nowhere."

She reached out and rubbed his cheek with her hand and smiled playfully. "St. Augustine was once a man like you, my sweet Fritz. He, too, spent his young life chasing the ladies. But he changed his ways and began using his head to think straight. So, there's still hope for you." She laughed.

"I'm only chasing one particular lady," he said, narrowing his gaze on her and grinning.

"Really, who is she?"

Herwald laughed.

"Tell me the truth," Fritz said. "Do you really find something worthwhile in what people like that Augustine fellow and all those other so-called religious thinkers had to say? What did they have to say about the world? About living?"

"That, my sweet friend, is where you miss the boat. St. Augustine and those other 'so-called religious thinkers', as you call them, were not speaking of things of this world."

"God you mean? That's even worse."

"The hereafter," she corrected him.

"I can only live in the here. The after will..." He paused. "What do your Jewish parents say about you poking into that cult religion? Or do they know what you are up to?"

"My parents don't speak for me any longer about such things, Fritz. I think for myself and make up my own mind about my actions, and my beliefs."

"And you're telling me that those Catholic writers speak to you? I'm surprised at you Gabriella. I thought you had more good sense."

"They speak to me more than you know," she replied.

He looked at her hard. "If I didn't know you, I'd say you are about to convert."

She smiled. "And become a nun possibly."

He laughed. "A Jew nun. That's a good one!"

"You think?" she asked.

Herwald thought he detected a resolution in the way Gabriella spoke.

Fritz would not let up. "You love life too much. You love your books too much. You love freedom too much. Admit it, you would never ever spend your life cooped up inside some convent somewhere following someone else's silly rules.

Besides," he said with a serious look, "How would I fare if my best loyal friend was placed out of my reach? I could not walk with you, hold your hand."

"You would find someone else," she replied, eyes sparkling.

Fritz collected his thoughts silently for a moment. "Why do you want to torture me this way with such nonsense about becoming a nun and going to hide away in some old stone building? You'd have to cut your hair and wear those awful, grotesque, shoes and cover that bo-" He stopped.

"I would still be the same person inside," she said.

"Not to me you wouldn't. How could you be?"

Gabriella took on a more thoughtful expression. She seemed to Herweld to be dreaming of some far off place.

Fritz spoke up again. "Don't you ever want children, Gabriella? A husband?"

Without changing her look she replied gently, "Who would marry me? Who would put up with me?"

"Stop playing that way!" Fritz cried angrily. "You know how I feel about you!"

Gabriella returned her gaze to Fritz's face. A friendly caring smile came across her face. "Dear Fritz, I'm teasing you. It is not...Christian. Forgive me."

Fritz found the resources to smile. "Throw that damn book away. Do your professors know you are reading that...garbage? Corrupting your mind!"

Gabriella stiffened. "When you have read it, then you can offer such opinions. You are supposed to be studying to be a scholar who is willing to allow his mind to explore. Shame on you, Fritz."

"There is not a single philosopher here at Gottingen who subscribes to the kind of thinking this...this Augustine peddles," he said. "Name me just one!"

"For once you are correct," she replied. "There are none to my knowledge."

"See?" Fritz replied as if he had won the argument.

Gabriella grinned, appearing to know something he did not. "One day they may wish they had."

Fritz threw up his hands. "You sound like a mystic, you know that?"

Gabriella smiled contentedly, "I suppose I do."

3

1934
CHICAGO, ILLINOIS, U.S.A.

Aristotle Gregory had not always been a wealthy man. He did not start out with a family inheritance. People often said that with wealth came fame. And it was true, the road to Gregory's wealth was strewn with incidents that certainly made him famous, or infamous, depending how one look at it. The popular opinion was that he was a cutthroat. Others said he was merely one of many of a breed who believed that manipulating the truth in order to gain an advantage, or monopolize a position, was standard business practice for men like Aristotle.

As practiced in the years just before and after the beginning of the twentieth century, the workings of big business in the United States was not a game for the weak of heart or for those with queasy stomachs and unblemished souls. Being on top one day and then fighting for your life the next was a state of existence that people like Aristotle Gregory understood well. In making their fortunes they had learned to lived with the danger of this up-one-day and down-the-next dichotomy. Some, like Aristotle Gregory, even relished it.

His sometimes competitor, John J. Rockefeller, understood this, too. In 1900 these two men (and a handful of others) saw themselves laying down the standards and setting the stage for the country's dawning new century. In their minds, a task of such magnitude and importance required that, in a manner of speaking, some throats simply *had* to be cut. Such was the order of nature. Darwinian capitalism was a process that should not be tinkered with and the men who practiced it to its full dimensions held no admiration for the soft hearted - those who recoiled from its seeming ruthlessness, and sought to curb it.

Continued attention to details and scratching out small percentages often made the difference in whether a deal truly paid off, or, sadly, took you down. Often, it was a payoff that came after years of toiling, and anyone playing the game had to have the stamina and intestinal fortitude to hold the field until the final reckoning. To Gregory and the men whose appetites yearned to build empires, recognizing the tiny openings in a potential venture and maneuvering between the political obstructions that might derail it was exactly the kind of work Aristotle and his kind did better than anyone else. The evidence was unmistakable. After so many years of hand-to-hand combat with the forces of this world while navigating its countless pitfalls, the results were in: Aristotle Gregory, along with a handful of like-minded contemporaries, had come to sit astride the nation like giant gladiators surveying the landscape strewn of unsuspecting victims. Gregory and his circle had reached the point where they were ready to claim their rightful prizes.

But, it was the world of such people like Aristotle Gregory that President Teddy Roosevelt had taken dead aim at as the twentieth century had dawned. Roosevelt was no fuzzy teddy bear himself, but he occupied a far different position and had a somewhat different upbringing than had most of the men like Aristotle Gregory. To Gregory's chagrin, Roosevelt was having considerable success in his meddling. Already this president had muffled and whittled away at too many of their advantages and was stifling their priorities. Already the imposing Roosevelt had forced them to alter their ways and was diminishing their advantages at every turn. As a result, one of them, Andrew Carnegie, was shedding large sums of money in order to enhance his name and clear his conscience; evidence that he was beginning to fall to what Gregory saw as a social malady. Others, too, were succumbing to this new sentimentality fomented by the bullying Roosevelt and a growing number of his followers.

Aristotle Gregory was the last holdout, but he was not delusional; he knew that in these times, an adjustment would be forced upon him.

Roosevelt had been too damn competent and too popular a personality to be pushed aside as Aristotle and the others had done so often before to those who had tried to challenge and alter their advantageous positions. As the masses of American people saw it, God was on the president's side, and furthermore, there were far more of *them* than there were of the likes of Aristotle Gregory, John J. Rockefeller, or Andrew Carnegie. Any way you looked at it, the tide of public opinion and the increasing indignation of the masses were carrying them out to the deeper parts of the ocean.

Aristotle Gregory had little choice but to give in and play the new game; but he would just play it with a few twists, that's all.

He wasn't going to go down the same road as Carnegie or Rockefeller, two men who had handed over much of their money and washed their hands of its final destination. That would not be Gregory's way of adjusting to this latest perturbation. Gregory was determined to have *his* money flow through the system in ways that benefitted *his* thinking. The spoils of his labors would not be dispensed without making some kind of contribution that was unique and meaningful, as he interpreted those words. To be sure, his wealth would also flow out to universities, hospitals, libraries, or foundations as had the resources of many of his contemporaries, but Gregory's would contribute by finding ways that respected *his* sensibilities and enlarge *his* image of what the world's order should be. Too much freedom can be a dangerous thing, he always said. If you make it too easy for people they will become weak, and eventually decadent, standing around with their hands out, looking for charity or whining for the easy fix to their so-called problems. Once the country reached that stage, very little progress would be forthcoming, society would begin to decay, then crumble to dust. By his reasoning, people like himself with their special business acumen should be encouraged and protected, not denigrated and despised. They should be bred, and bred again, improving the line. Indeed, if he had anything to do with it, that's what his money would help do. But it would take a special arrangement and a special place, one that was populated by sympathetic and like-minded officials with a mandate and charter to match. If he could not find such a place, he would create it himself.

Under that umbrella of thinking, in 1915 Aristotle Gregory launched *The Gregory Foundation.*

"Bless me Father for I have sinned ..." The words were coming from a pale and aged Aristotle Gregory, who, for the next several minutes, continued pouring out his many transgressions, both those of commission and those of omission.

Silently, just on the other side of the confessional screen, Father Joseph Kuntz listened. He had known Gregory for many years, or at least he had known his family, his wife, and his seven children. He knew that Aristotle Gregory was a troubled man and ready to make peace with his God. Gregory was in a state of near panic because he thought his life had been so unholy and sometimes so destructive to other human beings that he held out little hope that his God would take him back, would have mercy on his soul.

Gregory finished and fell silent, his burden lifted. Father Kuntz could almost hear the sound. He had heard it before as others had unburdened themselves in this traditional sacramental rite of the Catholic Church.

"Am I doomed, Father?" Gregory asked quietly, sadly. "I feel as if I am. Why shouldn't I be after all?"

"You have time to make some repairs to your life, my friend. I am going to give you a penance, but it will be a most unusual one. The again, much of your life has been an unusual life. You are an unusual man." Father Kuntz said.

The old man on his knees listened and said nothing in reply.

"As your penance, in addition to one Hail Mary and one Our Father, I want you to pay a visit to Cardinal Adrien McNamara in New York. I will let him know that you will be contacting his office. Do whatever he instructs."

Gregory blanched, feeling bewildered and surprise. "This... t... this... is my penance?" he stammered.

"I told you it would be unusual."

"But . . . "

"Follow the Cardinal's instructions, my friend."

"I don't understand."

"You will when you speak with the Cardinal," Father Kuntz told him.

"You have my word," Gregory said.

"Good," Father Kuntz replied. He then gave Gregorio absolution and blessed him as he mumbled his Prayer of Contrition. "Go in peace."

With those words, the tiny sliding screen door separating Father Kuntz from Aristotle Gregory closed.

1934
NEW YORK CITY

"Your Eminence."

Cardinal Adrien McNamara put out his hand; Gregory knelt and kissed the ring. The Cardinal touched Gregory's shoulder. The old man got up. "Aristotle, I'm so pleased you came to see me," the Cardinal said with sincerity.

Gregory looked into the face of the man whom he had heard much about. He had read about him in the newspapers. The Cardinal had disagreements with the official Vatican positions on several issues and had been called to Rome by the Pope himself to clarify matters, and to calm the waters, if possible. The Cardinal, according to the Vatican, was sticking his nose too far into politics, both those of governments and of the

Vatican. Word was that Adrien McNamara was "too visible", "too vocal on matters that should not concern him." His statements were causing embarrassment to the recently-recognized independent status of Vatican City.

The Cardinal motioned to the sofa. "Let's sit down."

He and Gregory sat by the window from which Gregory could see the small garden square outside, the line of stained glass windows, and their carved limestone frames that helped form the wall of the church next door.

"Your Eminence I - "

The Cardinal put up his hand. "Please."

Gregory fell silent.

"Aristotle, you have the means to do great service for some of your fellow human beings."

Gregory dropped his eyes. "Your Eminence, I'm afraid I've done little of that in my life."

"Well, you can possibly change that now," McNamara said. "if you accept my offer."

"Please," Gregory said, "Tell me what it is."

"Your life in the business world has provided you with considerable material wealth."

"The source of my present torment," Gregory replied with considerable gloom.

"But we are going to amend that," the Cardinal remarked.

"Tell me. Tell me how."

"You must now use your wealth for a special purpose. You must rearrange your finances and redirect the efforts of your foundation to accommodate a new mission."

Gregory tensed apprehensively. "I'm listening," he said.

"You will be working with the Church in this effort," the Cardinal informed him.

"You mean, the Vatican itself?"

"Well," the Cardinal paused. "Yes and no."

"I don't understand."

McNamara smiled a devilish smile; a smile like a small child might give his parent when he wants to please, but not admit to any wrongdoing on his part. "It's delicate," the Cardinal said to Gregory.

"The mission I'm referring to will be to use your foundation to rescue some unfortunate human beings who are in harm's way in the new Europe that I sense the Nazis are carving out for themselves. No telling for certain where it all might lead but I'm preparing for the worst." He shrugged. "If it doesn't develop, then, well there will be no harm done."

"Rescue?" Gregory asked. "What exactly does that mean, Your Eminence?"

"Get them to safe harbors. Get them out of Europe, away from the Nazis," McNamara said.

"But how?"

"The Church, unofficially of course, has several secret - let's call them 'conduits.' It's as good a term as any, I suppose. There are conduits, and people to staff and operate them through which individuals, let's call them 'the unfortunates,' might be moved along."

"To escape," Gregory said.

The Cardinal smiled approvingly. "Exactly."

"But - " Gregory said, beginning to digest the full picture.

The Cardinal continued. "Your foundation, Aristotle, The Gregory Foundation, with its assets, both financial and human, will be used to help such individuals make their way out from under the Nazis and away from the political regimes that I fear will be growing and increasing their reach in the years ahead. Your foundation should be ideal cover for our plan. For all intents and purposes your foundation will be the chief institution that will officially sponsor our refugee travelers."

"But how? I know nothing about such things."

"I have written out a plan of approach and provided you a list of some key personnel whose credentials fit our needs."

Cardinal McNamara got up from the sofa, and walked to the door leading to the next room, and stood for a moment. A man dressed in a priest's black suit and collar appeared holding a large leather-looking briefcase. The Cardinal took it, came back, and laid it on the table. When he opened it, he took out a manila envelope. Gregory saw the wax-like red seal affixed to the envelope's opening. "This comes from the highest authority, My Friend, but you will find nothing inside that would indicate that."

Gregory took it. He held it with utmost reverence.

"Everything you need to make your arrangements is inside. Guard this with your life," McNamara told him. "Can you do that?"

Gregory whispered, his mouth dry. "I can. I will."

"Lives are at stake."

Gregory swallowed hard.

"God be with you, Aristotle. And remember, you are doing His work, as sure as I am."

Gregory surprised himself by saying, "And if I - fail? Suppose I - "

"I have faith in you," McNamara said. As he did, he rested both his hands on Aristotle Gregory's head and whispered a blessing in Latin.

"You cannot fail, My Son. Remember, God is always with you. He will not allow you to fail. His will be done."

4

1934
BREMEN, GERMANY

"I have been trying to stay out of the clutches of the authorities for several months," Klaus Fuchs told Herwald Burkitz. "My past enthusiasm for the Russian Revolution and the communists has caught up with me. Herr Hitler, our beloved Fuhrer, and his henchmen don't appreciate my attitudes, or the people with whom I associate. They believe my associates and I were behind the burning down of the Reichstag."

"What will you do?"

"I've got some friends in the party who are helping me make my way to France. From there, who knows?"

"I would want to go to England. Study there. With Dirac maybe."

"Maybe show him your calculations; the ones on the electron," Fuchs said. "It's been nearly five years, Herwald. You have done nothing with it? Why not?"

Burkitz shook his head. "It's off the mark," he said.

"You have never shown the work to anyone?" Fuchs asked.

"Never. I was young. I look at it occasionally, but I tell myself it is missing something."

"You're finished with it? Really?"

"My mind is elsewhere now," Burkitz told him.

Fuchs shuffled his feet. He looked down. "Are you going to remain in Germany? Even now?"

"My mother. I can't think of leaving; she needs me," Burkitz told him. "Besides, why leave? Germany is the best place to do the kind of work I want to do. I have little money for travel. Things are hard. I have a small job in a shipbuilding laboratory. Very little mathematics now for me. I read what I can at night. Make some pretty calculations. I wish I could ..."

"I heard what happened to you. You can't beat them, Herwald," Fuchs fumed.

"Some say I got off easy, that I was lucky. I have to be around for my mother and baby sister."

"Things are going to get harder for everyone in Germany," Fuchs said. "For people like me for sure. It's already happened to you. More bad things will come to the Jews."

Burkitz did not address the remark. "If you leave will you ever come back to Germany?" he asked Fuchs.

Fuchs grinned. "Maybe when the Fascists are gone."

"Maybe they won't last. Nothing is forever," Burkitz offered. "They could be voted out next election."

Fuchs laughed sarcastically. "You will not vote in Germany for a long time, Herwald. Steel yourself."

5

Rudolf Peierls had been having mixed feelings about this day. He had not seen Klaus Fuchs for several years, and now that he looked at him across the table he saw that the young man had not changed in appearance. But what Peierls really wanted to know was if the man had changed or mellowed in his political leanings. It could prove important. It was something that concerned Peierls when approaching any of the recruits on his list.

"It's been a long time," he told Fuchs.

"Too long. Both of us here in England all these years, and we never got together until today."

"Now you have a new Ph.D. and are about to go off to work at Edinburgh. A new life, maybe?" Peierls offered.

Fuchs smiled satisfactorily at the thought. "I'll be working with Max Born. A fine opportunity."

Peierls nodded. "You could hardly do better."

"And you?" Fuchs smiled "Professor of Physics at Birmingham. A new life for you, too?"

Peierls nodded. "All thanks to the fellowship granted me several years ago by the Rockefeller Refugee Program. That turn of events saved me for *sure*. It allowed me to work with Bethe at Manchester. And that definitely helped me get the position at Birmingham."

"The Rockefeller Foundation was a salvation for many," Fuchs agreed, then added, "The Fascists are destroying Germany."

Peierls's eyes softened. "How is your family fairing?" he asked.

"As well as expected. At least they are not Jews."

"It is not so with my family," Peierls said, a considerable sadness evident in his voice and eyes.

"It's a heavy burden for you."

"I fear it'll get heavier," Peierls said dejectedly.

Fuchs was silent for a moment. "I guess that Born is caught in the same nasty snare as you and all Jews."

Peierls replied, "Max reached England in 1933, the same year I was scheduled to go back to Germany, the year Hitler came to power. That's when things took a turn for the worse. My stay in England was up and I had no good options. I was scheduled to return to Germany, a less than happy occurrence. That's when the Rockefeller group came to my rescue and awarded me the fellowship. With their help, I was able to remain and study with Bethe at Manchester." He smiled. "Now, you have been rescued, too; to have the opportunity to work with Max Born. Have you met him yet?" Peierls asked.

"No. Next week."

"What will you be working on? Do you know?"

Fuchs shook his head. "Not sure. How about you and Bethe?"

"Alloys," Peierls told him.

"Alloys?"

"James Chadwick was the one pushing for the program. You know Chadwick, I believe?"

"Yes."

"He came to see me at the Mond Laboratory, where I was working on superconductivity and doing a little work on liquid helium, too, when he recruited me to the Alloys Project."

"Will you continue your same work when you take up your professor's position at Birmingham?"

Peierls smiled, but didn't answer the question. "Maybe I'll look into electrons. I have a young colleague who once had some innovative ideas about their behavior," he teased playfully. "Maybe I'll go back to it."

"That was a long time ago."

"Yes, but from the little I could tell there seemed to be some real meat on the bone with those early calculations of yours. It seemed to be good thinking."

Fuchs grimaced. He shrugged and tried to deflect the remark. "I guess I could pay it another visit."

"I'll be looking forward to learning what you come up with."

6

FEBRUARY, 1939
BREMEN, GERMANY

The front showroom of the small jewelry shop on Humboldt Street was dark. Thin curtains covered most of the front window, concealing the almost bare display cases inside. It was a visible testimonial to the dismal financial state of the establishment's owner.

Herwald Burkitz sat at a table in the room immediately behind the showroom. The room served as a kitchen and eating area for the Burkitz family. Herwald's younger sister Anna stood at the stove, waiting for the water in the kettle to reach its boiling point. It was almost supper time.

"You say this man came to the shipyard?" Anna asked her brother.

"He came and sat at my table at lunch time."

"He is an American? Are you sure?" Anna asked.

"He speaks like one; seems to be one, yes."

"You have to be careful Herwald."

"His name is Sabastian Arceneau and he said his foundation wants to find a place abroad where I can study. Maybe even America."

Anna reacted harshly. "Herwald!"

"I know. I told him I couldn't possibly leave Bremen. Not now."

"Mamma is sick. She needs us," Anna fussed.

"She is dying," Herwald said softly, his voice trailing off sadly.

"And the doctor does not know how long it'll be," Anna added, speaking in hushed tones.

"I told him all that. I told him I could not leave."

"And still he is coming here to talk? What kind of man is he?" Anna huffed in a loathing tone.

"He wants to meet you."

"What in the world for? What possible reason?"

Burkitz shrugged.

Anna Burkitz turned back to the stove. "He is a cruel man to tempt you with such things."

"Maybe you should prepare some small meal for when he arrives?" Herwald said.

Just before seven o'clock when Anna Burkitz answered the knock at the front door she faced a tall man dressed all in black and carrying an umbrella and briefcase in the same hand. He tipped his hat.

"I am Sabastian Arceneau, and you must be Anna," he said.

She curtsied slightly. "Good evening, Sir. Please come in."

She led him inside and into the back kitchen and dining area. "Herwald is in the back with Mother. He likes to be with her when she has her meal."

Arceneau now had his hat in his hand and he placed it on the wooden rack; he put his umbrella and briefcase against the wall.

Anna thought Arceneau looked nothing like the image of the typical American she had gotten from the pictures in the many magazines she had read. On the contrary, Arceneau looked more like a British aristocrat. He seemed too refined in his manner and overall appearance to be an American, she thought.

The door behind Arceneau opened and Harwald Burkitz came through carrying a tray on which were several dishes and a glass and one vase with a flower in it.

"Hello, Mr. Arceneau," he said immediately. "You had no trouble finding our place."

"No trouble, no trouble at all. I'm rather familiar with Bremen."

Anna took the tray from her brother.

"Please, sit down," Birkitz said to Arceneau. "Is dinner about ready, Anna?"

"In a moment."

During their meal Arceneau talked about the Gregory Foundation and how he had come to work for it. He told them several stories about what he, himself, had been doing the past few years as he worked to fulfill the spirit of the Gregory's mission.

"I tend to freelance sometimes," he described. "Some of the other members of the Board of Directors get aggravated with me on occasion because of how I stretch things." He laughed. "Makes them nervous."

Arceneau did most of the talking. Herwald and Anna listened.

Arceneau's words and descriptions of the possibilities swirled in their heads. But things in Germany had changed and, for Jews, ideas of leaving were fleeting thoughts, a distant hope, if that.

Both Anna and Herwald spoke their doubts. Too much seemed to stand in their way.

For his part, Arceneau deflected all of their arguments although mildly conceding the legitimacy of their concerns. But he was persistent.

"Herwald, suppose I could get you a post in England?" Arceneau asked.

"What kind of position in England?" Herwald asked.

"Oh, for sure an academic position. You have much talent with numbers, Herwald, but you are not a bookkeeper, you are a mathematician."

Herwald's eyes fixed in the distance, his hopes rising. "A university?"

"Or a research laboratory. You have the required university training."

"But Anna and Mother would be here, alone."

Arceneau frowned. "It's a hard decision."

That's when Anna surprised them. "You must go, Herwald. I can care for mother."

Herwald stared at his teen-age sister.

"You have so much to achieve with your mathematics. You have been deprived for too long. Mother would want it this way."

Herwald wanted to cry. He then said to Arceneau, "Let me tell you the story."

But Arceneau surprised them by saying, "You gave the Nazi what he deserved. He was assaulting your mother. We all know what his intentions were." Looking over at Anna, he said, "You have a very brave brother."

She replied softly. "Mother was at the shop alone. It was a good thing that Herwald returned from the university for a visit when he did."

Herwald interjected; his tone showed his sadness. "I had just received word that I had graduated with high honors and had been admitted to advance studies at Gottingen. It's the only place I wanted to enroll. I wanted to rush home and tell my family of my good fortune."

"But your good fortune ended when you beat up the Nazi who was trying to rape your mother," Arceneau said.

"It was my bad luck that he was a local high official of the party. With influence." Burkitz muttered. "Beaten by a Jew no less!"

"Bad luck indeed," Arceneau agreed.

Herwald spoke with a slight choking sound. "I had just gotten the opportunity I wanted so much. To study with Professor Bore, Max Born. And then, because of my actions against that animal, it was taken away. I was dismissed."

Arceneau smiled. "I know Professor Born."

"Shortly after my dismissal Professor Born left Germany," Herwald said. "Do you know that?"

"He's in England," Arceneau replied. "My foundation helped him with his financial needs in 1933. It gave him the means to remain there, working. Rather like the Gregory Foundation wants to help you, Herwald."

Herwald sat silently, thinking: could he actually do what Arceneau was proposing?

Arceneau broke the silence. "Give me a few days to work some things out. What I have in mind might help with your decision."

Herwald smiled wryly, "A freelance," he said.

"Exactly," Arceneau replied.

Three days later Anna Burkitz once again answered a knock at the door of the jewelry store. It was an unexpected sight. She had never been this close to a nun before and she felt a strange sensation of awkwardness as the figure in black and white loomed in front of her.

The nun said, "You must be Anna Burkitz."

"Yes, Madame," Anna replied.

"I am Sister Katherine from the convent in Cologne. The woman's voice was smooth and rather lyrical, and surprisingly comforting, Anna thought. "I am here at the request of Mr. Sabastian Arceneau. May I come in?" she asked Anna.

"Oh, cer - tainly. You say Herr Arceneau?"

Sister Katherine smiled. "Some of us at the convent have known Sabastian for several years now. The convent has a ... relationship with him, or should I say with his foundation."

"About Herwald? About Herwald leaving?"

"Indirectly," the nun said. "He asked that I come speak to your mother."

Anna frowned. "Mother?"

"Your mother is here?"

Anna looked to the back room. "She is, yes."

The nun took on a compassionate expression. "My religious order is one devoted to medicine and to the caring of the sick. Sabastian informed us that your mother is ill and in need of care."

Anna's head dropped. "It is true, but Herwald and I take care of her."

"No doubt, but Sabastian believes there are other considerations to be concerned about," Sister Katherine said. "We probably don't have much time. Things will turn bad very soon, I fear."

"For us they are already bad."

Sister Katherine smiled reassuringly. "There is still time, but we cannot waste what we have."

Anna sounded uncertain. "You must excuse me. We must be very careful these days. You say you want to help, but why? We are Jews. We are not of your faith."

Sister Katherine showed no reaction but replied rather flatly. "So much more why we should help," she said. "Please, may I speak with your mother?"

Anna hesitated a moment, turning her head and looking at the back doorway for a brief second.

"Is she back there?" Sister Katherine asked.

"She may be sleeping."

There was a rustle and a voice that came from behind Anna. "I'm awake."

Sister Katherine saw a frail, gray-haired woman appear. She had eyes depressed deep into her head, fixed within dark, round sockets in which the surrounding skin looked like it had been smudged with charcoal. Sister Katherine went to her.

"Mrs. Burkitz, you shouldn't be up - not just yet anyway. Let me help you." She took Hilda Burkitz's arm. Through the nightgown she could feel the near fleshless condition of the woman's arm.

Hilda Burkitz gave Sister Katherine a weary, sad-looking smile as if even the smile was a movement that caused pain. Her eyes looked deep into those of the nun. "If you carry any special power my dead lady, I wish you to leave some of it with us."

"Any powers I have come from God, Mrs. Burkitz. I do what I can as His conduit."

Hilda Burkitz smiled again but this time it seemed she did so more to herself. "And your God was a Jew," she said.

"Indeed he was," Sister Katherine replied.

Hilda Burkitz sighed. "Yet for so long we have been at odds with each other."

"All of us are not at odds," Sister Katherine said.

"Too few to really make a difference."

"We cannot change the world all at once," Sister Katherine said. "As Saint Teresa instructed, to each little task of our living we must expend our maximum efforts. That is all God expects. Most of our lives are successive incidents of tiny endeavors, leading us to Him."

Hilda Burkitz moved toward a large cushioned chair whose cloth upholstery was well worn and dingy. She let her body fall into the chair. She grimaced and adjusted herself as best she could.

Sister Katherine wasted little time. "We want you to come live at the convent. We can care for you there."

The expression on Hilda Burkitz's face showed her surprise.

"You are puzzled, I'm sure," Sister Katherine said.

"I am fine here at my home. My children ... "

"Of course you are, but we can help your children as well. They may need our help more than you."

Anna came over and stood beside her mother's chair. "Help us how?" Anna asked the nun.

"You may need special papers and a good story if you are to leave the country. Sabastian is the man who can help when it comes to such things."

"Leave? I cannot leave. You can see that," Anna argued, her face showing her high emotion.

Anna's mother patted her daughter's hand in a calming gesture. "Permit the lady to explain, Anna."

Sister Katherine replied, "I do not know all the details but Sabastian and his people have ways. It has worked on other occasions. But there are things that have to be done, and your mother being cared for at the convent is one of them, an important one I might add."

"You will excuse me when I say I am confused," Hilda Burkitz said.

Sister Katherine drew closer. "Your residing at the convent under the care of the nuns makes it easier confusing the authorities that you are not Jews, but Catholics. When necessary it helps authenticate the papers one needs to get out of the country. It could provide believable answers for loose ends if an unfortunate incident arises and some eager bureaucrat begins checking too closely. That's all I can say about it. We have to be careful. It is dangerous to do the things we are doing."

Hilda Burkitz shook her head and looked at Anna. "Sweet Anna, would you leave us alone so that I might talk to this kind lady."

"Mamma?"

"Be a good girl. Go pay a short visit to your friend Freida. Just a short while."

Anna was gone a little over an hour. When she returned Sister Katherine was gone and her mother was back in her bed.

"You and Herwald will need the help of this nun and their priest," she told her daughter. "I am going to the convent tomorrow. You and Herwald will remain here until ... "

"Until when?" Anna asked.

"Until it's arranged for the two of you to leave," she uttered in a grated voice. "The time is close," she added.

"Things might get better," Anna said.

"I have been reading the newspapers, I have heard the radio. Our crisis is deepening, my dear."

"Oh, mother, what will happen to you if we are not here for you?"

Hilda Burkitz gazed on her daughter. She spoke with great sincerity and meaning. "There is little you can do for me now, sweet child. You have already done what God expects of you. Now you must think of yourself and see to your own well being. Herwald must do the same."

7

AUGUST 2, 1939
BREMEN, GERMANY

The three-story, ornate, gray-stoned building at the junction of Wandrahm and Contrescarpe streets looked much like any other building in this part of Bremen. For being so close to the middle of the city the entire layout of buildings and surrounding acreage was an ideal arrangement. For one thing, there was sufficient parking space off the street.

To the people of the neighborhood they were unsure about only one thing: how much of the business inside was civilian in nature and how much military. Like just about everything nowadays whatever it was it was surely controlled and managed by the Nazis Party.

It was noon. On the second floor, in a large office with a spacious window that faced the street overlooking the canal,

Major Fritz Eichenstat was reading over the file that Sergeant Markus Pond had laid on his desk bright and early that morning. Pond was a stickler for having things in good order and he always arrived early to have things ready for Eichenstat. The file Eichenstat was holding was an astonishingly revealing dossier on Sabastian Arceneau. Arceneau was a man Eichenstat and his security agents had begun keeping tabs on over the past year. In doing so, Eichenstat's operatives had done a modest job of monitoring Arceneau's movements throughout Germany, but his knowledge of Arceneau's movements elsewhere were blanks in the dossier.

On one level Eichenstat knew what it was that Arceneau was up to; on another level he was not sure just how he was able to do it so successfully. Eichenstat could not figure the man out completely but he wanted to in order to make his own personal plan work better. From his actions Arceneau seemed to show little concern that his movements were likely being monitored; he made little move to hide his travels. Eichenstat could only conclude that Arceneau functioned as he did because he knew he was being monitored, but didn't care. Why should he, he worked for the Gregory Foundation and was not officially attached in any way to any military or governmental espionage operation. Whether he was *unofficially* attached to some such organization was another question, and that was what Eichenstat would like to know.

But Major Eichenstat had another very private reason for wanting to learn more about this man. He was beginning to sense that, one day, he might need the man's expertise for a personal undertaking. In this Eichenstat knew he was working both sides of the street.

For the past six months Major Eichenstat's operatives had been telling him that Arceneau was tied into the Catholic

Church's involvement in the clandestine enterprise that was making it easier for certain Jews to slip though the Nazis' grasp and make their way to places where the Reich could not easily get at them. They also had a poorly defined list of suspects who, they thought, belonged to a band of clergy inside the Catholic Church who were using its labyrinthian maze of traditions and support institutions to help Arceneau. Or, was it the other way around? Eichenstat's superior, General Reinard, was pushing for more action from Eichenstat and his command to disrupt and close down these enterprises. His orders were clear on that.

Back in 1934, in the early days of the Concordat between the Vatican and the Third Reich, things were not as they were today. The Church and its clerical officials in Germany had abided by the conditions of the treaty when it was in its infancy. Now, however, it was clear that things had ramped up. Eichenstat felt that some elements in the Church were making plans to move into new territory when it came to aiding those who were seen as the enemies of the Reich. Eichenstat, in obeying Reinard's order, had decided for his own reason to center his attentions on the various convents throughout his district. Convents and monasteries were the area he had specifically requested when Reinard had given him a choice of assignments. His reasons were known only to himself. For the next few days he had his sights of the Carmelite Convent in Köln.

Eichenstat now found himself playing two separate roles but had to make it appear as if he were playing only one - the one officially sanctioned by the Reich, the one under the command of General Reinard and the one Eichenstat had taken an oath to obey. His other role involved a more personal enterprise; it was one Eichenstat had also sworn an oath to uphold and protect, but that oath was one taken long ago, and had been given to another authority.

Major Eichenstat stretched his neck and hunched his shoulders in an effort to get rid of the stiffness that had settled in. He closed the file. His mind focused, thinking back over how it was that he came to know of Sabastian Arceneau in the first place, but he was now thankful that he did.

Sabastian Arceneau's name had come to him from a high official in the Catholic Church inside Germany - the Apostalic Nuncio in Berlin, Cesare Orsenigo. Eichenstat knew that Orsenigo had close contacts inside the Vatican and had let it slip that there was a man whose communications were sent and received under the name *Crimson*. It was through *Crimson* that Orsenigo suspected Arceneau 's double line of occupation. Orsenigo, however, maintained he did not know *Crimson's* true name, or position.

Eichenstat leaned back in his chair. His thoughts focused on his upcoming visit to the convent in Köln.

8

JEPTEMBER 1, 1939
KÖLN, GERMANY

It was mid afternoon in Köln and the main building of the Carmelite convent stood with its front entrance bathed in filtered sunlight beneath a canopy of trees. Patches of sunlight danced on the surfaces of the old building's gray stone walls. Inside Sister Katherine hurried down the corridor heading for the office of Sister Marie Magdelene, the Mother Superior. She knocked lightly on the door.

"Come in, Sister."

She entered, closed the door gently behind her and faced the woman behind the desk. She looked older than her fifty three years but still retained a rugged, tenacious look about her.

"Sister Katherine," the Mother Superior said, "You have taken to your special assignment with great enthusiasm."

"Thank you, Mother."

"It seems as if only you have the way with our military protectors." She accentuated the word *protectors*.

"Thank you, Mother Superior."

"You seem to have a special way with Major Eichenstat."

"He is an old acquaintance," Sister Katherine told her. "Is it possible that you find some fault with him?" she asked warily.

Mother Superior replied, "I have observed the way he looks at you. It is the look of a ... suitor in a way," she said. "But I know that can't be the way you see him."

"Certainly not," Sister Katherine said.

"You say he is an old acquaintance?"

Sister Katherine suspected what Mother Superior might be thinking.

"Gottingen, the University, years ago."

"You were close friends?"

Sister Katherine smiled. "He wanted to marry me."

"And you?"

"I think in my heart I had already made my commitment to Christ, Mother."

"You are an especially talented woman, Gabriella. The Lord knew what He was doing when He sent you to us, and to this work. But be careful. This is all such dangerous business."

"I will Mother Superior."

"And I fear it will become more dangerous. I just received word that the German Army has invaded Poland."

"Oh, no!"

"It is true. This Hitler is a stain on our country. I do my best to be charitable, but I cannot find it in me to like this fellow."

"He has brought harm to some of my friends at Gottingen and to friends elsewhere," Sister Katherine said. "Jewish friends especially, even my family," she added with a sound of sadness. "Many of the professors at the University left long ago, after the Civil Service Laws were enacted making it illegal for them to hold their faculty positions. Only a few remained. No telling what will happen to them."

"Speaking of Jewish friends, how are our charges inside the convent holding up?"

"Mrs. Burkitz is declining steadily. Some of the others ... well, many have broken spirits. We need medical supplies, a regular doctor would be a Godsend. Young Anna Burkitz longs for her brother, Herwald. He is in England, studying."

"I believe Germany's invasion of Poland will be the last straw for the British, and the French too, perhaps. No telling what will happen to us now; what will happen to those we have as guests. Anna will likely not join her brother in England now."

"We must not forget that our convent is sacred ground, Sister. Our guests will remain our guests," she said resolutely.

Sister Katherine remained silent momentarily, then said, "Mr. Arceneau believes convents and monasteries might not always remain off limits to the Nazis."

Mother Superior's body sagged slightly. "I know. He has informed me of the possible outcomes and what we must do if those times come. We shall count on you, My Dear, if such troubles ever come to past."

"I shall do whatever is necessary, Mother. I have vowed to God that I would. And I have prayed for guidance."

"You are a saint, My Dear, I wish I could be like you. You will one day become the Mother Superior of this convent......no, of the entire Mother House. The Holy Father himself will acknowledge your work someday."

Sister Katherine smiled awkwardly. "The Holy Father will never hear of me, I'm certain of that."

"I will have a very hard time sleeping tonight," the woman said.

"As will I," Sister Katherine replied. "As will we all."

9

OCTOBER 30, 1939
BREMEN, GERMANY

Like almost every German officer, Fritz Eichenstat had known that there was a good chance that the invasion of Poland would bring on war with France and Great Britain. Now that war was upon them things were changing in his world. He had received word that he would be promoted to the rank of Colonel, and with that he might acquire a larger jurisdiction to oversee, and his responsibilities would increase. He would have far more authority than he now had. He would answer only to General Reinard directly

In the two months since the invasion of Poland there had been little military ground response from either France or Great Britain. He knew it would heat up soon enough. In the meantime he had to get on with his new assignments and one of those was to make a complete accounting of all the convents, churches, parish houses and monasteries throughout western Germany. He was also to prepare a report showing the locations of all such facilities in the countries to the west of Germany and the status of their inhabitants. The war would become larger, he knew; there would be other invasions and other conquests for the German military, other places he would be expected to administer in the same way he was now doing in North Western Germany. He also thought he knew the reasons for his new directives. It was already known that such places were becoming "safe havens" for refugees for all sorts of undesirables, as the Reich was describing them. Fritz Eichenstat knew this was a euphemism that was primarily aimed at Jews and those married to Jews, but it also included gypsies, the insane, homosexuals, communists, and sometimes the Christian clergy and their lay followers. Those who showed only lukewarm support for the Reich could be targets. There could be bad times ahead for such people. He thought of Gabriella. Images of her had been blazoned in his mind for a long time; he thought of her often, too often. He had seen her several times since she had become a Carmelite nun and each time it was painful for him. Being both a nun and a Jew kept her from him. Now, because of his new directive, she could be directly in his line of fire. His hand was being forced. He would surely be paying her a visit soon. She was a Jew housing other Jews as well as other individuals of questionable attributes, as the Reich directive described them. He was dreading the certainty that he would be the official overseer of any operations designed to cleanse the western country of such hiding places. He called for Sergeant Pond.

"Congratulations, Major," Pond said in a hearty voice.

"Or should I address you as Colonel?"

"Thank you, Sergeant. Olease note in my appointment book that I'll be away for a few days," Eichenstat said.

"Your destination? In case someone asks."

"Köln," he said.

"Will I drive you?"

"I'll go by rail. A more comfortable journey."

"Much more," the Sergeant replied. "Have a safe trip."

"Thank you, Sergeant. That will be all."

"Heil Hitler," the Sergeant saluted, and left.

Fritz Eichenstat stood there soaking in the gloom that he felt was beginning to surround him.

10

THE FOLLOWING AFTERNOON
THE CARMELITE CONVENT
KÖLN, GERMANY

The Mother Superior of the Carmelite Convent, Sister Magdelene, received Colonel Fritz Eichenstat in her office. He made her nervous; it was the uniform, the boots. He, himself, had striking features, clean cut and sharp. His eyes showed a depth that she admired in people, His face had a slightly ruddy complexion and his shaven face still showed a trace of beard. His uniform was well tailored and fit him expertly. She knew he was in his mid-thirties. His voice was pleasant and calm; his manners cordial.

She offered him a chair by the fire some slight distance from where she sat behind her desk.

"I must tell you, Colonel, I know why you are here," she said outright, as directly as she knew how.

He drew back slightly.

"You ... have me at a disadvantage, Mother Superior."

"Oh, I very much know why," she repeated.

He frowned.

"It's Sister Katherine," she said.

"We are old friends," he said. "I'm sure she has told you."

"She has."

"I have other business here, I'm sorry to say. Business that has nothing to do with Sister Katherine."

"And what might this business be?"

"I have orders to survey ... certain establishments to determine if the people living in them are well cared for and properly looked after, just in case..."

"In case of what, Colonel," Mother Superior asked deliberately with piercing, narrowed eyes.

"We are a country at war, Mother Superior. The Reich has an obligation to protect and care for its citizens. It cannot do that unless it has reliable information just where they are living, and how many there are, and who they are."

She stared at him disapprovingly. Her wits told her to appear conciliatory and accommodating but she just could not. "I too have obligations, Colonel," she then said.

"And I'm sure they will not interfere with those of the Reich," he replied.

She hesitated. Was he trying to goad her, she wondered. "Sadly, the Reich and the Church don't always sing from the same hymnal, Major, as you well know. However, each has a different sphere of responsibility, if you know what I mean."

"The Church in Germany cannot interfere with the Reich in many matters, Mother Superior. The Concordat lays out all that rather clearly. The Vatican signed and agreed to it."

"I have read the document, Colonel. I assure you I know what it stipulates, and what it does not," she replied.

He nodded politely.

Then she added, "I also know the things that persons such as I are obligated to do."

He frowned. "Are you implying that you have an obligation to stand in the way of the Reich's duty to protect its citizens? Do you believe you are exempt from the conditions of the Concordat. You are willing to go against the will of your own Pontiff?"

She smiled ever so slightly. "A conscience is so often a troubling thing with which to contend, is it not?"

He broke into a broad grin. "You sound so much like Gabriella," he said.

"Sister Katherine is a fine nun, a dedicated servant of God. You should leave her to that."

"Did she tell you that?"

"No, I'm asking."

"I cannot give up my friends that way, abandon them."

"I thought as much. Very well, I'm telling you before I tell her. I am going to give her full and complete authority in dealing with you and your Reich in matters of this convent. When it comes to such a thing she is a much wiser head than I. In making that decision you should know that she will have the full authority of the Church behind her."

"You have made an honorable and wise decision. May I see her now?"

"Tomorrow. She and I will have to have a talk before then. Besides, it is late and our hour of prayer before evening meal is nearing. You will forgive me for not inviting you to take part but the sisters might not understand. We cherish our one daily time together and besides we have our special rituals which I'm sure you have no desire to be subjected to."

He stood up. "I will see you tomorrow then, in the morning."

"No earlier than ten o'clock. Sister Katherine has her duties."

"He bowed. "Certainly, her ... duties," he replied.

As he began to leave he turned and asked, "Is Gabriella ..." he stopped. "Is Sister Katherine allowed to leave the convent?"

"Anytime she chooses provided all her duties are taken care of. No one is a prisoner here, Colonel."

THE FOLLOWING MORNING
KÖLN, GERMANY

When Colonel Fritz Eichenstat entered the office of Mother Superior it was Gabriella who greeted him.

"You frightened Mother Superior yesterday, Colonel," she told him directly before any friendly greeting.

"Please, Gabriella, we are friends. Do we need to speak to each other in so formal a manner?"

"You want me to address you as Fritz?" she asked with little emotion.

"It is my name," he said.

She smiled slightly, briefly. "Very well."

"Mother Superior told me she was ... directing you to be the person to act for the convent in its dealings with the Reich."

"She has."

"She has made a wise choice."

"We shall see, won't we?"

"Prudent decisions and proper behavior by you could save your convent from harm," he told her. "There's no telling what is coming down the road."

"I think we both have a pretty good idea what is coming down the road and won't be anything to make us happy," she predicted.

He dropped his eyes then said, "My duties and authority have been greatly expanded, Gabriella. It comes with my promotion to Colonel."

She nodded. "Congratulations. And how will you use your new authority?"

"I have a duty, Gabriella."

"A duty to whom? The Reich, or to those human beings who ..."

"I want *you* to be safe," he interrupted emotionally.

"I am safe."

"No you're not!" he stressed in a raised voice. "And neither are the others."

"The others?"

"You know who I mean."

She was silent. "I see," she finally said softly. "It is God's will, I suppose."

"Oh stop that!"

She did not react to his outburst.

"I want you to meet someone," she then said. "Wait here."

Several minutes later she returned. With her was a young girl whom Eichenstat judged to be about fifteen years old with her. "Colonel, this is Anna Burkitz. She's Herwald's little sister. You remember Herwald surely."

Fritz looked at the young girl. He could see the facial resemblance to Herwald.

"Hello, Anna. Your brother and I were friends a long time ago, at the University in Gottingen."

"They made Herwald leave the university," she said.

"Yes, I know," Fritz said. "Herwald is a very smart person."

"I miss Herwald. I was suppose to go away to where he is now but ... maybe ... Sister Katherine says I may not be able to do that now."

"Can you keep a secret?" Sister Katherine asked.

"Yes, Sister."

"Well, the Colonel and I are working on a way that will allow you to be with Herwald in his new home."

Fritz's head jerked around, staring at her with a startled look.

"You are!" Anna screeched. "It's like you always said, Sister. I've been praying so hard."

"You must not be too happy just yet, Anna. We are not yet sure we can make it happen, you understand. It could be some time but we wanted you to know that there are people who are doing all they can to help you. But times are difficult now, you understand."

"Yes, Sister, but having hope is a good thing. To have no hope is an awful feeling. It was so with my mother. You said so, remember?"

"Yes, you are right," Gabriella said sadly, peering sideways at Fritz from the headdress of her habit. "Now, would you please let me talk to the Colonel in private. I'll see you later. Hurry back to your studies."

Anna curtsied and left, closing the heavy door behind her.

Fritz glared at Gabriella. "Why are you telling her such things! Why get her hopes up?"

"She needs to have hope. I am Herwald's friend. His mother was here sick and she came here to the convent to ... rest and ... recover. She died several weeks ago. The child needs to keep her spirits up."

Fritz's appearance softened. "Does Herwald know about his mother?"

"He does," she said.

Her words made him give here a very hard, frowning look. "You are a very clever woman, Gabriella."

"Not clever enough to outwit the Reich's top official in charge of ... convents," she said with a look of determination.

"I'm not seeking to hurt you, Gabriella."

"I am only one person, Fritz. There are so many others."

"What are you getting at?"

"A bargain," she said.

He eyed her suspiciously, then said with all seriousness, "For you I would make almost any bargain."

"I'm glad to hear it. I will tell you my conditions tomorrow at this address." She reached into the inside pocket of her habit and brought out an envelope. "You will have no trouble finding the place. Tomorrow at seven in the evening."

"Evening? You can leave the convent at such an hour?"

"Of course. What do you think we are prisoners in here?"

"I ..."

"The sisters can get permission to leave," Gabriella said. "Our guests, on the other hand, are not so fortunate. They leave the convent and their lives are in jeopardy, am I correct?"

"Gabriella please."

"I'll see you tomorrow, Fritz. Let me walk you to the door."

At the door he reached out his hand. She took it.

"Until tomorrow, Gabriella."

Gabriella was up much of the night, unable to remain asleep for any appreciable length of time. She said the Rosary and once again asked for guidance, but she already knew what course of action she would take.

11

THE FOLLOWING DAY
KÖLN, GERMANY

It was late afternoon. Carrying a small bag, Gabriella left the convent through the back door and took the back streets in a roundabout route to the address where she was to meet Fritz. It was only three blocks from the convent. The street was deserted when she turned the corner; a single automobile went past her as she walked to the house. She unlocked the door and went inside. She turned on the small, dim light in the front room. She then went upstairs to prepare. She had an hour or so to wait. When she had finished her preparations she knelt down to say the Rosary. She wanted the Holy Mother to speak to her, woman to woman.

It wasn't long before she heard an automobile pull up. She went downstairs and over to the window and peered through the curtains. Fritz was standing in the street beside the taxi, looking around. He handed the driver the fare and the taxi drove off slowly. Fritz came to the door and knocked.

"It's open Fritz," she called but not too loud.

He did not immediately see her, his eyes strained in the dim light of the room, searching the opposite side of the room away from where she was standing. His eyes quickly found her.

The expression on his face left no doubt of his great surprise. "Gab ... riella?" he said quietly, yet with unmistakable wonderment.

Neither one of them moved. She said, "We came so close to this in years past, Fritz. It may be time to consummate our friendship in a more intimate way before it is too late. The world has overtaken us."

The expression on his face showed his puzzlement.

She walked toward him, her eyes fixed on his. As she did so she said, "You must promise me that you will protect my convent and those it takes in as its guests."

He threw his hat on the chair. "Do you know what you are doing?" he whispered.

"I do," she replied.

"But you are doing it for them, not for me."

"Fritz, I am truly torn in my feelings."

"I don't want you this way," he pleaded. "I want you to ..."

"Love you?"

"Yes, yes but you have gone off and done this nun thing. I've been sick over it for years, thinking of you."

"It could be that I've made a mistake," she offered.

He looked at her questioningly. "A mistake?"

"There are times when I think of you, and of this," she confessed truthfully.

In her preparations upstairs she had changed from her habit to a soft light green cotton dress with short sleeves. She had managed to find some shoes that were close to the latest style. They were a little too small and they hurt her feet. She put her arms around his neck. "Like old times," she said.

She kissed him. At first he just stood there but as her lips worked against his and her body pressed tighter against his and her thighs meshed with his he quickly gave way and put his two arms around her and embraced her hard. Her lips parted. She could feel the heat of his face close to hers. He pulled her tight against him. Her soft cotton dress covering her bare body underneath was no insulation to mask every curve and elevation. His hands moved up to her head and he caressed her hair, short as it was. She drew back slightly and looked directly into his eyes "I have prepared a place for us in the bedroom upstair."

He held back. "You are a nun," he uttered.

"I am also a woman. You can't have any doubts about that, My Dear Fritz."

His head was swimming. "But you are still doing this out of a duty to some other ... cause, or some ... other ..."

"I'm sorry Dear Friend, but that's where my life stands at the moment. We have to take our days as they are, one at a time."

"And us? How many days do we have?" he said harshly.

"As many as I can spare you, but in your position you will be the one who has a great deal to say about that." As she finished speaking she kissed him again, this time much more passionately. She felt his anxiety rising. It was then that she once again asked God to forgive her. It seemed all she could do at the moment.

Gabriella and Fritz met this way at that same house every time Fritz could arrange his schedule so as not to raise suspicion among his superiors and the others with whom he worked in Bremen. Gabriella, for her part, always brought an extra element of love-making and a sense of caring that pleased him. Every time they were together he asked her to abandon her sisters in the convent, give up the life she was leading, walk away from the Carmelites, marry him.

She shook her head and scolded him. "The Reich would not appreciate you marrying a Jew, Fritz."

He knew full well, more than most, having her as a wife was a dream that he could only wish for, never act on.

"They would crucify you," she added on one occasion. "Your wife would be a 'second-degree' Jew, and what do you think that would do for your status?"

He cursed the air, angry and frustrated, knowing there was no answer to his dream. What he had now was all he would be able to have as long as the two of them were in Germany.

"But by remaining in your present position you have great power to help; help me, help others," she always asked, always insisting.

It was torture for him. His only relief was when they were tangled up together in their love-making. What pleased him most about these times was the womanly way she responded to him, not at all in a way he imagined a nun could respond. He was surprised that nothing he initiated in their love-making seemed not to please her. Her movements and her words all seemed unmistakable signs to that effect. In fact, at times she behaved almost as a well-seasoned courtesan with every intention to please him in the bedroom. What he wouldn't do to have her always this way.

But their meetings were always all too fleeting. He always wanted more but she always told him that her trips away from the convent had to be planned judiciously. She always had to return at a respectable hour and with some small item or story about her travels. Being away from the convent so often this way would have been unusual under her former condition of Sister Katherine, but now that Mother Superior had given her to total responsibility of dealing with the officials of the Reich in matters concerning the convent it was easier for her to mask her travels, always labeling them as business with the Reich.

One day in her cell, early in the morning, Gabriella awoke before the usual hour. Perhaps for reasons known only to God she sensed that something about her was different. She lay there, praying to God, asking for His forgiveness. The feelings remained. They were in her head, she knew. It was nothing physical that she could tell. But she suspected, nonetheless. The voice in her head told her she was pregnant. Somehow she just knew it was a true voice. God's will be done, she whispered. In the weeks ahead some unmistakable symptoms might develop, she thought. Then she would know. She would know as a woman. Feeling these things, she did not panic.

It was a possibility she had considered. Fritz, however, had not. He wanted her love so much and so intensely that on their every encounter he devoured her with ravishing abandon. His fully naked body plunged with hers until his exhausted final moment pulsed through her insides in great vibrations of triumph and jubilation. No, she knew she was not mistaken, their child was growing inside her. She lightly rubbed her hand back and forth over her belly. Was it a boy or a girl, she wondered.

Then the awful thought hit her. Would Fritz see her condition as reason to run away from their agreement to help protect the convent and the people inside? Other convents and churches were beginning to feel increased pressure. Hers had somehow escaped and she contributed that good fortune to Fritz. But, now, would all that change? Should she even tell him about her condition? He would almost certainly propose that she have an abortion. For her, that was out of the question. She would die before allowing that to happen. She would have to tell Mother Superior and although she *thought* she knew how the woman would take the news she wasn't absolutely certain. A pregnant nun was almost certainly something Mother Superior had never faced before, especially a pregnant Jew nun. It could certainly bring a new circumstance to the convent. She had several more months before her secret would be hard to conceal but there could be a chance someone would discover her condition earlier than that. She would have to be careful. In the meantime she had to plan. She would continue seeing Fritz but what began to rumble around in her mind was the agonizing thought that the eventual end to all this could be calamitous. Her desperate course of action had produced an unusual, if almost predictable, turn.

12

JANUARY 10, 1940
BREMEN, GERMANY

Things were now building inside Fritz Eichenstat's command. Early that morning he had been handed several new directives. For weeks he had sensed they were coming. It closed the circle. He was now in the middle of something as odious and as repulsive as anyone could imagine.

He opened the door to his office and said to Sergeant Pond at his desk.

"You and I are going to Köln to make an inspection of the Carmelite convent there."

"When, Sir?"

"Is my car ready?"

"Always, Sir."

Early that afternoon Eichenstat stood in the office of the Mother Superior while Sergeant Pond waited outside in the hallway. He watched Sister Katherine approach and go into Mother Superior's office. Seeing Pond, she knew Fritz was inside, waiting.

"The Colonel is here to check on our patients and school children," Mother Superior said.

"I must see how well they are doing," Fritz said."

Gabriella nodded, peering at him. "Very well."

"My Sergeant will assist me," Fritz said. "He keeps some of my records."

For the next several hours Gabriella, Fritz, and Sergeant Pond moved through the convent, going from one room to another, sometimes stopping by a bed to take a look at the person, but saying little, if anything. The Sergeant stood always behind them and not too close. Occasionally the Colonel would ask for his briefcase, take out some papers, read quickly through some material, write something, and then put the papers back into the briefcase and handed it to Pond.

Fritz and Gabriella barely spoke to each other. When Garbriella did speak it usually was to describe various aspects of the endeavors that took place in the room in which they stood or tell him something about the occupants who were housed there. It was nothing but a walking tour of the premises which he had been on before. But this time it was different. He was making a final check to see just how he could maneuver the records that would get into the files at headquarters. At one particular stop Gabriella glanced back at the Sergeant standing a good distance away; she then came closer to Fritz and said, "You should have informed me that you were coming."

He replied quietly. "I was ordered to come this very morning by the Man himself. Seems someone has an interest in Herwald Burkitz's little sister."

"Gabriella's whole body stiffened. At that moment they were standing beside a small girl about six or seven years old. She was shaking, her eyes were riveted on the Colonel; they suddenly flashed a look of desperation at Gabriella. Gabriella put her arm around the little girl and pulled her close to her. The girl wrapped her arms around Gabriella's leg and buried her head in her flowing habit.

"It's all right, Liesel. Would you like to tell my friend what we have been talking about?" Gabriella asked her with a smile. "Go on, please. I'm sure he'd like to hear it."

Fritz bent down. The girl showed her face partially from behind Gabriella's long habit. She stared wide-eyed at Fritz.

"I'd much like to hear it," he said to her. "Please tell me."

Hesitantly the girl began. "Sister ... has been telling me stories about ... St. Augustine," she said.

Fritz threw Gabriella a quick glance. "And what about St. Augustine?" he asked the girl, abandoning his look at Gabriella and returning it to the girl.

"How he changed his life so much," she told him.

Again Fritz's eyes went briefly to Gabriella. He smiled. "Yes," he said, "I have heard these stories about St. Augustine myself."

Fritz then caught sight of Sergeant Pond who was now standing over by the wall some distance away from him. He had a curious expression on his face as if he were in the midst of struggling to solve a puzzle. He was looking over the large room at the many people concentrated across the way; some of them in beds. Pond could tell that they were in a shaky state, with many of their faces drawn into a near ghost-like countenance. Their eyes, more than anything, seemed to reflect their depressed state of mind. Pond knew fear when he saw it. Children hung around the outer limits of the beds; they were quiet. There was hardly any noise of any kind, only low hushed mumbling and some soothing reassurances coming from those who were attending to those who were bedridden. The scene gave Pond the impression that every person, both children and adult, was on watch, as if a tiger lurked in the bushes and they were waiting for it to lunge out and devour them. Their eyes kept jumping from watching him to looking off at the Colonel who had moved down to the end of the long room. Pond saw no smiles on their faces

Fritz said to Gabriella as they walked farther down the long room and farther away from Pond.

"Take me to see Anna Burkitz?" Fritz said to Gabriella.

"You say someone is interested in her? Who? Why?"

"Don't know," he replied. "But I believe what I have heard is real and she could be in danger."

"You cannot forget your promise, Fritz."

"You believe I have?"

She hesitated. "No. I'm sorry."

"You seem to want me to be like Augustine. Well I'm no saint! I'm just a mere man with no ambition to be a saint."

She did not reply.

He looked at her. "Would you think I could become a saint, Gabriella?"

Once again she did not reply.

He turned away from her, "Let's go see Anna."

As they entered Anna's classroom the children's nervousness was evident immediately as they stared at Fritz in his uniform and his black, heavy boots. As he walked around he asked a few questions of the children and then gave a personal account of some of his days as a schoolboy. After leaving he and Gabriella made their way to the front door of the convent.

"I hope you found no irregularities, Colonel?" Mother Superior said as she passed them in the long hallway.

He smiled. "None, Mother."

At the door Gabriella said, "Thank you, Fritz."

"One final thing, Gabriella. I suspect Anna receives letters from her brother so tell me how they arrive?."

For a moment she was puzzled.

"How do they get here?" he persisted.

"They ... just come."

"Here's how I believe they get here," he said. "Once the Gregory gets them from Herwald they come to the Vatican to the Apostolic Nuncio in Antwerp Belgium and then across the border to a church in Aachen and then to this convent," he told her. "The man coordinating and directing this at the Gregory Foundation is named Sabastian Arceneau. He has visited this convent at least three time the last time he was in Germany. The Gregory Foundation and the Catholic Church are working hand in glove in this endeavor. I suspect you, yourself, are deeply embedded in this." He stared at her. "Well, what have you got to say for yourself? And for my analysis?"

She studied him. "What if it's correct?"

"If I am going to help Anna, and any of the others, maybe even you, I have to have confirmation about this."

"Go on."

"I must have you verify that I am not overlooking something."

She waited for him to continue.

"You don't trust me, Gabriella?"

"I don't know all of the details. Sabastian Arceneau does not say any of the names. He alone knows them all."

"For security," Fritz said. "I suspected. Have you ever heard the name Konrad Schroeder?"

"No. Who is he?"

"A priest. A priest who takes big risks."

"You know him?"

He eyed her. "Soon, maybe."

"Be careful, Fritz," she said.

He wanted to take her in his arms, kiss her. He startled her when he said, "Don't tell Anna but you may like to know that I am hoping to get her out of Germany."

"America!"

"England. To be with Herwald."

"Is that possible?"

He shrugged. "I'll be back in touch when I have more information and more details. In the meantime continue all your routines as you have all along."

"Including the time I spend in the house on Lortzingplatz?" she asked in a soft voice.

He replied sadly, "That must stop." He opened the heavy wooden door. "I'm surprised you aren't pregnant already."

She watched as he walked away.

13

JANUARY 12, 1940
BREMEN, GERMANY

Colonel Fritz Eichenstat knew that the Reich and the German military were preparing to move quickly. The military push would come in earnest soon - a few months at best. Could he get his plan moving before it was too late? How did he get into this miserable situation? He knew the answer to that one - he loved Gabriella. He had no choice but to try what he was planning. It may work if all the stars and planets were aligned in his favor, he told himself, grasping at straws sort of. If not ... well, his life could be over.

Colonel Eichenstat and Sergeant Pond were now on their way to Aachen

Fritz Eichenstat was pensive as they drove. He sat with his eyes closed. A sudden rumbling noise made him open his eyes.

The road was now crowded with military trucks carrying troops and material. Pond slowed the car down and pull in behind one of them.

"Something big in the works, Colonel," Pond said.

Eichenstat looked drearily at the truck blocking their movement. He already knew what it all meant.

"What do you think, Colonel?" the Sergeant asked, eyeing him through the read view mirror.

"More maneuvers," Fritz replied dryly. "Possibly."

"The ranks are full of rumors," Pond said. "There's an offensive coming."

"Armies are always full of rumors," Eichenstat hissed. "You know better than to believe them."

"Everyone says it will be a short war, Colonel. The French don't want to fight. The British are good fighters sure, but they are a tiny island, no raw materials to make war, really. Almost all their materials have to be shipped in. Our U-boats will prevent that. The Fuhrer has that figured."

Fritz Eichenstat eyed the man through the rear-view mirror. "The British have conquered almost half the world at one time or another, Sergeant. What do you think they did it with, timidity, cowardice, and ignorance?"

The truck ahead of them pulled off and headed for the trees where others were already parked. With the road open ahead the Sergeant pressed down on the accelerator. An hour later they were driving through the outskirts of Aachen. Fritz had spent the past few minutes thinking of Gabriella, as he so often did when he had time to push all his other worries aside. He visioned her warm, sensuous body beside him. God, he missed that.

"Where to, Colonel?"

"St. Nicholaus Church," he told Pond. "Minoritenstrasse and Grasskolnstrasse intersection. It's near the market place in the center of the city. Keep straight, we shall come to the church soon, on the right."

The ornate church came into view. They drove up and stopped. The church had a small building which served as the living quarters for the pastor and other priests, if assigned there.

"Return for me in an hour, Sergeant," Eichenstat ordered.

He got out of the car. The front door of the building opened and a man came down the steps and walked toward him. From his collar Eichenstat knew he was a priest.

"May I help you, Colonel?"

Eichenstat thought: this priest knows military insignias it seems.

"I'm looking for Father Konrad Schroeder. I'm Colonel Fritz Eichenstat."

"I am Father Schroeder. I am the pastor of St. Nicholaus. How may I help you?"

"Well, you're the man I came to see."

"Is this a spiritual call?"

"No."

"I didn't think so," the priest replied dryly.

They began walking back to the building.

"What makes you say that?" Eichenstat asked.

"You have your driver with you."

"You have a sense about you, Father."

The priest nodded. "An attribute of human survival."

"You sound like a naturalist, not a priest."

"I could be both?" Father Schroeder said.

Fritz smiled. "I bet you are a chess player too."

"No, don't know the game at all."

"Really," Eichenstat said, eyeing the clergyman.

"Now what would you think of a priest who deceived? That could be contrary to my calling."

"Really."

"Without a doubt," the priest replied.

Fritz realized that this priest could not be easily intimidated and did not appear to be worried to see a German officer show up unexpectedly asking to see him.

They reached the building and went inside, up the steps

"Now, how may I help you, Colonel?"

A heavy table dominated the space in the living room, ten chairs with straight backs and upholstered seats were positioned around it. On the table were several stacks of papers.

"We just had our monthly parish meeting," Father Schroeder said.

There was a high cabinet against the far wall. The wall opposite the cabinet had two windows, each with heavy, dingy-looking drapes with faded red and purple flowers streaming throughout. Several lamps and upholstered chairs sat around the room. Two walls were nothing but bookcases filled to near capacity, books of all sizes and conditions, many with their titles in gold embossed lettering on leather bindings.

Father Schroeder went over to the fireplace and put a fresh log on the fire. He agitated the new assembly with a poker, nursing some larger flames to life.

The priest was a tall man with a reddish complexion and the beginning of grayness in his short hair. Fritz had noted the way he handled the heavy log. He had noticed the priest's hands as he worked; they were large and appeared to be heavily calloused. This man, Eichenstat sensed, had seen his share of manual labor.

Father Schroeder had spent several years in America studying at Notre Dame University in 1926 and 1927 and, according to the information Eichenstat had on the man had gotten himself into quite a bit of mischief the several times he visited Chicago. He had gone there often and, once, even got himself arrested for his efforts. The offense was uncertain, according to what Eichenstat knew.

The priest offered Fritz a seat in one of the upholstered, cushioned chairs while he, himself took the other.

"Maybe you would like a little Schnapps, Colonel?"

Fritz waved his hand. "No thanks. I'll get right to the point, Father. I've come here because I know what business you are in and I want to see if there might be a way you might assist me in a matter extremely important to me."

"You need spiritual advice, Colonel?"

Fritz smiled. He shook his head. "You are a parish priest and a spiritual advisor, true, but you are more than that. The new Germany has provided you a new vocation."

The priest's eyes studied Fritz as he pondered his words. "Really?" he asked eventually.

"I have not come here to bring an end to your activities or to arrest you, I assure you."

"You are certain you are addressing the right person in this matter, Colonel?"

"Do you know a man named Sabastian Arceneau?" Fritz asked, clearly stunning the priest. "Don't deny it, Father. You do work with the man. I need to get in touch with him. It has to be private and I have to be very careful. Can you help me."

The priest didn't reply. Some of the color had left his face but it was quickly returning.

"You can trust me, Father. I am not here to trick or deceive you. Like I said, I need your help."

"Hypothetically, what is it that you are trying to do, Colonel, that you believe that I, or this man you call Arceneau, can help you with?"

"I want to move a package."

"To where?"

"America."

"When?"

"As soon as possible."

"Just one package?"

Fritz thought for a moment. "Maybe several."

"All at the same time?" the priest inquired.

Again Fritz thought. "Whatever offers the best chance of a successful arrival," he said.

Father Schroeder studied Fritz's face with a steady, unflinching stare. "What might be the purpose of this hypothetical transport?"

Fritz was not sure what he should say about this. He finally said, "An obligation to a friend," he muttered.

"Humor me, please. Describe the package, or packages," the priest asked calmly. It's all hypothetical anyway."

"Female, fifteen years old, another female, thirty."

"Related?"

"No.

"That's all?"

Fritz hesitated. "The latter is a nun," he said, watching the priest for his reaction. He saw none. He then knew why this man was good at what he did.

"Why do these packages have to be shipped?" the priest asked.

Again Fritz was hesitant. "They're Jews," he told the priest.

Once again there was no mistaking the priest's reaction to hearing that bit of news.

"You say one is a nun?"

"Correct. A convert."

"Unusual," Father Schroeder remarked.

"She's an unusual woman. I believe she is going to be in real danger. If not immediately then in a year or two."

Father Schroeder sat thinking.

"Where are the packages located at the present time?" he asked Fritz.

"Köln, in a convent there."

"Let me ask you a very personal question but I have to ask it. You are not related to either of these packages, correct."

"Just ... friends," he uttered.

"Friends, yes."

The priest eyed Fritz. "Your interest is quite commendable in these times. I have another question, please. You describe this nun as an unusual woman. Did you know her before she became a nun, before she converted?"

"We were students at the University of Gottingen almost a decade ago," Fritz said.

"When did she become a nun?"

"Is that important?" Fritz asked.

"No, I guess not. I just assumed she was not a nun when the two of you were students at Gottingen; maybe not even a convert yet."

"She was neither," Fritz told him.

Father Schroeder said deliberately, "You are taking a real chance with this, you know. You must understand my bewilderment at your actions in this matter given your military position, which I am only guessing at because you have not told me anything about what your duties are. Tell me, what is your present assignment?"

Fritz described his duties and where he was stationed and some of the directives under which he was beginning to operate.

When he had finished the priest said, "You are facing a true dilemma, Colonel. Many of us are these days, I'm afraid. This whole business is going to get real nasty real fast unless people like you stop it."

Fritz tried to appear strong and determined as if the priest's challenge was off the mark, although deep down he knew the clergyman was not.

Father Schroeder then said, "Is it possible for me to see the packages to make some measurements about particulars needed for the transport?"

"I don't see why not if you think it is necessary, but I wish you would not say anything to the nun about her being one of the packages."

The priest looked very puzzled. "What is the problem?"

"She sees herself as the savior of her convent. She will not leave."

"So why have her leave?"

"She's ... in danger."

The priest narrowed his stare. "You love her, Colonel?"

Fritz's head jumped. "No!" he said. "No. She is a friend and I want to help her."

"Sounds as if she might not accept your help. She has obligations that maybe you don't appreciate."

"She is stubborn," Fritz said. "But you have to not say anything to her of our intentions."

The priest thought for a moment. "Because all this is hypothetical I'm not sure how I should proceed, but I'll think it over and come up with a hypothetical plan and let you know. But I must tell you something. The woman, the nun, has a right and a duty to make up her own mind in this matter. It's a matter of conscience, and conscience is a sacred thing, you understand."

Fritz nodded.

"In case the need arises, how shall I contact you?"

Fritz was ready for the question. "Call this number and say you have a report regarding installation 133. In our records your church is installation 133."

The priest glared. "Unsettling. We Germans are now spying and collecting information on each other. How hideous."

"I'm sorry," Fritz said with little enthusiasm.

"It will come to no good."

Fritz did not try to argue the point. He could not. He knew the man was correct. Things had gone too far. He stood up and bowed slightly to the priest. When he reached the door he turned and said, "What about Mr. Sabastian Arceneau?"

"Let me handle the hypothetical Sabastian Arceneau. You will have to accept my judgement, sorry."

Fritz nodded and turned and walked away. He had not gone very far when the priest said, "It took real courage to come see me, Colonel."

14

A WEEK LATER
JANUARY 20, 1940
AACHEN, GERMANY

Father Konrad Schroeder was no novice at this. Inquiries about Colonel Fritz Eichenstat and the story he had told him were in order. For this he had only one trusted source: Konrad von Preysing, the Bishop of Berlin. The man Schroeder had to stay away from was the Vatican's Apostolic Nuncio in Berlin, Cesare Orsenigo. Father Schroeder had plenty of evidence that Orsenigo was an admirer of Adolph Hitler and a bit too sympathetic to the Nazis regime to be approached. Schroeder had been informed that Orsenigo, or someone in his office, had suspicions about Schroeder and his 'after-hours' activities.

Father Schroeder's inquiries revealed quite a bit. The first and most important thing was that there was not just one

Catholic nun who was a convert from Judaism, but two, and they were both approximately the same age. However, one of them had already left Germany, having been sent to another convent in Holland for her own safety. The other nun had to be the woman Colonel Eichenstat was concerned about. She was a Carmelite nun living in Köln. He had the address of the convent. He also had the woman's name: Gabriella Sommers; she had taken the name Katherine.

What he learned about Colonel Fritz Eichenstat didn't greatly surprise him. Somehow it fit him. His was a family involved with the political happenings in Germany going back to his grandfather. There was also a healthy sympathy to Germany's military but there was no indication of any of the fanaticism that had now overtaken many aspects of it. Eichenstat had a brother, twelve years older, who had been killed in the Great War. His younger sister had died in the big 1918 influenza epidemic when Eichenstat was eight years old. With her death it meant that Fritz Eichenstat was the only remaining child. In 1933, after his university days were completed, he went into the military. After finishing the required preliminary training he was assigned to an ill-conceived and poorly defined intelligence unit. It was there that Eichenstat had developed his abilities to create schemes and plant false information to mislead. It became known as counterintelligence operations. His record was such that he received advancements regularly and was now seen as a highly efficient officer and a master of deceptions and ruses. He was also a man who would take risks, Schroeder had been told.

15

FEBRUARY 1, 1940
THE CARMELITE CONVENT
KÖLN, GERMANY

It snowed overnight in Aachen and the surrounding region and it slowed Father Schroeder's trip to the Carmelite convent in Köln. He found it comforting to sit in front of the large fire in Mother Superior's office. He rubbed his hands and let his body bathe in the heat.

"I received the letter from Bishop Preysing, Father," she told him. "I informed the sisters last night at supper."

"They understand?"

"I believe so, yes."

"Good."

"Your trip here must have been a tiring one, the weather."

"I'm fine," he said. "The fire is good."

"We have a custom, Father. Visiting priests, if they have the time, are asked to hear confessions. Is that possible?"

He pursed his lips. "Of course. Tell me when?"

"In our chapel, after you have refreshed. I'll inform the sisters."

Mother Superior left. A few minutes later she returned. "May I show you to the room we have prepared for you, Father?"

As the two were on their way to the room Schroeder said, "Tell me, please, in your opinion which of your nuns is the most unusual, the most outstanding?"

"That would be Sister Katherine," she replied immediately.

"You sound definite. No hesitation."

"She shines on many fronts. I will introduce you."

"No, no not just yet. Possibly at the evening meal."

"As you like. I'll tell the sisters you'll be in the chapel to hear confessions. In an hour?"

After unpacking his few belongings he walked through the convent, observing, saying little to anyone, nodding to those who passed him. When the time came he went to the chapel and quickly went to the confessional. There was one nun kneeling near the front by the altar. She did not turn around as the sound of his footsteps beat lightly through the chapel. He took his seat in the confessional. He kissed his sacramental stole and placed it around his neck. For a moment he peered through the open door at the nun, then closed the door. Soon he heard a faint creak of the wooden pew in the church as it yielded to the release of pressure as the nun got from her knees. He then hear her footsteps and the sound of her entering the confessional. He waited a brief moment and then opened the sliding door. He kept his eyes straight ahead, slightly shut, listening. He then heard her voice.

"Bless me Father for I have sinned. It has been ... several months since my last confession."

Immediately Father Schroeder thought this odd. Normally, the nuns' routine was to go to confession more often. Perhaps there was no priest available, he thought. But surely Mother Superior would have said something about that, if it were the case.

"Sister, has there not been a priest visit the convent to hear confession in all that time?"

"Father Phister comes regularly," she told him.

"I see. Go on, please. I'm sorry I interrupted you."

The woman let out a heavy sigh.

"Are you all right, Sister?"

"I have committed a grave offense, Father. A mortal sin of an unforgivable nature."

Father Schroeder stiffened slightly. The trembling voice of the woman just two feet away from him made his heart sink. She was deeply troubled; there was no mistaking that. What could he tell her?

"I doubt that your transgression is unforgivable in God's eyes, Sister. Don't be so hard on yourself." He then hesitated and wondered if he should ask what he was about to ask. "You have not murdered anyone, have you?"

"It could be worse than that," she startled him by saying. "I have violated my vows," she then told him.

"And how exactly have you done that," he asked her.

"I ... I'm pregnant," she said, her voice choking badly.

The revelation shook Father Schroeder but his years of hearing confessions had conditioned him to not be too shocked at the things he was sometimes told. This being a nun made for a difference, however. He recovered but he knew his silence would truly disorient and humiliate this poor woman who was clearly trying to find some acceptable path by which to navigate this heavy, almost unthinkable burden.

"Please, tell me how this happened, Sister. Just the generalities. Let me judge what questions to ask you about it. First, let me ask you, are you certain that you are indeed pregnant. Have you seen a doctor?"

"I'm certain, Father. I have not seen a doctor."

Father Schroeder thought for a moment, considering the possibility that the woman was somehow misreading her symptoms.

"How old are you, Sister," he asked her.

"Thirty years old."

Father Schroeder thought to move to another aspect of the exchange.

"Does the father know?"

The nun sniffled. "Excuse me," she apologized. "He does not know."

"Who is he?" he then asked her. "Can you tell me?"

"What good would that do?" she asked. "I was hoping you would ask God to forgive me of this sin and give me some peace. I have asked Him for guidance, but I need His forgiveness."

"If you could tell me more about the father I might be able to help."

"No one can tell him," she insisted. "You can't. You have a solemn oath. If you do it'll be a greater sin than the one I have committed. You have a most sacred obligation."

"So there is no danger in you telling me, is there?" he said. "I shall not tell him; you will have to do that yourself, My Child. That obligation is on you, I'm afraid."

She said softly, sadly, reluctantly, "Yes."

"Can you tell me something about him. Is he in a position to help take care of the child? What occupation does he have?"

"He's ... a German officer," she said. "A rather high ranking officer."

Father Schroeder's entire body stiffened and then he slumped. All his thinking seemed to evaporate; everything suddenly was jumbled. He did his best to recover, and continue. He heard the nun's voice.

"Father?"

"How do you know such a man? How did you meet him?" he was able to ask, having recovered his composure enough, although there was still a haziness fogging his brain.

"He comes to the convent to inspect. It's part of his duties," she told him.

"What do you think will happen when you tell him?"

The nun hesitated. "I ... don't ... know. But I'm frightened for him. It could put his life in danger."

"How could his fathering a child put his life in danger. You did say he is a German officer, rather high rank?"

"Yes," she said. "But ... I am a convert from Judaism, Father. I'm sure you can see the implications for him in that."

Father Schroeder instantly opened his eyes and jerked his head so that he was looking straight through the mesh of the wicker screen of the confessional's sliding door. He could not contain himself. The word came out too quickly.

"Gabriella?"

Gabriella's head popped up and she looked straight into the face of Father Schroeder. The wicker screen of the confessional could not hide either of their faces. Their eyes fixed on the other.

"Gabriella," Father Schroeder said again, this time more softly, sympathetically.

Tears began flowing from her eyes and down her face. Her eyes quickly turned a rubbery red color, her cheeks flushed bright red.

All of a sudden there were footsteps outside. Two nuns had entered and were making their way to the front of the chapel and were passing the confessional. Shortly after came the creak of the wooded pews the two were entering in the front of the chapel.

"Gabriella," Father Schroeder said, "I am here on a special mission that concerns you. We must meet later to iron out a few things. Other people are involved. Now say an Act of Contrition."

She began the prayer. "Oh, My God, I am ..."

As she was speaking Father Schroeder pronounced the words that his church proclaimed bestowed absolution and forgiveness of the transgressions she had willingly unburdened herself of. When she had finished he said to her, "You must come see me. It is imperative, now more than ever."

She did not respond.

Father Schroeder then said, "It will be your penance to come see me before I leave here tomorrow." He knew she could not ignore his wishes when he put it to her that way.

"Yes, Father."

Father Schroeder took the evening meal with the nuns. More then once he had his eyes on Gabriella at the far end. When the meal was over he thanked the nuns for a fine dining experience and lively conversation. He then announced that he was going to the chapel to say his evening prayers and then to his room where he hoped he would have a restful night's sleep.

Not too long after, in the chapel, he had almost completed his prayers when she came in. He felt the wooden pew give way as she sat down, then slipped forward and kneeled and crossed herself. She did not look at him. He said nothing, allowing her to stay concentrated in her prayer.

He heard her sob, then sniffle. He pulled out his handkerchief and held it out to her. She took it. In another minute she crossed herself and sat back in the pew, breathing a heavy sigh.

"Now tell me the whole story," he said. "It's important that I know. You are not alone. I'll tell you why later."

She relayed her story as best she could. He asked few questions. As she finished she said, "I thought I was doing the only thing I could. It was all I could think of to do. But ... things changed. I didn't expect to ... I don't know why ..."

He thought he knew to what she was referring.

"Do you love this man, Gabriella?"

She frowned. "How is it you know my name?" she asked, staring at him hard.

"Because I have met Colonel Eichenstat," he said. "The father of your child."

"Oh!" she cried. "Oh!" She began to sob. "Poor Fritz."

Father Schroeder let her cry. After a short while he said, "You said that things changed. Do you mean that you came to love this man?"

She shook her head and said softly, "That would have been too easy."

"What then?"

She smirked. "I found that I enjoyed the pleasures of being in bed with a man."

She kept staring at him, waiting.

"Are you waiting for some kind of denunciation from me?" he asked questioningly. "God made you a sensitive and caring, loving human being, Gabriella. Why should you not feel pleasure and joy in such a human relationship. Where is it written that it is wrong and sinful for a wife to be erotic and find pleasure in her lovemaking?"

She frowned; her look puzzled. "You are a strange priest," she said.

"Would Father Phister say anything other than what I have told you?"

She paused. "Maybe."

"Well, I cannot disappoint you. I am telling you what I believe to be the truth. My conscience is clear."

Suddenly she smiled. "But you are forgetting one thing, Father. It may be fine for a wife to be the way you say but I am a nun. I am the wife of Jesus Christ. I have my oath to prove it."

"We are not dealing with that. We are dealing with your femininity here. You found out that you enjoy sexual relations. It's who you are, Gabriella. You are God's creature. Are you saying that in His making you this way he made a mistake? That would be blasphemous, don't you think?"

She was silent.

"Think about it. It's the only rational conclusion. Your enjoyment is not a sin."

"But my vows?"

"You came to your course of action after giving the whole thing good, solid, honest consideration. You prayed. You asked for guidance; and then you decided in good conscience to carry on in order to help your fellow human beings who happen to be in a great deal of danger and in desperate need of help, help that many of them look to you to provide. I doubt God will find a way to condemn you for having acted the way you did. Decisions like that are not easy to resolve in one's heart. In a way, you could look at it in light of what Jesus said: No greater love has a man than to lay down his life for another."

"But what do I do about this baby?" she then asked.

He replied immediately. "We shall have to find a suitable course of action. Let me think about it. You keep doing what it is you have been doing. One thing for sure, you'll have to have a doctor examine you, provide you with some help. You have to stay strong."

"But ..."

"Yes, I know what you are probably thinking," he said.

"My condition will become noticeable eventually."

"It will, but we will deal with that in good time, before anyone can see your condition. We have a few months at least.

Your habit may give us a little longer. Your physical condition will not be all that noticeable."

"I worry."

"Of course. But I must tell you of another reason for my visit here," he said. "I want you to tell me about Anna Burkitz."

"Anna? Why?"

"Please?"

Gabriella gave him a brief description, telling him of Anna's life and her qualities as a human being and her affection for her brother, Herwald, now in England.

"Colonel Eichenstat believes she is in some kind of difficulty, maybe danger, because some governmental official has an interest in her, but he doesn't know what that interest might be. Do you?"

"No."

"Well, we'll have to wait on that for now," he told her. "But I still would like to see her tomorrow."

"That is no problem."

"Well, we are making progress," he said.

She hesitated, then asked him, "How did you meet Fritz?"

"He came to see me," he told her.

"What did he want?"

"To help you and Anna."

"How?"

He remembered that he had promised Colonel Eichenstat not to tell Gabriella the exact plans of what they were trying to do

"He wants to get Anna to America. He thinks the two of you could achieve that, or he used to think so. He realized that he, himself, might not be able to pull it off, so he came to see me. You see, he knows the business I am in."

She shook her head. "That's what he meant," she said, reflectively, remembering their conversation in the basement of the convent. "He said he wanted to get Anna to America and he said he thought he knew how. He must have meant you."

"But he doesn't know of the baby," he reminded her. "When he learns of it I'm certain he'll insist that you go with Anna."

"I couldn't!"

"You may have no choice," he said.

"I'm needed here."

"With the baby? Gabriella, your baby is in danger too. His baby."

She hung her head. "What have I done," she said remorsefully, dejectedly.

They talked a little longer but they were both drained of energy from the day. They soon left the chapel together. She headed up the stairs to her tiny room. He went down the hall to the room that Mother Superior had provided him. As he was undressing and preparing for bed he thought: Colonel Eichenstat you have handed me a very thorny challenge.

The following morning Gabriella took Schroeder to meet Anna Burkitz, although Gabriella told him that the convent rolls carried her as Anna Bumgartner. The priest was relieved to find Anna to be a girl who could understand and follow instructions easily. She was mature for her age.

The morning also allowed Schroeder to tour the convent, something he also wanted to do, for future reference. He was always looking for new outlets for his work, what he liked to call his missionary work. He wanted to get a feel for the place, to see it in its everyday operation, study the people. He wanted to sense the many levels of subterfuge and organization that held the place together and allowed it to function as it was. He knew one thing: the Nazis regime wanted to put as much of a human face on its public behavior as it could and, therefore, for the moment, it was biding its time. How much longer this would continue depended on many things but Schroeder felt the convent's days were numbered. He sensed Colonel Eichenstat thought the same.

16

FEBRUARY 3, 1940
AACHEN, GERMANY

Father Schroeder knew all too well that the Nazi regime had developed a rather formidable array of mechanisms to keep tabs on certain kinds of people, and that included clergy, especially clergy who happened to be engaged in shadowy business arrangements as he was. What other way could Colonel Fritz Eichenstat have known that Schroeder, a simple parish priest by all appearances, was the one to seek out for help in solving the kind of problem he wanted solved. Because of that, Schroeder began to think that maybe his normal channels of clandestine communication might be compromised. He was now thinking that maybe it was time to find some other avenue by which to communicate with the Vatican. He decided it was time to abandon using the office of Bishop Preysing.

His immediate need was to locate a qualified physician who would take Gabriella as a patient and be discreet in the process. A pregnant nun was not an everyday occurrence and, in this particular case, it was a pregnant nun who happened also to be a Jew.

It was out of the question to have a physician examine Gabriella at the convent. Privacy would be impossible. Even finding a physician inside Germany who would take her as a patient seemed risky; he knew of no one, no one he could trust.

Already Germany was beginning to see people walking the streets wearing those grotesque yellow Stars of David pinned to their garments. So far, Gabriella had been spared that, but for how long? He concluded that the physician had to be someone located outside Germany. But who, and where? How to find one.

Schroeder knew Belgium almost as much as he knew Germany. He had made a good number of trips there, to the cities of Liege, Antwerp, and Brussels to pick up letters and special papers to bring back and use inside Germany. So far, the German border guards seemed to dismiss his crossings as harmless. That fact was largely due to who he was and how he handled their questions. He had his routine well rehearsed and he had worked out all of the rationales that, so far, had satisfied the officials at the border. Belgium and Germany were not yet at war, and may never be, and given that fact, the border was still passable for a German without much difficulty, especially for a priest. Given all that, it seem best and easiest for him to seek out a physician in Belgium. If successful, he would make plans to take Gabriella back and forth across the border as a patient, until the baby was born, but that was his real fear. What course of action should they take *after* the birth? What would happen to the baby? What would happen to Gabriella?

But neither of those was the immediate problem. Finding a way to get Gabriella to a physician was, and he began to flesh out a plan. As with all his plans he knew it would likely take many turns and require many modifications as it unfolded.

The central rationale of his plan would center around his travels in order to inspect convents and monasteries. Working together, he and Gabriella would make a believable team and have a good chance of satisfying any questions that might be asked by German authorities who happened to question them. After all, the 1933 Concordat between the Vatical and the Nazi government gave jurisdiction over religious programs and services to the clergy. What Schroeder now wanted to acquire was official papers or letter from the Vatican authorizing him to conduct the inspections. He had already eliminated Bishop Preysing's office as a means to get these which meant he had to find some other conduit. His only possibility, he thought, was Bishop Clamente Micara, the present Internuncio in Brussels, Belgium.

Schroeder made the trip to Brussels to see Bishop Micara. He was met by the Bishop's secretary, a priest named Arnaud Dubois who told him the Bishop was not in.

"May I wait?"

"Certainly, but maybe I can help. You see, we have heard of your work, Father," Dubois told him.

"My work?"

"Moving people," Dubois replied.

"I'd better see the Bishop."

"The Bishop relies on me a great deal, Father."

Schroeder studied the man. "How long have you been a priest?"

"Five years. I have served the Bishop for the past year. So, what is it you need?"

What's the danger, Schroeder thought. "Official papers from Rome and the name of a reputable physician. I have a woman who needs care."

"What kind if care?"

Schroeder eyed Dubois, then said, "It's a pregnancy."

Dubois drew back slightly. "Oh?"

"The child is not mine, Father."

"I'm sure," Dubois replied.

Schroeder smiled.

"Do you think you can get both? The papers and the physician?"

"Papers for what purpose?"

Schroeder described what he was after.

"A good strategy, Father. Very ingenious."

"Thank you. When can I get them? Time may be short."

Dubois thought for a moment. "I'll put a special seal on the request. The Bishop will know who to direct it to so it doesn't get lost or misdirected."

"The Bishop will approve?"

Dubois smiled. "Sabastian Arceneau speaks highly of you, Father."

Schroeder replied, "Sabastian is a good man."

"Let me check on a physician," Dubois said. He then went into a back room. It did not take him long. When he came back he handed Schroeder a card. "Dr. Julien Remy is your man. He has a loyal heart and a tight-lipped mouth. He's the best we have."

Schroeder frowned. "We?"

Dubois grinned. "We Catholics, who else."

"I see."

"I'll tell Dr. Remy to be watching for you."

17

ONE MONTH LATER
MARCH 1, 1940
KÖLN, GERMANY

Mother Superior finished reading the letter Father Schroeder had handed her.

"So, the Vatican wants you to make a series of inspections of the convents in Belgium, Luxemburg, and western parishes of Germany?"

"And for that I'll need Sister Katherine to assist me. Rome has authorized me to select whichever sister I feel would be the best to assist me. After all, no one better to determine the status of a convent than a sister. I'm rather a novice at this."

"Sister Katherine is needed here. Suppose Colonel Eichenstat shows up wanting to make one of his inspections? Also, I fear the British bombs will reach us soon. We hear them exploding close by all too often. Sister Katherine needs to be here at such times. To me she is indispensable."

"The Holy Father has a sacred obligation to make preparations to care for his flock, Mother. Yours is not the only convent under stress, surely you know that."

Mother Superior sagged in her large desk chair. "When?"

"Today, if possible."

TWO DAY/ LATER
MARCH 3, 1940
BRU//EL/

Father Schroeder sat in the outside waiting room while Gabriella was with Dr. Remy in his office. She had been with the doctor for nearly an hour.

"Well, Sister, you are indeed pregnant. I'd say two months," Remy informed her. "All your vital signs are normal and you seem to be in top physical condition. That's good. I see no problem with the pregnancy provided you follow my advice and take care of yourself. You must eat well."

"Thank you, Doctor," Gabriella said calmly, almost with no emotion.

"You are not happy to have this child?" he asked, hearing her voice and seeing her expressionless face.

"Have you forgotten what I am, Doctor?" she said with great pessimism, and some anger which she could not hide.

"No," he replied. "I just want all my patients to be pleased about having a child. It helps make for a good outcome."

She smiled. "Forgive me, Doctor, but that is something only a man could say while believing that it made sense. As a woman I may be happy; as a child of God I am happy for this baby; as a nun I am mortified and I couldn't be more frightened."

"I'm sorry. It was irresponsible of me to speak in such a manner and very much out of line. I apologize."

She smiled. "I forgive you," she said.

"Come and see me again, if you can. Next month," he instructed.

"If I can. That depends on Father Schroeder."

"Of course," Remy said. "Schroeder seems like a good man."

She thought she knew what he was thinking. "He is not the father of this baby, Doctor."

Remy recoiled slightly. "Of course not," he said, showing his embarrassment.

Gabriella managed to smile at his embarrassment.

APRIL AND MAY, 1940
GERMANY

Events moved quickly. Germany invaded Denmark, then came Norway. In May, Germany sent its forces into the Netherlands and Belgium and then into France. By June it was all over on the continent. The Germans ruled supreme.

Stories began circulating about the heroic actions taken by the British at a place called Dunkirk along the French coast only days before France surrendered. It seemed that the British had managed to rescue thousands of their troops and thousands of French troops who were trapped and had gotten them back across the channel to England. With the British off the continent and the French surrendered, Germany was now in control of much of the European continent. The only thing that stood against them was the British Empire, and it was now reeling, waiting just over the horizon on the other side of the English Channel, preparing for a German onslaught.

JUNE 10, 1940
AACHEN, GERMANY

Father Schroeder had just finished saying morning mass and was feeling a great sadness and great anxiety over the events of the previous few months. The world around him had been blowing itself up at a rapid pace as the Germans roared across Western Europe all the way to the English Channel. During those short few months of Germany's conquests Father Schroeder kept thinking of Gabriella and what she might be going through. He wondered if her secret was still a secret inside the convent. He wondered if she had told Colonel Eichenstat that he was going to be a father. He wondered how Eichenstat would react. What would he say? He wondered also what role the Colonel had played in his country's offensives of April, May, and June. Was he still assigned to the same unit, having the same orders, following the same course of action? He wondered what would be Eichenstat's future role now that Germany dominated Europe as it did. Events had moved so fast. It was hard to think straight, hard to be calm, to have steady nerves. But Father Schroeder knew he must. If he slipped up he would be putting himself at risk. More than that, he knew, those he was trying to help would pay an even greater price, a consequence he tried his best not to think too much about.

For two days he had been mulling the idea of visiting the convent in Köln to determine how things had changed relative to what he knew of the new circumstances in Aachen and from what he had picked up on his communication network, as ragged as it had become. But the situation had changed; the Germans were feeling more confident, more belligerent, more demanding, more bullying following their easy, quick victories. It had all been too easy for them, Father Schroeder groused. There was no telling what they were up to now, or what they were planning. The rhetoric he had been hearing from inside Germany over the past several years did little to engender a feeling of ease on his part now that the generals and politicians had seen what was possible. They must be having thoughts that nothing could stand against them. He clenched his jaw. He had to visit Köln and see Gabriella, he told himself. He feared that his time was running out.

THE SAME DAY
JUNE 10, 1940
BREMEN, GERMANY

Colonel Fritz Eichenstat's anxieties had been festering steadily for the past few months, ever since he had gone off to see Father Konrad Schroeder. In spite of it all he still managed to stay alert. He watched his superiors carefully, trying to gage their intentions, trying to anticipate their orders and always hoping he had already put in place a maneuver that would deflect any suspicion away from him and make it unlikely that any one of them would discover his deceptions. The various ruses he had put into place and the false trails he had cleverly developed seemed to be holding up, but he could not help but feel that things were becoming more and more risky. Any day now he could be found out, but so far, he was still in the game and still ahead of any potential pursuers. It was too late to turn back now.

He had not seen Gabriella in nearly a month but during that last visit he felt there was something she was trying to tell him. Theirs had not been the usual kind of conversation. She had not been herself, he felt. He had asked but she had put him off, claiming she was just under so much stress and was a little disoriented and confused about all the things that were happening around her and all the things she had to get done. The convent relied on her good sense and strong personality and there were many who were coming to her for help and advice. Many wanted to be reassured and calmed. It was more than any one person could handle, he felt. He had tried to comfort her as best he could. He had wanted so much to hold her.

And then too, Eichenstat had his request to Father Schroeder on his mind. He had wanted to go back and see him again but Germany's big military push to the English Channel had gotten in his way. He feared he might be reassigned now that Germany's sphere of influence had increased.

A knock at the door interrupted his thoughts. He looked up to see Sergeant Pond.

"Yes, Sergeant?"

"General Reinard is here, Sir."

Fritz looked startled.

"Could be a surprise inspection, Sir," the Sergeant offered.

Fritz Eichenstat stiffened, seeing Bruno Reinard come through the door. Reinard had a pale complexion and leaden eyes with blond eyebrows. His eyes were gray, like those of a wolf. He had a predatory way of looking around at his surroundings, like he was seeking a victim, measuring what he might have to face and what might be lurking to disrupt his intention. His body was small. He had a haircut that paid tribute to Adolph Hitler, Eichenstat thought. His icy demeanor tended to intimidate people which put many who dealt with him on edge. His intolerance for sloppiness and laziness was legendary. His conversations often changed direction abruptly, deliberately. Eichenstat knew that General Bruno Reinard was a man to be wary of, and a man to be feared.

Fritz stood up and saluted. "Heil Hitler."

Reinard returned a perfunctory salute. He held his gray gloves in his hand and his hat was tucked firmly beneath his arm. He had a big grin on his face.

"A great day for the Reich, huh Eichenstat?"

Eichenstat knew what he meant. ""Our forces have moved quickly," he said. "France is done."

"Britain is all that is left."

Eichenstat nodded. "They could be more of a challenge," he said, knowing he had to watch his words. Besides, Eichenstat suspected Reinard had other things on his mine than to talk of the recent glories experienced by the armed forces of the Reich.

"Please, sit down, General," Eichenstat said. "I'm sorry but I was not expecting anyone this morning."

Reinard sat down. The grin left his face. "I was in the neighborhood," Reinard said. "Thought I'd stop by and see how you were doing."

Eichenstat did not believe it. The man was too methodical, and too well organized for that.

"It's a pleasure to have you."

"I've been back at headquarters grappling with all these new directives from the Furher's people, Colonel, trying the coordinate the work of all my officers like yourself."

Eichenstat did not want to show any alarm on hearing this but he was certain the General was looking for any sign.

"Reinard continued. "Your numbers look satisfactory but I find some confusing elements that none of my other officers seem to have. It is imperative that we have accurate numbers in order to make our resettlement program run efficiently. You read the plan, of course."

"Of course."

"I hope your efforts have not slowed, Colonel. We want to be fully ready to move to Phase II as soon as the Fuhrer gives the word. "

Fritz frowned. "I'm not familiar with Phase II, General."

The General raised his hand and smiled. "It's in the final stages of formulation. It's a big operation; bigger still now that we have to include our newly acquired coverage." He grinned.

"Understood," Eichenstat replied, hoping to sound supportive.

The General eyed him. "Tell me, Colonel, do you enjoy your work?"

"I serve my country, General."

"You mean you follow orders."

"Of course. I would be a very poor officer if I did not," Eichenstat replied.

The General smiled. "I take it then that you have followed your orders in the handling of the convents and monasteries that are under your jurisdiction?"

"I believe I have, yes, Sir," Fritz replied, beginning to feel a little queasy wondering just where this exchange was headed, or what its true purpose was.

"Well, the reports you submit testify to that fact. I go through all the records submitted by my officers."

"I would expect nothing less, General."

There was a noticeable pause. The General's wolf-like eyes searched eerily somewhere off in the distance. "I must say though that this Carmelite convent in Köln does seem to show some oddities."

"How so, General?"

"Well, for the size of the area it serves it does seem to have a larger number of Catholic children in its school, and a rather large number of ... infirmed."

Fritz was grateful that he found the wherewithal to laugh. "That's because many are not Catholic; they are of many faiths, most of them are Lutherans."

"Really?" the General said, showing genuine surprise. "But they are listed as Catholic on the roster that your office submitted to headquarters. How is that?"

"Because it's easier to secure extra food and incidentals from the parishes by listing them that way. The Bishop has a way of sending extra rations. He has Vatican support I assume. All I can say is that he thinks they are children of Catholic parents."

Reinard frowned. "When you say Bishop, are you speaking of that Bishop Preysing in Berlin? The one who constantly criticizes the Reich?" he growled. "The Furher should ..."

"It's not Preysing," Fritz said.

"Lutheran you say?"

"Sorry for the deception, General. Would you like for me to cease the practice?"

The General laughed. "I like that you're pulling the wool over the eyes of these Church officials. Excellent ruse, Colonel."

"Thank you, Sir."

The General rose from his chair. "You'll be receiving our Phase-II plan soon. Get on it promptly, Colonel."

"Yes, Sir. Anything else you need, Sir?"

"No, Good day, Colonel." He turned without a salute.

18

THE FOLLOWING DAY
JUNE 11, 1940
KÖLN, GERMANY

Mother Superior sat in her office facing Father Conrad Schroeder. Her mood was somber. She knew she had little choice. Sister Katherine was going to be taken away, if not today, very soon. Whether it would be a temporary absence or a permanent one she could not say, but she had her worries.

Father Schroeder had presented all the justifications as best he could. He ended by saying, "Mother Superior, Germany is not fighting Great Britain, Germany is in a death struggle with Satan himself."

Mother Superior nodded but said nothing.

"And that is why those in the Church *must* do what they can," Father Schroeder added.

"I'll miss her."

"She will be back. You will have her for another few days."

"Does she know you are here?"

"No," he said, checking his watch. It is getting late. Where is she? We must talk about our visits and what we'll need to do."

Mother Superior said with noticeable sorrow. "I should tell you, she has not been feeling well. It is something new with her. I have never known her to be this weary, almost despondent, as if she is losing faith in her work. Yet, despite it all, she carries on."

Schroeder let the analysis pass. "I am going to the chapel to say a prayer. She can come to me there."

A short time later Sister Katherine came into the small chapel, dipped her hand into the font of holy water, crossed herself and came to the pew where Father Schroeder was sitting. He had no trouble seeing what Mother Superior meant. Gabriella's face, normally so bright and cheerful, was instead drawn and unexpressive, as if she were too tired to waste the energy to even move the muscles that would cause her face to brighten. Her eyes were noticeably glassy.

"You must get out of the convent," he said immediately. "You must get some rest. I won't ask how you are doing."

"I'm so pleased to see you," she said, sitting down with a heaviness in the pew beside him. "I am not well," she added.

"I have a plan that should change that," he told her.

"I have not told Fritz about his child," she said. "I am afraid how he will react, what it will mean for him."

"You haven't much time." He studied her carefully.

"My habit is becoming snug, too snug," she said, examining herself as she sat.

"You must see Dr. Remy again," he said. "We will get to that as soon as we leave the convent. Mother Superior understands."

Her face blanched. "She ..."

"No, no," he quickly dispelled her fear. "She believes that you and I will be away in order to inspect convents and monasteries again, just like before, for the Bishop, for the Vatican and the Holy Father."

She clasped her hands together. "What do I ... say to Fritz?"

"We shall work on that, In the meantime let me tell you my plans."

After he had finished she said, "So, I go with you back to Aachen?"

"To Brussels to see Dr. Remy."

"And stay at your church residence?"

"Yes."

"What happens to Anna?"

"I will come here for her later. Now is not the right time. That's where Colonel Eichenstat comes in."

"Is this before or after I tell him about ..."

"Maybe at about the same time."

She lowered her eyes. "What's to become of me, of Anna, of this baby?" she asked, sounding as if she expected little in the way of any positive answer.

"We must have faith," he said.

"My prayers could not be more fervent," she said.

"The baby can be born at my residence. I have parishioners who can help. Dr. Remy can attend."

"And then what?" she asked.

"I'll have to make some arrangements."

"Fritz has spoken of getting Anna to America. That can't be possible, can it?"

Schroeder shrugged. "The Colonel may have his ways; we can't be sure of just what they might be. Also, we still have friends of our own who might help."

"If only this baby could make it to America," she pondered out loud.

"And you as well," he said.

She smirked. "I am convinced that my fate resides here, with my fellow sisters and my convent, and the people we look after."

Schroeder felt he knew the error in her analysis. He told her, "You must come with me today. We shall begin our visits to the other convents as the letter from Rome instructs us to."

"Rome!"

Schroeder shrugged. "I'm not all that convinced it came directly from Rome but it serves our purpose and, besides, we have no other choice. I just pray it works. Are you up to it?"

She shrugged.

19

THE NEXT DAY
JUNE 12, 1940
AACHEN, GERMANY

Father Konrad Schroeder had a lot on his mind. The series of actions he was piecing together still had too much uncertainty to give him confidence of a good outcome. Maybe he was asking too much. He had learned from experience that no matter how carefully he planned these things there was always a need to improvise once things got off the ground, and all he could do if that happened was hope that whatever he contrived on the spur of the moment would carry him through. It would be the same this time.

One other thing bothered him: the man assigned to Colonel Eichenstat's staff, Sergeant Markus Pond, seemed to have been probing for information the last time Schroeder had called

Eichenstat's headquarters. The Sergeant always answered the call and passed him through to Eichenstat, but the last time it had been different. Schroeder thought Pond had asked too many questions that he thought out of line. He mentioned his concerns to Eichenstat when they had talked but he wasn't sure how Eichenstat had taken his concerns. Schroeder would mention it again when they next met, which was going to be in a few days.

TWO DAYS LATER
JUNE 14, 1940
AACHEN, GERMANY

Colonel Fritz Eichenstat had taken Father Schroeder's concerns about Sergeant Pond to heart. This was no time to be trusting; his was a precarious state. Suspicions about Sergeant Pond was only one of his worries at the moment, however. He had learned something the previous evening from General Bruno Reinard who had called all his commanders together. Things were ramping up. The message was the same. General Reinard had stressed that for Germany to fend off its enemies and fulfill its destiny as Europe's leading peoples it had to shape itself into a well-honed race that was agile and single-minded. Malcontents, detractors, and free-thinkers only stood in the way and had to be pushed aside, by any means. Any true German would not question that task. "You," the General had addressed the group, "are at the forefront of that mission."

At the moment no one had any official written orders to put Reinard's directive into action but Eichenstat knew that such orders would not be long in coming to his desk. When that day arrived any obvious delays on his part would be hard to hide. But he wasn't sure just what he would do in carrying out those orders. His depression was growing. His thinking was taking him down several avenues at once, several different courses of action he might take. If he could only be like some of the other commanders, suppressing their personal conscious, or hiding their true feelings from the others while managing to still live with themselves. Maybe they too were struggling with this issue the same as he. He envisioned their faces, thought of their words and how they spoke of things when they met. There was no question, some of them were enthusiasts for their tasks, the hard liners; others, he guessed, rationalized that a soldier simply carries out orders whether he agrees with them or not and tries to forget. That was too easy for Eichenstat in this particular case. Choices would have to be made, and the time was fast approaching when Colonel Fritz Eichenstat would have to make his. And choices had consequences.

In the back seat of his automobile Eichenstat sat nearly motionless, staring at the passing countryside but not seeing much of it. The hum of the wheels of the staff car against the pavement sent small vibrations up through his body. One thought kept surfacing. Had Father Schroeder called him to Aachen because he also knew what was getting ready to descend upon them. Eichenstat thought that Schroeder might possess a sixth sense that told him the same thing.

From some far off place he heard Sergeant Pond's voice.

"That's what I heard," the Sergeant was saying.

"What?" Eichenstat said.

"I was saying that I heard some of the men at headquarters saying that some priest got arrested for hiding some Jews in his house."

Suddenly Eichenstat was on high alert. He thought quickly. "Forget it, Sergeant. I have personally investigated Father Schroeder. He is one of us. He gives me good information. Why do you think I deal so much with him."

"I see."

Eichenstat thought to add credibility to his ruse. "How do you think we arrested that priest, the one you are talking about?"

Sergeant Pond laughed. "Maybe our priest will be given a medal."

"No, no, Sergeant, we don't publicize our informants. That ruins them as a source, don't you see?"

"Of course. How stupid of me."

Eichenstat laughed. "Father Schroeder has some unique habits that go along with tending to his flock, but he has to keep it hidden."

An hour later, at ten o'clock sharp, Sergeant Pond pulled the car into the parking area of St. Nicholaus Church. There was only one other car parked. Sergeant Pond jumped out and opened the rear door. As Eichenstat stepped out he heard the heavy latch on the front door to the church's residency open and he saw Father Schroeder come out. The priest stood watching from the small porch and steps. Eichenstat put on his hat and headed for the priest's residence. Sergeant Pond got back in the car and drove toward the main street and headed down the street.

Father Schroeder and Eichenstat shook hands as Eichenstat came up the steps.

"Is your Sergeant going far?"

"Petrol. He always wants to keep a full tank, if possible. He's a dedicated aide."

Schroeder eyed the car as it disappeared from view. "Do you trust that man?" he asked.

"I watch him," Eichenstat replied.

"Carefully, I hope."

"Don't worry, I have laid down a clever story about you. He can't help but believe it."

"For our sakes I pray. Please, let's go inside."

Eichenstat smiled. "You hinted that my visit today was urgent."

"Things are moving fast, yes," Schroeder replied.

Eichenstat felt his muscles tighten. "You can still help? Please, tell me you have not failed."

Schroeder closed the front door behind them. "Put aside your anxiety, Colonel. But before we move on there are some circumstances about which you must be aware, but I will let Gabriella tell you herself."

Eichenstst's face showed his surprise.

"She is in the adjoining room," Schroeder told him.

Eichenstst's eyes jumped to the door. "In ... there?" he asked.

"She's expecting you. Go in, please."

Eichenstat paused a moment then put his hat on the table. He slowly opened the door, not at all sure just what he would see, or what might happen. He closed the door quietly. Gabriella was on her knees on a small kneeler adorned with intricately carved forms of religious figures. She was facing a statue of the Virgin Mary. Gabriella's head was bowed and it seemed as if she had not heard the door open and close behind her. He hesitated, watching her, thinking, admiring.

"Gabriella," he said softly.

When she turned around he saw that she had been crying. She wiped at her eyes. "Hello, Fritz," she whispered. "You look handsome," she said as she stood up, blinking repeatedly and then wiping her eyes.

He came closer. "I am confused. Why are you here? Why ... are you crying?" He inspected her more carefully. "You ... don't ... look. Are you ill?"

"Come, sit here," she said, sitting in one chair and motioning to another beside it.

He sat down. "You don't look yourself," he said.

"I'm very tired.'

He studied her, shaking his head.

"I have been praying for you Fritz," she said calmly. "and for me too."

He did not want to tell her that he did not believe in such things. He saw himself as an intelligent, modern, man of education. But it was not necessary to tell her these things because the two of them had argued about it on countless occasions when they had been students. Now, all he wanted to do was to reach out and hold her hand. He was surprised when *she* took *his* hand, then the other.

"Fritz," she said ever so softly. "You must prepare yourself for what I am going to tell you."

He blinked and breathed deeply. His brain burned. He said irritably. "First Father Schroeder, now you? Both of you are speaking in words that are clouded with a darkness, it seems. The two of you are talking in ways that are as mysterious as the ciphers I have to deal with every day."

Her gaze dropped from his eyes. "I'm sorry."

He then spoke as if boasting, "I am fully prepared for whatever you have to say to me."

She looked at him squarely; a look of tenderness came to her eyes. Her grip on his hands tightened noticeably. "Fritz, I have your child growing inside me."

For an instant there was no reaction from him, his eyes remained fixed on hers. Then he blinked several times quickly as he fought to take in the meaning of what she was telling him. His eyes jumped down to her body as if he hoped to see some manifestation of that possibility beneath her habit.

"Fritz," she whispered. "It will be all right," she added, leaning forward as if to provide added assurance.

"How ... what ... will we do?

She smiled.

Seeing her smile, he frowned. "Gabriella?"

Still with a slight smile she said, "Yes, Fritz?"

"Gabriella ... is it wrong for a man to say he loves a nun?"

She squeezed his hand between both of hers. "I am happy now. I am happy that you now know."

"What do we do?" he asked.

"And I am happy that you said *we*," she told him.

"Did you believe I would throw you to the wolves?"

"No," she replied. "But it is gratifying for one to learn that one's instincts about a person are correct."

"I'm not so sure you really know me, Gabriella. The kind of person I am inside."

"You are in a difficult position, Dear Fritz. Circumstances have grabbed you up and put you in an unhappy place. Your family status, The Eichenstats, and the noble heritage born by its name and how its family members are expected now to honor that heritage and serve the Reich in its march to glory. But the march has taken us all down a road we would best not travel, but we have little say about it. You have little say and that frightens me terribly. I am also frightened because my condition could jeopardize your well-being."

"I will help you," he said. He wanted desperately to hold her, to kiss her. God was torturing him, he thought. Why could he not kiss the mother of his child? Why could he not caress her? It was not natural! His insides were on fire suddenly. He stood up abruptly. He said, "Father Schroeder knows ... of this?"

"He does," she said. "He is a good man. He has helped get me to see a doctor. In Brussels. I am to see him again tomorrow."

"There is no problem? You, the child, are in good health?"

"Yes," she replied. "Our son is all right."

"Son?" Eichenstat asked. "You cannot be sure."

"It pleases me to think so," she said.

"A boy with no true name," Eichenstat said. "A boy with no ... father."

"You are his father, Fritz."

"I cannot openly claim him, can I?"

"No," she said sadly. "No, I suppose not. But you and I and God know who his father is," she said. "And we must make sure he is safe. We must get him out of this place!" she said angrily. "We must make it possible for this child to survive. It is God's will," she added.

Eichenstat was angry at hearing her words. "Well then, God damn well better offer you and Father Schroeder some real avenues of action to bring that about!"

"Don't blaspheme, Fritz, please. You can't fight God. When are you going to understand that? You used to talk that way when we were students, remember?"

"I'm sorry, Gabriella. "I just can't see your God the way you do." He got up and began pacing about the room.

"God will take care of me," she said. "And of you."

He looked at her, at her innocence. Here she was buried in the middle of the most unhappy circumstance and still she could talk that way. Did she really believe it, he wondered? Maybe for a former Jew, a German citizen, now a Catholic nun, who was pregnant with an illegitimate child fathered by a German military officer serving Nazi Germany in the middle of wartime it was rational to believe in such a thing. He could not; at least that's what he told himself as he stood looking at her.

"It is Father Schroeder who will take care of you; that's my guess. It should be me but I am almost completely helpless in this. And that ... angers me greatly," he said with considerable emphasis. "I will speak with the good father. Maybe together we can come up with something. I have a feeling he has already started a plan. The man is a marvel, and a mystery."

"I'm ... so sorry, Fritz. I feel this is all my fault. I tempted you and I should not have. It is my greatest sin."

"Stop it! Please, stop it!" His voice was firm but not loud.

"Don't you know how much I love you?"

Her eyes dropped. "Yes. I have no doubt about that."

"Yet I can't have you. You will be leaving me if all goes well. It will be over for us. Wherever you are you have your church, I will have ... I have ... Germany."

She could not mistake his aching sense of hopelessness. She stood up and walked to him. She put her arms around him and pulled him against her. There were tears in her eyes. "Forgive me, Fritz, please. You must. Don't hate me, please don't hate me."

He could not help himself. He held her tight and kissed her passionately; she made no attempt to pull away or prevent him. He wanted desperately to do more, she knew. For a brief moment she too wanted his naked body against hers. Once again she had no illusions that she too had a wide streak of womanly passion that he could instantly ignite. She had discovered that fact the first time they had made love in that cottage a few blocks from the convent - that first time when she had set her unholy trap that led to this ordeal that was starring them in the face, and which could consume them both, along with others. As they embraced she could feel his face heated against hers.

"Fritz, we must ..."

He drew back. "I hope your God knows what He is doing!" He was breathing hard as he spoke.

"No one else can save me, Fritz," she said. "I know that you would like to be the one, but you can't and that is no fault of yours. In my condition, only God, Himself, can render me a safe landing."

"With Father Schroeder as His helper," he replied.

"As God's instrument," she corrected him. "We should be thankful we have Father Schroeder. Our baby needs him."

"I wish I could learn more about what that man is thinking of doing. He is cautious and he tells me little about such things. I guess it's his nature. He has to be careful. He ... he is a better man than I am."

"You forget what it is you are doing with the convents, the people inside? For that, you, yourself, must survive."

He laughed derisively. "In the Germany of old maybe I could manage to survive. In my role in the new Germany my survival has little chance. Soldiers often think that way, but for me, it is true."

"Can you resign your commission?" she asked.

Again he laughed. "How can you be so naive, Gabriella?"

"Yes, stupid of me."

Eichenstat turned away. "I must speak to Schroeder." He opened the door. The outer room was empty. Eichenstat walked to the outer door and went outside, looking for the priest.

Father Schroeder was bent over tending to one of his plants in his garden. He looked at Eichenstat as he stood a short distance away on the steps and said, "I suspect you are now fully aware of the seriousness of our present enterprise. You will pardon me if I do not offer you my fullest congratulations. You have a heavy burden, my friend."

Eichenstat came down the steps and over to the priest. "I must know what you are planning."

Father Schroeder stood up. "We can talk over here. I have a small rock garden."

The two men talked for nearly a half hour. Before he left Eichenstat told Garbiella what he was sure his coming orders would be regarding her convent in Köln.

"Somehow you must save Anna," she pleaded. "Our friend's blood, his only sibling. She is so young. Fritz, you must!"

"I will," he answered, not knowing exactly how. All he knew for sure was that it would be risky, for both of them.

On the trip back to Bremen Eichenstat sat silently thinking of Gabriella and his child. It was another aspect of his life with which he had to confront, and deal with. His mind was churning. How might he possibly maneuver through the maze of challenges that were now his unhappy life as a German officer in a politically sensitive position in a regime that tolerated no mishaps. Deceiving the likes of General Bruno Reinard would be a formidable task. In his dark moments he didn't think he had much of a chance.

20

JUNE 15, 1940
BRUJJELJ, BELGIUM

While Gabriella was seeing Dr. Remy Father Schroeder made a trip to see Climente Micara. There was a large automobile parked outside.

Father Arnaud Dubois answered the door. "There's been a bad turn," he said. "The Nazis want Micara out of Belgium. I'm right now packing some things."

"How much time? When will he be departing, do you know?"

He shrugged. "Soon."

"Where will he go? Do you know his travel plans?"

"Eventually Rome, I suppose."

"I saw the large automobile outside. Will he be going in that?"

"Yes."

Schroeder fell silent.

"What are you thinking?" Dubois asked, watching Schroeder.

Schroeder grimaced. "Seems I don't have as much time as I first thought."

"How much time do you need?"

Schroeder thought. "More than a few days."

"To do what?" Dubois asked.

"Do you remember the female patient for whom you helped me find a physician?"

"Indeed. I hope Dr. Remy served your needs."

"She is seeing him at this very moment."

Dubois eyed Schroeder. "I have the feeling there is much more to this."

"She needs to get out of Germany; along with a young woman companion. They will need papers. Might Rome help? No, there is not time for that."

"What are you thinking, Father?"

"I have heard there are ships leaving Lisbon," Schroeder said suddenly. "A long way off, I know. I don't see how it would be possible."

Dubois frowned. "Papers to get a person across France, into Spain, across Spain and into Portugal and all the way to Lisbon? And then on a ship to ..."

"I know, I know. A long trip where so much could go wrong, but I am at a loss."

"Maybe Sabastian Arceneau?" Dubois said suddenly.

"Yes! Of course! The Gregory Foundation!"

"But where is Arceneau now?" Schroeder said.

"The Vatican will know. Micara can contact the Vatican," Dubois said.

"Would there be time enough?"

Dubois shrugged. "What else have we? Maybe he could secure passage from Lisbon for your travelers. They'll need it."

Schroeder's mind jumped. "To America?" Would that be ... they couldn't be that lucky."

Dubois stiffened. "You're getting ahead of yourself, Father. Many poor souls want to make it to America. That has proven a very elusive goal."

"I know, I know, but I made a promise to try. I must pursue every avenue in this matter if I am to keep my conscience clean. You understand."

Father Dubois looked through the window and saw the car pulling off. "The Bishop has just been dropped off."

When Bishop Micara came through the front door he gave both men a hurried look. "I hope your day is going better then mine," he said.

"Father Schroeder requests a few minutes of your time, Bishop. It is important."

"In my office, please."

Schroeder followed the man. Once inside Schroeder wasted no time. He rattled off the particulars. He just let them pour out. It was a nearly irrational litany but the Bishop seemed to grasp the point.

"A clever rouse, inspecting convents," Micara said, a small grin appearing.

"So far."

Micara was a ball of nervous action. He picked up one piece of paper after another and made a quick decision after examining it, throwing one in one box and a second in another box. "In essence you want Vatican travel documents to take you to Portugal?"

Schroeder nodded. "At least two, maybe three; one for me to act as official escort."

"All the way to Portugal?"

"If possible, yes. I can't see them traveling alone."

Micara eyed Schroeder. "The name Father Konrad Schroeder is spoken proudly in certain circles, Father, if you know my meaning. But I must say that your efforts in this case seem to be taking things to a much higher level. It seems very risky to me. Of course, I am not the expert. This case must be special."

"These are special people, Bishop."

Micara gave Schroeder a careful look. "Sabastian Arceneau has mentioned your name."

The comment surprised Schroeder. "I don't understand, Bishop."

"My guess is that your passengers are Jewish?"

Schroeder's mind stumbled a moment but he quickly caught himself. "One is a Catholic nun, Bishop, but, yes, she is also Jewish. It is a long story. The other passenger is also Jewish; she is fifteen, almost sixteen."

The Bishop looked over at him and then went back to his sorting of files and papers. He said nothing. Then, "Does Father

Dubois know all the particulars about your needs, about the nun and the girl?" Micara asked.

"I believe he does, yes."

"All of them? You sure?"

Schroeder thought for a second. Should he inform the Bishop about Gabriella's condition. He could sense that his hesitation had made the man stop with his papers and look up. "The nun ... is pregnant," Schroeder uttered.

The Bishop displayed little reaction. He then looked back down. "I believe I've heard enough, Father. You seem to have your hands full. I wish you well but I have been ordered out of the country, remember. I don't think I have enough time to ... "

"I take it you will be traveling in your automobile?" Schroeder interrupted him. "The large one parked outside?"

"It is my only transportation," Micara said. "The Reich do not much care how I leave as long as I leave. Why do you ask?"'

Schroeder was thinking fast. "Well . . ."

"Speak your mind, Father."

"It's possible you might take along passengers?"

Micara stood up from his desk and eyed Schroeder. He then smiled. "Would you use a Bishop to deceive our German masters, Father?"

Schroeder could not help himself. "I do it all the time."

"Mr. Arceneau says you are a clever man," Micara said.

"A tool of the trade, Bishop. If one wants to remain alive."

The Bishop smiled in reply. He then said, "I will be traveling across France, to Spain to visit a friend in Madrid. Then on to Rome."

"An ideal route, I ... think." His eyes were playing with his thoughts. "It has ... possibilities, if you are disposed."

Father Schroeder then laid out his thinking.

"Work it out with Dubois," Micara said when he had finished and then went back to his sorting of papers.

Father Schroeder opened the car door for Gabriella.

"What did the good doctor say?" he asked her.

"Other than gaining six pounds I'm in excellent health. The same for the child."

"We may be close to moving," he told her. "I saw Bishop Micara and I believe we have a plan formulating. Still some loose ends."

"Tell me."

He laid out his thinking for her as they began the trip back to Aachen.

Father Schroeder's residence next to St. Nicholaus Church in Aachen was a welcome sight. Gabriella was tired. She said goodnight and climbed the stairs to the guest bedroom. The small bathroom was cozy. She turned on the water and waited for the tub to fill. She tested the water cautiously and then climbed in and slowly sank beneath the warm, soothing water. She rested her head back and closed her eyes.

"Blessed Mother, I am at your mercy. You have a grave responsibility to permit this child to survive. It is through my own reckless actions that helped bring him into this world and you cannot punish him for what he had no part of. He will be a great man one day and serve you and your Son, Our Lord, with great distinction. He is here inside me for a reason just as your Son was inside you. Your Son did not let this happen for no reason. I am His servant, He is my master whom I serve. I trust Him. He will not abandon me. Knowing that, allows me to be at peace. But my friends are not at peace; they are in danger and part of that is my fault. Father Konrad Schroeder, Anna Burkitz, and my dear friend Fritz Eichenstat are all in grave danger because of me. Hold them all in your heart and give them courage. This I pray to you with a tormented spirit. Amen."

Downstairs, Father Schroeder put in a call to Colonel Eichenstat.

21

JUNE 16, 1940
BREMEN, GERMANY

Once again Colonel Fritz Eichenstat was on his way to Köln; Sergeant Pond was driving. Eichenstat tried to clear his mind and forget, but he was not having very good results. When they arrived Pond jumped out and opened the door. At the main entrance to the convent Eichenstat pulled the wrinkled, frayed cord attached to the brass bell. A young nun opened the door. He followed her down the hall.

Mother Superior sat behind her desk and did not get up when he entered.

"I have the feeling that this is an ominous visit, Colonel. I can read it in your bearing," she said bluntly. "Am I correct?"

He sat down and unlocked his briefcase and removed one of the files.

"I have an order here for the removal of one of your ... guests. The name is Anna Bumgartner."

"Order! What order!" she asked indignantly "Whose order!"

"That is no concern of yours," he said.

She glared at him.

"This Bumgartner is a special individual," he said.

"They are all special, Colonel," she barked, still glaring at him with an increasingly repulsive look on her face.

He smiled a faint smile. "You have taken on a new demeanor, Mother Superior. That surprises me."

His admission forced her expression to quickly became noticeably less dire, softer looking. The look did not last long. She flared, "I won't give up the girl until Sister Katherine returns."

"Oh, she is not here?" he said, a statement which was only meant to help him continue his stratagem and hide his knowledge about Gabriella.

"She is not, so you will have to come back when she is here."

He shook his head. "You don't seem to understand. You have no legal authority in this matter, Mother Superior."

"I have the authority of the Church! Of God Himself!"

He smiled. He wanted so much to play the part of the harsh, uncaring, unmoved Hun. He said, "Do you have in your possession any documents to substantiate such a contention, Mother Superior?" His words spat out with as much contempt as he could muster.

There was total loathing in her expression. "Someday, Colonel you will feel the full power of God come crashing down around you, burying you."

Her fight was amazing, Eichenstat thought. A mother protecting her young; a warrior ready to go to the very end. It was admirable, he thought.

"Well spoken, Mother Superior. But your beliefs are foolish. This is the twentieth century. Intelligent people . . . well."

"You are an evil man, Colonel. You are doing evil things."

"Yes, possibly, but I must have the girl. If you refuse I will have to call for extra men to come an inspect the convent more thoroughly. No telling what illegalities they might discover. Maybe even some forged papers?"

Her face hardened.

"What are you going to do with Anna? Where will she be taken?"

"I cannot tell you that," he replied. "But let me ask you, do you trust Sister Katherine?"

"You know I do," she replied as if the question was ludicrous.

"And does she trust me?" he asked.

Mother Superior frowned, "She ... seems to. But why I do not know."

"She does, and you know she does."

"And I should trust you too, is that your meaning?"

Eichenstat raised his eyebrows and cocked his head. "You just might consider it."

She did not offer any comment.

Eichenstat reached into his briefcase and took out a folder. "Here is a form stating all the relevant facts about the subject, Anna Burkitz. You have her as Anna Bumgartner. No matter. We know who she really is and that's all that matters. Most of the people here are not truly who they say they are or by what names you call them. But just to keep everything in good order you will sign this form stating that I have taken one Anna Burkitz, known to you as Anna Bumgartner, and that you have released her into my custody. That way you are no longer responsible if anything happens to her, or if she disappears and turns up in some other place, in some other country even. So many people are moving around these days."

"Ohhhh," Mother Superior growled. "You are a beast for sure."

"Please sign," he ordered.

As Colonel Eichenstat and Anna reached the front door to the convent Mother Superior appeared and said to Anna, "Do not be afraid, Anna. God is with you."

When Anna and Colonel Eichenstat got outside Anna said, "I *am* afraid. I know more about things than you might think."

Eichenstat put his arm around her as they walked. "You must listen to me. This is important. When you get in the car with me you must say nothing. Do your best not to cry. There may be some things said that you might not fully understand. Ignore them. I am your friend; I am Sister Katherine's friend. Remember that."

As they reached the car Eichenstat said to Seargent Pond, "We have a passenger, Sergeant."

Sergeant Pond gave Anna a disrespectful smiled and took the suitcase from her. Anna glared at him and then dropped her eyes as she got in the car. Eichenstat followed and climbed in behind her. The Sergeant carried the suitcase and put it in the front passenger seat as he got in.

"We are going to Aachen, Sergeant."

"The Church, Sir?"

"Yes, I believe we have enough petrol."

"Plenty, Sir. But we will need some extra to make the return trip to Bremen."

As they drove the Sergeant kept glancing up in the mirror, watching Anna. Eichenstat did not miss the man's checking movements. He then decided it was time to play out his next move.

"Sergeant, what do you think of our passenger?"

"Sir?"

"She is pretty is she not?" As Eichenstat said this he squeezed Anna's hand as a reminder to say nothing. He felt her stiffen.

Sergeant Pond half turned and looked quickly at Anna as if to make a final inspection so he could correctly answer the Colonel's question. "Yes, Sir, she is."

"She will be staying at the Church with Father Schroeder," he told Pond. Once more he squeezed Anna's hand.

"Oh, yes, I see. Yes indeed. That will be ... "

"Are you getting the picture, Sergeant?"

"I believe I am, yes, Sir."

Anna sat firmly and straight through the exchange. Suddenly her fear was not a guise; she began to feel a rising nervousness at what she was hearing. Eichenstat sensed it and squeezed her hand again, then patted it gently. She looked at him. He gave her a faint shake of his head, barely moving it. She thought she then understood.

"Does the priest know we are coming, Sir?"

"He does. He is most anxious to meet our passenger."

"I'm sure, Sir."

As they drove Colonel Eichenstat was surprised to see very few military vehicles on the roads. Traffic was light. When they reached St. Nicholaus Church it was late in the afternoon. Eichenstat said to his Sergeant, "I'll be staying the night here, Sergeant, with Father Schroeder. You find yourself quarters in the center of town, down by the market. There is an attachment of infantry there. We could be some bombing tonight, so find a secure place."

"Yes, Sir."

"Return here tomorrow morning, early, by sunrise," Eichenstat instructed further. "If I am not ready to leave you may have to wait, or find some other duty around town. Understood?"

"Yes, Sir."

Pond smiled as he opened his door. He reached over and took Anna's suitcase and dragged it behind him as he slid out the seat and stood beside the car. He straightened his uniform before opening the rear door for Eichenstat.

"I'll take the suitcase, Sergeant," Eichenstat said as he got out holding his own briefcase. He then reached back to help Anna get out. Eichenstat had his hat tucked under his arm. He put it on. He and Anna then walked to the front door of Father Schroeder's residence. Pond watched until they were inside.

Father Schroeder shook hands with Eichenstat and gave Anna a light hug. Anna's eyes took in her new surroundings.

"Don't worry, Anna," Father Schroeder said. "You have nothing to be afraid of here."

Anna offered up a weak smile.

"Do you know where Sister Katherine is?" she asked.

Father Schroeder looked at Eichenstat. "Yes I do, Anna."

"I wish I could be with her."

"Soon maybe," Schroeder told her. "I'll take you to your room upstairs. You rest a while. We will talk later. We'll have something to eat soon."

When Father Schroeder returned he found Eichenstat standing in front of one of Schroeder's two massive bookcases full of books. He had taken one down and was now reading.

"St. Augustine," he said to Schroeder. "Confessions."

Schroeder grinned.

As Eichenstat closed the book and replaced it on the shelf he said, "I have been facing this man Augustine and his influences in one form or another for a long time, it seems."

"And where do you stand now after all these encounters?"

Eichenstat grimaced. "I'm where I am in life. Here, waiting. Waiting for who knows what."

"You sound as if you are drifting; lost maybe?"

"Aptly put, Father. Now can you tell me where Gabriella is?"

"Next door, in the Church."

Eichenstat came closer. "May I ask what is your intention? What is your plan?"

Schroeder hesitated. "You will likely not see her again after tomorrow, Colonel."

"For God's sake, Father, don't you know I know that!"

"You did request that I help get her to safety, remember," Schroeder said.

Eichenstat backed off some. "I'm sorry. How will you do it?"

"Colonel, it is best for everyone that you do not know. Besides, all the parts are not in place yet."

Eichenstat did not protest. "I must see Gabriella," he said. "To say goodbye."

"Go through the side door near the front of the church." Schroeder instructed.

Eichenstat entered the Church. It was dark, the only light was provided by the burning candles that gave the place an undertone of faded illumination throughout. Deep shadows loomed in the far corners. He saw Gabriella sitting alone a few rows from where he entered. As he approached her from the side he could see her trance-like attention to the crucifix suspended above the spacious, ornate alter. There were two woman sitting in separate pews much farther back. Another woman with her head draped with a black, lacy shawl was walking toward the rear, on her way out of the church.

He moved closer. "Gabriella," he whispered.

She turned instantly. "Fritz, you have arrived. Is Anna with you?"

"In Schroeder's house," he replied, sitting down. "Must we talk here?"

"It's quiet. I'm comfortable here. Does it unnerve you?"

He looked up at the altar. "The slightest whisper seems to reverberate everywhere," he said. He looked back at the women several rows behind them.

Gabriella took his hand. It startled him. "I am sorry for what I have done to you, Fritz."

"We have been through all that, Gabriella. We are past that. We are here. It is now. Half the world is in turmoil and we are caught up in it along with millions of others. Everything is changing from one day to the next. Nothing is for certain anymore, if it ever was."

She squeezed his hand. "Our child is growing fine," she told him. "Dr. Remy said so."

He looked at her belly but, dressed as she was in her Carmelite habit, all he saw was bulky fabric and a string of rosary beads.

"Go ahead," she said, smiling. "You can touch him." With that she directed his hand to her abdomen. She released his hand and he slid it back and forth, lightly across her habit.

"You don't show much," he said.

"When I am without clothes one can see a change," she told him.

"How long now?"

"Five months about."

He hesitated. "Where ... will the baby be born? His voice was dispirited. "Do you know? Did Father Schroeder say anything. He would not tell me anything about what is to happen. I can't stand this," he cried softly.

She grabbed his hand and held it tightly. "Forgive me, Fritz! Please, please, please forgive me!" Her voice trembled. "I anguish over my actions every minute of every day. I have put so many people in danger. I have a great penance coming."

"Stop it! Stop it, Gabriella! I love you. I love you. I've always loved you." He wanted to hold her close. He glanced behind him. He was sure the woman had heard him. But she was not looking at them. She was still kneeling, her head bowed.

Gabriella began to choke up. She swallowed hard. She knew what he wanted.

"Come to my room tonight, Fritz," she said softly.

He shook his head. "It is not proper," he replied. "It is not right. I will not defile Father Schroeder's house that way, I will not defile *you* that way. I have done enough!"

"If I must end this part of my life by leaving you and taking your child away then maybe it is right. God will punish me appropriately I am certain, but, as I believe, it is for Him to decide. If I do this out of my own weakness then it is my failing."

He looked at her, shaking his head. "Dear Gabriella. For all of your knowledge there are some things you do not know. I am the one who came to ask Father Schroeder to help find a way for you to leave this country."

She replied quickly, "Yes, you did but that was before you knew I carried your child inside me."

"All the more that you should leave," he said. "All the more."

"God will not allow ... your child ... you will see him ... when this ... when ... when ..." It was no use. She could not finish. Her head was swirling with uncontrollable thoughts, each one climbing over the others, twisting and intermixing in ways she could not adequately sort through. She managed to say, "I have brought so much anguish into the world." As she spoke tears began to seep from her eyes and run down her cheeks. Suddenly she stiffened and pointed her finger at the crucifix and addressed it in a demanding way. *"You keep this man safe. You keep us all safe."* With that she looked at him. Their faces were close. He wanted to kiss her but he could not make the final move.

She shivered noticeably. "I ... I believe I have just blasphemed," she said. "My God, what have I brought upon myself, upon everyone?"

Later, when they left the church and returned to the residency, they found Father Schroeder and Anna already eating dinner at the large table arrayed with decorative bowls of food. There was a sweet smell of fresh bread throughout the room. The room was bright and warm, a complete contrast to the church they had just left.

"Sister Katherine!" Anna yelped and jumped up and ran to her. The two embraced.

"I am so pleased you are here, Anna," Gabriella said, hugging her.

"The Colonel brought me," Anna told her. "Mother Superior was angry that I left. I think she does not like the Colonel."

"No, no, Anna. She only worries about you when you leave her care. And she seems not to like Colonel Eichenstat only because she does not know him as we do."

Both Anna and Gabriella glanced at Eichenstat who was shaking his head. "Someday, Sister, you will have to explain the full meaning of all this to Anna."

"I understand things, Colonel. I told you."

"Do you understand enough to know that Colonel Eichenstat and Father Schroeder are trying to help you, Anna," Gabriella asked.

"Most people don't like us, the Jews," Anna then said. "Why is that?"

Father Schroeder interrupted. "Enough of all this. Our food is getting cold and I labored long and hard in preparation."

"No housekeeper, Father?" Eichenstat asked.

"I gave her today and tomorrow off."

"I understand," Eichenstat said.

"I thought it best," Schroeder added.

22

JUNE 18, 1940
AACHEN, GERMANY

There was still a darkness to the sky overhead. The sun was still below the horizon but there was still a faint contrast to the grayness just overhead. Eichenstat and Father Schroeder stood outside near the church, both silently peering into the distance. Schroeder knew that Eichenstat had spent a restless night.

"My Sergeant should be here any moment," Eichenstat announced, interrupting their silence.

Schroeder could tell from the man's tone that he was suffering; he could see it too in the way he stood. The precise military appearance which Schroeder had seen so often in German officers in uniform was noticeably less precise with Eichenstat now.

"I have seen her for the last time, I'm afraid."

"Colonel," Schroeder said, "You are a good man caught square in the middle of a horrible predicament. You have my deepest sympathy, and my total respect. You are in my prayers, Colonel."

Eichenstat looked at him with his haunting, bloodshot eyes. He swallowed. "Father, see that she ... is looked after properly. And, please, if you can, inform me of the final outcome." He put out his hand to the priest who took it in a firm grip.

"You do not want to see ... her?"

"And prolong my torture? It is bad enough. She says we shall see each other again, but I ... can't see how that's possible. I am a fatalist about that, you see."

"Does she know you are leaving so early?"

Eichenstat shook his head. "I told her I would see her in the morning."

"She ..."

"Of course she will," Eichenstat said, sensing what the man had on his mind.

As he said this a car came through the gate. Sergeant Pond was behind the wheel.

"Goodbye, Father," Eichenstat said, picking up his briefcase. "Thanks for . . ." He got in the car quickly.

"Quickly, Sergeant," he ordered. "Move!"

As the car began to move he could not resist. He looked back, up at the window. There she was. She was there looking down at him, standing at the window in a white gown covering her body, a white scarf covering her head. white.

"Quickly, Sergeant!" he ordered harshly.

The car shot forward and was almost immediately at the gate.

Upstairs at the window Gabriella was in panic. She rushed downstairs and outside. Her heart was pounding; she was breathing hard; her eyes peered out at the gate. The rear of the car was just disappearing. It was quickly out of her sight. She slumped.

Father Schroeder ran toward her but before he reached her she turned and was back in the house quickly. Schroeder followed but when he got inside she was already up the stairs.

A few minutes later Anna came down.

"Sister Katherine is crying, Father. Her door is locked. When I knocked she would not answer. What is wrong?"

Schroeder decided to be truthful. "Her friend Colonel Eichenstat is gone. She may never see him again. He is a soldier and he cannot be sure where he will be sent."

"He could be killed?"

"Yes, he could be killed."

"German soldiers make me scared."

"Colonel Eichenstat is one of the good ones, Anna. There are many others too but ... it is a hard time. Many people are scared."

"Am I going to stay here?" Anna asked.

"No, all of us are going to Brussels."

"That's in Belgium."

"I have a friend there who is going to help us. We are going to take a trip with Sister Katherine. I will be going too."

"Where are we going?"

"Maybe France, maybe even Spain," Schroeder told her.

"We will stay there ... forever?"

"No, probably not, but it will give us time to think of what is best to do next. We will wait and see what happens here in Germany. There is a war, you know."

"Sure, I know. I know many things. I hear the bombs."

The stairs behind them creaked as Gabriella came down. "You sure ask a lot of questions, Anna," she said.

"Sister, why were you crying?" Anna asked straightaway. "I heard you crying."

"I told her that you were crying because your friend went away," Schroeder said quickly.

"Father Schroeder is correct, Anna. The Colonel and I have been friends a long time. Now we must part. He is a soldier and I am a nun. Our lives are different. Our paths are different. It is God's way, I suppose, and one cannot fight God, can one?"

"If it makes you sad why does God let it happen?" she asked.

Gabriella looked at Father Schroeder. "I'm not sure anyone can really answer that one, Anna, except that maybe God is testing me to see just how strong my faith is. We all must be strong in these times, Anna."

"Father says we are going to Brussels today," Anna said to Gabriella.

"That is right. We must get ready."

"We have to be at the Bishop's residence by noon," Schroeder said. "I'll prepare some breakfast. The two of you get ready."

Colonel Eichenstat was feeling ill. He was choking.

"Stop the car, Sergeant!"

Pond hit the breaks. They were not going fast and the vehicle stopped instantly. Eichenstat opened the door and leaned out. He vomited onto the pavement. He closed the door before Pond could get out.

"No need, Sergeant." He wiped his mouth with his handkerchief.

"Sir?"

"Too much to drink last night," he said. "We can proceed now."

"A party, Sir? Last night?"

Eichenstat knew he would have to engage the Sergeant and continue his lies. "The girl, she was not unreasonable. I was surprised."

"The priest, he was pleased?"

"Very much so. I have the feeling we shall not see the girl for a while."

"What will become of her, Sir?"

Eichenstat was having a terrible time concentrating. Images of Gabriella would not leave his mind. He guessed they never would but it could not remain like this, a burning agony blazoned within his head. He was feeling intensely angry, yet he knew he had to maintain his composure and continue working on Sergeant Pond so that in the days ahead Anna's disappearance would not seem too unusual. Just how Father Schroeder handled that part of their charade he was not sure. He would do everything he could to help cover for him but he could not be sure that whatever he did would shield Schroeder if anyone began inquiring further into this matter. As far as the record was concerned Father Schroeder was the last person in Germany with whom the girl was seen. Pond, himself, could be considered a witness to that.

23

JUNE 18, 1940
MID-MORNING
AACHEN, GERMANY

There would be only one point of their trip from Aachen to Brussels that worried Father Schroeder: the border crossing from Germany into Belgium. He was counting on the fact that the Germans were so delighted that under the Concordat the Vatican had agreed to stay out of the political life of the Reich provided the Reich allowed the Vatican to tend to religious matters that it deemed under its direct care. Convents and monasteries certainly qualified in that regard and Schroeder was counting on the Reich's officials in the field not standing in the way of his travels because of that agreement. Still, he could not help thinking that he might have to bluff his way through this time. He always felt that there would be some official of the

Reich with aspirations for advancement who would pop up and upset the apple cart.

When they reached the German-Belgium border Schroeder held his breath. He informed the soldier who came to the car of their business in Belgium. A second soldier, barely twenty years old by his appearance, came over close to the car and looked admiringly at Anna through the side window, adjusting the strap of the rifle that hung on his shoulder. Anna looked back at him nervously. He smiled. As he peered through the open window his eyes suddenly left Anna and settled briefly on Sister Katherine. She gave him a stare that made him divert his look and step back a little; he quickly gave Anna one last look before walking back around the car to take up a position next to the soldier who was still talking to Father Schroeder through the front window of the car.

The guard folded the papers and handed them back. Schroder smiled and shifted the car into gear.

The border disappeared in the rear and Schroeder breathed a sigh. As they drove on he said to himself: one day this talent of yours might fail you if you happen to run up against an adversary who could see through it all, or catch what sounded like a serious inconsistency in your story, if those stories become too convoluted. If that day ever came, your days will surely be kaput, priest or no priest.

They arrived at Bishop Micara's residence in Brussels just fifteen minutes before Micara's luxurious automobile came through the gate, Father Dubois behind the wheel. The car Schroeder had driven to Brussels was now parked beside the residence, near the back, under a tree. He had already taken out the two small suitcases belonging to Gabriella and Anna and his own one small traveling bag. He had locked the car and the keys were now in the side pocket of his jacket which he had zipped closed. He would need the car for his trip back to Aachen when he returned from wherever Micara was about to take them. Right now he did not know when that time would be exactly.

From here on out Bishop Micara and Father Arnaud Dubois were running the show. Schroeder hoped the two men possessed the guile and cunning that he thought would be necessary to get Gabriella and Anna to their final destination in one piece.

They spent the next hour packing things in the car's trunk and on its roof. Schroeder helped Father Dubois fasten the boxes on the carrying racks on the roof.

Bishop Micara came out of the house. His housekeeper was with him and she was crying. He spoke to her as they stood just outside the door. He hugged her, then came over to the car.

He had a sad, disappointed look on his face. "Are we ready, Father?" he said to Father Dubois.

"Ready, Bishop."

Micara turned and looked back at his residence and the housekeeper who was still standing near the door, watching, wiping her eyes.

The Bishop, Gabriella, and Anna sat in the back with Anna in the middle, Father Schroeder up front with Dubois behind the wheel.

"We should reach Paris by nightfall," Dubois said as he started the engine.

In the back seat Gabriella whispered a prayer and quietly caressed her stomach.

On the other side of the car Bishop Micara pondered the plans he and Father Dubois had scrambled to put together a few days ago. Getting to Paris was the first step. They would stay overnight at the residence of the Nuncio Valerio Valeri. They would then travel through Bordeaux, then along the coast of the Bay of Biscay to Bayonne, then on to the Spanish border at Inun. There they would be met by a representative of Bishop of Madrid, Gaetano Cicognani. He would take them to Madrid. From Madrid they hoped to make arrangements to make a run to Lisbon. Once in Lisbon everything was up in the air. Getting passage on a ship was a longshot, especially one to America. For one thing the women had no visas, no papers to permit this. Success seemed a long shot. They could easily become stranded, he thought.

He was sure he had gotten his message to the Vatican describing their route and the official documents they might need. However, he carried little hope that any of it had gotten to Sabastian Arceneau. He grimaced inwardly, knowing how circuitous could be the route of such a message once it arrived inside the walls of Vatican City. He could imagine how many such pleas arrived there every day.

Hardly anyone spoke as they made their way across Belgium into France, headed to Paris. They passed some trucks filled with German soldiers. Anna asked Sister Katherine a question and it was clear that she was nervous. Bishop Micara patted her hand for reassurance.

"Take heart, Anna. Nothing will happen to you if you are with us. We are all safe in God's hands."

They were fortunate in one way: the large size of the car had a roomy interior and they were not cramped at all. The seats were cushiony and there was plenty of room for their outstretched legs. The ride was smooth thanks to the car's large tires and heavy-duty shocks. Once, as they approached Paris, they had to pull over to allow a convey of German vehicles pass.

The machines made an angry, grinding sound and their passing reverberations shook the car.

They had sufficient petrol to get to Paris but they stopped twice in order to walk about and stretched their legs and find suitable bathroom facilities. At their second stop several young men fixed their eyes on Anna as she emerged from the car and stretched her arms upward. She didn't notice them, but Gabriella did. It triggered her memory. It was reminiscent of the looks that Fritz used to send her way when they had been students and she would be walking across the campus toward him, or sometimes when she walked away. They were looks that boys her age often sent her way when she was in school, teenage looks of aspirations and desires.

There was only a peek of sunlight still holding in the sky when they drove into Paris. There was no mistaking that the city was no longer in the hands of the Parisians. Concentrations of German soldiers stood about, laughing, joking, relishing in their new circumstance. Some were unloading material from trucks, preparing quarters for those who would occupy the city and take up their positions and reside among the ordinary French population. The occupation had begun. It looked as if the Germans were preparing to remain for a long time. It was hard to think of Paris as a German city without cringing.

The Bishop's oversized automobile with its boxes and luggage on top looked to be an anomaly among the numerous military vehicles which now dominated the streets. Micara had the address of Bishop Valeri's residence and they made it there in just under an hour.

"We have rooms waiting for you," one of the men who came out of the house to help them said.

"Is Bishop Valeri here?" Micara asked.

"Shortly," the man said. "He was called away by the German authorities."

"Trouble?" Micara asked.

"Who really knows with the Germans, but I don't think so. There seems to be some confusion on the roads south of the city."

The house was large, three stories tall. The Bishop was given his own room; Father Schroeder and Father Dubois another to share; Gabriella and Anna shared a third.

They began their evening meal without Bishop Valeri. They were nearly finished when he showed up. He apologized as he came in, then Micara introduced him to everyone.

"These are very ugly times," Valeri said.

"Has any word come to me about a man named Sabastian Arceneau?" Micara asked.

"Nothing."

"Nothing from the Gregory Foundation either?"

The Bishop shook his head. "I'm sorry."

Micara said nothing. His silence became awkward after a while. Micara then said, "How are the Germans conducting themselves? We were told they called you away."

"More like I called on them," Valeri said. "Just today we heard reports of some disturbing activity around Bordeaux and along some of the main roads into the city. An unusual number of people trying to get to the Portuguese Consulate there. People wanting visas. We are trying to monitor the situation but it is so difficult. From what little information we have it sounds as if there is some real despair, people are frantic. There are stories of suicides."

Micara and Dubois looked at each other.

"We were hoping to go to Bordeaux," Micara said.

"That will be ... risky perhaps."

"We have no choice. All our plans hinge on getting to Madrid through Irun," Micara told him.

Father Schroeder flinched. He, himself, would not have informed the Bishop of that. Schroeder then said to Valeri in an attempt to dampen that piece of information. "We could also cross at San Sebastian. The border can be crossed at many places. It may be Irun, it may be elsewhere."

Micara stared at him; so did Valeri. "You speak as if you know this for a fact," Valeri said.

Schroeder was quick to answer. "I have gone there to hike in the Pyrenees countryside. Crossed the border many times. Many places to cross, if you know how to go about it, and have the stamina. The mountains are high."

Valeri asked, sounding as if he knew something. "Did you do your hiking before or after the revolution?"

"Both," Schroeder said. "Most of it after."

Valeri dwelled on that for a moment and then turned to Micara. "You informed me that you are going to Madrid to see our old friend Cicognani."

"We are. I am hoping he can help us get Sister Katherine and Anna to Portugal, to Lisbon where they might find ship passage."

Once again Father Schroeder thought Micara was saying too much. His experiences told him that the least said the better. Did Valeri need to know these things? If Micara felt free to tell

Valeri then maybe it was all right, he thought. He tried to relax. Maybe he was just too cautious.

"Cicognani is resourceful," Valeri said, smiling. "He just might help you. But these times are so challenging."

"Well, yes, but we still have Sabastian Arceneau and the Gregory Foundation," Micara replied.

"Sabastian is a good man," Sister Katherine said, bringing everyone's attention to her. "I know him."

"So do I," Anna added.

"Well," Valeri said. "From the admiring looks on your faces this man must be quite something."

"He works through the Vatican," Micara said.

Father Schroeder was ready to throttle Micara. He talked too much.

"Do you know Arceneau, Bishop Valeri?" Schroeder asked, interrupting the direction of the conversation. "Have you ever had the opportunity to work with him?"

The question seemed to baffle Valeri for a moment. "Well, no, I'm not even sure what business he's in. What does he do?"

"He works for the Gregory Foundation. And, the Gregory works with the Vatican sometimes," Micara interjected.

"Doing what?" Valeri asked.

Schroeder wanted to answer before Micara said anything more. "Mr. Arceneau facilitates," Schroeder answered quickly.

Valeri smiled. "Is he any good at it?"

Schroeder replied, "Good enough."

Valeri eyed Schroeder. "You have first-hand experience of this, Father?"

Schroeder thought quickly. "Once he helped me with a situation."

"One like your present situation?"

"No," Schroeder said, "Sabastian helped arrange for an individual to win a fellowship to study in England."

"My brother," Anna said excitedly. "He helped my brother."

"That he did," Schroeder confirmed. "Under the auspices of the Gregory Foundation."

"I must learn more about this man Arceneau and the Gregory Foundation, Valeri said. "I, myself, could possibly have need for his services one day."

"I will tell him to contact you when I see him next, Schroeder said.

"I too," Gabriella added.

Valeri turned to Micara, addressing him by his first name. Clamente, are you still planning to go through Bordeaux and on to the Spanish border?

"We are, yes. No other way for us, it seems."

"I must tell you, Clemente, we have received word that the roads are clogged with people fleeing the Nazis. Jews mostly. You will be in the middle of all that if you go."

"I have no choice, Bishop," Micara said. "The Germans want me gone."

"That doesn't mean Spain."

"I have other responsibilities and they take me to see Cicognani in Madrid first. After that I shall likely serve my Belgian flock from an office in the Vatican. That is what I have informed the Vatican I would do, and they have agreed. They are expecting me."

Later, when they finally broke up and were heading back to their rooms Valeri took Bishop Micara aside. "Father Schroeder is an interesting man. I get the feeling from his words that there is more to his history than a simple ordinary parish priest. Sister Katherine and the girl, is there something special about them? I feel that Father Schroeder spoke as if to cloud the issue."

"Father Schroeder is a man with special skills, Bishop. He is putting them to good use as he goes about doing the Lord's work."

"He is not going on to Rome with you, is he?"

"No, he is not. He cannot. Too many people in his church need his guidance."

24

JUNE 19, 1940
PARIS, FRANCE

They were anxious to get going again. All their luggage was packed away. Micara thanked Bishop Valeri for his hospitality as the two shook hands.

"God go with you," Valeri said as Micara climbed in the back seat beside Anna.

The morning was bright and sunny, one of those mornings with a scent in the air that gave an extra special meaning to being alive. Father Dubois drove through the city slowly, somewhat cautiously, heading for the main road south of the city that would take them to Bordeaux. There was more of a German presence today than there had been yesterday. As they had seen yesterday on their drive into the city there were few civilian vehicles being driven on the street. Civilian pedestrians outnumbered soldiers on foot, however. One could only speculate how quickly the Parisians would adjust to their new circumstances.

Within an hour Micara's car was on the open road outside the city. Here the scene was more rural and the German presence was less noticeable. Several times they came upon a truck carrying troops or supplies to outlying areas. They spotted an army half-track parked under a clump of trees with a soldier sitting behind a menacing-looking large machine gun perched on top.

Soon they were traveling at a steady clip having to slow down on occasion when some slower moving vehicle appeared, or some wagon or bicyclist blocked their way. For the most part the road was open. They drove through Orleans, then Tours, and then Poitiers. The town of Noirt was now up ahead. No one said much. Bishop Micara's large car offered them a comfortable ride thanks to its heavy, reinforced suspension and balloon-like tires.

Gradually the scene outside began to take on a little different look. There was more traffic, they were passing more people on the road, civilians walking and pulling carts and wagons. Father Dubois tapped the breaks, slowing down for this one, then for that one. They were coming up on the town of Noirt. It was shortly before noon.

"Time for a short rest," Bishop Micara said.

"And some food," Father Dubois added.

I see some buildings up ahead," Father Schroeder said. As they get closer they couldn't miss the beautiful flowered garden adjacent to the buildings. They looked in at the three, single-story structures. Dubois slowed the car to a crawl.

"Shall we stop, Bishop?" Dubois asked.

"Looks to be an inn of some kind," Schroeder said.

"Maybe there's a restroom," Gabriella said.

Father Dubois pulled the car over and stopped and they all climbed out. Father Schroeder and Father Dubois went inside to look around while the others waited near the car. When they entered, a man came up to them; he introduced himself as Patrice Fournier, proprietor.

"Have you seen many Germans this way?" Schroeder asked.

"A few speeding trucks come and go," he said. "They do not stop."

A woman came over to them.

"This is my wife, Juliett," Patrice Fournier said. She smiled.

"Do you have a rest room our friends outside might use?" Father Schroeder asked.

Juliette looked through the window at the car. "For the nun and the girl, and the priest?"

"Yes. That is Bishop Micara. He is the Bishop of Brussels. The nun and the young woman are members of his staff."

"You are a long way from home," Patrice said.

"The Bishop thought it best under the circumstances if he left Brussels," Father Dubois said.

"The Germans," Patrice Fournier said knowingly.

Dubois nodded.

"We have toilet facilities you may use," Juliette said.

As she said this she looked back out the window at the people passing on the road. "Jews," she said. "They are all fleeing."

"We have passed many," Schroeder said.

"Many passed yesterday," Patrice told them.

"They don't come in here," Juliette said. "They keep to themselves. They have no time to waste."

"Too bad," Patrice said with a pout. "We could use the business. Do you intend to have a meal?" he asked them.

"No, we have brought some food from Paris. We would like to sit in your garden and eat if you would allow us," Schroeder said. "We will pay for the privilege."

"Of course, but no money," Juliette said

"You are generous. We should not be long. We must be on our way if we are to get to Bordeaux by nightfall."

After they had each used the toilet facilities and eaten lunch in the garden Gabriella and Anna strolled among the flowers and shrubs as the men checked over the car to see that all was packed securely. Gabriella breathed in the fresh air and felt the gentle breeze drift over her as she walked. The aroma of the blooming flowers was in the air. God's creation, she thought. In her mind it was another turn of God's annual cycle of growth and beauty. She then thought of Fritz Eichenstat and the time years ago when the two of them had walked through an entire field of wild flowers on their way to hike up a small mountain during a weekend excursion a group of students from the university was taking. She wondered what Fritz was doing just now?

"Sister, it's time to go," Father Schroeder called from near the car. "Let's go, Anna."

They once again climbed in and tried to make themselves comfortable. Father Dubois said, "Next stop, Saintes."

Half way to Saintes the road seemed more crowded then before. Motorized traffic had increased some and more people were walking, some with sacks on their backs; many carrying suitcases and containers of possessions. Children were laboring in their walk to keep up with the adults. Micara's car passed wagons loaded down, often being pulled by one or more people or by horse or mule; some cyclists struggled in their peddling, some were off their bikes and walking beside them. Automobiles, loaded down much like Micara's, were becoming more common. All of this humanity was flowing in the same direction - south, toward Spain..

The entire spectacle of human migration was a dismal reminder that this part of the world was on the verge of something unholy.

They passed through Saintes and were now moving steadily closer to their destination - Bordeaux. The traffic flow remained a steady stream. At the top of the hill they encountered a slowdown. A group of men were pushing a broken down car off the road and out of the way. As Micara's car came up and slowed, then stopped, Father Schroeder leaned out. "Trouble?" he asked in French.

"Petrol," the man said, throwing up his hands, His twisted face showed his panic. Inside the car children cried and a mother tried to calm them. "No petrol!" the man cried, looking around in desperation at his family inside the car.

Father Dubois waited a brief second then put the car in gear and moved forward. As he did so he looked into the mirror to see the man yelling and gesturing at the children as they climbed out of the car.

"Say a prayer," Sister Katherine said.

Not long after they once again encountered a delay. Two cars had collided and the people were standing about, arguing while all around relatives were grabbing up the items that had been scattered about on the ground and throwing them back into whatever containers they possessed. Passers-by, preoccupied with their own plight, walked around them with little comment, or notice.

"Look at it," Father Schroeder said in a horrified tone.

Micara commented, "What thoughts must be going through the minds of all these people? The anxious looks on their faces."

"And fear," Schroeder added angrily. "The blank stares."

"Can we help them?" Anna asked.

"I don't see how," Micara replied. "Except to say a prayer and ask for God's help."

It was a depressing scene: human beings struggling to stay ahead of what they envisioned as the awful terror that lay behind them. They were being hunted, and they knew it. Certainly these experiences would brand dark images on their minds that would be impossible to exorcize.

It was the same relentless stream of humanity all the way into Bordeaux.

"There's the Pierre Bridge up ahead," Micara said, pointing forward over the seat. "An elegant structure."

They drove across the bridge and down the Cours Victor Hugo, leaving the Pierre Bridge behind them. Unexpectedly the traffic began to thin as one by one the cars and carts and people began to peel off onto the side streets. For some reason they seemed to be abandoning the wide boulevard.

"What is everyone doing?" Micara asked.

"We should find a place for the night," Father Dubois said.

"I never imagined we'd face all these people," Micara said.

"Better keep going straight ahead, Father."

Dubois replied, "We could be in for a nasty, uncomfortable night if we have to spend it in the car. It could be dangerous. No doubt there are some desperate people out there."

"The only thing we can do is head for the Cathedral Saint-Andre," Micara said. "I visited there several years ago. If my recollection serves me right this avenue should intersect with Cours Pasteur. The Cathedral is on that street, I believe. We might get some help there."

They were lost. Father Dubois drove slowly.

"Ask that woman over there," Father Schroeder said suddenly, pointing. "She looks as if she belongs here."

Father Dubois eased the car over to where she was standing.

"Madame," Bishop Micara said.

The woman came closer, but it was obvious she wanted to keep her distance.

"We are lost and need some directions. I am Bishop Micara from Belgium, Madame."

She gave him a sleepy look, an expression that said she was unimpressed by his title and his office, or, maybe, she didn't believe his story about who he claimed to be.

She huffed. "What do you want from me?" she asked, peering up at the great heap of material on top the car. "Why are *you* on the run?" she said unexpectedly.

He smiled at her. "Well," he said, "I've been expelled from my diocese by the Germans and I am trying to make my way to Rome."

She raised her eyebrows. "At least the Huns gave you a choice. Our streets are suddenly filled with people who seem to have no choice."

"We have seen many of them," Micara said.

"More than enough," she replied. "All day. Are any more back there?" she asked, twisting her head.

Micara frowned. "I believe so, yes."

The woman shook her head. "Too bad, but I guess they brought it on themselves."

Micara's mind went blank for a second, then he recovered. He knew the prejudices that lurked in some of the French. "They deserve our pity, Madame," Micara said.

"Of course, Bishop," she grinned. "Of course."

"Can you tell us how to get to the Cathedral Saint-Andre? I feel we are close to it?" he asked her.

She pointed. "Straight to Cours Pasteur. Go right. You'll see the steeple."

He thanked her, and they drove off.

"Unfortunate comments, ladies," Bishop Micara said.

Neither Gabriella or Anna said anything.

They found the Cathedral with no difficulty. It seemed strange but there were only a handful of cars parked and the place seemed almost lifeless. A subdued glow of candle light issued through the stained glass of the cathedral's windows. The adjacent building close to the cathedral was nearly dark, only two windows in the back showed any light.

Father Schroeder and Father Dubois both got out of the car and surveyed the scene around them. Bishop Micara got out right behind them, shutting the rear door.

"I'll make some inquiries," Micara said. "Wait here."

Micara left and was soon back. There was a priest and another man with him. Micara introduced Schroeder and Dubois to Father Chabot whom, he said, would put them up for the night.

They took from the car what they would need for the night.

"After you are settled come to the kitchen and you can eat," Father Chabot told them.

A short time later they were seated in a small dining room next to the kitchen. Father Chabot had arranged to have a variety of meats, cheeses, and breads and several bottles of delicious wine waiting for them. When they had finished Gabriella and Anna said good night and went to their room; the men remained at the table talking to Father Chabot. Bishop Micara wanted to know anything about what might be ahead for them tomorrow. They drank more wine. Micara brought up his worry about not possessing the proper papers for the women. They had left Brussels so hurriedly with so much of their plans up in the air he told Father Chabot.. Father Chabot was about to say something when they heard the thunder off in the distance. The first sound was a sharp bang followed quickly by more bangs that rolled through the air in quick, overlapping succession. It was then they realized it was not thunder they were hearing. Just then the building vibrated as the shock waves from the distant booms reached the church area. They scrambled to the windows. In the distance they saw the once quiet darkness being assaulted by angry explosions bursting out in orange and white. The skyline was aglow. The stone church vibrated again as the shock waves rolled in once more. The glasses and utensils on the wooden table pulsed with tiny dancing oscillations; the chairs bounced across the floor. Then came the drone of airplanes overhead.

"They're bombing!" Father Chabot cried with a bilious twist of his mouth and disbelieving expression. "God Almighty they're bombing us!"

"Who?" Father Dubois asked.

"My countrymen!" Schroeder cried angrily. "Who else could it be!" he said sadly.

Father Chabot cried again, "But we have no army any more, no anything!"

They all were frozen at the window staring in dismay at the not too distant brightness.

Schroeder whispered, "Those poor people." He then crossed himself. "Helpless children in their beds." He wanted to cry knowing it was Germans who were doing this.

"What should we do?" Father Dubois said almost to himself.

Just then Gabriella and Anna appeared in the doorway behind them.

"We heard the thunder," Gabriella said excitedly. "Then we saw it was not thunder!"

"I must go to them," Father Chabot said.

"I'll go with you," Father Schroeder said.

"We'll all go," Gabriella said.

"No," Micara said, surprising everyone. "We cannot afford to get stranded here in Bordeaux. Our movement to the border is touch and go as it is. If anyone gets hurt, or worse there's no telling what we'd then face. Too much can happen to prevent us from reaching our destination."

Father Schroeder though that Micara's point was well taken. It also brought to his mind his own promise to Colonel Eichenstat to get Gabriella and Anna to safety. As for himself, Schroeder knew his role in this matter was essentially completed. He was not going to be the one to take Gabriella and Anna all the way to Portugal anyway. He was along only to the border. After that it would be Micara and his friends who would have to finish the job. At the border Schroeder would leave and head back to his church in Aachen. For him, he could only hope Micara could pull it all off and get Gabriella and Anna to safety.

"The Bishop is right," Schroeder told Gabriella. "My role is about over. I will go with Father Chabot, the rest of you should remain here. If something happens and I do not return by morning you can continue on without me." He then smiled. "But I'm pretty sure I'll be here waiting for you and ready to leave in the morning. Let's go Father," he said to Chabot.

No one argued and the two of them left.

JUNE 20, 1940
BORDEAUX, FRANCE

True to his word Schroeder was waiting for them the following morning. He had gotten little sleep and his face showed his weariness. Micara and the others questioned Schroeder about what he and Father Chabot had seen and done when they had reached the location of the bombing. Hearing what Schroder described made Gabriella feel a morbid anger at her countrymen; she was certain he had not told them the full story.

Through it all Bishop Micara was pushing them to depart. Schroeder understood his anxiety. Last night's bombing had unnerved the man. Schroeder suspected the Bishop was rightly having thoughts of the border being closed at any moment. The Germans had shown their level of hardheartedness and they could only guess at what other plans they had in store for the near rabid stream of people heading south to the Spanish border.

Just before they were ready to get in the car Father Chabot went up to Bishop Micara with a basket.

"Some food and some of our special wine. As I told you last night, we make it here in our vineyards. Also, what we suspected has been confirmed. It was the Germans who did the bombing. Many people are running south, to Spain. No one is sure why the Germans did it but it could be part of a plan of some sort."

"The reason we must get back on the road quickly," Micara said.

"I have been thinking of what you said last night just before the bombing started, about your lack of official papers to cross the border and get to Lisbon. I didn't have time to tell you to look for a man by the name of Sousa Mendes. I know him. He is the Portuguese counsel here in Bordeaux. He might be able to help you. He is the reason so many people have come here. It is to get Sousa Mendes to give them papers to Portugal. The Portugese Consulate is located here and they need visas to get them across Spain and into Portugal. The people have heard that Sousa Mendes is handing out safe passage documents and visas at will."

"Things are beginning to make more sense now," Schroeder said, listening in on their conversation. "Those people we saw leaving the avenue yesterday when we came into the city were heading for the Portugese Consulate."

Chabot continued. "I made an inquiry this morning, trying to find Sousa Mendes. The Consulate said he took to the road just a few minutes before I called. They told me he is headed for Bayonne."

"Sousa Mendes, I'll remember that name," Bishop Micara said. "But if we can get to the border and then to Madrid and Bishop Cicognani my hope is he can somehow arrange for us to get to Portugal, and Lisbon."

Father Chabot nodded. "Yes, but in these times it would be wise to have some backup in the pocket. Sousa Mendes might be a good backup. Look for him. He is a good man. You may not realize it but the Germans might have plans to close the border. Last night might not have been all to what they have planned."

Micara replied, "But to go looking for this man might get us gobbled up in this mayhem of human commotion. No telling where that might take us and we have to be in Irun at a certain time. I have no way to communicate to the Bishop's representative who will be waiting in Irun. If anything goes wrong and we get derailed looking for Mendes it could smash all out efforts. I feel I must stay on schedule."

Chabot said. "It was just a thought."

Micara shook Chabot's hand, then Father Schroeder did the same. "We thank you for everything," Schroeder said.

"You have been a blessing," Micara told Chabot.

Ten minutes later Father Dubois had Micara's car back on the open road on their way to the next town. Once there they would head to Castets, then Bayonne, and then to Irun at the border crossing into Spain. If all went as planned Bishop Cicognani's representative would meet them there and escort them to Madrid. That would put them closer to Lisbon.

The crowds on the road looked a little different, a bit more numerous and bearing more anxious, fearful looks on their faces. The two times they stopped to stretch their legs they overheard the name Sousa Mendes in the agitated conversations of those around them. The pulse of the people was definitely quickening inside their lethargically moving bodies. Micara and the others sensed that they knew that Sousa Mendes was the only one who could get them to Lisbon and, maybe, a lucky passage off the European continent. It didn't matter just where that passage might take them as long as it took them away from the grasp of the new Europe. Of course the destination everyone wanted was America but, as most of them knew, that was the longest of long shots. Just about any other country would do for the present but everyone knew that most countries had erected formidable policies against admitting Jews. The easiest ports of entry were any number of South American countries. South Africa was a good bet as well.

As they drove along it was not hard to read what they were seeing. As they had seen the day before they saw now the same dreaded expressions on the faces of the people they passed; they moved with the same haltering steps; they bore the same watchful eyes darting about, warily suspicious of those who looked at them. Many turned their eyes away and quickened their steps, wanting no part of any outsider. The thought crossed Father Schroeder's mind that he was seeing people in the throes of losing their minds. The fear that was lurking inside them was slowly strangling their ability to reason sanely, to think logically, and calmly. Watching them, Schroeder thought that all sense of reality was seeping out of them. They had lost just about all trust they might have once possessed. Panic was building.

By late afternoon they were closing in on Bayonne. The road was more clogged. The unhappy struggle was magnified here. All the emotions were concentrated in one tight place.

They stopped a few miles outside the main part of the city to rest and gather their thoughts. Gabriella and Anna walked away from the car and over to the shade of some trees, still close to the road. The people came down the road and passed them in broken clusters, families; they were sweaty, and so many seemed to be fighting for every breath, bending, pulling the belongings. It was the old ones having the most difficult time. The stress was taking a toll.

Gabriella saw a woman and two small girls standing in the road. The woman's flashing eyes looked one way than another, straining to locate something.

"Joel," she yelled. "Joel."

She frowned and moved back slightly as Gabriella approached her.

"What is it, Madame?" Gabriella asked.

"My. . .husband. I have lost him!" Her voice was shaking.

Anna drew close to them.

The woman stared at them. "You sound German?"

"We are, Madame.

She frowned. "Why. . .you are not. . . Jewish."

Gabriella said nothing. The woman gave Anna a stern look and Anna knew what it meant. Anna remained quiet.

There were tears in the woman's eyes now. "Joel ... he has our visas, and ... we have ... become separated. He was helping a neighbor and ... I don't know where he is."

"He'll find you," Gabriella said.

Then from back down the road there came a shout, "Eliana, Eliana!"

A man was running waving his arm in the air. "Eliana!"

"Joel! Oh, Joel!" the woman yelled heading toward him in a hurry. They embraced with great elation. The two little girls were soon huddled around, jumping up and down with happy giddiness, clutching at the man. The woman was now weeping uncontrollably. "Jo … el." She kissed him as she threw her arms around him. Gabriella and Anna watched the joyful reunion.

"This is my husband Joel," the woman said holding tight to his arm as they walked toward Gabriella and Anna.

"I am Sister Katherine. This is Anna," Gabriella said.

"We are the Gutmanns," the man said. "We are going to Portugal. We have visas thanks to Mr. Sousa Mendes."

"You are some of the lucky ones," Gabriella said.

"And you?" Joel Gutmann asked. "Where are you headed?"

"Madrid first," Gabriella replied. "Then Portugal, we hope."

"Lisbon?" the woman asked, looking at Anna. "For the girl," she added, returning her look to Gabriella.

"We are going to visit Bishop Cicognani in Madrid. He may be able to get us into Portugal," Gabriella told them. "Lisbon, yes. If we can."

"Try to find Mr. Sousa Mendes," Joel Gutmann said.

"We shall try," Grabriela said. "But he seems to be a man besieged with pleas from so many. He could be hard to locate."

"They say he is somewhere in the crowd that is heading south. They say he left Bordeaux last night after the bombing," Gutmann said.

"We heard the bombing," Gabriella said.

It was then that a yell came from father Schroeder. "Time to get back on the road, Sister, Anna."

"Coming, Father."

They said their goodbys and the woman gave Anna a hug. "Shalom," she said.

Anna did not reply.

Back on the road their progress was as slow as before.

"Maybe we should try to find Mr. Sousa Mendes," Anna suddenly said.

Without turning, Bishop Micara said with a quiet tone of resignation, "Where would we look, Anna? Besides, we don't have the time. We have to get to Irun on time."

Anna looked down. "I'm sorry."

Micara patted her hand. "We'll get you to Lisbon," he said.

Anna looked over at him.

Micara smiled. "All we have to do is get to the border. We'll go straight to Hendaye, cross the river to Irun. The border guards will admit us. Bishop Cicognani will have the necessary documents waiting to let us enter. His personal emissary will have everything we need. The Bishop understands our special situation. I talked to him personally."

"Maybe this is a good place for me to leave you," Father Schroeder surprised everyone by saying. "I have no authority to go into Spain. It would jeopardize my standing back in Aachen. I have work to do there. My parish. These are people who rely on me."

Micara frowned. "How will you get back?"

It was strange but they had never discussed this.

Schroeder grinned in his usual confident manner. "Sometimes I think maybe I missed my true calling. I live now with so much subterfuge and slight of hand."

Father Dubois grinned to himself, then said, "Maybe you could hitch a ride in a German military vehicle."

Schroeder laughed. "After I get back to Paris possibly."

Dubois looked over at Schroeder. There was no smile now, there was only seriousness. "Don't become too complacent," Dubois warned.

Schroeder knew Dubois was right. He then had a thought which disturbed him: *things had been too easy lately.*

"Well," Schroeder said, "I'll leave you."

"Here!" Micara said.

"You'll be stranded," Gabriella added.

"Are you sure?" Dubois said. He slowed the car but did not stop.

Schroeder assured them, "There are vehicles going the other way. I'll catch a ride."

Dubois hit the brakes. Schroeder opened the door half way. He looked at each of them. "After the war ..." He got out and reached up and pulled down his bag from between two of the suitcases on top the car. He threw it over his shoulder.

"Father," Gabriella said. "May I speak with you a moment in private?"

Schroeder looked at her. "Of course," he said. She got out and walked off to the side.

Schroeder lowered his head and looked through the window of the car. "God be with you," he said to those inside, then turned and walked to where Gabriella was waiting.

She said with a soft, caring voice, "How will you fare?"

"God will be with me, Gabriella."

She dropped her eyes. "Yes," she whispered.

"You have Anna to look after as well as yourself," he said. "God has given you a heavy burden."

"All will be better when we reach America," she said.

"A long way away. Much could stand in your way."

"We are in good hands."

"God's hands."

"Father," she then whispered in a faint choking tone. "See about Colonel Eichenstat. He will have difficulties too, I am certain." She wiped at her eyes. Emotion was taking over.

"We will find a way to communicate," Schroeder told her.

"Maybe Mr. Arceneau," she offered. "He has ways, doesn't he?"

"I will find a way. When you get to America you might find people who ... could help get information to me. I could get it to the Colonel."

She began to cry openly. "Oh, Father, I have done such a very bad thing and I wanted to be such a good nun, a good ..."

Schroeder grabbed her hands. "I prefer to believe that your actions were guided by the Holy Spirit, Gabriella. You acted out of love for people who were counting on you for their survival. God put you in that place for a reason."

"But ... I ... enjoyed ... being with Fritz, Father. I told you! I told you!"

Schroeder reached out and drew her to him.

"Of course you enjoyed it. You are a creature of God. I told you before. Being the person He made it would have been impossible for you *not* to have enjoyed it."

She sniffled and pulled away from him slightly.

"Should I have been a nun? Had I not been a nun I could not have violated my vows. I would have taken no vows!"

"Gabriella, you have not been listening to me," he said with a slightly raised voice. "You must stop torturing yourself with your feelings of guilt. If you feel the need for forgiveness God has already forgiven you. You have confessed with a sincere conscience believing in the validity of your transgressions. It is up to God to make the final determination. It is always that way. I believe that He already has. I have given you absolution. Now my sweet Gabriella, you have to continue along the path God has set before you. Do you believe that all this that we are witnessing going on around us is mere chance; you carrying this child, conceived under these circumstances? Think about it. There is no possible way you can fail, Gabriella, no matter what hardship awaits you. No matter who confronts you."

She replied with a choking voice, "Pray for me."

He smiled. "We shall meet again in this life, Gabriella."

She left him standing there alone. She did not look back, although she desperately wanted to.

When she climbed back into the car no one spoke to her. Her's had been a private matter. Father Dubois started the car and drove off. As he did he checked the rear-view mirror. He saw Father Schroeder standing, looking after them; then he saw Schroeder turn and begin walking in the opposite direction. Dubois watched him as he disappeared on the other side of the hill.

It was not long before they were at the river Bidasoa, the border between France and Spain. Irun was just on the other side less than a mile away. The bridge across the river carried a steady stream of people and vehicles.

"The crowds will get worse now," Father Dubois remarked.

It was slow going but they finally worked their way across the bridge. They were now completely mixed in with the hundreds, maybe thousands, of people trying to get into and across Spain and on into Portugal and finally to Lisbon. There was only one thought on their minds now: get through the border crossing at Irun. Outside the city, as the mass of people waited, their behavior was noisy and a little pushy but not riotous by any means. No mistake, there was tension just below the surface. Anxieties were high and tempers flared here and there but there were no serious altercations other than a little yelling and cursing between small groups. Everyone was on edge; it was impossible not to feel it. Survival instincts were now lurking just below the surface, ready to react at any hint of being put off or losing out now that they had come this far.

Micara instructed Father Dubois to drive off to the side away from the main part of the crowd and park. Dubois quickly found a good spot and shut off the engine.

"I think if I go on foot we'll have more luck locating the officials in charge of controlling border crossings. I'll also try to find Bishop Cicognani's representative. He should be somewhere up there in one of those buildings. He's probably waiting. I'll be back soon."

Micara left the car and headed in the direction of the gate. Spanish guards flanked each of the three large gates and fenced corridors that had been put in place to control the movement of people; other guards patrolled the long stretches of fence that ran either side of the main gates. When Micara reached the fenced area he then learned that no one was being passed through. Guards were standing stiff and determined, but some of them looked nervous and uneasy. The faces of the younger ones seemed especially tense.

He worked his way up to the fence just beside the gate. He eyed the cluster of military vehicles parked beside the main building along with a large dusty Renault and a Mercedes. Several motorcycles were parked close to the wall of the house. From behind him Micara heard several short angry yells of protest from the crowd; people were becoming increasingly restless, and irritable. Then someone yelled a nasty insult, then another, aimed at the guards, but it was more the frustration at the situation and the waiting with no sign of progress to allow them to pass through to the other side and be on their way to Portugal. The thought that at this late stage something might go wrong and their desire to leave this place was not going to be fulfilled was getting to everyone. Still the guards stance remained unflinching. Micara noticed the eyes of several of the guards kept making sideways glances at the lone officer standing nearby, as if waiting for his signal. Micara studied the officer, a dark, handsome individual, the picture of a Spanish aristocrat in looks and bearing. The man was paying particular attention to the main building, not the crowd on the other side of the fence. Micara focused on the building. Through the front windows he saw several men inside, gesturing as they moved past the windows facing the front. Micara made his way along the fence, trying to get a better look.

"You should wait your turn!" an angry voice said to him. "Everyone wants to be in the front!"

Micara apologized. "I'm sorry." His movement continued, edging closer to where the officer stood. He squeezed himself past a woman who must have noticed his collar.

"What are you doing here, Father," she asked. "I'm sure they'll let *you* in."

She was a tiny woman and he looked down into her face. Her weariness was evident. She was a young woman, yet old, he thought.

"I'm suppose to meet someone here," he told her. It was a mechanical reply.

"Aren't we all," she replied. "But with little success."

"Oh," he replied, frowning. "Who is it you are seeking?"

"Sousa Mendes. They say he's in that building," she nodded. "But I haven't seen him. Wouldn't know him anyway."

Micara's eyes jumped to the building he had been looking at earlier. "In there?"

"Someone said he went there to see if he could arrange with the authorities to open the gates so we can cross into Spain."

Micara said to himself, "So, the near legendary Sousa Mendes is only a few hundred feet away." Then, for no apparent reason he had another thought: what was happening here must be similar to what it must have been like in ancient Palestine when crowds of people struggled to see Jesus to ask for healing, or to hear his teachings. With that thought he now knew he had another reason to meet this man. He inched himself right up to the fence, as close to the officer could get. He wasn't certain but he thought the officer had the rank of captain.

"Captain," he yelled, holding his neck high so as to make his collar easily visible. The officer's eyes narrowed, as if focusing. He came over.

"Father? Why are you out there?"

"I'm Bishop Micara from Brussels."

"A Bishop! Why are you in this crowd!"

Micara grinned. "The Reich has expelled me. I'm on my way to Rome by way of Madrid."

"You have papers to that effect of course?"

"Of course, but they are with my belongings and the members of my party back there in my car. I am expected to meet Bishop Cicognani's representative from Madrid here in Irun. Has he arrived? Is he here, do you know?"

The officer indicated with a movement of his head. "He could be in there."

"With Mr. Sousa Mendes?"

"You know that man?"

"Heard of him."

"Yes, hasn't everyone."

"I'd like to meet him," Micara said.

"If, as you say, you have papers then you have no need of his services," the Captain said.

"Nevertheless, I'd like to meet him. Might you help me do that?"

The Captain grinned. "He's a bit busy now, Bishop."

"What is he doing in there?"

"Trying to get approval to allow these people through. He has his hands full dealing with the two officials sent here to handle this," the officer described.

"Will he succeed?"

Again the officer grinned. "If not, your church will be disappointed, I'm sure. Hitler will applaud us, but the Vatican ... well."

"I take it that my church is not your church," Micara said.

There was no reply.

"What is it that you would have me do for you, Bishop?" the officer then asked.

"Get me through the gate and have me meet Sousa Mendes. At the same time I could see if Bishop Cicgonani's representative has arrived."

The officer hesitated. "Of course I will let you through in order to see if your party from Madrid has arrived. Go to that gate over there," he pointed.

Micara did as he said. The officer opened a single, small gate and Micara went inside. Together they walked to the building.

As they walked the officer said, "You mentioned that you are traveling with a party? How many?"

"Three. They are back there in my car. We have come a long way today. It has been tiring."

"Are they all clergy?"

Micara thought. "Yes," preferring to leave it at that.

"Priests?"

Micara decided to lessen his fabrication; it seemed apparent that the officer was going to keep asking his questions. "One nun, one priest, he's my secretary, and a young girl who is studying to become a nun."

The man smiled. "How young a girl?

"Sixteen," he said. Then, he wasn't sure why, he began fabricating again. "She is also my niece," he said. "Her parents are deceased. I promised her mother to get her to Rome. Her uncle, her mother's brother, lives there."

"And the nun? She going to Rome too?"

"Eventually. First she will visit several convents. She is on a special mission for the Vatican to inspect convents."

"This war has changed many lives, hasn't it?"

"Mine for certain. I'm afraid my people in Brussels will need me in the years ahead, but I had no choice but to leave. The Holy Father instructed me not to disobey the Reich's decree against me."

"Wait here, the officer said. He went inside leaving Micara standing off to the side, less than fifty feet from the building. The men inside were easily visible from where he stood; one window was partially open at the bottom, the other pulled all the way up. Three men were seated at a table. Their voices could be heard but they were not all clear. One of the men got up, then another, one was much shorter than the other, the short one threw his hand into the air. Micara heard him say "Impossible," as he swung around and faced the table again.

The man seated smiled at the man walking and splayed his hands as if explaining something. The man walking grinned; then they all laughed.

When the officer returned he told Micara," You are in luck. The man you are supposed to meet is in Hendaye. There must have been some misunderstanding. He is on his way here to escort you to Madrid."

"Is that Souse Mendes in there?" Micara asked.

The officer looked through the window. "The one seated at the table."

"Distinguished looking isn't he?" Micara said.

The officer grinned. "I have heard that his government in Lisbon is not at all pleased by his actions. His President Salazar is screaming mad, I hear. And the Germans are unhappy too."

"All these people want to do is get across Spain to Portugal," Micara said. "What harm is there in that?"

The door to the building opened and an immediate rumble seeped through the crowd outside the fence as they saw the men come out.

"Sousa Mendes," the officer said to Micara.

Mendes shook hands with the two men who accompanied him out of the building. One of them gestured to the officer with Micara to come over. The man who had gestured came forward a few steps as the officer walked up to him. They conversed for a while. Mendes came over to the officer and the two walked to the gate. The officer said something to the guards at the gate. Mendes spoke to the people close to the gate. The guards then swung the gates open while other guards moved forward and formed a tight corridor to keep the people confined and moving along once they had gotten past the fence. People began slowly filing down the corridor of soldiers. Behind this, as the crowd began to funnel toward the gates, some shoving began from the back as people pressed forward. Mendes yelled to the crowd. It seemed to have an effect as the shoving decreased; the flow began to smooth out and become more orderly. After each person passed by Sousa Mendes they went straight into the building. They remained inside for a short while and then filed out another doorway on the side. The process continued for some time with the Spanish officer keeping his eyes on the proceedings. Sousa Mendes stood at his side. As they made there way through the gate some individuals would stop beside Mendes and he would write something on a piece of paper and hand it to them. Their faces lit up as he did this.

"Visas," Micara said to himself.

Some people grasp Mendes's hand and kissed it. Everyone who passed greeted Mendes with much enthusiasm and affection. After a while the officer looked up and over to Bishop

Micara who had not moved. The officer put his face close to Sousa Mendes's and said something. Mendes looked over at Micara. Micara saw Mendes's eyes focus on his Roman collar.

Cars and carts, bicycles and wagons along with people on foot continued to pass through the gates. Each of these various vehicles had to be parked over under some trees as their owners and passengers left them to go inside the building. Soldiers stood around watching them. This went on for several hours. Soon the crowd had dissipated considerably. Micara could now see his car back past the fence where he had left it. He started to walk back to it. That was when he heard a voice call to him.

"Bishop."

When Micara turned Souse Mendes was almost upon him.

"I was told you wanted to see me."

"I wanted to meet the man I have been hearing so much about ever since I arrived in Bayonne yesterday and all along the road here. I am Bishop Clamente Micara, Bishop of Brussels," he told Sousa Mendes.

Mendes looked puzzled. "What are you doing here in this crowd?"

Micara spent the next few minutes explaining his peculiar circumstance. When he had finished he added, "Strange as it might sound I do have need of your help."

"Surely you have no travel problem," Mendes said.

"I do, yes."

Mendes drew himself in. "How so?"

Micara hesitated a moment. "Mine is a strange story."

"I'd like to hear it," Mendes replied.

Micara looked back at his car. "Could you walk a short distance with me and meet some people who have been traveling with me. They are the reason for the strangeness of my story. You might like to hear it, and meet them."

Mendes visually checked back at the last of the people still moving through the corridor of soldiers at the gate. "Let me tend to some business, over there," he said. "Come along. Afterward I *would* like to hear your story."

The two walked to where the Spanish officer was still standing, attending to his duties, watching the guards and the people coming through. The numbers had diminished. As Sousa Mendes took up his position again nearly everyone had something to say to him.

"God go with you, Souse Mendes."

"You are a holy man, Sousa Mendes."

"God bless you, Sousa Mendes."

"My children and grandchildren will honor you all their days, Sousa Mendes."

Micara was overwhelmed with admiration for this man, seeing the outpouring of affection directed at him. Mendes then broke away, telling the officer, "If anyone needs a visa give them one of these, please." With that he handed the officer a hand full of small papers. The offcier looked at them, then smiled.

As Sousa Mendes and Micara walked to Micara's car Micara told him, "Bishop Cicognani in Madrid is trying to help but I'm beginning to worry that even the Vatican cannot help in this matter. I have some people who have to get to Portugal."

Mendes stopped. "Jews? You?"

Micara nodded. My story is much more unusual than just that."

Mendes grinned a broad grin. Then he said, "We do what we have to do, don't we?"

"We do, with the guidance of the Holy Spirit."

They reached the car. Father Dubois was standing outside watching the two men approach, wondering who the man with the Bishop was. Sister Katherine and Anna were standing on the other side of the car.

"This is the man we have been hearing so much about. This is Mr. Sousa Mendes, Father," Micara told Father Dubois.

"An honor," Dubois said.

Sister Katherine and Anna came around the car. Micara could tell the Mendes was indeed considerably puzzled when he saw that one of the women was dressed in a nun's habit. He looked at Micara for some explanation.

"Yes," Micara said, "She is a nun in the Catholic Church."

Mendes smiled. "You did say your story was a strange one," he said as he introduced himself to Gabriella.

"Your name is on everyone's lips," she said. "Everyone is looking for you."

"They are. I do what I can do," he said.

"God bless you for it."

"Thank you." He looked at Anna. "And this one?"

"This is Anna," Micara said.

Anna curtseyed slightly. "Sir," she said politely.

Mendes looked around. "Any more?"

"Only these two," Micara answered.

"I'm assuming you need visas?"

"We are," Micara said.

"Let's make these really official looking. I will use some names and I have my official stamp," he smiled.

"You are saving many lives," Micara then said. "So many."

"I'll need your real names," he told Gabriella and Anna.

"Gabriella Summers."

"Anna ... Burkitz. I have my certificate of birth and my school papers if you need them, but they are hidden in a secret place with my belongings."

"No need," he told her. "Better keep them well hidden. Well hidden."

He wrote out the same kind of paper for Gabriella.

"Good luck to you all," Mendes said as he put away his pen. "Now, I have to return to the people still going through the gates."

"God bless you," Micara said. "I'll keep you in my prayers."

Mendes suddenly looked sad. "I will need them when I return home. My government is not sympathetic to ... the current situation. And my role in it."

"I heard as much," Micara said.

"Your Vatican could help possibly."

Micara nodded. "I'll bring it up when I get there, but I am a mere Bishop."

"But you have seen first hand," Mendes replied. "Tell them."

"I will, but they must already be aware of what is happening."

"Mendes pouted. "Maybe not the ones who sit in Rome, those who never get out. You know, the professional bureaucrats. It can be a good life for some."

Micara had to smile. This man knew his Vatican. He reassured Mendes, "I'll tell them."

"They need to know."

Micara and the others watched him walk back to the refugees and their hurried passage through the gates into Spain. Would they all make it to Portugal? Would they all get to Lisbon? How many would find a way to leave Europe and find safety somewhere?

Micara got in the car.

25

JUNE 21, 1940
ROME, ITALY

Sabastian Arceneau left the noise of the streets and climbed the stairs to the second floor of the Hotel Principessa located on Via Sardegna, several miles from Vatican City. A week earlier Mussolini's Italy had entered the war on the side of Germany and suddenly Rome, and that meant Vatican City, had become a far more important center of information and diplomatic crossroads where information might be gathered and arrangements might be *arranged*. Sabastian Arceneau was here to see if he could do just that. The man he was here to see was Myron C. Taylor, President Franklin Roosevelt's new representative to the Vatican.

Arceneau had never met Taylor but he had formed some opinions about the man from the things he had been told by the people at the Gregory Foundation and what he remembered from newspaper and magazine articles. Taylor was a lawyer by training, a graduate of Cornell University, but his fame and fortune had come from his position as Chairman of the United States Steel Corporation. Arceneau also remembered him as being the United States representative to the 1938 Evian Conference held in France where he had been elected chairman, some said largely because of his friendly, outgoing manner. The conference had been suggested by President Roosevelt to address the issue of Jewish immigration and to get the participating countries to change their policies regarding such immigration. For Roosevelt the conference turned out a disappointment. When it ended there had been no substantive new policies, no meaningful changes in policies, or positions. In fact, the whole thing had been a gigantic publicity coup for the Nazis who crowed that all these countries criticize and condemn Germany for its policies toward the Jews but when given the opportunity to alleviate the situation by altering their own immigration policies they did nothing. The Germans wasted no time declaring that the conference had been all one great hypocrisy. Arceneau could not agree more. Even the Congress of the United States failed to pass any new or revised laws addressing this issue. Public sentiment throughout the nation was to stand pat and offer no helping hand. Roosevelt, the consummate politician, could do nothing but honor the mood of the country in spite of what might have been his personal desire.

Arceneau reached the top of the stairs to the second floor and walked to room 233 and knocked on the door. The man who answered was dressed in coat and tie and looked to be ready to head out to a fashionable gathering of some sort. Arceneau recognized Taylor from his photograph. The two men shook hands and Arceneau was invited inside.

"Would you like something to drink, Mr. Arceneau?"

"No thank you."

"Sit, sit," Taylor offered a chair. Arceneau sat down. "So you work for the Gregory Foundation."

"Correct."

"With Crandell Overstreet no less."

"You know Crandell?"

"We were once competitors of a sort," Taylor replied. "He left the commercial world and went to work for the Gregory Foundation. He used to be one of the directors of one of Aristotle Gregory's commercial enterprises. That was before the old miscreant got religion and overhauled his foundation to become the modern one it is today."

Arceneau grinned.

Taylor unbuttoned his coat and sat down in the chair opposite Arceneau. "What is it you and the Gregory want of me, Mr. Arceneau?"

"No need for formalities," Arceneau said.

Taylor grinned. "Of course. Well, Sabastian, if what you are here to ask of me is not against the law I'll do what I can to assist you, but you must understand I am new at this."

"I'm trying to solve a problem and have not much time," Arceneau said. "I have just begun to seek solutions and my thinking is still evolving. I'm sure you know how that goes. I'm after two things. First, I need visas for two people to permit them to enter the United States. I wanted to run it by you first because I figured it'd be the easiest solution. I'm ignorant of what special influence you might have at your disposal regarding such a thing. Who knows, you may be able to solve my problem with a phone call. If not, I'll move to my other options, but they could prove more troubling for me."

"Visas are beyond my authority, or influence, Sabastian. I'm sorry."

"I suspected as much. I thought maybe the State Department might honor a special request from you."

"It's an all too common request these days, but I'm afraid the State Department does not appreciate my being here in Rome, doing what I'm doing."

"Understood."

"So, what are your other possibilities?" Taylor asked.

"Maybe the Vatican. It's a more tenuous approach, however," Arceneau said. "Mine are not always officially endorsed procedures. I have to be careful and watch my step. One never knows when working inside the Vatican who is really on your side."

Taylor smiled. "I was informed of the mysteries of the Vatican hierarchy. So, what about the other thing you are after?"

"Ship passage for two to the United States," he said. "Out of Lisbon."

Taylor thought for a moment. "You're thinking the White House might make a special request to the right people?"

Arceneau grinned.

"Tell me about the two people for whom you are seeking these items," Taylor said.

Arceneau thought a moment. How much should he tell Taylor? He had to be honest here. "One of the persons is a Catholic nun who happens also to be Jewish. Her activities on behalf of the Jews in Germany has put her in a precarious position. The Nazis will soon want her out of the way. Right now they don't have the necessary fortitude to make a move like that because of the Concordat agreed to by the Vatican and Hitler. However, I fear that in time circumstances will nullify that agreement and her life will then be in jeopardy."

Taylor's expression grew more contemplative. "What has she done to upset the Nazis?"

"Well, for one thing, she became pregnant. She is carrying the child of a German officer who has been helping protect Jews in her convent. I don't think I need tell you what outcomes are waiting people who do such things."

Taylor's surprise at the revelation was evident. "That's quite a pedigree."

"I've worked with the woman. She is a special person, for many reasons."

"What about the other passenger?"

"A young German girl, also a Jew. She is residing at the nun's convent. The nun has a special, personal responsibility for the girl. It's a long story. The girl is the sister of a scientist presently working in England. My foundation helped him get there and has been supporting him financially. He is someone I believe the Germans would like to tap into and they would likely dangle the girl as incentive to cooperate. My guess is he probably would succumb."

"It's no secret that a lot of Jewish scientists and intellectuals have left Germany."

"The Nazis deprived them of their livelihoods. Kicked them out of the universities. But Germany still has many good ones. Gentiles like Heisenberg."

"The Fuhrer may come to regret his policy."

"I believe it's already happening."

"Let me say, even if you get ship passage, securing visas to enter the United States for Jews is nearly impossible in this political climate."

Arceneau frowned, knowing the validity of the statement.

"Besides, there are damn few ships leaving Lisbon heading to the United States." Taylor said. "The newspapers are full of stories of Americans trying to get out of Europe and back home, but can't because of a lack of ships."

"Which magnifys my problem."

"At least Portugal is neutral," Taylor said. "If the two get stranded there it might not be all that terrible. Better than Germany."

"For the time being Portugal is neutral, but that could change. The Germans have their eyes on Gibraltar. Several high-ranking German officials have made visits to Spain recently for the purpose of convincing the Spanish to permit some kind of move."

"To grab Gibraltar from the British," Taylor said.

"Don't forget, Spain owes Hitler for helping in its civil war. If Spain suddenly goes with the Germans Portugal would be up for grabs. If Portugal goes German then the two women could again be at the mercy of the Germans. Along with many other Jews," Arceneau said.

Taylor pondered the description. "It could be the Jews are herding themselves into one big holding pen waiting to be rounded up."

Arceneau nodded.

"Let's say your two people reach Lisbon," Taylor said, "U.S. citizens are given priority for passage. And there are few ships making the trip now. Too damn dangerous."

Arceneau signaled his agreement. "If I've not forgotten how Washington works your appointment tells me you have a special relationship with President Roosevelt."

"You could say that," Taylor replied. "But are you asking me to go directly to the President on this!"

Arceneau smiled. "Not directly. I'm asking that you cable Mr. Michael Duncan in the White House. He works there in some kind of troubleshooting capacity for the President. Do you know him?" Arceneau asked.

"No, I do not."

"Well, I believe he might be able to cut through some red tape and help us here with ship passage. If you personally made a request to him."

Taylor pondered the suggestion, then said, "Can't hurt, I suppose."

Arceneau got out of his chair. "I'll stay in touch. I'm staying at the Hotel Nardizzi at 38 Via Firenze, room 277, if you need me."

26

JUNE 22, 1940
WHITE HOUSE
WASHINGTON, D.C.

When anyone asked Michael Duncan about his job he often told them that he had a government position and that one of his duties was to look after certain things surrounding the security measures around the White House, to monitor things. He never elaborated. His reference to security made it easy to avoid having to go any further. People understood. If, however, it became necessary to expand his story he would always then say that he also acted as kind of a liaison between certain personnel, minor officials to be sure, who worked in the White House and their dealings with other agencies of the government. Most of his story was a ruse. To even say of it was fifty percent accurate was a stretch.

President Franklin Roosevelt was a man who played things close to the vest in many matters and, Duncan knew, was a man who took a prankster's-like pleasure in circumnavigating the system. Sometimes such circumnavigations came close to breaking the law, which Michael Duncan had heard Roosevelt being warned about on more than one occasion. The President often laughed wryly and replied, "It's all in the manner of interpretation, my friend."

Duncan had little doubt that in these times playing things close to the vest was a good way to be if you were the President of the United States. But the man's occasional maneuvers often caused Michael's job to become a tangle of knots when dealing with people. At the present time the President was walking a tightrope on several issues and Michael had his hands full helping to get the President through the mine fields. Duncan worked directly through Harry Hopkins. As almost everyone knew, Hopkins often acted on the President's behalf but never without the President's approval, stated or unstated.

To Harry Hopkins, Michael Duncan was a valuable player on the Washington political landscape. If one wanted to stretch things it was okay to say that he worked for the White House, but then again there was no listing of his position on any official government roster that would substantiate that. He had come by this arrangement in a way that was not all that unusual when one remembered that this was Washington D.C., the nation's capital, and the roads traveled by different people could be circuitous and filled with seemingly happenstance occurrences that all added up to explain how it was they had gotten there. This was certainly true for Michael Duncan.

His path to Washington really started with his temporary job at R. H. Macy's Department Store years earlier. It was September of 1929 and Macy's President, Jesse Strauss, was planning a special dinner and reception for a prominent New York politician. As the time for the affair approached, preparations began to sour. One thing after another began to unravel, minor glitches at first, then several major ones. Up until that time Michael Duncan was an innocent bystander to all of this; he was not involved in any way with the party at all. He was drawn in when he came to work very early one morning to find Strauss's administrative secretary sobbing and completely distraught over the fact that she thought Strauss and his wife would blame her for everything going wrong which, she said, was not her fault at all. People were backing out for the flimsiest of reasons, some going back on their word, altering their agreements in ways that would guarantee the party an awful mess. She was most fearful of losing her job, but also she would be humiliated. It didn't take long for Duncan to learn all the details about the original plans that were seemingly coming unglued. The woman gave him all the names of the significant perpetrators causing the most trouble and what their roles were to be. With that information Duncan went to work, using what skills and contacts he had. He told lots of stories and stretched the truth to where it never was meant to go, he made many promises, but, in the end, he got what he needed, in reasonable amounts anyway. It wasn't perfect, or clean, but it did the job. Mr. Jesse Strauss and his wife never knew. The reception was a success, and the secretary received a large bouquet of roses from Strauss for a job well done, plus a bonus at the end of the year, which was almost unheard of at the end of 1929. While many people were losing their jobs, she kept hers. So did Michael.

Growing up in New Orleans, Michael Duncan had always put together solutions gotten what he wanted by being innovative and, when needed, cutting corners. All the kids in the neighborhood tried it, it was part of everyone's survival training, but none were better at it than Michael. Part of his success, and his charm, was his storytelling demeanor. He could fabricate with the best of them. In the strictest sense it probably could be considered lying. His Irish roots gave him that quality of storytelling; the lying just came naturally with it, he figured. His parish priest told him he should stop and although he tried, he seemed unable to completely shut down that element of his being. Michael's solutions were always wrapped up in a story, if only in his head, but he needed that story to have a chance of making everything work. It guided him in his actions; it was his blueprint. All this gave Michael Duncan an unusual leg up when it came to solving problems quickly. The thing he had to solve problems without bending the law too much, or cause great injury to people. Michael Duncan was not a cheat and he did not want to hurt anyone; that is, unless he thought they deserved it. His Catholic religion told him he should not be this way for he had learned from his upbringing that "vengeance is mine saith the Lord," and Michael, being a mere human, should stay out of the revenge business. Being a human being, he failed at this too many times.

In a short time Michael Duncan's temporary job turned permanent at Macy's and that proved beneficial. In 1931 Mr. Jesse Strauss was named by President Franklin Roosevelt to be president of one of Roosevelt's new social programs of the New Deal; it was the Temporary Emergency Relief Administration, or the TERA. Strauss quickly named Harry Hopkins, a New York social worker he had come to know, to be both administrator and TERA's executive director. In this job Hopkins needed an assistant to help work out things in setting up and running the program and he asked Strauss if he could recommend anyone who was smart enough to figure new things out and quickly solve problems on his own. The inquiry from Hopkins to Strauss came when Strauss's secretary was present in the room. Listening to what Harry Hopkins was saying she thought immediately of Michael Duncan. He would fit the bill just fine, she thought, and said so to Hopkins. Hopkins arranged to talk to Michael Duncan and liked what he heard and saw. For one thing Duncan had an intimidating look about him and he had a boldness in his expression that Hopkins thought might take the young man a long way. He spoke with a cadence and a confidence that told Hopkins he had the makings to be a great help to him. For one thing, Hopkins concluded that no one would have to hold Michael Duncan's hand. Duncan was his own man, even though he was a rather young twenty-seven. Hopkins quickly hired Duncan as his personal assistant.

In 1933 when Hopkins was summoned to Washington by Roosevelt to take over the running of two more New Deal programs Michael Duncan went with him. But he never had a regular appointment, he was not a civil servant, he was hand picked by Hopkins just as Hopkins was by Roosevelt. By the standards of most jobs in Washington one would have to say that Duncan's job had to be described as offbeat. Duncan, himself, often mused about this when juggling things, trying to put together some ad hoc solution to a problem that happened to be on his desk at the time.

When Hopkins was appointed Secretary of Commerce in 1938, Duncan tagged along, unofficially. It gave Duncan more time and exposure to the things that made Washington go round. When Hopkins left as Secretary of Commerce Duncan was still with him, wiser and more connected to Washington's power brokers than ever before. Duncan could now move within the Washington system better than almost anyone else.

Michael Duncan had a mail drop and the smallest of offices at the White House and he had come by to pick up what was there from the previous day. As he flipped through the envelopes, reading the addresses of origin, he stopped when he saw the Western Union envelope from Myron C. Taylor posted from Rome. Duncan had never met Taylor but he knew the position he held and why Roosevelt had appointed him. He also knew that Roosevelt had instructed Taylor to bypass the State Department. However, Duncan knew that those instructions did not mean for him to go through Duncan. For one thing, Duncan had no instructions to watch for such communication. This could be interesting, Duncan thought.

He opened the telegram.

TO: Mr. Michael Duncan

White House

Washington, D.C.

Awkward situation here **STOP** Can't explain fully this time **STOP** Request two ship passages to U.S. out of Lisbon **STOP** Subjects are not U.S. citizens **STOP** German nationals, one Catholic nun, one Jewess **STOP** Situation complicated STOP. Request comes from Arceneau at Gregory Foundation **STOP** Can you help **STOP** Subjects trying to get to Lisbon presently **STOP** Please advise on possibilities **STOP**

M.C. Taylor
Hotel Principessa Tea
Via Sardegna
Rome, Italy

Duncan checked the time. It was six forty-five, maybe a little early to call the State Department. Fact was, he wasn't quite sure whom to call. What the hell, he thought and picked up the phone and dialed the main number. There was a long wait but on about the tenth ring someone came on the line, a woman's voice answered.

"Good morning, Department of State."

"Mike Duncan at the White House," he told her. "Could you connect me to the person who might be able to provide the White House with information about ship passage from Europe to the United States?"

"Naval?" the woman asked.

"Civilian."

There was a short pause. "That would be Odom," she said. "I'll give him a ring, see if he's in."

A raspy voice came on. "Odom here."

Duncan told him his name and what his government position was. He then asked about ship passage from Lisbon.

"Lots of that going around," Odom said. "Americans scrambling to get out of harms way. Our embassies are being deluged by both citizens and non-citizens. We have bits and pieces of reports coming in now about some nasty business going on in France and Spain. Jewish refugees in a mad rush to get out of France and into Spain and finally to Portugal, Lisbon to be exact, looking for any way to get themselves out of there. From what we are hearing it is a real mess."

"What about ships?" Duncan asked. "Can you help me? I need information."

"For our people we're working on it. For the others, they're on their own. The Jews are . . .well, they're in no-man's land. It's pretty hopeless."

"What if they have the proper visas? Can they be admitted to the U.S.?"

Odom did not answer immediately. "That's dicey. We have rather tight requirements. Congress has been specific on that."

"Jews you mean," Duncan said.

"Right. Very strict."

"Even with the proper visas?"

"Our embassies have their instructions. How would they get visas?"

"I see."

"Some of the South American countries are taking them in. South Africa as well, we've heard. A few other African countries."

"So what is our government going to do about the stranded Americans? Will the Navy get involved?"

"It's being discussed," Odom acknowledged. "Our people are working with the passenger liner companies to see if they'll make a few more runs to Portugal and Galway to bring home the last of them."

"With naval escorts?"

"I guess that's possible but I have no first-hand knowledge. I don't believe that has been decided yet, but doing so might be dangerous. Too much chance of something going wrong if one of those German subs shows up and her captain wants to push the envelope, if you get my point."

Duncan agreed silently. "Listen," he said, "I need some solid information as quick as I can get it. The White House has just received a request from some people connected to the Vatican. The President assigned the task to me to inquire if we can honor their request. He thinks it's important."

"I don't recall any of our people posted to the Vatican. Our embassy in Rome has unofficial connections, of course, but nothing too strong at our level. Of course there's this fellow Tyler who's now over there. Is Taylor the guy you're dealing with?"

Duncan was on high alert. "All I know is that the President ask that I get information so he can proceed with the Vatican's request, as I said."

"I'll get back to you as soon as I have something on passenger liners," Odom said.

Odom was true to his word. The following morning his call came.

"Looks like the owners of the United States Lines have agreed to make two more runs to Europe, the first leaving in a few days headed to Galway, Ireland; the second and last will be to Lisbon. I'm guessing from the timetable that the ship will arrive in Lisbon around July 1st."

"What's the name of the ship?"

The *Washington*."

Duncan laughed. "Who's the Captain?"

"Don't know," Odom answered.

"July 1st, thanks."

"Give or take a few days. The 3rd at the latest, I'd say. Everything is being done on the fly it seems, day by day."

"This helps, thanks," Duncan said.

"I hope the President's Vatican people have all their papers in order, visas and all."

"I'm sure," Duncan replied, knowing there was no purpose in getting into a lengthy discussion over visas with Odom, or tell him that one of the passengers was a Jewess.

His reply to Taylor took only a few minutes to compose.

Mr. Myron C. Taylor

Hotel Principessa Tea

Via Sardegna

Rome, Italy

Passenger liner S.S. Washington arriving Lisbon on or about July 1 **STOP** Could be last U.S. vessel available **STOP** Still working on passage **STOP** No success on visas seems likely this end **STOP** Suggest you keep trying your end STOP. Approach Rome Embassy with care **STOP**

M. Duncan

JUNE 23, 1940
ROME

Myron Taylor read Duncan's telegram and called the number that Sabastian Arceneau had left but there was no answer. He asked the manager to ask Arceneau to contact him first thing. He had no idea when Arceneau would get back to him so all there was to do now was wait.

But Taylor was not much of a waiter. He began thinking the unthinkable: he might like to make a run at the U.S. Embassy and see if he could shake something loose. He thought of himself as a pretty persuasive guy although his personal art of persuasion had been honed and tested only in the business world of arranging working contracts and making deals, not in the government arena of bureaucratic formalities where those in charge bowed down and worshiped rules and time-honored procedures. Such people were not of a mind to horse trade. But, as he saw it, he had little choice if he was going to exhaust all his options. Besides, this whole matter had gotten his blood up. Everything he knew of the circumstances said the odds were stacked against him, approaching the Embassy was a long shot. Nevertheless, if this job that Roosevelt had persuaded him to take on carried any meaning at all why not play his cards until he reached the point where he was forced to fold. No one could blame an amateur for coming up short as long as his actions did not stumble or blunder, bringing embarrassment to his country, and the President.

At the entrance of the U.S. Embassy he identified himself to the official at the desk and was escorted to a room upstairs where he was asked to wait. The sign on the desk read: *Robert*

Clairmont Winchester. Taylor was seated when the man entered the room.

"We heard that you were in Rome, Mr. Taylor," the man said, going directly to the chair behind his desk.

"You're ... Winchester?" Taylor asked in a tone that matched Winchester's entering arrogance and impoliteness.

"I am. It's nice of you to come by our place to see us."

There was no mistaking Winchester's unhappiness over his being in Rome. Roosevelt had warned him about such bruised feelings. Taylor couldn't blame them, really. Makes them feel the President thinks they can't do the job. No self-respecting agency would easily accept such a left-handed play without some resentment. But the point in fact was that Winchester and Ambassador William Phillips were in Italy to deal with Bonito Mussolini and the Italian Government, *not* the Vatican. The United States had no official government representatives to the new state of Vatican City. There was no U.S. Embassy in Vatican City, no ambassador, no representative at all - until now. That representation, as fledgling as it was, was the presence of Myron C. Taylor, personally appointed by the President of the United States. Taylor had not yet met the present U.S. Ambassador to Italy, William Phillips, and he didn't know if he held the same sentiments that Winchester seemed to be conveying by his statements and demeanor.

"I understand my being in Rome makes it look like the President believes he can't count on you fellows."

"No, no, Mr. Taylor. You being in Rome is no problem. However, poking around inside the Vatican can surely be. That's not a job for an amateur. Even a professional could inadvertently screw things up."

Taylor wanted to object at the description but he held back. He needed to placate this man if he were going to get anywhere. He laughed. "No one *pokes around* inside the Vatican, Mr. Winchester. That is not why I was sent to Rome. That is not why I am here."

"I saw where you presented your letter of introduction to Pius," Winchester said with an almost mocking smile. "I hope your audience went well and you found the man in good spirits."

"The Holy Father seems well, yes. His words to me and the President were most cordial, and reassuring."

"Of course they were," Winchester replied. "And what might those words have been, if I may inquire."

Taylor smiled. "Please, Mr. Winchester, I am not that much of an amateur."

Winchester picked up a pencil and began tapping it on his desk. He gazed past Taylor's face for a moment. "I'm disappointed. I thought you might be here to report on your visit with the Holy Father."

"Sorry. No I'm here to see what the government's position is on the issuance of visas."

Winchester hesitated a moment. "Really?

"If I had someone who needed a visa quick what might the process be?"

Winchester smiled. "How quick?"

"A few days."

Winchester eyed Taylor suspiciously. "Our immigration laws are rather strict, and specific."

"I've heard. I only want to make sure I have all the particulars."

"You have some ... special case maybe?" Winchester asked.

Taylor suspected that as soon as he told the man about his case he would delight in informing him of the absurdity of it all and that his request could not be honored.

"What provisions does the U.S. have for emergency situations?"

"Depends on the emergency. Conditions still have to be met."

"Give me an example, please," Taylor asked.

"We haven't had any emergency cases recently," he replied. "Not while I've been here."

Winchester's attitude was annoying Taylor, and Winchester knew it, which made it particularly irritating to Taylor.

"What does the Department's play book say?"

"Play book?" Winchester blanched.

"Your manual. Surely you have a manual, an instructional manual, a statement of dos and don'ts," Taylor replied in a matter-of-fact manner with no revelation of his true annoyance with this insufferable man.

"I think that I should hear your story first," Winchester said. "You must have a story. I can't believe you came here to inquire solely about hypothetical situations."

Taylor looked at the man scornfully. "Who is your superior, Mr. Winchester?"

Taylor was struck by how little Winchester flinched, if he flinched at all. The question seemed not to bother him. Instead, he grinned. "I am the one and only final say in visa disbursement at this embassy, Mr. Taylor. The Ambassador himself, Mr. William Phillips, is my superior, but others have tried traveling that route. They've had little if any success. He always defers to my judgement. He's a stickler for obeying the law."

Taylor could see that Winchester was convinced he held all the cards. Taylor decided to soften his approach but he had the feeling that he had already gone too far and there was no reasonable chance he could squeeze out even an once of good will from Winchester. In spite of his meager chances he decided to give it one last attempt even though deep down he felt that this career bureaucrat would go to the very end to thwart Taylor's request.

"Look, Mr. Winchester, I am not a career diplomat like you, trained in such matters. I am a mere civilian doing a favor for a friend of mind, the President. He is a man walking a tightrope and all he wants is for me to give him a fresh assessment of what Pius might be up to and how he feels about certain relationships in other countries with which he has dealings. It's a matter of another window into a very messy world, and getting messier by the day. You surely can appreciate that. At this stage of the game the President didn't want to send a career diplomat who would attach himself officially to the U.S. Embassy here in Rome. It's not to undercut anyone at the Embassy. The President has more to do than to create internal conflicts and hard feelings among those who operate the levers and make the wheels go around in our relationships with the Italians. It's just that the politics and the mood of our country are not yet ready to accept formal recognition of the Vatican as an independent state worthy to receive a full ambassador from the United States. Surely you know that. Right now we have no recognized ambassador to the new independent state of the Vatican. I'm filling that role for the time being. You have to admit that the President deserves all the eyes and ears he can muster in these perilous times. I'm a small cog in all this."

"You underestimate your position and I believe you know better, Mr Taylor."

"All right, I'll grant you that, but can't we work together?"

The smile Winchester gave Taylor still did not diminish the disrepute Winchester held, although Taylor thought for a moment that the man might be making the effort.

"So," Winchester began, "Tell me about the person for whom you wish to secure a visa to enter the United States."

"There are two people," Taylor told him. "And I don't know much about them personally."

"Let me save us a lot of time, Mr Taylor. Is either one of them a Jew?"

"Both are. One is a young woman, a teenager, I believe; the other is a Catholic nun."

"A Jew who is a Catholic nun!"

"Yes."

"Christ! That's a new one!"

"I'm sure it's happened before. The first Pope was a Jew, remember? St. Peter."

"Spare me, Mr. Taylor.

Taylor could not help himself. "Then there was St. Paul."

Winchester stared angrily at Taylor.

Taylor grinned. "I guess there's no hope for my two candidates?"

"My hands are tied, Winchester claimed. "There is no legal way to issue visas to persons of the Jewish faith, Catholic nun or no Catholic nun. Even your new friend, Pius, can't change that."

Taylor stood up. "I thought I'd give you people the first shot at it. You have enlightened me a great deal on this issue. I now see how rigid these things are."

"They are indeed and they are that way because that's how the U.S. Congress wants it. It's the law. Criticize the Congress if you like; I'm only carrying out its legal mandate."

"Your point is well taken, Mr. Winchester. Good day."

Taylor left without shaking hands with the man.

27

JUNE 22, 1940
MADRID, SPAIN
RESIDENCE OF BISHOP GAETANO CICOGNANI

Bishop Micara and his party had met Bishop Gaetano Cicognani's representative at Irun and traveled much of the night, arriving in Madrid early on the morning of June twenty-first. They spent much of the day resting. That evening Bishop Micara and Bishop Cicognani had a long private conversation. Micara told Cicognani of their experiences along the road, the plight of the people on the road, the bombings in Bordeaux, his meeting Sousa Mendes and their official authorization to enter Portugal.

"So, Lisbon is within reach," Cicognani said.

"It will all be meaningless unless we can find ship passage and visas for Sister Katherine and Anna."

Micara then described to Cicognani the unusual circumstances surrounding Gabriella and Anna.

"Definitely most unusual," the Bishop said. "Let me think on it."

The following day Cicognani told Micara. "You might remember that I have a brother in America, Amleto Cicognani. He's the Apostolic Delegate to the United States. Has been since 1933. He has gotten to know many government people in Washington. Now let me tell you what I'm thinking might solve your situation."

After Cicognani had finished with his proposal he eyed Micara with a look of mischief.

"Quite an unorthodox proposal. Is it possible?" Micara asked.

Cicognani smiled. "I'd say it has a good chance. I know something about these things. Working back channels is my speciality. If nothing else it keeps my juices flowing."

"And you say you are certain your brother will play his part and go along?"

Cicognani grinned. "He's as much a back-channel cleric as I am. Sometimes you have to be. He's already sent several unofficial messages to certain people in Rome, instructing them what is needed."

JUNE 23, 1940
AFTERNOON, PRINCIPESSA TEA HOTEL
ROME, ITALY

"I hit a brick wall at the Embassy," Myron Taylor confessed dejectedly soon after entering Sabastian Arceneau's hotel room.

Arceneau smiled. "I suspected you wouldn't be able to resist making a try."

"The Embassy people resent my being here, no question."

Arceneau smiled further. "It was hopeless to begin with."

"But I have heard from Duncan, the man you said to contact. I learned that a ship, the *Washington*, will be making a special run at the request of the State Department and will arrive in Lisbon around July first. It could be the last ship returning to the States."

"Well, that *is* a step in the right direction. It gives us a target. Now to see what we can come up with to make it happen."

"But he said visas are out of the question at his end."

"I figured as much."

"He's working on ship passage, however. I sense that's still a possibility."

"Easier than the visas."

"So, what now?"

"Tomorrow we meet a man from the Vatican," he replied.

"What for?"

"I'm hoping papers. Official documents for the two women," Arceneau told him.

Taylor looked at Arceneau warily, yet with a bit of playfulness showing. "I presume the man we are to meet is not the Holy Father."

"Heavens no! The Holy Father would know little of how such papers come into existence."

"I suppose it's part of the Vatican intrigue?"

28

**THE NEXT MORNING
JUNE 24, 1940
ROME, ITALY**

At ten o'clock Sabastian Arceneau was back at the Hotel Principessa Tea to see Myron Taylor.

"Good news. As I expected I have received word from the Gregory. It relayed a message saying Bishop Cicognani in Washington has made contact with Vatican personnel.

"What does that mean?"

"It means we can go ahead with our meeting," Arceneau said.

"You mean with the man who is not the Holy Father?"

Arceneau grinned. "No, he is a Jesuit priest named Paolo Rochelli. He works inside the Vatican."

"In what capacity?"

"He's an artist," Arceneau said dryly.

"One of many, I imagine."

"Not what you think. He's an engraver, and a forger, and extremely good. He is a man who can produce authentic looking signatures of just about every important Vatican official - including Pius XII himself if need be,. He can also affix the proper seals to the proper papers."

Taylor laughed. "Such chicanery. Who would think such things go on inside such a sacred place."

The end of Arceneau's lip twisted up in a wry grin. "You are not Catholic, are you?" Arceneau asked.

Taylor shook his head. "I thought you knew that I wasn't."

"I don't think I ever thought about it. It's just your last comment. Your surprise."

"President Roosevelt thought it best for political reasons that his first appointment to the Vatican not be a Catholic. I assume that you are a Catholic."

Arceneau nodded. "Born to it."

"Devout?"

"Depends," Arceneau replied. "When I have to be."

Taylor laughed. "I take that as a maybe."

Arceneau laughed.

Sabastian Arceneau knew that Father Paolo Rochelli maintained an apartment not far from the Vatican which he used for his hobby and for special occasions when he had to be away from the Vatican. Arceneau told Taylor he had already sent the needed coded message that would bring Rochelli to his apartment.

"How do we know when he'll receive the message?" Taylor asked. "And why the code?"

"Vatican mail is delivered several times a day," Arceneau began. "If you put a letter directly in the Vatican box outside the wall today the person will get it today. As for the code, one cannot be certain about whose eyes might look down on a letter. They might not be the eyes of the addressee."

Taylor showed feigned surprise. "In the Vatican?"

Arceneau smiled. "My friend, Catholics see the Vatican as the manifestation of God's presence on earth. But they sometimes forget that it is also an institution comprised of human beings, and when human beings are left to function as human beings then the seven deadly sins, along with a few other kinds of sins, are surely to manifest themselves in various ways. All you need to do is look at its history. Human frailties can't be kept out of a human institution, any human institution. I needn't tell you that. The Vatican is no exception. A piece of mail can be opened and read by anyone at any time, if they have the mind. We're just taking precautions by using this code, as you call it. Never can tell who might be failing to effectively cope with his temptations and decide to make the wrong moral decision and open a letter that's not addressed to him. It comes down to that age-old problem of free will. We humans like to believe we are the only earthly creatures possessing it, and all the evidence seems to say that we are, but we also have our natural instincts and those instincts often cross swords with free will, and our spiritual side."

Taylor stood digesting the intricacies of what Arceneau had said. "At the moment I cannot find any real fault with your analysis. Maybe if I studied it," he grinned.

"It will do you no good," Arceneau smiled back confidently. "But you're welcome to try."

Taylor fell silent for a moment.. "I wonder how many Germans are battling with this dilemma right now?" he then said.

"A lot, I hope."

"I'm glad I'm not in their place," Taylor added.

"That makes two of us."

That evening when Sabastian Arceneau and Myron Taylor arrived across the street from Father Paolo Rochelli's apartment building the light was already on in the window.

"He's at home," Arceneau said, looking up at the building.

The elevator in the building was old and shook when it moved. Much of the paint had been worn off the inside. When it stopped on the third floor Arceneau pushed aside the gate.

"It's down this way," he said.

There was light coming from the opening beneath the door to the room; the sound of someone walking came from the other side of the door. Arceneau knocked.

The man who opened the door was dressed in a gray sweat shirt and black pants; he was wearing black slippers. He was a short muscular man with short salt-and-pepper hair cut flat across the top.

"Hello, old friend," Arceneau said. "Did you receive the gift I sent?"

"Generous as usual," the man replied.

Arceneau introduced Taylor to Father Paolo Rochelli. The two shook hands.

"Mr. Taylor is President Roosevelt's special representative to the Holy See, Paolo," Arceneau added.

"A distinguished position. But a vexing one I bet. The place can be daunting, even for those of us on the inside." Rochelli commented, twisting a grin at Taylor.

"I'm getting a lesson on just how vexing it can be," Taylor commented.

Rochelli then said. "I have received word that you need me again, Sebastian."

"It's another rush job, Paolo. What else."

"Excuse me," Taylor said. "But you sound as if you are an American."

Rochelli and Arceneau both laughed.

"Raised in Baltimore," Rochelli told Taylor

"How . . .?

"Did I end up here at the Vatican? Doing what I do?"

"Why, yes," Taylor said.

Rochelli looked at Arceneau. "Well, I often ask myself that," he said. "After my ordination someone must have discovered that my father and grandfather established and operated one of the biggest manufacturers of printing and engraving equipment in the entire northeast United States and that I knew something about printing and engraving."

Arceneau already knew the story and he grinned. "Tell him the rest," he said to Rochelli.

"Well, why not. A man by the name of Frank Lazzaro was the foreman at the plant in Baltimore; he instructed me in the rudiments as well as some of the finer points of engraving. Seems Frank Lazzaro received his early training while working for the United States Treasury Department before he ran into Salvatore Luciano and struck out on his own. In case you don't know . . ."

"Lucky Luciano?" Taylor interrupted. "The gangster."

Rochelli smiled wildly. "The same. After Frank Lazzaro finished serving his jail time, my father hired him. He still works at the plant in Baltimore. Frank Lazzaro gave me my training. Of course, I picked up a few finer points on my own. I found I was good at it. Someone over here thought I could be of some use to them, so, here I am, working for the Holy Father but also working backroom deals for people like Sabastian Arceneau and his damn foundation," he said with a good-natured chuckle.

"Free lance," Taylor described.

"A fair description," Rochelli said. "So, Sabastian, fill me in on just what it is you are looking for. I need names, dates of birth, you know."

For the next few minutes Arceneau laid out the details and gave Rochelli all the particulars.

"Some of this Cicognani did not know," Rochelli said. "Good to double check these things. Too much can go wrong."

"Indeed," Arceneau said.

Rochelli nodded. "So, we need visas that appear to have originated from your own State Department as well as a letter from ... some high official here in the Vatican?"

Arceneau nodded. "Who is the required Vatican official who signs off on such an appointment?" Arceneau then asked.

Rochelli shrugged. "One of several."

"Who do you suggest?" Taylor asked.

"Would you like it from Pius, himself?"

Taylor and Arceneau looked at each other, then back at Rochelli who was grinning. He said, "That might be too ambitious."

"Too," Arceneau agreed. "Much too ambitious."

"We'll make it from Raffaele Cardinal Rossi, he's the Prefect for the Congregation of Bishops. The most appropriate official in such matters. It'll be his seal on the letter. And his signature."

"Time is of the essence, Paolo," Arceneau said. "These people are headed to Lisbon. There is a ship. It might be the last. They'll need to have all their papers before boarding. First of July."

"Where are they now? Did you say Madrid?"

Arceneau nodded. "Madrid. I can transport the documents there in time if they are in my hands by ... let's say ... day after tomorrow?"

29

JUNE 25, 1940
WAЅHINGTON, D.C.

Michael Duncan had called ahead and made sure that the Vatican's nuncio in Washington, Bishop Amleto Cicognani, would be available to see him. Duncan took a cab to Georgetown and arrived at the residence precisely on time. The housekeeper ushered him into the library, where he waited. He went over and looked at the large photograph hanging on the wall. It showed Cicognani and President Roosevelt standing together, alone.

Duncan had met Cicognani several times before and had a pretty good idea of the kind of man he was. Bishop Amleto Cicognani was 57 years old and had been the Vatican's nuncio for seven years. During that time he had made himself knowledgeable about the ways of Washington and about the people who inhabited the halls of government, a talent in which the Bishop took great pride. He was short, barely reaching five and a half feet tall. He had a round, friendly face that sported a gregarious smile. His brown eyes glistened with curiosity. Duncan had already decided that the man enjoyed being alive, and especially relished engaging people and making things happen when called upon. Duncan had already concluded that Bishop Cicognani was a consummate politician.

"Michael, my friend," Cicognani said, coming into the room.

The Bishop extended his hand and Duncan bent and kissed the ring as every Catholic was expected to do. Behind them the Bishop's secretary closed the door and left the two men alone.

"Let's sit," Cicognani said. "You have some information?"

"I have been directly in contact with the Captain of the ship, the *S.S. Washington*, that will arrive in Lisbon on or about July first."

"Excellent."

"This will likely be the final run by any United States passenger ship to that part of the world, so your two people must be there by that time. If they are late they could be stranded in Lisbon."

"Trapped along with others."

Duncan looked away. "Most likely."

"How's the President handling all this?"

"Congress has the big say, I'm afraid," Duncan said.

"Yes, yes, I understand your government's ways. I read the newspapers."

"We can only hope the two women have the papers they need."

"I believe they will," Cicognani said. "Getting a ship is the main thing now."

"Tell me, Bishop, are these people that important?"

Cicognani hesitated. "No more than anyone else," he said.

"Then . . ."

"Why the effort?" Cicognani asked. "I suppose because we have been asked."

Duncan did not respond.

"I have a favor to ask," Cicognani said. I don't suppose you could meet them when the ship docks and bring them back here?"

Duncan grimaced, caught off guard. "Surely someone from the New York Diocese . . ."

"Those people do not know the full situation here, Michael. Besides, I'd rather keep this in my backyard, as you say. Please, as a favor to me."

Duncan knew the final outcome here. "I'd be happy to, Bishop. As a personal service."

"Bless you, Michael. Bless you. That is a big weight off my shoulders."

Duncan eyed the prelate. "You don't play fair, Your Excellency."

THE FOLLOWING MORNING
JUNE 25, 1940
THE WHITE HOUSE

A note had come to Michael Duncan's desk when he checked his mail that morning. It was from the President.

Mike:

I fear we have been working you too hard. I suggest that you work your schedule so as to plan to take a short vacation and enjoy yourself, maybe in N.Y. City. While you are there please do this old man a favor and meet some people who are coming in on the *S.S. Washington* from Lisbon on or about mid July. MyronTaylor informs me that it would be an appropriate gesture if we could assist in helping with their arrival. I believe you are familiar with the details.

Have fun in N.Y.

F.D. R.

Duncan shook his head in admiration, concluding that Cicognani must have called the President directly.

30

JUNE 27, 1940
ROME, ITALY
JUST OUTSIDE VATICAN WALLS

It was mid-morning when Sabastian Arceneau met Father Paolo Rochelli. He laid the documents out on the table to inspect them.

"You are a good man, Rochelli," Arceneau said.

Father Rochelli smiled. "If my mother had any inkling of some of the things I'm doing, her rosary beads would never be out of her hands."

Arceneau laughed.

The two shook hands. "Until the next time, friend," Arceneau said.

Two hours later, Sabastian Arceneau was on his way to Madrid. By the time he arrived he was only a few hours behind schedule. There was little time to waste; July first was just around the corner and it was still a long way to Lisbon. Much could happen.

Arceneau was a born worrier. He worried routinely about his appointments and keeping to schedule. On this particular assignment, he thought things were being cut too close, but what else could he do? The Madrid-to-Lisbon trip had to come off with no delays. If that happened, the three days that were left would get them there in time. But, if they got delayed with car troubles, or some official wanted extra time going through their papers and kept them around to ask more questions, they might arrive in Lisbon sometime *after* the first of July. And in the mean time the *Washington* might have sailed.

Portugal sat in a geographically strategic position on the Iberian Peninsula and the political pressures were coming from both sides in this war, causing the Portuguese to have to juggle a mix of considerations. No one could say just which way the country might go. Would it remain neutral as it was now? Or would it formally declare for one side against the other? Where did its sympathies lie? What was in its best interest? Britain? Germany? Neither? At the moment the Portugese government, and its people, seemed to be leaning toward the Nazis, but not officially, as yet.

For Arceneau, the main issue now was the arrival in Lisbon of the *S.S. Washington* from America. He was hoping it would be behind schedule. That would give them some breathing room, the pressure to make it to Lisbon would be lessened.

Arceneau carried his nervousness along with him. He checked his watch often as he pushed on toward Madrid.

When he arrived at the residence of Bishop Cicognani he quickly discovered that their plans had changed.

"Bishop Micara and Father Dubois have been ordered to Rome," Cicognani told Arceneau. "They left a few hours ago.

Now we have no escort for Sister Katherine and the girl. What is more, I am having trouble getting someone from the Portugese government to meet them at the border and take them to Lisbon. I thought I had this worked out but the confusion over all the Jews rushing to Portugal has caused Prime Minister Salazar to become hesitant. He has never been all that friendly to foreigners anyway, most especially Jews. This is troubling."

"There is no need. I have the needed authority to take the women all the way to Lisbon."

Cicognani looked wide-eyed. "How is that possible?"

Arceneau shrugged. "The Vatican. Here are the papers." He reached into the inside pocket of his coat and took out an envelope.

Cicognani took it, opened the folded paper, and read it. He smiled. "You and the Vatican seem close on these things. Are they authentic?"

"Do they appear authentic?"

Cicognani smiled as Arceneau put the papers back in the envelope.   "Where are Sister Katherine and the girl now?" Arceneau asked.

"Upstairs," Cocognani replied. "From the way they talk I believe they know you."

Arceneau nodded. "Old acquaintances." He then thought it best to add, "I also know Sister Katherine's condition."

"Most unfortunate," Cicognani said. "The poor woman."

"How does she seem to be handling it? Can you tell?"

"Hard to say but I detect no ill effects in her manner, at least outwardly."

"She's a strong woman."

"What can you tell me about how she became . . . how all this came about?"

Arceneau frowned. "Is it pertinent?"

"I was just curious."

There was the noise of running on the stairs. "Sabastian!"

It was Gabriella. She ran to him like a teenager heading for a waiting special birthday gift. She hugged him.

"Such a long time. How have you been?" she asked, flashing him a big smile.

"You look splendid, Sister," he said. "In good health, I hope. We have a long trip ahead of us."

"I'm ready, so is Anna."

"We have to arrange things carefully, and get ready. We have to leave early tomorrow morning."

"Anna still wants to get to England."

Arceneau drew his eyes away. "America is on the horizon for you both. That is, if we can arrive in Lisbon on time and the *Washington* shows up as scheduled. We have no time to waste."

"Is that the name of the ship?" Gabriella asked.

He nodded.

"Go get Anna so that we can sit down and go over our final plans," he told her. "Let me be the one to tell her about not going to England."

She hugged him again. "She will be sad. She and Herwald have been away from each other for so long."

"Just one more sad casualty of this horrible war," he said.

At supper Gabriella and Anna learned all about their new status as Bishop Amleto Cicognani's staff in Washington D.C.

Arceneau told them, "Your host, the Bishop here, has a proclivity to toy with the Vatican hierarchy." He gave the Bishop a wry grin with a raised eyebrow. "He enjoys pulling the wool over their eyes when he gets the opportunity. Is that correct, Bishop?"

The Bishop laughed, pleased at the revelation.

"My brother, Amleto, and I have always been disposed to mischief. It's a wonder we made it this far in the ranks of the clergy. Pastors of a parish was about the best we had seen for ourselves."

Their table talk quickly moved to Gabriella telling Arceneau and the Bishop of their experiences on their trip through France.

"We saw many desperate people," she said.

"Jews," Anna added. "Like me."

"We have heard some terrible stories. Utter despair, and suicides," Cicognani told them.

"I have heard the same, Bishop," Arceneau said.

"The people were all looking for a man named Sousa Mendes. He was handing out visas to enter Portugal," Gabriella said. "It was both wonderful and terrible."

"This man will pay a heavy price for his charity," Cicognani said. "I know Prime Minister Salazar. He could be the kind of man who would decide to have Portugal join Hitler in this madness."

"You, Bishop, had better hope that Franco does not decide to get too close to Hitler either. The war could come to you very quickly."

Cicognani grimaced. "Gibraltar. Everyone is aware of that possibility."

"The Germans want it. The only thing now that keeps them from it is Spain's neutrality, and that could change quickly."

Cicognani did not reply.

"Franco owes Hitler for the help he received during Spain's civil war."

"True," Cicognani said sadly. "All too true."

"All the more reason why we should leave Spain," Arceneau said. "Too much uncertainty here. Things could break against us."

These were not comforting thoughts to have just before bedtime.

31

JUNE 28, 1940
MADRID, SPAIN

The following morning Bishop Cicognani greeted Sabastian Arceneau with a smile. "I received a phone call this morning, Woke me. My friend in Lisbon, Bishop Pietro Ciriaci, will have someone meet you at the border and take you to Lisbon."

"Good news indeed," Arceneau said.

"He didn't give me a name but the man knows you will be on the train."

"We should be going then."

"God be with you," Cicognani said.

An hour later the train to Lisbon pulled away from the station. The small, private compartment that Bishop Cicognani had arranged for them was comfortable but a little cramped. The trip to the Portuguese border took six hours and there were no incidents. The letter from Bishop Cicognani that Arceneau carried never had to be shown. No one offered any interference. It was an easy trip, so far.

Just before they passed into Portugal, in the Spanish town of Badajoz, the train stopped. They did not get off, although some of the passengers did. They remained inside the private compartment, choosing not to even walk around. Arceneau felt that that could be asking for trouble. Within minutes there was a knock on the compartment door.

"Mr. Arceneau," a voice came from the other side.

Arceneau opened the door. He saw a man in a business suit. His hair was jet black. He looked to be in his late twenties, maybe younger; he was broad shouldered.

"I am Duarte Casal," he told Arseneau. "Bishop Ciriaci sent me to accompany you to Lisbon."

The train gave a jerk as it began moving again and Casal lost his balance and threw his arm against the wall to catch himself.

"Come in," Arceneau said. "Sit down. It was kind of the Bishop to have someone meet us."

"A courtesy to Bishop Cicognani."

Arceneau introduced Casal to Sister Katherine and Anna.

He gave them a small bow. "An honor," he said.

With all four of them now inside the compartment space became a problem. Finally they managed to adjust themselves. Casal had the most trouble finding a suitable position for his legs while sitting. After taking several positions he found one that satisfied him. Anna laughed. Casal smiled.

"We should be in Lisbon a little before nightfall," he said.

EARLY EVENING
LIJBON, PORTUGAL

At the Lisbon railroad station an automobile and driver were waiting for them. The driver took their luggage and loaded it in the trunk of the car as they all got in. Casal sat up front next to the driver. They left the station and were soon out on a wide street.

"The docks for the ships are just over there," Casal pointed. "Less than one hundred kilometers."

"Is the Bishop's residence far from the docks?" Arceneau asked.

Casal half turned around in his seat. "You will be staying well within walking distance of where the ships dock. But it is not the Bishop's residence. That is too far away and we thought it best to be close by the docks. Just in case."

"Not a bad idea," Arceneau said.

The driver turned off the main thoroughfare and down a narrower street. They continued for several blocks. A large structure loomed in front of them.

"There's the Lisbon Cathedral," Casal said.

The sun had just disappeared over the horizon and the beginning of evening light was throwing gray shadows across the massive gray-beige colored limestone blocks that made up the walls of the cathedral. The Cathedral's two tall towers flanked the massive wooden doors of the main entrance.

"The priests offer several masses each day," Casal said, looking at Sister Katherine. "You will be staying on Rua da Conceicao," Casal told them. "Just around the corner."

A few minutes later they stopped.

"Your new home," Casal said. "Top floor. You'll have a splendid view of the city, and the harbor."

Small groups of people were standing around on the sidewalks and in some doorways, talking, gesturing, or silently observing the happenings on the street. There were people carrying suitcases and bags.

"They look like the people we saw on the road in France," Gabriella offered.

"A good chance," Arceneau agreed.

"They look so weary," Anna added.

"Lisbon is teeming with refugees all looking for ship passage. It's a madhouse," Casal said.

They stood looking for a moment.

"This way, Casal said, opening the front door to the building. "Take your things."

As they entered the apartment on the top floor Casals said, "This is the home of a friend of the Bishop. They are away."

"Will we see the Bishop? "Arceneau asked.

"I can't say, Sir," Casal replied. "The housekeeper will be back shortly."

Arceneau thanked them.

"I'll be leaving you now. Is there anything else, Sir?"

"No, we can make our way. These are splendid accommodations. I would like to thank the Bishop personally, but if I do not see him please . . ."

"I will, Sir. God speed."

Shortly after Casal left a middle-age man arrived and identified himself as Erico, the housekeeper for Mr. Diogo Reis and his wife Teresa. He said they were in Brazil, tending to the family business.

That evening, late, he prepared an exquisite meal for them. Sabastian Arceneau thought he had not eaten food that was so savory.

Gabriella was up early and attended mass at the Cathedral.

Sabastian left the apartment several times during the day to apprise himself of the neighborhood and to make certain he could get to the ship easily when it arrived. He spent time down by the docks observing the people and the routine. He did not think it a good idea for Gabriella and Anna to leave the apartment. Erico again prepared scrumptious meals for them, the evening meal was better than the one he had put before them the day before.

"I have had more time to prepare," he said when they lavished him with praise for his efforts.

Bishop Ciriaci showed up the following day. He was on his way to meet with some high official in the Portugese government, but he wanted to pay them a visit and offer his blessing for their journey. It was a courtesy to his good friend Bishop Cicognani in Madrid, he told them.

Ciriaci had an elongated face, weak chin and receding hair line. He had eyes that reminded Arceneau of those of a bulldog's and they looked out at the world from behind steel rimmed glasses. His nose was long and straight.

Arceneau did not miss Ciriaci's glance at Gabriella's abdomen as he took her hand in greeting.

"Bishop Cicognani tells me your trip across France was a most unpleasant one. I have been hearing a lot about some of what went on. Many of the people who crossed with you are here in Lisbon now, and Prime Minister Salazar is not pleased that they received authorization."

"Sousa Mendes," Arceneau said. "Jews."

Ciriaci growled, "Salazar wants me to condemn Sousa Mendes's actions."

"Sousa Mendes is a saint," Gabriella said with surprising assertiveness.

Ciriaci smiled. "In your world, maybe, Sister. In Salazar's, Sousa Mendes has brought much trouble."

"What will happen to Sousa Mendes?" Gabriella asked.

Ciriaci's mouth drew down. "He'll be removed, and scorned. He will have a hard time, so will his family, I fear."

"Can you help?" Gabriella. "Will you?"

"My hands are tied, Sister. The Church can only do so much."

"You'll be doing even less if the Germans come," Arceneau said.

"They don't have an interest in Portugal," Ciriaci claimed.

"They have an interest in Gibraltar."

"Maybe," Ciriaci said with a voice that trailed off.

"Pray you are correct, Bishop. You don't want the Nazis sharing the territory here in Portugal, or being your neighbor in Spain."

"I fail to see your real meaning, Mr. Arceneau"

"If the Germans try for Gibraltar national boundaries will be meaningless. They have proven that already elsewhere," Arceneau said. "Portugal and Spain *are* Iberia; the two are one."

The Bishop frowned.

"Hitler is working both Franco in Spain *and* Salazar in Portugal. Either one gives in, the other will have no choice but to go along," Arceneau said, becoming tired of this personal lesson in geopolitics.

"You speak as if you seem certain," Ciriaci said. "I hope not."

Arceneau smiled. "I'm a pessimist, Bishop. Always have been."

"I am an optimist," he replied proudly.

"Then God was more generous to you than to me. I can only live with what He gave me."

They bantered this way for a while longer and then the Bishop left after giving them his blessing.

32

JUNE 31, 1940
LISBON, PORTUGAL

It was a spectacular sunset. Gabriella was standing by one of the windows, watching. Her eyes were drawn to a ship and from the appearance of its stacks it did not look like a freighter. It soon was about to pass under the bridge. She called Anna.

"That could be the *Washington*," Gabriella said as Anna came up beside her.

For the next few minutes they both watched in silence as the ship slid through the water. Now they could see it was a passenger liner.

The door to the apartment opened and Sabastian Arceneau came in.

"The *Washington* is coming in," Arceneau said.

"We see it!" Anna said excitedly. "There it is; it just passed under the bridge."

Arceneau came over. "A beautiful sight."

"Can we go see it?" Anna asked.

"We'll be boarding tomorrow morning," Arceneau said. "We must get ready."

That night, after Gabriella and Anna had gone to bed Sabastian slipped out of the apartment, telling Erico that he would be gone for a while.

When he was still several blocks away from the dock he saw what he feared he would see. The street and the alleys were crowded with pockets of people with their belongings, families, moving toward the docks; there was some occasional pushing and harsh words. It was a mild commotion. They were frightened people lining up to get a chance of boarding somehow, to escape this land. There was no way to be sure but he guessed a good number in this crowd did not have the proper boarding passes and papers that would permit them passage, but they were there trying to find a way all the same.

Sabastian made his way closer to the ship. He wanted to get a better look at the mechanism the shipping line had for boarding passengers. He looked for men wearing the uniform of the United States Line, the owner of the *Washington*. Several were visible. They seemed to be standing about, measuring the behavior of the crowd.

The police suddenly came down and began moving people along, trying to calm things, but it had little effect. Then more came and the crowd became less angry. Sabastian knew it was because these people knew full well the power of the police and what they might end up having to contend with if they resisted.

They quickly reduced their noisy, pushy behavior, wanting to shrink themselves to near invisibility.

Sabastian approached one of the uniformed men from the ship who had just gotten free of a woman crying wildly in a language Sabastian knew the man in uniform didn't understand. He did, however, know that the officer knew the meaning of what the woman wanted. It was what they all wanted.

"Sir," Sabastian said.

The man eyed him.

Sabastian smiled. "I need information, please. I have authorization to board tomorrow. I want to know the best place. It is for two ladies. If we can, I want to avoid this kind of thing tomorrow, if possible. Will it be like this tomorrow?"

The man shrugged. "We should have help from the local people tomorrow to keep order. We have many more people booked than we have standard accommodations, cabins, beds. Bring some kind of bedding, and warm clothes. Some people will possibly be living on deck and sleeping inside on the floor. The captain has his hands full on this run. We still have to go to Galway and pick up passengers, refugees, children mostly. We will be over capacity this time, for sure. This could be our final run to Europe."

"Yes, but where should we board?"

The man pointed.

"Thank you, Sir."

THE FOLLOWING MORNING
JULY 1, 1940
LISBON HARBOR

Everyone was up early. The housekeeper prepared a large breakfast. At seven o'clock they were headed for the *Washington*. Sabastian went to the gate the officer had indicated the previous evening. There was already a line forming when they arrived and there were many people moving along the dock, both passengers and workers.

"Our tickets should be waiting for us at the gate," Sabastian said.

"What if they aren't?" Gabriella asked.

"Don't worry."

The line moved forward as those ahead of them made their way through the gate where the attendant took their tickets and whatever personal information was required and then sent them up the walkway and onto the ship.

"When we get to the gate let me do all the talking."

Their boarding went smoothly, not even a near mishap. Sabastian was surprised but greatly relieved. They were shown to a small cabin that had a minimum of furnishings, but it didn't matter. They were aboard.

By evening the *Washington* was only a few minutes from sailing. Sabastian, Gabriella, and Anna were on deck, watching preparations for departure and watching everyone crying and saying goodby. Emotions were high, and there was a low tension in everyone's words.

"I shall see you again in America," Sabastian told them.

Gabriella took his hand. "You have been a Godsend."

He smiled. "I am rather good at what I do if I must say so myself. This was a most pleasant mission, Gabriella. We worked well together."

"How true." Tears began to form in her eyes.

"But, this time I had a lot of help," Arceneau said.

"I pray for you, and for all those who helped us," she said.

"I will do my best to try and stay abreast of Colonel Eichenstat," he told her.

Her tears grew larger. "Poor, Fritz. It is all my fault. Please, if you can, tell him where I am. And how I'm doing."

He squeezed her hand. "Don't be too hard on yourself."

Anna watched them.

"What are your plans now?" Gabriella asked Arceneau.

He shrugged and looked off into the distance. "Contact the Gregory. See what assignment awaits."

She smiled.

Arceneau looked at Anna. "Remember, Anna, you are being given a special opportunity. Do not waste it. Use every opportunity. Do not dishonor all the souls who have helped you this far."

"No, I won't. I'll work hard."

"I'll tell your brother, Herwald, where you have gone and how you are doing," he told her. "I'm sure he will write to you soon."

The ships whistle blew. With it, Sabastian turned and walked away. He did not look back until he was on the walkway almost at the bottom. He waved as his eyes spotted them at the railing above. Gabriella's black habit stood out. She returned his wave, as did Anna.

For Gabriella Sommers and Anna Burkitz, America now waited.

33

JULY 2, 1940
THE S.S. WASHINGTON

Gabriella and Anna had come up from their cabin to walk around. It was a climb of several flights of stairs. They made it to the ballroom where canvas cots were being laid out. It was the same in the swimming pool area. Gabriella asked one of the attendants what was the meaning.

"Kids," he said. "Sleeping places for the kids we are to board when we dock in Galway. They say we'll take on about nine hundred. We'll be almost double overloaded. British kids mostly, I suppose. Escaping the bombing."

After a further climb they made it to the top deck which was open to the morning air. The air was cool but not cold. Numerous people milled about or walked briskly, trying to unwind and gain some change of pace from their tight quarters, although, Gabriella guessed they, like herself, were grateful for just making it aboard the ship and now heading to America.

"Good evening, Captain," someone said from behind them.

Gabriella turned to see the captain tip his hat. He kept walking. He appeared to be coming right for them. He tipped his hat as he stopped.

"Good evening, Sir," she said, taken by his brilliant blue eyes. She thought they were well suited for a captain of this fine ship..

"You are Sister Katherine?" he asked.

Gabriella was caught unsuspectedly. "Sir?"

"I am Captain Henry Manning. I was informed you would be aboard. Mr. Michael Duncan in Washington spoke to me about you, and the girl. This is Anna?"

"Yes, this is Anna. You say who spoke to you?"

"He said his name was Michael Duncan. You know him?"

"No, I . . ."

"Well, I told him I would make sure you were well cared for while on board my ship and see if you needed anything. Please call on me if you do."

"We have all we need, Sir."

Anna kept staring at the medals on his chest.

Captain Manning smiled broadly. "You take interest in these, young lady?" he asked.

"We've come all the way from Germany," Anna blurted out.

Manning looked at Gabriella. "The two of you?"

"Yes," she replied.

"I hear it is bad," he said.

Gabriella lowered her eyes. "Desperate people."

"That's why we are here," Manning said. "This is a special run we are making. It may be the last."

"We have heard that. We are happy to have made it. Now, we have a new life waiting in America. Thanks to people like you, Sir."

Manning nodded his appreciation and began walking again, greeting passengers.

"We are in good hands, Anna," Gabriella said.

The truth of that statement came early the following morning. Captain Manning had just gotten to the bridge when a German submarine surfaced and flashed a signal that the ship would be torpedoed in ten minutes.

"Get your passengers into the lifeboats!" the submarine's flashing signal read.

The alarm spread through the *Washington*, waking the passengers from a restless sleep. They were being instructed to move to the main deck where the lifeboats were hanging, fastened down in their respective positions.

"Get in, Anna! Get in!" Gabriella yelled as she pushed Anna up. Someone's hand reached out and Anna took it and was pulled into the lifeboat. Gabriella climbed in beside her. Others followed. They soon sat shoulder to shoulder, waiting. Others scrambled to get themselves into the other boats. There was loud shouting, instructions being yelled out. Some people were sobbing but generally everyone remained in good order thanks to the calming hands of the *Washington's* officers and men who were assisting. Watching them, Gabriella guessed they had practiced this drill before. It was a smooth operation.

On the bridge, Captain Manning was giving orders to his signalman. The signalman sent the flashes for the submarine commander.

W-A-S-H-I-N-G-T-O-N   A-M-E-R-I-C-A-N

The German seemed not to understand. The next series of flashes read:

I W-I-L-L S-I-N-K Y-O-U

Again Manning sent:

W-A-S-H-I-N-G-T-O-N   A-M-E-R-I-C-A-N

There was a lengthy pause.

"He's translating," Manning said.

Passengers continued to pile into the lifeboats, nearly full by now. Gabriella looked out and saw the submarine, seemingly motionless in the water. She saw the German swasticka.

On the bridge the Captain received a new message:

I W-I-L-L S-I-N-K Y-O-U

"Damn!" Manning cursed. "Send American ship!"

"Aye-aye, Sir"

A-M-E-R-I-C-A-N S-H-I-P   A-M-E-R-I-C-A-N S-H-I-P

Agonizing minutes passed. Then flashes came from the submarine.

T-H-O-U-G-H-T   Y-O-U   W-E-R-E   A-N-O-T-H-E-R S-H-I-P

P-L-E-A-S-E G-O O-N

"Full speed ahead," Manning ordered. "Don't unload the lifeboats just yet."

Gabriella and the others watched the German submarine shrink in size and slowly slip back beneath the surface of the Atlantic Ocean.

"Bastards!" someone cursed.

"Jesus, that was too damn close!"

A small boy asked, "Will it come back, Mommy?"

Gabriella saw a man several rows down take out a silver flask, unscrew the top, tip it nearly straight up and swallow what remained of its contents.

Half and hour later, after moving at nearly twenty-two knots, the big ship slowed.

"Get the passengers out of the boats," Captain Manning ordered.

Immediately several versions of what had happened began to circulate. Making their way back to their cabin Gabriella heard one of the seamen say to his companion, "That Manning is one cool customer."

34

JULY 5, 1940
BREMEN, GERMANY

General Bruno Reinard was in no mood for pleasantries. He got right to the point and when he had finished Eichenstat had all the evidence he needed to know that Sergeant Pond had been talking too much. Father Schroeder had been right about the man, he was not to be trusted.

"So you can see why that convent in Köln has me a little concerned, Colonel," Reinard said.

"How so, General?"

"People have gone missing from that place."

"I don't follow you, Sir. Pardon me, but I don't."

"Do you want me to cite specific cases?"

Eichenstat knew what was coming. "If you believe it is necessary, Sir."

"Very well, let's take the girl, and the nun. What has happened to them?"

Eichenstat did his level best to present Reinard with a genuine look of no concern. He tried to speak casually.

"First, the nun, I can't remember her name, went on a trip to inspect convents in Belgium and I believe France as well."

"Yes, yes, with that priest fellow, that ..."

"Father Schroeder I believe," Eichenstat said. "He had papers from the Vatican giving him that authority. He took with him the nun as his assistant. She is an expert in such things, at least that's what I was told by Schroeder."

"So you say!" Reinard cracked.

"So the Vatican says," Eichenstat shot back, but not defiantly. "It has that right, I suppose. It oversees all convents, as I understand our present arrangement. So you see, I could find no reason to prevent them from leaving. It was a simple thing to me."

"And the girl? What about the girl?"

Eichenstat shook his head. "There you have me, General. I may have been out of line but I did it for a good reason."

Reinard glared at him. "I want to hear it."

"Well, Sir, the priest ... has a ... he likes young girls."

"A religious man?" Reinard said, his face cringing in disgust.

"It happens, Sir."

Reinard shook his head "Degenerate," he hissed. "So why the hell provide ... are you telling me that the girl ... you provided this degenerate with ... the girl!"

"I had my reasons," Eichenstat said calmly.

"I'd like to hear them."

"I thought I could get information from the man. He hears things. If he was making his way around inspecting convents I thought it would be a way for us to gain information about what was going on inside. Things we might not hear otherwise. It was a backhanded shakedown, I suppose."

Reinard remained silent. His eyes focused on several different places in the distance, mulling what he had just been told. Eichenstat was not sure from watching the General's demeanor whether he would believe his story. On the surface it was perfectly plausible. But would Reinard swallow it?

"So," the General finally said, still showing some skepticism. "What did you learn?"

Eichenstat grimaced. "It was a mistake, I'm sorry to say. Both I and Father Schroeder have been taken advantage of."

"That needs an explanation, Colonel!"

"Yes, Sir, it does. The nun and the girl have disappeared, it seems. After I drove the nun and the girl to Aachen to be with Father Schroeder, he subsequently took both of them to Brussel. I assumed that it was the first stop on their inspection tour of convents."

"I assume you checked to see."

"I did, Sir. They stayed at Bishop Micara's residence in Brussels. The good Bishop had been told by our governing people in Belgium that he would be no longer welcome and that he would have to leave the country immediately. Our people saw him as a disturbance to Brussels tranquility. He was voicing openly against us. In obeying our declaration to leave Belgium, Sir, Bishop Micara took the nun and the girl with him."

"And what in the world was the priest doing all this time while this Bishop was making his departure out of Belgium, do you know?"

"He went with them, Sir."

"Christ!"

"The priest did not know what the Bishop was up to, Sir. I have checked with him. He was just following orders, Sir. You can appreciate that, General. You understand the need for subordinates to follow orders of a superior. It's the same in the Church, maybe more so. But all the while the Bishop was deceiving Father Schroeder."

General Reinard sat in silence. The fingers of his hands flexed in and out in a nervous reaction. Eventually he said, "We have to assume they went to Spain. We can check, maybe."

"Father Schroeder said that was their plan."

"But why? Why do this?" Reinard asked. "There's only one reason I can think of that makes sense."

Colonel Eichenstat went rigid, waiting.

"What were their names, the nun and the girl?" Reinard demanded.

Eichenstat went to the folders on his desk, pretending not to recall immediately. "The ... nun's name is Sister Katherine."

"And I am *Rumpelstilzchen*! What is her given name?"

"I'm not sure, Sir."

"Isn't that in your records?"

"Somewhere, I suppose. I'll have to look. Is it important?"

Reinard slapped his gloves in his hand irritably. Eichenstat knew he had overstepped.

"My instincts tell me she is a Jew!" Reinard fumed. "You didn't know?"

"I believe you're mistaken, General. She's a Catholic nun. It's not possible."

"You have a better explanation?"

"Yes, Sir, I think I do. She was escorting the girl. The girl is a Jew, we know that."

"Christ! Dammit!"

"And why was the girl taken along. Does the Bishop appreciate young girls as well. Both the priest *and* the Bishop!"

Eichenstat forced himself to laugh and throw up his hands. "It could be, Sir. I believe the fact that she is a Jew only makes it more exciting for them. To bed a Jewess, especially if she is a virgin?"

The General gave Eichenstat a curious look. "Have I possibly misjudged you, Colonel?"

"I fail to understand your meaning, Sir."

"Is it possible you have such ... deprivations. Does a Jew girl excite you, Colonel?"

"I believe you'll find that my record and my behavior show no such inclination, as you say."

Reinhard laughed. "Of course."

"Thank you, Sir."

Reinard took on a repulsive expression. "Imagine it," he said. "Imagine the nun as this Bishop's concubine. Traveling with him. It makes one squirm." He sat silently and Eichenstat could only believe he was forming an image in his mind of what he had just described about Bishop Micara and Garbiella. Reinard then said, "Do you have a photograph of the nun in your files? Is she pretty?"

The question about Gabriella catalyzed Eichenstat's own imagination and he pictured Gabriella; he felt her embrace, her fragrance, a true womanly body fragrance, not any perfumed contrivance. Smells are a powerful remembrance in the minds of most people; they can trigger intense emotion and Fritz Eichenstat was no exception. He remembered Gabriella all too well. He could hardly stand it now.

"What's the matter, Colonel?"

"Nothing, Sir."

"You had a very peculiar expression."

"Sorry, Sir."

He could not escape the grip his thinking had on him. He felt his loins begin to ache. These thoughts of Gabriella drove themselves deeper into Eichenstat's consciousness. Even with Reinard looking at him, Eichenstat could not prevent them, he could not discard them. He wanted Gabriella for his own. Suddenly, as it always did, the dark thought raced through his mind: his life on this earth would be over before he saw Gabriella again. He would never hold her again; he would never breathe in her fragrance. He would never see his child.

As the General was leaving he said, "I'm looking forward to reading your physical fitness report, Colonel."

"I'm in fine shape, General."

35

JULY 7, 1940
BREMEN, GERMANY

Colonel Fritz Eichenstat stood on the scale in the doctor's office dressed only in his underwear. He was there for his annual physical, ordered by General Bruno Reinard for all officers under his command.

"You have lost weight, Colonel," Dr. Gerhardt Schenck said. "Six pounds to be exact. Are you working too hard maybe?"

Eichenstat had a sullen look about him as he stepped off the scale. "Let's get on with it, Doctor. I know what condition I'm in, and whether I'm working too hard."

A half hour later Eichenstat had dressed and had just finished adjusting his boots. Doctor Schenck, sitting at his desk, was writing in Eichenstat's file. A moment later he put down his pen and got up. "The General says you may be worried about something," he said, approaching Eichenstat. "He's worried it might be affecting your performance, getting in the way of your duties. Might that be the case?"

"Is it part of your duties to pry, Doctor?"

Schenck glared at him. "The General also said that you have an independent streak."

"Do you and the General talk a great deal about the physical health of all his officers, or am I a special case?" Eichenstat asked in a ringing tone of arrogance.

"Maybe the General and I talk, maybe not," Schenck replied. "The General wants all his officers in the best of condition."

Eichenstat grinned. "Are you telling him that I am not?"

"No, no."

"Good, because losing a few pounds still puts me in far better condition than most of the other officers I've seen under the General's command."

Schenck frowned. "Shall I inform the General of your view?"

Eichenstat gave the man a stern look. "I am a professional, Dr. Schenck. I would hope you would practice your profession with similar decorum."

Schenck drew himself up. "The General keeps up with all the files on his officers. I do not have to speak to him personally. He sees everything in your file. You are a member of the Army of the Reich. In civilian life the protocol may be different. You must be aware of that fact."

It was something Eichenstat could not refute.

"Write what you will in my file, Doctor."

Schenck then stunned him by asking, "Tell me, Colonel, why is it that you are not married? Do you have a female companion somewhere, or, maybe ... several. No one seems to see you with anyone special, or has heard you even speak of anyone."

Eichenstat reached for the man and grabbed the edge of his white coat, pulling him slightly forward. "Tell the General I will provide him with the names and addresses of several former *companions* if he feels the need to authenticate the status of my libido!" He then released the grip. "Are we through?"

It was clear that the doctor was flustered. His face was flushed, but he recovered some. "The General will hear of this," he said slowly.

Eichenstat grinned. "I have no doubt. Good morning, Doctor."

As Fritz Eichenstat walked out of the office he was having unhappy thoughts about his mental state. Was he going mad, or was he on the verge of a nervous breakdown? His actions with the doctor just might get him re-assigned, or dismissed from the military outright. No, he quickly concluded, that was not likely. He was too valuable an asset. Even with all his shortcomings and independent tendencies he was too valuable to Reinard to be disciplined or dismissed for so minor an offense. At least he liked to tell himself that. But, he had to admit, there was an outside chance that there could be serious ramifications from his behavior. He had little doubt that his job performance was under scrutiny. The General had been asking curious questions lately. And then there was Sergeant Markus Pond who had said things to General Reinard, or one of the General's staff. That seemed clear. Father Schroeder picked up on Pond early on and had good instincts about such things; he had to have, given the nature of the work he was doing outside of his standard church duties. But as long as Pond was assigned as his aide there was very little Eichenstat could do to avoid having his actions watched. It would not be easy for Eichenstat to maneuver successfully around this impediment. He had to watch himself and what he had to do today was going to be a tricky test of just how careful and wily he could be. Eichenstat had a trip to make and making it without taking Pond along would almost certainly get the Sergeant's curiosity working overtime. Eichenstat had planned this day with as much care as he could think of and he thought he had a way to keep Pond in the dark on the real objective in what he was about to do.

"Did you pass your physical, Colonel," Sergeant Pond asked as Eichenstat reached the waiting car.

Eichenstat threw out his chin in a show of toughness. "An iron man," he said.

The sergeant had the door open. "Glad to hear it, Sir."

"We'll be making a trip today, Sergeant."

Pond faltered for a brief moment. "I didn't know, Sir. Did you say? Did I forget?"

"No, no. I've got to see about something in Hanover. I brought a map with me so that we can find the place I am looking for." Eichenstat began unfolding the map in the back seat as they drove.

Soon they were away from Bremen and on their way. "In Hanover we will be going to Goethestrasse. There is a plaza nearby. I'm hoping we'll have no trouble finding it."

They arrived before noon. They drove into the city along Vahrenwalder Strasse, then across the railroad tracks and finally to Goethestrasse. The apartment building was on their left close to Goethe Plaza. Sergeant Pond parked on the opposite side of the street from the building.

"Wait in the car, Sergeant," Eichenstat ordered.

Inside the building Eichenstat began looking for Apartment 311. On the third floor he walked down the long hallway. At 311 he stopped and knocked. As he waited a door across the hall opened and a woman peeked out. The door quickly shut just as he turned around. His knock had brought no response. He knocked a second time, this time with more force. Still no answer. He then turned and walked over to the door that had just opened and closed. He knocked. A short, elderly woman stared out at him. He tipped the visor of his hat.

"I am looking for the Sommers," he told her. "They do live across the way do they not?"

The woman only nodded and then began to shut the door. Eichenstat prevented her by pushing back.

"Have you seen them today?"

The woman shook her head.

"When did you see them last?" he asked.

The woman's eyes widened.

"Do you know where they are now?"

Again the woman shook her head. At that moment an elderly man appeared behind her. He was dressed in a coat and tie. Eichenstat saw the yellow Star of David sewn to his coat.

"Eliana we have not seen in a few days." There was a fright in his voice. Eichenstat tried to look less menacing but he knew that was impossible given his uniform and boots. He had seen that look before.

"I have a message for them," he said to the two. "It is important."

The man shrugged. The woman looked at the man and then back at Eichenstat, still with that stare of anxiety and fear.

"Eliana has been ill, I believe," the man said.

"Oh, I'm sorry," Eichenstat replied.

The man looked puzzled by his show of concern.

"She has no one," the man said. "She is all alone."

"Her husband?"

"He died a few weeks ago," the man told him.

"Oh, I see," Eichenstat said. "How did he die, do you know?"

The man looked down. "In the Plaza," he said. "Just down the street."

"What happened?"

The man raised his eyebrows. "They say he walked in front of a large truck carrying soldiers."

"An accident?"

The man dropped his eyes. "Perhaps. They did not say."

"Was his wife with him?"

The man shook his head.

"I'm sorry," Eichenstat said. "I would like to see her if I could. It may be the last chance I'll get to give her this message."

The man looked puzzled. Eichenstat knew that his confusion was being caused by this German officer behaving as if he were a dear friend of this woman, something the man had not seen happen in quite some time. It seemed so out of character that it must be some kind of deception that would bring harm in the end.

Finally the man said haltingly, "I ... could ... give it to her ... maybe."

"Thank you, but I must do this myself. I made a promise to someone."

The man knew better than to press the issue.

"Tell me, does Mrs. Sommers go out often?"

The man and woman checked each other for some kind of confirmation. The man replied, "Her husband was the one who went to market. She was ..."

"She was what?" Eichenstat asked quickly.

The man looked uncomfortable.

"Please, tell me. It's all right.

"She was sad all the time. Her daughter ... her daughter left the family several years ago. She's in a ... became a nun."

"Mrs. Sommers told you this?"

The man nodded.

"It is true," Eichenstat said. "I know her daughter. We were in university together. That was many years ago."

"We did not know the daughter."

"If Mrs. Sommers rarely leaves her apartment why is it she does not answer the door when I knock?"

The man shrugged.

Eichenstat went back over to door 311 and banged as loud as he could. He shouted out an order, one that would arouse any German.

"Gestapo! Open up!"

He waited, listening as the echo of his shout faded down the hall. The door where he had just been slammed shut instantly. Still, from behind 311 there was no sound at all. He began to have an unhappy thought. He then stepped back and raised his leg and slammed his foot against the door. It broke open and swung back hard on its hinges. He looked around from where he stood. He went inside. The front room was empty. He went to the door leading into the next room and peered inside. There she was, sitting in a large green upholstered chair, staring out the window that overlooked Goethestrasse. She did not move. Eichenstat rushed over to examine her more closely. The way she looked he thought she could be dead. She then grinned a sinister grin. It was a contemptible grin, a grin, that told of a final resignation of her recognition of just how humorless life had become, how it had drained everything of meaning right out of her. Eichenstat then went back and shut the door to the room. He came back and bent down.

"Mrs. Sommers, you must come with me," he said gently.

His new attitude made her blink and she almost looked over at him. He began to think on his feet, an exercise he was not all that bad at. It had been his original plan to tell her what he knew about Gabriella, where she was, and how she was. Now, he felt he had to alter that approach. He was grappling with all the possible ramifications, hoping he could accurately measure most of them.

"Gather up some of your personal things, your keepsakes and put them in your suitcase and come with me," he ordered.

She raised her eyes slowly and looked at him. She said nothing right away. Then, "Kill me here. Here in this place you people have forced me to come. I had a nice home once. I will not move. Take out that ... gun of yours and shoot me here and now. You took away my ..." she stopped.

"Mrs. Sommers," he said with added emphasis. "I am not here to harm you. I want to help you."

She smirked. "German soldiers cannot help me," she uttered contemptuously.

"I am a friend of your daughter's," he then told her.

He saw her stiffen.

"I have no daughter," she whispered.

"You will come with me nevertheless." He reached out his hand. "Gather your things." His grip on her arm tightened. She twisted and grimaced, he relaxed his hold. "Please. If you do not come with me without a fuss your daughter will be in considerable danger. You are the only one who can help her now."

That got her attention.

"What have you done to her?"

"Nothing. I am her friend but you must listen to me and do exactly as I tell you."

She labored to get out of the chair. Once on her feet she walked to the closet and took out a modest size suitcase. The handle was nearly broken off and it hung loose. He took it from her and threw it on the bed and opened it. She began putting clothes inside. Grabbing up some framed pictures and a small photo album she carefully placed them on top of everything. She stood and scanned the room with a look of purposelessness.

"Anything else?" he asked.

She went over to a dresser and pulled open the top drawer and took out a small leather box.

"Gabriella's," she said. "Some ... things"

He wanted to see what was inside. She placed it in the suitcase.

"We must go now," he said.

"Where are you taking me?"

"You will know soon enough. But when we get to my car downstairs I warn you not to say a word. My driver is not to be trusted. I tell you this for your own safety. Whatever I say to him you are not to say anything; make no comments. Do you understand?"

She looked at him. "Why should I believe you?"

"Because you have no other choice if you want to have a chance to survive all the madness that is going on in Germany now."

"You can't frighten me. I am already dead."

"That is your choice but you should know that I am doing this for your daughter, Gabriella, the person you claim no longer belongs to you."

She frowned, looking confounded, then asked, "You love her, is that it?"

"Never mind, it is of little importance now."

"Where is she? Do you know?"

"We must leave. Remember what I told you."

He picked up the suitcase and they left. The door to the apartment of the man and woman he had talked to opened a crack. A half face appeared in the opening, then shut quickly as Eichenstat glanced sideways at it.

Outside, they walked across Goethestrasse and headed for the car. Sergeant Pond jumped out and swung the read door open. He stood straight, watching them approach.

"We'll have a passenger, Sergeant."

Pond gave the woman a rather nasty look.

"One of them, Colonel?"

Eichenstat motioned Eliana Sommers to get in. He handed Pond the suitcase. "Stow it up front, Sergeant."

Back behind the wheel Pond asked, "Where to, Colonel?"

"How are we on petrol, Sergeant?"

"More than enough to get back to headquarters."

"Can we make it to Köln?"

Pond hesitated. "Köln, it'll be close."

"The convent. The shortest route."

"I'll have to check."

After checking the map he said, "We may need petrol along the way."

"I want to get there well before dark, Sergeant."

Pond put more determination into his driving. Eichenstat knew that he liked to drive fast and was all too pleased to get the order to move along. It would keep him concentrating on his driving and draw his attention away from Eliana Sommers, which was Eichenstat's intention.

Just outside Köln when they had slowed down because of traffic Pond asked, "Has this one committed an offense, Colonel?"

Eichenstat was ready. "No, Sergeant, she is going to help me with my little problem with the General."

"Sorry to hear you are having trouble, Colonel."

"It's a minor problem but I don't like having even minor problems get in the way of serving."

"I see, Sir."

"This lady is going to provide me with information about a certain Carmelite nun who has disappeared. 'Escaped' is more like it," he said this hoping that Eliana Sommers would recognize the hidden meaning in his words and react as he had told her. She said nothing. As he had hoped, she sat rigid, stiff and unmoving just as she had been in the apartment when he had burst in.

"How would this one know the whereabouts of that nun, Sir?"

Eichenstat laughed as though he had some secret knowledge. "She is the nun's mother. She must know."

"You are a smart man, Colonel. The General surely will be pleased about your progress."

"This will restore my standing with the General if I can learn the nun's whereabouts."

"You fooled me, Sir. I was wondering all day why it was we were going to Hanover."

They arrived at the convent at just before five o'clock. "We shall stay the night in Köln and start back to Bremen in the morning, Sergeant. Now I have to speak to Mother Superior about this woman and inform her about my intentions for her."

"Shall I go inside with you, Sir?"

"No, you go find us lodgings for the night. And some petrol. Get back as soon as you can. I shall not be long."

Eichenstat and Eliana Sommers got out. Eichenstat took the suitcase from Sergeant Pond and they headed toward the convent entrance.

"I do not know about Gabriella," she suddenly said as they approached the convent entrance.

"Of course you don't," he replied.

"Then why ..."

"Hold your tongue, please. Let me do the talking. I am trying to help you."

"Why?"

"Because of Gabriella," he said. "No more questions."

Mother Superior's office was empty. The sister rushed off to fetch her, almost floating down the corridor.

Moments later Mother Superior appeared in the doorway. She stared at Eliana Sommers. Eichenstat introduced the woman as Eliana Sommers but said nothing else. Mother Superior showed a hint of confusion.

"Colonel?"

"Yes, Mother Superior."

"What ... is it you want?"

"I want you to look after this woman."

"We are filled to capacity, Colonel. We have scarce supplies, barely enough to get by. Another mouth to feed."

Eichenstat then said, "Surely you can accommodate Sister Katherine's mother."

Mother Superior shot Eliana Sommers a sharp look of astonishment. The woman said nothing.

"Colonel? Is this true?"

"Ask her?"

Mother Superior again looked at Eliana Sommers. "Is it true? Are you Sister Katherine's mother?"

"Her name is Gabriella," Eliana Sommers then said.

"Your ... daughter is the finest nun I have ever known," Mother Superior said. "I wish I knew where she has gone to. She was taken away by Father Schroeder and the Vatican to make inspections of convents throughout Belgium and France. I have not heard from her; I have heard nothing about her since then." She looked over at Eichenstat. "Do you know?"

"I have a pretty good idea," he said. "But I cannot be sure. I may have a way to find out something but it could take awhile."

"Where is she?" Mother Superior asked again.

"My best guess is that she is in America, or on her way there."

"America!" Mother Superior cried out. "That is not possible!"

"America," Eliana Sommers whispered.

Eichenstat looked at her. There was a faint glow in her eyes and some pink color had surfaced in her cheeks.

"I must be going," Eichenstat said. "You *will* take care of Gabriella's mother, won't you Mother Superior." She has a few things in her suitcase," he added, lifting it.

As Colonel Eichenstat headed for the door Eliana Sommers surprised him by speaking. "Will Gabriella return?"

He replied, sounding official, and certain. "I don't see how that's possible. Besides, America is the best place for her now."

36

JULY 8, 1940
KÖLN GERMANY

Eichenstat had thought this through and knew what he was going to tell Sergeant Pond that morning as they ate breakfast. It was part of the plan to camouflage his reasons for bringing Eliana Sommers to the convent. What he had in mind was something that would throw Mother Superior into a spin when she learned of it. But for it to work he had to have her play a part. He was counting on her to understand this need and go along, but convincing her was the element in Eichenstat's plan that still could derail everything. If that happened Eichenstat would be squarely in the cross hairs of General Reinard.

"We are going to return to the convent, Sergeant." Eichenstat told Pond as they ate.

Pond drew in his chin. "Today?"

"As soon as we finish here."

"Did you forget something, Colonel?"

"No, I want to interrogate the old woman we brought here yesterday." Eichenstat thought that the slightly wicked smile on Pond's face showed his approval.

"May I participate, Colonel? I've some experience in that sort of thing."

"Maybe next time, Sergeant. This first encounter I want to experience alone. I guess I want to see if I can be successful at such things. Remember, I have to show the General that I am one of his officers who has the will to get results."

"You have not done one of these before, Sir?"

"Not to a woman," Eichenstat replied, lying. He had never done such a thing to anyone, male or female.

"Women are especially satisfying subjects," Pond volunteered. "It can become rather exciting, especially if the subject is a young female. It can be a rather erotic experience. But this woman is old. It will not be the same for you."

The description was an insight into Sergeant Pond's makeup that Eichenstat had never known about. He wondered if maybe he had missed something in the man's file.

When they arrived at the convent he ordered Pond to remain outside.

"Do you think you will be long, Sir?"

Eichenstat shrugged, then grinned for effect. "Depends, Sergeant. It depends."

Once he was let inside the convent he walked directly to the office of Mother Superior, assuming she would be there. She was surprised to see him back.

"Maybe you should have stayed the night with us, Colonel."

"Listen to me," he began right off. "I have little time to waste and I have to make my point so that you understand my meaning fully. We are going to perform a little exercise in deception, Mother Superior."

She recoiled in utter bewilderment. "Have you lost your mind, Colonel? What ..."

He held up his hand. "Listen carefully to what I am going to tell you." He then went through a lengthy, detailed explanation. She listened but he could see that she was in a steady state of difficulty as she tried to digest all that she was hearing.

"You are mad! You must be!" she responded.

"You were not listening, Mother," he said harshly.

Again, this time more emphatically and more slowly, he repeated what he had said. This time she eyed him with a determined stare.

"Have I misjudged you, Colonel?"

He answered with a slow, methodical speech. "Mother Superior, this entire period of mayhem that we are embroiled in is just in its infancy. When it is all finally over, if you and I are still alive, then we may be able to make some final judgements about that. For the here and now we can only do what we think we have to do in order to possibly have a successful and honorable outcome."

"Successful? Honorable?" she said. "Whose success, whose honor?"

"Yours. Mine."

She blanched. "They are not the same."

"Oh, but they are. Mother Superior."

She faced him with a blank look. "So you say now."

He nodded. "You will have to trust me."

"You? Why?"

"You have no choice."

"We all have choices, Colonel."

"Then choose the one that will give you a chance to save your convent and some of the people in it, and possibly yourself."

Once again she had that look of uncertainty on her face.

Eichenstat continued. "Do you remember that I once told you that if you trust Sister Katherine you should also trust me, do you remember?"

"Oh, I remember," she replied.

"From your expression and talk I thought for a moment you had forgotten."

She seemed to think about that. "What do you want?"

"You can no longer haggle with me over this. You must throw yourself into this role or else it will not be convincing. If it is not, then, well, both of us may be in a real fix."

After a thoughtful pause she said, "You shall have my cooperation, Colonel."

"I knew I could count on you."

A hour later Colonel Eichenstat emerged from the convent. Mother Superior was right behind him. She was yelling something but Sergeant Pond was too far away to hear exactly what she was saying but he could see that she was greatly agitated. He dropped the newspaper he had been reading and quickly headed toward them. At that moment Eichenstat stopped and turned to face Mother Superior who closed in on him. Pond then saw her reddened face growling at Colonel Eichenstat. She yelled, "God will surely punish you for treating that poor woman the way you did. She is old and sick at heart over her daughter. You are a monster. Your words to her were foul and cruel!"

Pond was close now.

Eichenstat said to Mother Superior, "I am a man who does his job, Mother Superior."

Pond was now right beside him. "Colonel?" he said, seeking some sign about what he should do.

Eichenstat raised his hand to the Sergeant who stopped immediately.

Mother Superior glared at Pond for a second then looked back at Eichenstat. She said, "That poor woman will surely not recover from the cowardly things you did and said. You, Colonel, have no soul!"

Eichenstat grinned and turned to Sergeant Pond. "Sergeant, what do you think of this foolish woman and her reference to my soul, or lack of one?"

"Foolish indeed," Pond replied dutifully. "There is no such thing."

"I want you never to come back here," Mother Superior was now saying. "Never!"

Pond grinned, appearing to enjoy the moment. "Losing your soul? She is losing her mind, Colonel."

"A distinct possibility, Sergeant."

Mother Superior glowered at him; it was a hateful look. She then drew back her arm to full length and swung, slapping Eichenstat solidly across the face. His officer's hat slipped sideways from the blow. He grabbed his face, then dropped his hand. Sergeant instantly jumped toward her but Eichenstat blocked his way.

"She is one tough female, Sergeant. Reminds me of a butcher's wife I remember as a child," he told Pond. Then he said, "We are finished here, Sergeant."

When they drove off Mother Superior was still standing outside glaring at them all the way out the main gate. It had been a great performance.

Sergeant Pond was chuckling. "I wish I could have witnessed it, Sir," he commented, looking back through the rear view mirror.

"She's frail and frightened. If she knew anything she would have said so."

"So, you got nothing?"

"Nothing but a little pleasure. You were right, Sergeant, a woman can be quite enjoyable."

"A young one is much better, Sir. Stripped and writhing in pain is a sight ..."

Eichenstat tried to hide his disgust. His aide was revealing a side of his nature he had better remember. He would check his file again back in Bremen.

"Now I have to go to Aachen to see the priest. I must see if he has any new information about the nun, and the girl."

"When will we make the trip, Sir?"

"I'm not sure yet."

"Will you want me to drive you?"

"Of course, Sergeant."

"Thank you, Sir. I always like getting out in the field."

Eichenstat did not reply.

They drove on in silence. Eventually Pond said, "Sir?"

"Yes?"

"I guess I should tell you that I will be requesting a transfer."

The statement startled him. "Did I hear right?"

"Yes, Sir, I think you did. A transfer."

Eichenstat looked up into the mirror. He had an almost detached look on his face now. This was good news.

"And your reason?" he asked Pond.

"I'm not suited for desk work. I know that now."

"What branch will you request?"

"Tanks, Sir. It's my hope to be with Guderian. I would like to work the radios. I'm rather good at communication devices. But there is much I can still learn."

"I will support your request, Sergeant, if that is your desire."

"I'll still be with you for a while longer. These things take time."

"I met General Guderian once," he told Pond. "He's a man who demands perfection. You'll have to watch yourself."

Pond straightened up as if demonstrating his commitment to serve.

"He is not like me, Sergeant. I run a less rigid operation. It may be the thing General Reinard does not appreciate about me. That's why I have to get to the priest in Aachen to provide me with information regarding the nun. It could improve my reputation with the General."

"Yes, Sir."

37

**JULY 13, 1940
NEW YORK, U.S.A.**

That afternoon passengers lined the deck of the *S.S. Washington* as the great ship slipped through the calm waters of New York Harbor. There was excitement all around brought on by the anticipation of seeing their homeland and families and loved ones again after their nerve-wracking departure from a continent overrun with the miseries of all-out war and the near sinking by a German submarine. For a few of those passengers, reaching America was more than seeing familiar surroundings that gave comfort and happiness; for some it was the gift of life itself. But it would be a life changed from what had gone before. For Sister Katherine and Anna Burkitz, landing in America meant a new life among strangers, a new life each could only wonder about. For Sister Katherine it had already become a trial that she could only pray about, to ask God to protect her and her unborn child. Her baby would be born in America. That seemed certain now. But what was to become of him after that? Thinking of this baby as a male was something she had become accustomed to. She could remember only one weak moment what she had confessed the possibility that the child could be a little girl. It all seemed so long ago.

"Look, Anna," Gabriella said, pointing. "Lady Liberty. You have heard of it?"

"Oh, yes, Sister, yes I have."

"Think of what a symbol it is and what it means to people," Gabriella said, shading her eyes from the glare. "It means the start of a new life, a fresh start for people."

"Is that us, Sister?"

Gabriella felt her abdomen with her hand. "A new life," she said to herself. "Yes, Anna, I guess it is us."

"Are ... we never ... going home again ... to Germany?"

"If God wants us to, yes we will return someday. I told Captain Manning that I believe I would return."

Anna was silent, watching the Statue behind them getting smaller.

"What do we do now, Sister?" Anna then asked.

"We wait. The Captain said Mr. Michael Duncan would meet us."

Out of the corner of her eye Gabriella caught Anna staring at her.

"Why are you looking at me that way?" Gabriella asked.

"You are a pretty nun," Anna said before deflecting her eyes away.

Gabriella smiled. "Does that strike you as peculiar, me being pretty, as you say?"

"I wish I was pretty."

"Anna! You are pretty."

"No I'm not, not really pretty."

"Everyone is pretty in the eyes of God, Anna."

The end of Anna's mouth turned up slightly. "Boys like pretty girls. Sometimes big hairy old men like them too. They want to ... hurt them. I know about that."

Gabriella put her arm around her. "We have talked about that, Anna. You must understand that some men, boys too, will treat a nice girl that way."

"Did anyone ever treat you that way?"

"I was spared such treatment," Gabriella said. "I was fortunate to know only nice boys. But even nice boys will ... they'll want to hold you, kiss you, be close to you. We have had some long talks about such things, remember?

"Yes."

"You are becoming a pretty young woman and as you do you'll meet and know many young men. You will probably fall in love and get married and have children."

"I could be a nun," Anna said sharply. "Like you, couldn't I?"

Gabriella smiled and pulled Anna close. "Of course, but you have to talk to God about that. If He convinces you that that is what he wants you to be then, yes, you can become a nun. But you must have a true calling to it and only after you have considered your feelings. But don't forget you are a Jew and to become a nun like me you will have to become a Catholic. That is one other choice you will have to make. That's what I had to do."

Anna looked away and did not reply.

"What's the matter, Anna?"

"All those people who helped us were Catholics."

"Yes they were, but not everyone who is a Catholic would have helped us. Some would have chosen not to."

Anna seemed to think about that. "Why?"

"I don't know, Anna. All people are not alike. Some do things that others would never do. It's called free will. One is free to make up one's mind to do what one wants, a personal choice. But almost always that choice has some consequence, or several consequences. Sometimes that choice hurts someone else. That's why when making choices a person has to consider all the possible effects it might have. You have to ask yourself: what hurt might your choice do to others, to the people you care about."

"Did becoming a nun hurt someone you know?" Anna asked.

"Yes, Anna, it did, but it was not my intention. I ..." She could not finish.

"Who did it hurt?"

"My mother."

"How?"

Gabriella shrugged, but not because it was any inconsequential matter. She wanted to be truthful with Anna. It still hurt. "My mother ... wanted me to marry and have a family, to have children; she wanted to be a grandmother. It's not too unreasonable a thing."

All the while Gabriella was telling this she was thinking of her mother and the fact that she would never know about her grandchild soon to be born. Gabriella felt a surge of extreme dishonesty move through her, a disgusting hypocrisy engulfed her. The hypocrisy lay in the fact that it was her conversion to Christianity that angered her mother so, not for the reason she had told Anna. It was a lie. She was still sinning and she couldn't help it. Her conscience was yelling at her.

"Sister, your face is red. You are crying. Why are you crying, Sister?"

Gabriella turned away and wiped her eyes.

Shortly before four o'clock the walkways went down and the passengers began getting off. Cheers and cries of recognition flew through the people waiting and those coming off the ship. Gabriella and Anna waited at the railing just outside their cabin, watching the people.

Soon the crowds thinned. Gabriella continued looking around, seeing if there was someone who might be the person who was supposed to meet them.

"A steward approached them pushing a dolly. "Sister Katherine?" he asked.

"Yes."

"There is a gentleman waiting. I will take you," he said.

"We have several suitcases," she told him.

"I'll get them."

The steward got the suitcases and placed them on the dolly. "The gentleman is down on the dock," he told them.

They went down the walkway and onto the flatness of the dock and headed toward a man standing near one of the dock's support pillars

He was a big man with a ruddy complexion, brown eyes and thick eyebrows and an immense, appealing grin. His hair was a rusty brown color.

"I'm Michael Duncan. The Bishop asked me to meet you and get you on your way to his residence without too much trouble. I hope I am up to it."

He put out his hand.

Gabriella took it. "We would be lost had you not come," she said. "This is Anna. I am Sister Katherine."

"I'm happy to be of help."

He handed the steward a dollar bill. "May I use the dolly?"

"Certainly, Sir."

As they headed off, Duncan pushing the dolly, he asked Gabriella, "You have your papers?"

"The ones we were given."

"Getting through customs will be a formality. Everything has been cleared. All we have to do is present you two to the person in charge so he can verify that two actual human beings did indeed come ashore and that you are who you say you are. There should be no trouble."

When they arrived at the proper office Duncan asked for Mr. Dan Altobello. As they waited Duncan said to them, "This fellow's real name is Dante but he Americanized it to Dan T. There's a lot of that kind of thing in America. Original names changed, either on purpose or accidentally, misspellings become permanent. It's crazy." He laughed.

Altobello came through the door.

"These are the two people I told you about," Duncan said.

Altobello's look was one of casual inspection. "Two flesh and blood people," he muttered, smiling. "Good."

"Is everything in order? The Bishop is anxious to see them."

Altobello gave Duncan some papers. "Copies," he said. "Hang on to them."

"Thanks," Duncan replied, sticking the papers haphazardly in the side pocket of his jacket. "Are we through here?"

"I'll have to inspect the luggage."

Duncan looked at the three suitcases on the dolly. "How about my word?"

"Which is?"

"No contraband."

"Your boss will vouch for you?"

Duncan grinned. "Read this," he said to Altobello. Duncan then reached into his other side coat pocket and took out the memo he had received from the President. Altobello read it.

"Anyone could have written this," he said playfully.

"You haven't the guts to challenge it."

Altobello laughed. "I'm too good a Democrat."

"Let's go ladies," Duncan said, returning Altobello's laugh in kind. "I'll leave the dolly."

He grabbed two of the suitcases by their handles and tucked the smaller one under his arm. He led them out a side door and down a short hallway to a much longer one. It was becoming crowded again. Everyone was heading in the same direction, up two flights of stairs. Sunlight streamed in through a host of wide windows as they reached the top. In front of them stood a line of large marble columns, the floor was marble. Duncan kept walking but Gabriella and Anna stopped and stood still, taking in their surroundings. Duncan looked back. He let them experience the sensations they were feeling. It was something many people felt when first making the move to the street. The room echoed with the sounds of people greeting people; there was hugging and kissing and occasional screeches of joy; there was a smattering of crying.

Duncan walked back to where the two were standing. "America awaits you, ladies."

Gabriella grinned.

"I have a car waiting," Duncan told them, adjusting the suitcase under his arm.

"Let me take that one, please," Gabriella said. "I am not helpless."

Duncan smiled.

"My kind of . . ." He caught himself.

38

JULY 13, 1940
BIJHOP AMLETO CICOGNANI'J REJIDENCE
WAJHINGTON, D.C.

Bishop Cicognani, himself, greeted them at the door. "So glad you have arrived, Michael. My new staff members," he continued, eyeing Gabriella and Anna. "Welcome, welcome."

They entered the large foyer.

"In here," Cicognani said, leading them into the large living room. "Michael, put those suitcases over by the wall. We'll deal with them later."

He stood back and inspected them. He laughed. "I bet you're tired."

Gabriella smiled. "Thankful we are off the boat."

"Mr. Duncan has treated you well?"

Gabriella looked at Duncan; she smiled. "He has. He made everything so easy."

Cicognani then asked. "Did my brother treat you well in Spain?"

"He was very gracious," Gabriella said.

"Yes he was," Anna agreed.

"I believe you will like America. It is a fascinating country; of course I have seen only a small part of it."

"Everyone seems in a hurry," Anna said.

Duncan and Cicognani laughed. "That was New York," Duncan told her. "There are other, slower places."

"The buildings seem ... so different. New."

"Many are, yes, compared to those in Europe. We are a young country," Duncan said.

"A vibrant country too," Cicognani added. "But it is in some bad times now. Money is scarce and people are in distress in many places."

"It is the same in our country," Gabriella said.

"Are there many soldiers in America?" Anna asked. "I did not see any."

"There are a few," Duncan said. "But I don't believe it's like it is in Germany."

"There are many soldiers in Germany," she said.

Gabriella thought of Fritz. "America will be different, Anna," she then said.

"It even smells different," Anna then said. "I think so."

"Maybe it does, Anna," Cicognani said. "A newcomer might sense that. I have been here long enough not to think of myself as a newcomer."

"You are an institution almost, Bishop," Duncan said. "Some say you call the President directly on occasion."

Cicognani eyed Duncan with a buoyant smile. "You exaggerate, my friend."

"It is a town in which people survive on influence, and you have learned well the workings of the place."

"I had good training in Rome, remember," Cicognani laughed.

"It is needed sometimes, influence. Take our two guests here, for example," he said, looking at Gabriella and Anna. "It did not hurt to have influence, did it?"

Duncan nodded in agreement.

"Much in the world seems not to be able to function without it," Cicognani went on. "Would things be better if it were not that way? Could the world work any other way? I have often thought about that. The way I see it, human beings being human means that the world could never be a world without influence. It is the human condition."

"Is there influence in heaven, Bishop?" Duncan asked, in a more festive and playful mood.

Cicognani laughed. "Your Jesuit education is showing, my friend."

"On that comment I'll be going," Duncan said, laughing.

"Stay for supper, please," Cicognani said. "My cook has prepared a special pasta dish tonight."

Duncan accepted the Bishop's invitation. He was grateful for the opportunity to get a better picture of this nun he had escorted to Washington. He sensed there was something noble about her. It was more than casual curiosity, he told himself.

During supper their conversations remained lighthearted. Gabriella was thankful for that. She was sitting next to Michael Duncan and he remained rather quiet as they ate. She had the feeling he was preoccupied with something. Bishop Cicognani did most of the talking. At one time he asked Gabriella about some of the things he had heard were happening in Germany. She described to him a few of the things she had seen or experienced herself, but none of it in too much detail. She wanted to keep the evening as pleasant as she could. Although her words were glossed over descriptions, in her mind her thoughts were different. She could never forget.

Cicognani took some time to explain what he expected of them as members of his staff.

"It sounds ideal," Gabriella said.

Cicognani then gave a large laugh. "Pay no attention to any of it. It's all a ploy to get you into the United States."

Gabriella was taken aback on hearing him. "So, what is to become of us?"

"I have made some arrangements to accommodate the uniqueness of your situation, Sister," he said.

"This is all so unsettling. For one thing I cannot see how it is that Mr. Roosevelt would take note of our small problems when ... he has ..." She looked at Duncan beside her.

Cicognani answered her question. "Sabastian Arceneau is the key instrument here, Sister, or I should say the Gregory Foundation. Along with me and Michael, of course. As conduits of movement if you will." He laughed again.

"I have known Mr. Arceneau for a good while, in my convent days, in Köln, especially. That's where I got to really know him."

"Mr. Arceneau and the Gregory Foundation have deep tentacles inside many organizations," Cicognani said. "And governments," he added. "That is what I have heard. He may have penetrated the Vatican itself." With that comment he laughed more robustly than before.

"Maybe even the White House?" Gabriella asked.

Duncan grimaced to himself. "I doubt it."

Cicognani said, "No one can really be sure just where Sabastian and the Gregory Foundation have influence." He nodded with a wistful expression. "But the White House? Probably not, at least not yet." He laughed. "What do you say, Michael?"

Duncan shook his head.

"He seems to move around Europe with ease," Gabriella said.

Duncan looked at her through thinning eyes. "You said you knew him there?"

"I did."

"Can you say what it was that you did there to know him?"

Gabriella smiled and gave him a steady stare. She said slowly, "I believe you have already figured that one out, Mr. Duncan."

Duncan shook his head a second time. "You and Arceneau?"

"And others."

"We have said enough. It is time to get some sleep," Cicognani said from across the table. "Tomorrow, Sister, we shall have a talk about what we are planning for you and Anna for the next few months. I think it will please you."

He called for his housekeeper.

JULY 14, 1940
BISHOP CICOGNANI'S RESIDENCE
WASHINGTON, D.C.

Gabriella and Bishop Cicognani were in his study, talking.

"I have sent Anna off with my housekeeper. They will be looking for some clothes for Anna. There are things she will need for her new life in America. Now, how about you, Sister? Is there anything?" Bishop Cicognani asked. "You must need some things."

"We have little money."

Cicognani smiled. "The Gregory covers such things. You will have to make a list."

They spent the next hour talking. Gabriella learned that Sabastian Arceneau and the people at the Gregory Foundation had made arrangements for her and Anna to travel to Nashville, Tennessee, a place about which she had no knowledge. She and Anna were to live in a convent, St. Bernard Convent, the home of the Sisters of Mercy.

"It has been arranged. They know of your situation. Your child can be born there and they can help you until you decide what it is you want to do. No use thinking of all that now. There is time for that later. The immediate thing is to have a healthy baby."

She was speechless. The suddenness of it all, the matter-of-fact way he laid it all out, was awkward to digest.

"Having you stay here as members of my staff was a fabrication. No one will inquire."

Gabriella's mind was whirling. It was all coming so fast.

Cicognani smiled. "Many have helped you, Sister. Especially Sabastian Arceneau, but there have been others along the way. I am only the last one. I am at the end of a long line."

"Sabastian," she said, seeing the man's face in her mind.

"A true servant of God."

"When do we leave?" she asked.

"As soon as you are ready. I'd say maybe day after tomorrow. The Gregory has someone who will escort you. His name is Crandall Overstreet and he is coming to meet you tomorrow. He says he is a friend of Sabastian's."

"I hope Anna likes this new home," she then said.

"I understand there is a fine university nearby. She may be able to enroll although she is a little young."

"But she is smart. She would like that."

"I'll see what the Gregory might arrange. Those people have considerable influence. I'm sure they can work some arrangement for Anna."

Gabriella smile. "Thank you, Bishop. This has been a . . . wild few months. I can't imagine it becoming more wild."

The following morning Gabriella, Anna, and Crandall Overstreet boarded the *Baltimore and Ohio* and headed for Cincinnati, Ohio. Later that day they changed to the *Louisville and Nashville.* It would take them to Nashville, Tennessee, their final destination.

They talked of many things on the trip but what Gabriella appreciated most was the things Overstreet told her about Sabastian Arceneau. It made her appreciate and admire the man even more than she had before.

39

JULY 14, 1940
AACHEN, GERMANY
FATHER KONRAD SCHROEDER'S RESIDENCE

"That's quite a story, Father," Colonel Fritz Eichenstat said to Father Konrad Schroeder.

Both men were standing in Schroeder's living room. "It's the way it all happened," Father Schroeder replied dryly, as if it should not be doubted.

"You say Bishop Micara deceived you. He took Gabriella and the girl and ... let them *slip* away into Spain?"

"I would not use the word *slip*."

Eichenstat shook his head. He went to the window and looked out. "And that's the story you'll tell? Always?"

"If anyone asks, yes."

"Even General Reinard?"

"That's the way it happened. Bishop Micara fooled me."

Eichenstat looked reflective. "Have you heard whether Gabriella has actually reached America?"

"I've heard nothing, sorry."

"Do you believe you will?"

"Possibly. If she got to Lisbon there's a good chance she made it to America, or will do so soon."

"I think of her constantly."

"I can imagine."

"Well," Eichenstat said with a determination. "She is now safer than she would have been in Germany."

"And so is your child."

"I located Gabriella's mother," he then told Schroeder. "She was in Hanover. I took her to Gabriella's old convent. There she might survive this . . . time."

Father Schroeder put his hand on Eichenstst's shoulder. "I pray for you, Colonel."

Eichenstat scoffed. "I told Gabriella I didn't believe in such things."

"Yes, she told me once in confession."

"Isn't that against your rules? To reveal?"

"Only one's transgressions. She was concerned about you and the trials you were facing. The decisions you were having to make."

He hesitated, then said, "Tell me, Father, do you believe Gabriella loved me? Does she still, maybe?"

"I can only say that she spoke of you with very great affection, but you must remember she is carrying a heavy burden herself. Maybe almost as heavy as yours."

They remained silent for a long time.

Eichenstat finally said, "I think you will be happy to learn that I am going to get rid of Sergeant Pond. He is transferring."

"You will be better off."

"Yes. I also told him a fabrication about you. I hope you can live with it if the story gets around. I told him you like young girls."

Schroeder laughed.

"Let me guess. Anna?"

Eichenstat pointed his finger at him. "My Sergeant thinks you are a sick man. So does General Reinard."

"I'm getting some reputation, I see."

"It helps as cover. It's all I could think of to get Anna here."

Schroeder laughed again. "I'll suffer the bad reputation if it helps me do my work."

"Be careful."

JULY 15, 1940
ROME, ITALY

Michael Duncan had sent the following telegram to Myron Taylor.

Date: July 14, 1940
Time: 10:35 A.M.
Location: White House
From: Michael Duncan

Both packages soon to be lodged in convent in Nashville Tennessee STOP St Bernard Convent STOP All is well STOP Gregory has full information STOP Job well done your end STOP

Duncan STOP

As one of his last acts before leaving Rome to return to the United States Myron Taylor made arrangements to see Bishop Micara in the Vatican in order to pass along the news he received from Michael Duncan. When he arrived at the room where Micara was setting up to conduct his business he found Micara dressed in civilian clothes. The sleeves of his shirt were rolled up and there was sweat on his brow. He was busy arranging the limited bits of furniture and equipment he had been provided and unpacking the things he had brought with him from Brussels. Father Dubois was helping along with one Italian worker who seemed to be trying to wire up some kind of instrument. Taylor introduced himself as he stood in the doorway. Micara shook his hand, so did Father Dubois. The Italian worker continued fumbling with the wires, seemingly confused.

"An honor to meet President Roosevelt's special representative to the Vatican," Bishop Micara said.

Taylor told him why he had come and gave him the news conveyed by Michael Duncan.

"Duncan thinks you might get word back to let people know what had happened to the nun and the girl,"

"Father Schroeder should know, yes. I'll see that he gets word."

"My job here is finished," Taylor said. "I'm returning to the United States. I wish you success and I wish your people in Belgium the same."

"The Belgian people will fight the Germans any way they can," he proclaimed. "Many of them will be killed, I fear," he said sadly.

"I'm sorry."

"Tell me, what do you think your president will do in all of this? In the coming years."

Taylor frowned. "That is a question a good number of people are asking. I bet the Germans are. But the President is in a tight spot. His options are limited."

"The Nazis will not stop, you know that. Somebody is going to have to do something."

"What's the Pope going to do? The Concordat between the Vatican and the Reich has many people worried that it gives the Germans too much of a free hand."

Micara hesitated for a moment. "It could be seen that way, yes. They say Pius is more worried about the godless communists in Russia, than he is about the Germans."

"The two are about equal in their unpleasantness," Taylor grunted. "Both are dangerous to the world."

"It puts Pius in a tight spot, like your president. Neither man has many good options."

"I suppose."

"I'll tell you, there are some in the Vatican who want the Germans to attack Russia and get rid of Stalin and let the people return to their former way of life."

"Life before the revolution."

"Yes."

"The Czar? A monarchy?"

"Well, maybe that would be better than what is going on there now," Micara offered.

Taylor smiled slightly, "We in the United States have a hard time seeing monarchs. It's our history. We had our revolution too, remember. The U.S. is a different country, different sensibilities and complexions of thought because of our mix. That makes the place very unique. We are new and don't have much baggage. People want to start fresh and throw off much of their bad history. Besides, times are so bad economically for so many people now that they're not thinking about what happens in Europe. People don't empathize much with the problems of those in Europe and elsewhere. They have their own problems. President Roosevelt has to deal with that all the time. As a politician it ties his hands, if you know what I mean."

Micara nodded. "Thanks for the history lesson."

"My guess is that Roosevelt sees America at war in a few years," Taylor then said, adding, "Now that the Brits are just about on their own he'll really be tested."

Micara sighed and rolled down the sleeves of his shirt. "We are such tiny pawns in this great commotion. A great realignment could be coming, I believe. On a more spiritual level I have been thinking lately that it might be like the transformation that occurred after the birth and death of Jesus."

Taylor eyed Micara. "Except now we won't have to wait centuries for the transformation to take effect and be felt. Things move too fast nowadays. Then too, that transformation two thousand years ago had a far different foundation than what underlies the Nazi and Russian philosophies."

"Far different," Micara admitted sadly.

Taylor said his goodbye. "You and your people won a small victory with what you accomplished. The nun is safe and so is the girl. What happens to them now is out of our hands."

40

AUGUST 13, 1940
ST. BERNARD CONVENT
NASHVILLE, TENNESSEE, U.S.A.

The tiny shrub-hidden patch of land a short walk from the main convent building offered isolation where a person could sit and contemplate peacefully. Gabriella was there waiting for Crandell Overstreet. She had asked him to visit her, if he could. He had written, telling her of his arrival.

"It's right at the end of this path, Sir," Gabriella heard one of the nuns tell him.

"Hello, Sister."

"Thank you for coming. I know you are busy."

"Bishop Cicognani will appreciate hearing how you are doing. He is pleased that Anna will be going to the university."

"Vanderbilt, yes. They have been very understanding. The Gregory has helped."

"It has good relationships with several universities, both here and abroad."

"And you, have the nuns treated you well?"

She smiled. "A more charitable group I have never met before. I am most fortunate. My son will be born in a safe place."

"I assure you they will help care for the child until you get your bearings. That will take time."

"That's what I have to discuss with you. I need your help. I have decisions to make, arrangements."

"Of course."

Gabriella looked away. "I know I cannot remain a nun when my child is born. I probably should have left the order already."

"What do you envision?" Overstreet asked.

"Move. Rent a house. Anna should not have to live at a convent?"

"Why not? The place is full of women, some not much older than Anna. For the time being anyway."

"My baby."

"The nuns want to care for the child. For the time being."

"Until when?" she asked him.

"You will know when the time comes. You cannot jump too soon. Have you thought about what you might do . . . as a civilian, if you leave the sisterhood?"

"That's the other thing. I have, yes. I believe I would make a fine nurse. I have some biological training from my university days. It is a noble profession. I could possibly work at the university down the street."

"Vanderbilt Hospital?"

"There are others. There is St. Thomas."

"You'd probably have to receive additional training."

"I could do that while the nuns care for . . . my baby. Until I get on my feet."

Overstreet sat thinking.

"What are you thinking?" she asked.

"Let me see what the Gregory can do."

"You approve?"

"You have thought out a reasonable course, I believe. Let me discuss it with the Bishop. He might have some ideas, but I doubt he'll have any objections."

"There's one thing I worry about. Anna and I are supposed to be members of the Bishop's staff."

Overstreet grinned. "No one in the State Department is going to come around to check. Besides, you fit all the criteria as refugees and that carries great weight in this country. I wouldn't be surprised that after your child is born you will become a naturalized citizen."

"Citizen!"

"Didn't you know that your child will be an American citizen the moment he is born?"

"No!"

"Well, he will be, or she will be."

"Are you sure?"

"Ask anyone."

"I . . . would almost have to become an American then," she said. "Anna too, maybe."

He smiled. "Welcome to America, Sister."

SEPTEMBER 15, 1940
NASHVILLE, TENNESSEE, U.S.A.

A little less than a month after Gabriella and Crandell Overstreet had talked Colonel Fritz Eichenstat's son was born. The birth occurred on September 7, 1940 at 10:44 in the morning at Vanderbilt Hospital in Nashville, Tennessee, U.S.A. Of the particulars on the record of birth were the following: **Name**: *William Steffan Eichenstat*, **Father**: *Fritz Eichenstat*, **Mother**: *Gabriella Sommers*.

It was a difficult birth and Gabriella was in the hospital for eight days. During that time Anna was a daily presence at her bedside. Half a dozen of the nuns from St. Bernard Convent made regular visits, arriving always in twos and threes. In addition, Gabriella received a long-distance phone call from Bishop Cicognani in Washington who offered her and the baby his blessing. She also had a phone call from Michael Duncan. A few days later, a bouquet of one-dozen roses showed up in her room. Word got around that the phone call had been placed through an operator from the White House. One overly curious, gossipy nurse on the floor traced the roses through the local florist who had delivered them. The flowers had been ordered by a customer through a shop in Washington D.C. The card read: *Your Friend at the WH.*

On the day Gabriella was to leave the hospital Dr. Daniel Gordon, the man she had talked to on several occasions about enrolling at the university to begin her studies to acquire certification as a nurse, came to see her. He too was curious.

"Seems you have friends in high places, Gabriella," he said.

"It is a long story, Dr. Gordon, But there is nothing sinister in any of it. My personal history lately has been rather unusual."

He smiled, raising his eyebrows. "I bet it's quite a history too."

She started to say something but was interrupted by the door swinging open. A nurse came in holding the baby. "Oh, sorry," she said, startled for a moment at seeing Dr. Gordon.

Gabriella smiled wildly as the nurse approached. "Little William," she beamed.

"Not so little," Dr. Gordon said. "His chart says eight pounds two ounces at birth."

Gabriella grinned as the nurse placed the child in her arms.

"He *is* a big boy."

"He'll have big blue eyes, I bet," the nurse said, adjusting the blanket covering the child. "Beautiful."

After the nurse left Dr. Gordon said, "Will you be back, Gabriella? Will you still take those nursing courses we talked about?"

"If you'll still have me."

"With your background, you bet I will."

Gabriella smiled. "You have been so kind, and understanding. Almost everyone has."

"Classes begin in a week," he said. "You should put it off until next year. It would be too much for now."

"September 1941 is a long way off."

"You should be settled by then. This child is a big change for you."

She knew he was right. "I suppose. This coming year could be a hard one for me to get through. I want so much to ..."

"Of course," he said, patting her hand. "You have a fine baby. You take care of him and we'll see you next year."

When he had said his goodbyes he headed down the hall. He stopped at the nurses station and asked, "Is nurse Doris Wills on duty?"

"Shall I page her?" the nurse asked.

"Please."

Doris Wills was a short, robust woman from the rural South. On this day she was wearing her hair pulled back which was unusual of her. A surgical mask dangled from around her neck. Dr. Gordon thought she appeared harried. As she came down the hallway toward him her steps were short and quick and her heels hit the floor hard as usual.

"Doctor?"

"The rumor about Gabriella Sommers and the White House? You've heard it I'm sure?"

"Almost everybody has."

"You believe it's true?"

She shrugged. "I suppose. Why do you ask?"

"Miss. Sommers is a unique case, on several fronts."

The expression on Wills's face changed. "Are you speaking of her medical condition, Doctor?"

"No, no. Nothing like that."

Wills stared at Gordon. "What then, I don't follow you?"

"Nothing," Gordon said. "Just trying to clear the air."

She gave Gordon a hard look. "The woman has captured the attention of others beside yourself, Dr. Gordon. For one thing, she is quite pretty, very ... elegant if that's the right word. No question of her beauty. I have no doubt you have noticed," she said with a smart little twist of her mouth.

Gordon fixed his eyes on the woman. "You have a dirty mind, Wills."

She laughed. "Well, there's another very believable rumor. Some are saying she is a nun. You believe that?"

"No."

"She has had visits from the sisters down the street. And where is her husband? No one has seen him around."

"He's in the military," Gordon replied.

"Yeah, the German military, that's the story."

"She's been through a lot, Wills."

Nurse Wills grinned. "I bet she has. Especially if it's true and she really is a nun."

Gordon threw off the comment. "Next year she will be a student with us, training to become certified as a nurse. She has a heavy dose of training already, from her college days in Germany, I've been told. Seems the woman is smart."

"I wouldn't know of such things," Wills replied coldly.

"You will treat her courteously, Wills."

Wills replied dryly, "When and if she gets here next year and if she takes care of her duties the two of us should get along fine."

"She may need some extra help," Gordon said, giving Wills a look. "At learning our system."

"With a baby to care for and no husband around?" Wills commented. "I bet she will need help."

"I don't think that'll be a problem," Gordon said.

"How she manages that end of her life is her business," Wills said, disinterestedly.

Dr. Gordon stared at the woman, "I'm so pleased to hear that you see it that way, Wills."

"Is that all, Doctor?"

"I have nothing else," he replied, then added for effect, "We may need to have this conversation again next year."

Nurse Wills walked away, the heels of her shoes making their customary sound as they hit the marble floor. Dr. Gordon watched her go and thought: In medical matters magnificently competent, yet so unforgiving as a human being. An unhappy woman is my guess.

41

SEPTEMBER 18, 1940
KÖLN, GERMANY

The British planes always came at night. Since the war began in September a year ago the British had made a good number of nighttime bomb runs on Köln. Last night's raid, like all the others, had shattered the warm quiet darkness and had sent people to whatever shelter they could find. Now that daylight had arrived the damage was visible. Besides Köln, the city of Aachen had been hit, producing on the ground the same scenes as in Köln. It was the same in any German city being hit.

For months now the British had been employing incendiary devices and the Nazi government was yelling that Winston Churchill was deliberately targeting civilian neighborhoods and ignoring military targets with this hideous form of warfare. The Germans labeled it a terror campaign. In fact, these descriptions were largely true although much of the errant damage to civilian areas was not entirely deliberate but instead was due to a host of difficulties. All too often the bomber crews had to cope with poor visibility and navigation mistakes in zeroing in on the specific targets of military value. Sometimes, navigation and the recognition of landmarks were so misguided that bombs were unloaded on the wrong city entirely. Nighttime bombing was imprecise to say the least, and hounded by problem after problem. Nonetheless, the British seemed incessant in their efforts. It was little comfort to the German people on the ground to have their government repeatedly tell them that their own Luftwaffe was punishing the British people in an even worse way.

The Carmelite Convent in Köln had been damaged by only one bomb, but there had been several close calls. Windows had been blown out and many of the tiles on the roofs had crashed down due to the force of the concussion of those nearby hits. For the people inside the convent the basement was always the place of refuge when the bombs began to fall. The minor damage inflicted by the close calls was nothing compared to the direct hit on the convent, but even that hit was not as severe as would have occurred if the bomb had been larger. That one had been a mere one-hundred pounder; a five-hundred pounder, making a more direct hit, would have destroyed a large portion of the building and the death toll would have likely been substantial. If people were inside, direct hits were something that almost always resulted in deaths. Fires from incendiary bombs were too horrible to think about but everyone knew that being trapped inside a burning structure likely meant certain death. The horror was unthinkable and everyone tried not to think of it, but it was impossible if one's mind still functioned properly. Insanity was the only thing that could completely blot out what was happening. As it was, whenever the nightly drone of the planes over the city was heard that fear intensified; the screech of falling bombs sent the terrified people scrambling, but by then, if you could hear the screech and you were not already in an appropriate shelter, it could be too late. They had now been through enough such attacks that they had reconciled that there was nothing anyone could really do about any of it except huddle in a safe place, and pray.

Every day, as nightfall approached, the children became increasingly nervous and jittery. Their playful chattering which could be heard during the daytime fell quiet at night and their eyes seemed to be moving in anticipation of the coming noise and ground vibrations that always could be felt as they huddled in the cellar rooms. They waited, their eyes instinctively scanning upward, expecting. On many nights, fortunately, they were spared, for no planes sounded overhead.

Adults too trembled; they cried to themselves and tried to hold their fears out of sight of the children, but they trembled not from fear of bombs alone. The bombs were secondary. Their fears came from the German authorities and the stories they had been hearing from the outside. But silently, inwardly all of it took its toll and few, if any, could hide their anxieties completely. All of it presented them a new dimension of life that none had experienced before.

SEPTEMBER 18, 1940
BREMEN, GERMANY

At Colonel Fritz Eichenstat's headquarters, General Bruno Reinard was complaining about the status of his command and what some of his officers were and were not doing.

"Like you, Eichenstat, there are few other officers who seem to be moving slower than usual. Not many, but enough. Things must move more quickly!"

"I am using my best judgement, General. I assume those you speak of are doing likewise."

"Not good enough! Not good at all! The people under our care must be moved along faster!" Reinard bristled.

Eichenstat snarled inwardly at the way the General used the term "under our care." He tried to fight back without calling attention to his motives. "It is not efficient, General," he claimed.

"You have sent along how many now?" Reinard asked, his eyes narrow.

"Whatever I can, General. Whatever is appropriate."

Reinard waved his hand angrily. "Your heart is not in this, is it?"

"I am a good soldier," Eichenstat replied in his defense.

Reinard laughed. "How would you like to become a member of the SS, Colonel?" he asked without warning.

The question startled Eichenstat. "There is no need for that, General."

"That's not what I asked."

"I am happy where I am, General. Serving my country."

Reinard fell silent. He walked to the other side of the room and looked out the window. He turned and picked up a photograph from one of the bookshelves and stared at it, then asked, "Who are these people, Colonel? They look to be teenagers. Is this you?"

"Some friends from my university days," Eichenstat told him nervously.

"The university at Gottingen?"

"That's correct, General."

"The girl here is a pretty one. Were you and she ... close?"

"Friends, General."

"Are you still in contact with them? What became of them?"

Eichenstat had a bad feeling now. Did Reinard know who these people in the photograph were? He might. What should he say?

Was Reinard leading up to something? Was he laying a trap? What?

Eichenstat had to chance it.

"The girl ran off to Russia. She sympathizes with the communist. I suppose she is in Russia somewhere; maybe fighting our forces there right now."

Reinard laughed. "She could be dead already. Our advance through Russia has been devastating. We should be in Moscow in a matter of weeks it seems. These are glorious times, Colonel. The Fuhrer is very pleased."

"As he should be."

Reinard looked at the photograph again. "What about the fellow here? You still see him?"

"I'm not sure where he is now. It was a long time ago, General."

Reinard frowned. "Why keep their pictures?"

Eichenstat laughed. "Those were good times for me, General. It's strange, I know, but it reminds me of how life can be so meaningless. Friends one day, strangers the next, even enemies. It's the times. Frankly, I don't want to form any close bonds with anyone and that photograph reminds me of the reasons why. Too many disappointments, and broken promises."

Reinard smiled as he replaced the photograph. "Are you telling me that you are a man who likes to work alone? To remain alone?"

"I am not married, and plan never to marry. Does that answer your question?"

Reinard mulled the comment. "There could be another reason, Colonel."

Eichenstat knew what the General meant. He grinned. "I believe you are aware of the women in my life, General."

Reinard nodded. "I have heard. You know, Colonel, you being a man who is comfortable to stand alone, forming no close personal associations, you seem to have the essential marks of a good spy. I think maybe you could be used in other capacities."

Eichenstat wanted to laugh, knowing the things he had been doing. Maybe, he thought, Reinard also knew. Once again he was in water that could become hot. The General may be setting him up, to catch him. Was he about to be called out? He decided to play along. For a brief moment he didn't care what became of him.

"How could I become a spy, as you say?" he asked Reinard.

"You speak English with little accent," Reinard said. "And you are fluent in several other languages, according to your records."

Eichenstat nodded acceptance of the statement. "A chance talent I have."

"You are accomplished, there is no doubt. Very intelligent. That's why you are in the position you are in. But the times have changed. Your present assignment might not be the best way to serve the Reich."

"Do I have any say in the matter, Sir?"

Reinard's face took on a stern look, "You are a soldier. Orders, Eichenstat. We follow orders."

"Of course, Sir. I'm sorry."

"You always were one who was not afraid to speak his mind, Colonel. You do things as you see best."

"Within the confines of my orders, Sir."

"True, I suppose, but you do have a ... certain way."

"My failure, Sir."

"No, no, it is sometimes good. It is essential for a good intelligence officer, or a good spy."

"Sir, are you speaking seriously about a change in assignment?"

Reinard didn't answer immediately. Finally he said, "Colonel, I am getting requests and being asked by people in Berlin about personnel. Everything is shifting and our forces have to remain malleable; our needs are changing. We may be wasting your real talents in your present position. There are others besides you who may in positions that do not match their true talents." He laughed. "Take Sergeant Pond, your former aide, he has won several medals already with Guderian's tanks. Who would have thought."

Eichenstat thought of Pond, then asked Reinard, "Is there a chance I could be reassigned soon, General?"

Reinard shrugged. "Perhaps. But for now, it is out of my hands. I only provide the details about my subordinates, others make the final determinations."

"Yes, Sir."

42

JUNDAY, DECEMBER 7, 1941
JT. BERNARD CONVENT
NAJHVILLE, TENNEJJEE, U.J.A.

William Steffan was now fourteen months old. The surprise birthday party given by the sisters two months earlier was now a cherished remembrance in Gabriella's heart. The fourteen months since William's birth had gone by quickly and the warmth of life inside the convent and the affection shown by the sisters had provided Gabriella and Anna the beginnings of a new life. Those fourteen months had moved them both down new paths toward futures they each could only hope would be meaningful. Gabriella prayed every day for guidance. She thanked God for the good fortune she had experienced during this turbulent time; she prayed for the safety of family and friends back in a Europe at war. She prayed for her mother and father of whom she thought about sadly, thoughts that made her heart ache. She prayed for her Carmelite sisters in Köln. She prayed for Fritz Eichenstat and wondered every day what he might be doing. As always she asked God to forgive her for causing him the anguish she had brought by her actions. Her daily prayers included all those who had helped her and Anna get to America. Strangely, she felt, so much of her present existence seemed to be still tied to all of them. One thought she could not escape: would she ever encounter any of them again.

Gabriella was now engaged full time as a nursing student at Vanderbilt. She had been enrolled since the summer. Dr. Gordon had arranged for her to be admitted as a special student and, from the beginning, she had approached it with great passion. She was grateful to be doing something productive; her life had purpose once again. It gave her a certain piece of mind to feel she was using her talents and moving toward a worthwhile end where she could again begin helping people. At the hospital everyone saw how quickly she learned new things. She took instruction easily. She excelled in her formal classes but it was in the practical training inside the hospital where she really shined. The way she dealt with people, her quiet kindness and soft, encouraging voice brought commendations her way. However, one source of trouble made itself know almost immediately, and it came from nurse Wills who was in charge of all student nurses inside the hospital. Dr. Gordon had warned Gabriella that she might find Wills difficult.

"Nurse Wills is a no-nonsense professional," he had said when she was first admitted to the program and was trying to reassure her.

"I have probably faced more difficult challenges, Doctor," she had replied. "In some ways I see all of the things in my life as tests from God," she laughed lightheartedly. "I shall approach this the same way."

He had smiled. "Well, I just want you to succeed and become a member of my team."

"I'll do my best not to disappoint you."

Nurse Wills had turned out to be just as Dr. Gordon had described. But the more she demanded of Gabriella the more Gabriella welcomed the challenge. The students watched this confrontation with great interest and what they saw only increased their admiration for Gabriella. In time the students began seeking out Gabriella for advice, and help; they wanted to be close to her. This was another element of her new life that gave her considerable pride and satisfaction, and a quiet comfort. It quickly became apparent that Wills resented all this yet seemed to find little that could dampen it. While Wills was a demanding task master and held a superior position within the hospital she knew just how far she could push things without running into difficulties with Dr. Gordon. She was aware of Gordon's plans for Gabriella, and his fondness for her. The students whispered that Wills's behavior toward Gabriella was because Gabriella was physically attractive and accomplished in a worldly way and Wills saw her as a rival for the students's loyalty. Gabriella had heard this and could only wonder whether it could really be what was driving the woman's animosity. As a counter, Gabriella had begun saying a prayer, asking God to grant her patience and compassion for the woman.

Early on the nursing students had learned that Gabriella was a refugee from Germany but she had never gone much further in telling them many of the details of her life. She guessed that some of the them, as well as the staff, had heard the story about how she had a baby and lived at the convent and may have once been a nun, but they were left in the dark about the other circumstances of her life. Gabriella had always signaled that she wanted many of the personal aspects of her life to remain private. So far, no one had crossed that line, and asked. But no one could stop the rumors and the most intriguing one was the one that told of her baby's father being a high-ranking German officer still in Germany, a story that only enhanced Gabriella's mystique.

Anna, too, had found a new direction. As a student at the university she was studying round the clock almost, except for occasional breaks to spend some time with William and get a little sleep now and then. The rhythm of her days was far different then her life in Germany and she adjusted well. For one thing, her longing to be with her brother Herwald had diminished as her new life put more enjoyable options on her plate and kept her busy. She had received several letters from Herwald, thanks to the help of Sabastian Arceneau, and she had sent him several in return. Their exchanges served to calm their worries about the other. Each now knew that the other was safe and working at things they loved.

In the months since her arrival in America Anna had grown more mature and confident in her behavior and her natural attractiveness seemed to shine through more vividly. Males were paying her more attention and there were many more of them on campus than females, a fact that had not escaped Gabriella's notice and she vowed to discuss this with Anna; most likely when classes were over and the demands on their time slowed. The Christmas holidays would be a good opportunity, she concluded. The end of the year was approaching fast. The year 1942 was just around the corner. Gabriella wondered what it might bring. Sadly, the signs did not look comforting.

It was the tradition of the sisters at St. Bernard's to celebrate Mass early every morning in the convent chapel. On Sunday mornings, however, Mass was celebrated a little later than it was on the other days of the week and it drew a modest number of civilians from the city. Because of the presence of the civilians, Sunday was the Mass that Gabriella most enjoyed for it let her blend in. Since the birth of her son she no longer wore the traditional nun's habit but dressed in civilian clothes, most of which she purchased at one of the local second-hand shops in the neighborhood near the convent. At today's Mass she wore a light blue calico dress and a simple solid white scarf with a blue border that covered her head. On her feet she had on a pair of black, soft-leather, low-heel shoes. Anna was in her room studying and keeping an eye on William Steffan who slept soundly nearby.

Another Sunday custom for the sisters of St. Bernard's was to eat a more elaborate noon meal than they ate during the week. As they sat around the large, massive dinner table the conversation went back and forth. It quickly focused on the coming of Christmas school pageant put on by the students of the school.

"Little William can be the baby Jesus," Sister Mary Ursula suggested abruptly, as if she had just thought of the idea and had to let everyone know it.

The nuns all looked at Gabriella.

She smiled and surprised them by saying, "William has blue eyes. Did Jesus have blue eyes, Sister? I wonder."

Sister Mary Ursula frowned, then laughed.

From the far end of the table Mother Superior said, "You are curious about the most unsuspecting things, Gabriella."

Gabriella grinned. "Is that a good or bad thing, Mother? I'm never quite sure."

"Using the mind that God gave you is never bad, Gabriella."

"That's what I think."

"So, it's all right for me to plan for William to be in my pageant?" Sister Mary Ursula asked.

"Of course it is, Sister," Gabriella said.

There came a moment of silence and then one of the older nuns, Sister Mary Jerome, asked, "Gabriella, what do you think will happen over in Europe? I remember the Kaiser and the things people said about him during the big war. This Hitler seems a far different sort of man."

Gabriella's expression hardened. "Hitler is not a good man, in my opinion, but many in Germany like him."

"Can you tell me why?" Sister Mary Jerome continued. "He has brought them war. Why would they like that?"

Gabriella shrugged. "You may find this hard to understand but they see him as someone who can bring pride back to Germany. It's complicated."

"He turned on the Russians after agreeing not to."

"Double-cross," said the young Sister Mary Ursula.

"You are well informed, Sister," Gabriella said, smiling. "That's what he did. He did trick them. Hitler cannot be trusted. He tricked the British; Neville Chamberlain was taken in."

"Maybe he will rule all of Europe soon," Mother Superior added.

"He will not have us," Sister Mary Louise said with conviction in her voice. "He'll never get across the ocean. My brother is in the navy and he says the Germans will never be able to launch an attack against us like they've done to England."

Gabriella commented, "Anna's brother is in England right now. He doesn't believe the Germans can beat the British. He could be right."

A sheepish looking Sister Teresa Ann seated several seats down from Gabriella commented, "England seems such a tiny island."

"A strong people, the British," Mother Superior said. "I spent some time over there."

All the sisters looked at her. "You did, Mother? When? Why?"

"Before I entered the order. My father sent me on a trip to broaden my horizons. He was not in favor of my becoming a nun."

The statement made Gabriella think of her mother and the unhappiness she had caused her when Gabriella had told her of her decision to convert to Catholicism, and a second time when she joined the Carmelite Order.

The thought made Gabriella ask, "Did your father ever have a change of heart?"

"He did," she replied. "He said he should not try to live my life for me."

"He spoke with great wisdom," Gabriella said.

"He was a hard-headed German," Mother Superior described with an affectionate grin. "Sorry, Gabriella."

Gabriella laughed. "I know the kind."

"What of your parents, Gabriella?" Sister Mary Ursula asked.

The question caused Gabriella's facial muscles to tighten slightly and her lips to purse noticeably. She looked at the young nun. "They are still in Germany," she said softly, sadly.

"Sister Ursula," Mother Superior said. "Please, we should not pry. Gabriella has had a trying experience and she is struggling with her new life here in America. It can be hard but from what I know of her and what I have heard I believe she is making a big impression on the people at the hospital. And, of course, we know what kind of impression she has made on us here at the convent."

Gabriella's eyes jumped to Mother Superior, wondering how it was she knew enough to say this.

Mother Superior recognized Gabriella's wondering. "My father was a physician, Gabriella. My family has many friends who work at the University. They speak to me occasionally."

"I see," Gabriella said.

"Oh, we are not checking up on you, Gabriella. We sisters have taken an oath. We know our responsibilities in this matter."

"Thank you, Mother. I never doubted. You and the other sisters have been so generous and so kind. Anna and I can never repay you."

"There is no need for any repayment," Mother Superior said.

"I'm so sorry, Gabriella," Sister Mary Ursula said. "Forgive me for my intrusion?"

Gabriella smiled genuinely. "You are a fine group of sisters. You do me honor in accepting me so willingly, and my baby. But it is so hard."

No one spoke for a moment. Then Mother Superior said, "We can all see, Gabriella, that you are a very good person, one to be admired, and maybe emulated. You have great qualities. Someday we may know more about you. Until then, you will receive all the privacy you want here. Just let me know."

"Thank you, Mother. All this is going to make me cry."

After their meal Gabriella looked in on William and Anna.

"I must get to the library," Anna said. "Is it all right?"

"And I have to get to the hospital. Sister Mary Ursula is coming to look after William. She is thrilled that I agreed to let her use him to play the part of baby Jesus in her Christmas pageant."

Anna looked at William lying on his back and kicking his legs, grinning at them.

"A blue-eyed Jesus," Gabriella said, smiling.

"What?" Anna asked.

"I don't believe Jesus had blue eyes," Gabriella said. "Do you?"

Anna looked confused. "I ... never thought of it."

"You get to the library."

Anna grabbed up her books and left.

A short time later, well bundled up against the cold, Gabriella left the convent. When she got to the hospital she headed straight to the nurse's station on the third floor. There was a patient case she was following and she was anxious to learn how he was progressing, if indeed he was. Yesterday all the signs said he was improving better than expected. The post-operative treatment regimen prescribed by Dr. Gordon was something new and he had asked her to check it on Sunday; he was not expected to be in. When she reached the hallway at the top of the stairs she was surprised to see him. Her first thought was that something had gone wrong with the patient.

He saw her coming.

"Gabriella, have you heard?"

"Your treatment is not working?"

"No, no, no," he said excitedly. "We have just received word that the Japanese have attacked our fleet at Pearl Harbor. The news is all over the radio."

She then began to notice the people around her. Some had stunned expressions, one woman was crying, a little boy and a man walked by and the little boy asked, "Why is Grandma crying, Grandpa?"

Dr. Gordon acknowledged a fellow physician as he passed by. "We're in it now, Dan," the man said.

"How ... are you sure?" Gabriella asked. "It ..."

Gordon shook his head. "It's all confused," he muttered, "but it looks to be the real thing."

"What does it mean?"

Gordon shook his head. "I guess it means we're at war, or soon will be."

"Against the Japanese?"

"Yes."

"Not the Germans?"

Gordon looked at her with a blank expression. He shrugged. "I can't see how. They have not attacked us."

"What shall we do now?"

"Keep doing what we're doing. Take care of our patients. You keep going to school, work here in the hospital. Everything will likely become very different for all of us in the coming weeks, months. The nation will change. This is a real tragedy. Bad, very bad."

"More killing," Gabriella uttered to herself sadly. "There will be war everywhere."

Gordon turned to her. "The nation will need physicians and highly trained nurses, Gabriella. You keep up with your training."

Her look was one of utter astonishment. "What are you thinking!"

"I've seen what you are capable of doing. You now have an obligation. The unit could use you."

"There is not time," she said.

"You may have time to get enough training. You may not get the usual official certification but you can get training in surgical procedures sufficient to make you more useful. All my people should get better training now. It will be needed."

"You are moving so fast," she said.

"It's my job. I want my unit to be ready when the time comes."

"What will happen? What do you mean?"

"We'll get activated at some time. That seems certain. The more training my people have the better. You could end up being one of my most qualified people."

"I am not ... am I one of your people, Doctor? How is that? I don't understand?"

"You will be soon. I'll see to it. I must plan to have everyone ready when the time comes."

When Gabriella returned to the convent for supper the nuns were in the chapel. Mother Superior had called for a prayer vigil. Afterward, all the talk was about the coming speech by the President. Everyone knew he would ask the Congress for a declaration of war against the Japanese.

Later that night, when Anna returned to the convent, she was crying.

"All the boys are saying they will join the army, or navy. Some say they will go to the marines. I know several who say they want to fly airplanes. Everyone is talking, planning to leave school."

Gabriella tried to comfort Anna and explain what she understood of the situation. "I don't know for sure what's going to happen, Anna."

That night Gabriella lay in her bed thinking. She wondered what would it all mean for William if she were not around. Dr. Daniel Gordon was so sure of himself. He wanted her as a member of his unit. That much was out of her hands. He would have to make the arrangements for that. What did all this mean for Anna? Most likely, she thought Anna would probably remain in school, provided it remained open. She thought it would, but with limited curriculum and enrollments, who could say. There would be many fewer men around, for sure. Could William remain at the convent if she were away, as Dr. Gordon seemed to be telling her would happen? He was sure that his medical unit would be activated, as he put it. She lay there watching William sleeping in the small bed beside her. She didn't think he looked anything like baby Jesus but, she thought some more, what did Jesus look like as a baby? There was no positive indication of what he looked like as a man so anyone was free to conjure up any image. Mother Superior was right, she had the strangest of questions floating around in her head as she tried to fall asleep. As she lay there, her eyes closed, still unsure what this day meant.

43

DECEMBER 25, 1941
NAƒHVILLE, TENNEƒƒEE, U.ƒ.A.

For most people in the world Christmas 1941 was not a joyous time. Much of the news was bad. By most measures conditions were steadily deteriorating. Germany and Japan were on the move and seemed to be doing so at will.

Three weeks earlier, one day after the Japanese attack on Pearl Harbor, President Roosevelt had given his address before a joint session of the Congress of the United States. In response, Congress granted his request for a formal declaration of war against the Empire of Japan. Days later the Germans seemed to play right into Roosevelt's hands by declaring war on the United States. With that declaration all the international legalities were in place and the major combatants were ready to formally square off.

But for the United States, things didn't look all that favorable. Almost every aspect of making war had to be formulated from the ground up or, at best, from meager holdovers from the previous world war that had ended a short twenty years earlier. Most equipment was outdated. New, updated weapons were on the planning boards, or just coming into production, and were not fully tested so no one could say for certain what would work and what would not. In most things, the United States was starting this war from scratch. No doubt, the branch of service most ready for combat was the U.S. Navy but it had taken a terrible beating at Pearl Harbor and its resurrection was only in the beginning stages. One stroke of luck for the United States was that its two aircraft carriers based in Hawaii, the *Lexington* and the *Enterprise*, had been away at sea when the attack occurred, thus saving them from any damage.

AUGUST 1942
NASHVILLE, TENNESSEE, U.S.A.

Having his unit prepared was the one thing Dr. Daniel Gordon spent a good deal of time thinking about. He had trained his people hard for the past eight months. Now his unit had been ordered to assemble and move out in two weeks. They would be attached to a newly-formed fighting force, the 101st Airborne Division - paratroopers. Gordon and his small unit of surgeons, nurses, and orderlies would join others in the 326th Airborne Medical Unit that had been assigned to the new 101st. It was an elite assignment and Gordon got it because his people had been judged highly fit for this kind of operation. They were intelligent and, as the military had judged, possessed considerable skills at improvising. Gordon had been told that being able to think on your feet and solving problems that inevitably arise in combat situations was a key factor in getting the assignment. The division to which he was being assigned was being formed with just that element in mind. Being behind enemy lines, often surrounded and cut off, would require just such capabilities if success was to be the final outcome.

For now the members of Gordon's unit were in the dark on all this. He would give them the word tomorrow.

44

APRIL 20, 1943
COLOGNE, GERMANY

The city of Cologne was bombed just before ten o'clock in the morning. It was the first time bombs had fallen during daylight. The Americans, unlike their British allies, liked daylight bombing and Bomber Command was now sending more of the American B-17s deeper into Germany, testing the loss rate of longer and longer flights. Losses were considerable, but in most cases, according to the people running Bomber Command, acceptable so far. Fighter escorts could only stay alongside the big planes for so long before having to turn back for England. The debate was always just how far and for which targets should the U.S. risk its crews and big planes.

Cologne was a city not too far inside Germany and the American B-17 bombers could make a run at it with only limited exposure because of an absence of fighter cover. But it was dicey and the Americans paid a price that some would say was too high.

On this day the American raid dropped bombs far from the Carmelite convent, unlike the last raid by the British who managed to make two direct hits, the first time ever that the convent had been shaken so violently. Three people had been killed, one child and two women. The sisters buried their bodies on the convent grounds. A small plaque had been placed over each grave. The names of each had been recorded in the convent's official historical record book. In that book was written the victim's name, age, and religion. The record showed the three to be Catholic. That was a fabrication, of course, part of the deception that had been going on ever since 1940. The victims' true names and religions had been recorded in Mother Superior's Bible which she kept in a small space carved out of the stone wall behind her bed. The names she recorded were: *Ada Kupner*, age 6, Jew; *Cayla Spiro*, age 27, Jew; and *Leya Feldshuh*, age 53, Jew.

Their deaths were just another sign to those still living in the convent that the war was closing in on them. Trying to stay alive, hiding as they were, was becoming harder and harder, in spite of what Colonel Fritz Eichenstat was doing.

The war was also closing in on Colonel Fritz Eichenstat as well, but for different reasons and in another way. The past year had been painful and worrisome for the Colonel; he was now at the end of the line, he felt. No longer could he make useful alterations in the orders he was receiving from General Reinard in order to minimize the effects of the Reich's programs to exterminate the Jews of Europe. Over the past year he had been finding ways to slow down the movement of people out of a few of those places over which he had jurisdiction. The convent at

Köln had received most of his help. It was the one convent that he could call a success, so far. The other places under his jurisdiction had fared more poorly. He had to sacrifice them in order to cover up the Carmelite convent in Köln and make it less conspicuous when the numbers were being tallied. Now that contrivance was waning, he felt. Eichenstat had been playing a dangerous game indeed and he was surprised that he had been able to conduct his charades for as long as he had. He had Father Konrad Schroeder, from his church in Aachen, along with his small band of accomplices, to thank for that. But now, Eichenstat was running out of time and out of tricks and his association with Schroeder was becoming more tenuous, and more dangerous. He had already warned Father Schroeder about his latest worry, telling him that he had been called to General Reinard's headquarters in Berlin. The time for that meeting had now arrived.

Eichenstat was shown into Reinard's office. He had to be on his best behavior.

"Heil Hitler," Eichenstat saluted stiffly. He wanted to show his best military bearing.

Reinard did not return his salute. "Good to see you again, Colonel," he said pleasantly enough.

Eichenstat then noticed that the General had redecorated his office.

"I hope you had a pleasant trip from Bremen."

"My new aide is not as talkative as Sergeant Pond, but yes, my trip was easy enough."

Reinard pouted. "Sergeant Pond, yes. The poor fellow."

"Sir?"

"He is in Russia. He thanked me for helping get him his assignment. He's either dead or a captive of the Russians. Which would you'd rather be?" His grin was telling.

"I didn't know he …"

Reinard grunted and sat down. "Now, I believe I have the assignment for you," Reinard said. "Sit down, Colonel."

Eichenstat found the chair in front of Reinard's desk and sat down, waiting for the next surprise to hit him. "Sir?"

"Over a year ago you might remember I told you I thought you might be suited for other types of work."

"I remember."

"I think I've found it. It's new and the man heading it is a true patriot, and an original thinker when it comes to unusual operations."

Eichenstat braced himself. "Yes, Sir."

"His name is Otto Skorzeny."

"Yes, Sir?"

"The Fuhrer has a fondness for what Skorzeny can accomplish, or claims he can accomplish. He hasn't done much yet, but he is making preparations, and that is where you come in. He's collecting qualified personnel for his unit. I think you could be one of those who might join him."

Eichenstat could hardly think straight but he knew he had to think fast. He knew he could not voice any objections without knowing more specifics, so he had to remain calm and analytical as he fought to contend with this new development. "What does this Skorseny do, exactly?"

"Clandestine operations will be his speciality. Small unit operations, behind enemy lines."

"Assassinations?"

Reinard shrugged. "Abductions, destructions. I'm really not all that sure but it will require people of many special skills. You have good language skills. People like that are hard to find."

"Yes, Sir, but what you're saying sounds to me as if Skorzeny needs young, agile people who are in top physical shape. Look at me," Eichenstat said, peering down at himself.

Reinard laughed. "You're in better shape than you make out, Colonel. I've read your medical reports. You were a top athlete in school."

"Yes, Sir, but ... that was a long time ago."

"You'll need some extra training, of course, but it could be a big boost to your career. Pay and rank would be better. Of course, you already outrank Skorzeny but in these things rank is not always the main concern. Skorzeny will be in charge, no matter his rank."

From the sound of Reinard's words it sounded to Eichenstat that he had his mind made up. "Is this definite, Sir? Am I being transferred to this unit?"

"That's up to Skorzeny. He wants to look over all the records of all the people recommended to him. He'll be contacting you if he wants you. If not ... well, you stay where you are, I suppose."

"I must tell you, Sir, I am not too pleased about this but I will, if ordered."

"Of course you will, Colonel. I would expect nothing less."

"If it please the General, I am happy in my present command, if you are so disposed."

Reinard looked down. "Skorzeny is responsible for searching the records for the people he thinks could help him. We have all been ordered to help in the selections. I can't go against orders, Eichenstat, you know that."

"Does Skorzeny have my records already?"

"I think so."

"He has the ultimate say?"

"As I understand it, yes. Are you thinking of going to a higher authority?" Reinard asked, eyeing Eichenstat. "I would recommend against that."

"No, no. I would not do such a thing."

"Think of it this way, Colonel. Skorzeny would be quite a change from what you are doing now. Exciting. Being in the field. Are you really the indoor type?"

"No, Sir," Eichenstat replied submissively.

"Good. Now I want to speak to another matter," Reinard then said.

"Sir?"

"Himmler is insistent in stepping up operations. You know what that means."

"What does he want, specifically?" Eichenstat asked, desperate to learn whatever he could and see what Reinard was thinking when it came to carrying out Himmler's coming directive. If he were forewarned about that he'd be better able to adapt to whatever might be coming from Berlin.

"Himmler says there are still too many vermin infecting Germany. He's doubling the numbers."

"I am sending out as many as I can, General."

Reinard looked at him. "Double your efforts then."

"They aren't there, General. Not in my district."

Reinard smiled. "I will make that determination after my inspection, Colonel."

Eichenstat stiffened but quickly relaxed. "No officer likes having his judgement questioned, General, but if you believe an inspection is necessary I will be happy to cooperate."

"If I doubted that, Colonel, you would be reassigned and sent to the Eastern front." He laughed.

"So, I have your confidence?"

"I shall tell you, Colonel, there was a time back a year or so when I was having my doubts."

"When was that, Sir?"

Reinard waved his hand. "It doesn't matter. I have other troubles now, and so do you. Himmler wants his flesh. Do your duty."

"Yes, Sir. Is that all, Sir?"

Reinard stared down, then smiled as he looked up again. "Maybe being a member of Skorzeny's unit would be less wearing on your conscience, huh, Colonel?"

45

APRIL 26, 1943
KÖLN, GERMANY

Sergeant Stut Uber had replaced Sergeant Marcus Pond and been Colonel Fritz Eichenstat's new aide for some time now. Uber was a true son of the Reich. He had served in the German army since 1932 and had been in every major campaign from Poland to North Africa to Russia. His wounding in the retreat from Russia left him with a battered left face that included a shriveled ear and a slightly sunken cheek, and a jaw bone that pained him whenever he chewed his food. He had been lucky, his eyesight, miraculously, had not been impaired. The explosion that had gone off near him had not permanently damaged his brain either; his mind was still as good as ever. His temperament had always been to keep his personal thoughts to himself and handle his own problems. These were attributes that Eichenstat appreciated. He seemed a fatalist, like himself.

This was the first time that Sergeant Uber had driven the Colonel to the convent in Köln so once they had reached the city Eichenstat had to instruct him which roads to take. Eichenstat had not been here in over three months and as his car drove onto the grounds and approached the convent buildings he could see that the complex of buildings looked even more damaged than he had imagined. The homes and buildings in the neighborhood were in much the same shape, but there were some structures that had escaped damage completely, or were only slightly scratched. The massive British bombing in the last days of May, 1942 had left the convent severely damaged. Remarkably, only one person inside had been killed during that devastating British onslaught. What was even more remarkable was that the nuns still carried on their work afterward, and people continued living here. But what else were they to do? Everyone was beginning to make do, scraping by, some were leaving if they could find shelter outside the city. But leaving was not a wise option for those who were hiding inside the convent. During the past year Köln had been bombed several other times and some additional bombs had landed close enough to the convent to further damage the already weakened structures. But to Eichenstat's eye, the place looked about as bad as the last time he had seen it. He knew that several more people had died in the last raid when a small wall had collapsed. The convent had been fortunate in one way, there had been no large fires like the ones that had been ignited in other places.

Sergeant Uber maneuvered the car around several small piles of stone and broken up pieces of wood as he worked his way closer to the main entrance. He stopped.

"Wait here, Sergeant," Eichenstat ordered as Uber started to get out to open the rear door for Eichenstat.

"Yes, Sir."

Eichenstat had not notified the convent that he was coming. There was no one to greet him. The right side of the front wall and part of the roof showed a large hole; the wood and stone that once comprised it were now a pile. On the left side of the main door the bell and cord still hung. He rang it. There was no reply. He pulled the cord again, then struck the wooden door with his closed hand. He heard footsteps.

When the door opened he saw the same young nun who had opened it for him on other occasions. He quickly noticed that she seemed out of character. Her eyes were red and bloodshot as if she had been crying, and her habit was torn in several places and quite dirty.

He tipped his hat. "Sister."

She stepped aside. "Come in, Colonel."

She did not look straight at him. She spoke softly and he was barely able to hear her. "This way, please." She led him down the hall, her head bowed, walking lethargically, her hands folded in front of her against her habit.

"I have to see Mother Superior," he told her.

She motioned. "She is out on the grounds. This way."

There were several gaping holes in the roof, and dust and considerable debris everywhere. They made several turns and passed several handfuls of people scurrying about, children in tow. They stood still and watched him with wary suspicion. Mothers pulled their children closer to them. There were few men about. Just about everywhere Eichenstat looked there was something to say that this place had been struck by something powerful. But a lot was still in place, still usable. Dark shadows and dingy looking corners existed in every room he could see into. On visits before the massive British raid he remembered it as a brighter place. The only brightness now was the sunlight that came through some gaping hole above, or a side wall that had been penetrated.

"How many ... times has the convent been bombed?" he asked.

"Several," she said.

"Anyone killed since I was here last?"

"Too many," the young nun said, sounding as if she had a lump in her throat.

They reached the door to the back of the convent, its window broken out. He opened the door for her. They went out onto the grounds. He saw Mother Superior across the way. "I can manage things from here, Sister," he told the young nun. There were two elderly men with shovels a slight distance farther on. They looked up and stood watching him as he approached.

Mother Superior's sideward glance saw him coming but she continued checking in the book she held.

As he reached her he removed his hat. "Mother Superior." He looked around. "What are you doing here?"

"Dead people buried, Colonel."

"All these? How many?"

"Nearly all. In a few days they'll all be here in the ground."

He frowned.

She grinned. "All dead and gone. No one can then harm them."

"I ... don't understand."

"Come." She began walking. "I have devised a method," she said. "If these people are killed in an air raid we must give them a decent burial, a final resting place. Here they are," she spread out her arms.

He looked down and around. "But I saw people inside. A good number."

She smiled. "You don't understand. They are there, but they are here as well, or soon will be. For the record, as seen in this book, they'll all be here in the ground. We nuns will have buried them."

He then began to get the picture, he thought. "Unless someone comes and exhumes their ... bodies. If there are any bodies, that is."

"You're a smart man, Colonel. Do you think anyone will want to exhume them if the Church says they are buried here? What's to be gained by that?"

He thought a moment, eyeing her. "And what about the people I saw walking around inside? Who are they?"

"They are who we know they are. But our records will show them here in the convent cemetery. If anyone asks." She watched his expression. "Your records could show the same, Colonel."

"Why should I do such a thing?"

"Because you are a decent man. And because Sister Katherine trusted you. I've have come to see you in a different light, Colonel and I have come to understand better why it was she thought of you as she did."

He looked away. The mention of Gabriella made him sad, very sad. He had been living his life trying not to think of her, and of his child. He knew nothing about where she was. "I explained all that to you over a year ago. We were students together."

"She is an attractive woman, Colonel. I bet she made a striking appearance when attending the university."

Eichenstat's throat tightened. "What are you saying, Mother Superior?"

"I think you know."

He tried to reply. His mind only filled with images of Gabriella.

"All of us here miss her, Colonel. I can tell that you do as well, in a special way, I imagine. Is it possible you know where she is?"

"No," he said emphatically. "No. I wish I did."

"As I recall, you seemed rather certain she would wind up in America. That's what you told her poor mother."

He shook his head slowly, his eyes fixed in the distance. "I still believe that, but I have no definitive word."

"I see. Well, her mother is dead. She's buried over there as you will see if you saw our records. She died with a happy heart knowing her daughter made it to America. It was you who made her happy. It was you who brought that news to her."

"How many have you buried here?" he asked. "I came today to get my records up to date before I am reassigned," he told her.

"Reassigned! Why?" she asked with a distinctly worried expression.

"It's not a certainty yet, but I have to plan for the worst. I want all the names of the dead."

As they walked back to the main building he asked, "Why don't you try to clean up the rubble, Mother Superior?"

"I would like for the place to appear as torn up and damaged as possible. How can people be killed by bombs but not have the buildings in which they were housed show no destruction?"

He laughed weakly, impressed with the woman, a true leader, always thinking ahead, he thought. When they got inside she gave him the complete list which showed the names under which each of the individuals was buried. He looked at them.

"These names ... "

"Yes, they are all the 'non-Catholics' who were housed here. You have their correct names and, ages, and birth places right there. They are all dead, and there will be others as this war goes on. As long as we continue to be bombed people will die here."

He then told her, "I can't be certain how long they will be allowed to remain here. I have ... deceived far too long."

"Colonel, there are only us nuns and a few Catholic lay people here."

"You are burying Jews in a Catholic cemetery? What does the Church say about that?"

She shrugged. "I consulted a priest in Aachen," she said. "Is that Church enough for you?"

"I'm not Catholic. You tell me. Is it?"

"Probably not, but who can readily communicate with Rome at this time to get an answer?"

"If I am reassigned my replacement could come calling on you," he advised.

"Not if your records show officially what has happened here."

"I wish I could ..." He stopped. He wanted to say that he wished he could apply the same deception to the other convents and monasteries under his jurisdiction but to do so would have risked calling too much attention to the entire matter. He could not. At least he was doing what he could for Gabriella's convent in Köln. In dealing with the others he was practically helpless. Jews in those places were fair game for the likes of Himmler who was now showing his contempt for the Concordat with the Vatican, if it ever applied to Jews in Catholic convents. Eichenstat's reassignment would put someone else in his place and he would likely funnel all these people to Himmler with no questions asked, maybe move them out with glee. There surely were enough men who would oblige. Was he any different? Was he really better than they were? He knew many of them. Was he really all that righteous. He would have to talk to Father Schroeder about that. It made him wonder how Schroeder was getting along. He had not heard from him lately.

46

JUNE 1, 1943
WASHINGTON, D.C., U.S.A.

When the United States officially entered World War II on December 8, 1941 Washington changed quickly. By then, Michael Duncan had been there ten years and he had put those years to good use getting to know the landscape and the people who walked upon it. He had gained valuable knowledge and, now, in this new Washington, he had become a very busy man. Harry Hopkins, the man who had brought Michael Duncan to Washington as his assistant years ago, was now one of the most powerful men in Washington and Roosevelt's leading advisor on many fronts. That made Michael Duncan, as Hopkins's close associate, a powerful man as well. But Duncan worked behind the scenes and there were many who wondered just how much the President relied on him. Most people saw him as a trouble shooter, a problem solver, a person who could smooth the bumps and cut through red tape. The one thing he didn't do was take bribes or act unlawfully. In that regard, he turned down half the requests that came to him.

Today, while on his way to work, Duncan thought about how his role had become more frightening. The nation was at war, the stakes were now as high as they could get, crises loomed everywhere, lives could be snuffed out by ill-thought-out processes and poor planning. There was a lot going on now that was depressing, yet, for his own well-being he had been moderately successful in maintaining an upbeat disposition.

Duncan's phone was ringing as he entered the Smithsonian and made his way to the rather lavish office which Hopkins had arranged for him. He picked up the receiver.

"Duncan," he answered.

"Michael." Bishop Cicognani's voice was unmistakable. It possessed the friendly, gracious, Italian lilt that was his trademark.

"I believe I know what this is about," Duncan said. "You and I probably received the same request from the same person."

"Yesterday, late, from Sister Katherine, yes," Cicognani said. "She writes to me only out of respect," he added. "When she left the sisterhood that took me out of the loop, as they say. This thing she is asking seems to be right up your alley, however."

"She is asking for strings to be pulled," Duncan said with a slight laugh. "I've already had conversations with two of the medical people involved. One is her immediate commander, Dr. Daniel Gordon; the other is Gordon's commander, Major William Barfield. Sister Katherine must have told Gordon about me. Gordon told Barfield and that's how he came to call me.

Everything is a rush now because the unit is assembling at Camp Shanks in Orangetown, New York, getting ready to depart for England any day."

"How does it look to you? Is it possible? From the tone of her letter she sounds determined."

"I've already made some phone calls," Duncan said. "I think we can get this done."

"Did you know she had become an American citizen? The girl, Anna, too, she wrote me."

"I knew about it, yes."

Cicognani gave out a low laugh. "I bet you helped."

"An easy request," Duncan said.

"Have you spoken to her?"

"Several times, regarding the citizenship issue." As he said this Duncan thought of the flowers he had sent her when William was born and the note of thanks she had sent him. It all seemed so long ago.

Cicognani's question brought him back. "Could she be in danger if her request is granted and she does become a military nurse with this unit?"

"It's a paratroop unit, Bishop. It will be very dangerous I suspect."

"She could end up back in Germany," Cicognani said. "That must be a little frightening for her. Do you think she has thought about that?"

"I'm sure she has thought about it, but that's what she wants. Well, today may be the day she gets her wish. I have a call in for the division's chief surgeon, Dr. David Gold."

"I'll leave it with you, Michael. Keep me informed, please."

"Good day, Bishop."

It was just after noon when Lieutenant Colonel David Gold called. "I must say, Mr. Duncan, I am unclear as to what it is Major Barfield wants of me here. He's under a lot of pressure preparing his people. I understand he wants some new personnel assigned to the 326th?"

"Just one person, Colonel."

"A nurse."

"An exceptional nurse. An exceptional individual. I want to tell you a story to make my point, Sir."

"I'm listening."

"Maybe after hearing it you'll better understand why I believe this assignment *must* be done."

It took Duncan nearly twenty minutes to complete his story. It was clear to Duncan that Gold was taken by the many elements of what he heard. Duncan did not interrupt the silence that ensued as Gold thought of the things Duncan had just told him.

Finally Gold said, "I've seen the reports Dr. Gordon has sent to Major Barfield. He says the woman is the best he has been associated with in his career. That's high praise, I suppose."

"You would know more about that than I would, Colonel."

"That's all well and good but how do you arrange for the woman to secure military status?"

"I'm not sure, but I will make it my business to find a way. All I need to know is that this request has your approval."

"You have it," Gold said.

"Thank you."

"It is a remarkable story, Mr. Duncan. I look forward to meeting this woman."

"You won't be disappointed, Colonel."

47

JULY 20, 1943
BIRMINGHAM, ENGLAND

The man showed his badge to Herwald Burkitz. It identified him as Jeremy Underwood, a security agent for the British government. They sat down at a table in Burkitz's small office.

Just doing some final checking," he said. "I want to ask you about Klaus Fuchs."

"Oh?"

"What can you tell me about his political leanings?"

"Is he a communist? Is that what you want to know?"

"We strongly suspect he is, but how dedicated is he?"

"I've not found him secretive about his sympathies for the Russians," Herwald said.

"How about you?"

"Never had such sympathies. Klaus and I have discussed it on several occasions, not often, but that was a number of years ago."

"Has he ever tried to recruit you?"

"Not in any serious way. Not overtly."

"Fuchs has already been sent to America to work with the Americans. You could be next, I guess."

"I'm ready."

"Well, that's not my business. My purpose for being here is to get some things cleared up about you. You were dismissed from the University of Gottingen, correct?"

"I was."

"For what reason? Was it for striking a Nazi official?"

"It was."

Underwood smiled. "You get him good?"

"I should have . . ."

"Killed the bugger?" Underwood finished for him.

"They would have killed *me* if I had. As it was, I'm surprised they didn't."

"Yes, I guess they might have."

"My mother and sister would have been alone then."

"Of course, I see. Sorry."

"Are you sure I might go and work with the Americans?"

"A good number of my assignments have been on that list but, like I said, it's not my business. I only gather the information used. You are German, after all, but so are half the scientist and mathematicians we send. All I know is I interview them and the next thing you know many of them are over in America."

"My sister is in America now."

"We are aware of that. Are there any other relatives?"

"No. Just Anna. The Gregory Foundation helped get her there."

"That too we know," Underwood said.

"The Gregory got me to England."

"We know."

"What don't you know, Mr. Underwood?" Herwald asked.

Underwood smiled. "How good a mathematician are you. Mr. Burkitz?"

Herwald couldn't help himself. "Better than Klaus Fuchs."

Underwood threw back his head, laughing loudly.

Herwald could not help but see the bad teeth.

48

OCTOBER 1, 1943
BIRMINGHAM, ENGLAND

It had taken Gabriella several days of inquiring to find out
exactly where Herwald Burkitz worked and to get a message to
him. Burkitz was still having trouble processing the fact that she
was now in the U.S. military assigned to the 326th Medical
Company of the 101st Division stationed just a few counties west
of London.

They had arranged a meeting for Sunday. There was much
catching up to do.

He had been waiting for nearly an hour now. When he first
caught sight of her he felt a hard tug in his stomach. She did not
look anything like what he remembered. He would never have
readily recognized her had he unexpectedly run into her on the
street. He remembered her as she looked dressed in her nun's

habit, the rosary beads dangling at her side. Now, seeing her, he was a little embarrassed, thinking to himself how beautiful she looked, even in her army uniform. He felt his face redden. She was smiling wildly as she approached him. He didn't know what words to use in greeting her but she quickly solved his uncertainty by giving him a huge bear-hug.

"Ohhh, Herwald," she said. "It's so good to see you."

"I ...," he fumbled, trying to recover.

She drew back and looked at him. "Your shock is evident, Herwald," she laughed.

"I ... you ... I am feeling good all over seeing you," he grinned. "I am so, so very happy. You and Anna are safe in America."

"Well," she said. "I am back in Europe, but Anna is very safe and making a considerable mark for herself. I know she has written you about all that has been going on in our lives in America."

"She has, she has, yes. She tells me all that is happening. She tells me you are doing well in your scientific work."

He straightened up a little to show his pride. "I may get to go to America soon."

Gabriella's face brightened. "Herwald?"

"It's possible," he said. "I cannot say much about it but I am working for the British Government and they may send me to America to work. But it may never happen," he ended sadly.

Gabriella took his hand. "I pray for that day for you, Herwald. It would make Anna so happy. She misses you. She is growing up."

"I have a picture of her she sent me."

"Do you think she has changed?"

"Oh, yes," he said. "She says she has many friends."

"Oh, you can believe me when I tell you she is popular, but she spends much of her time studying. She is so anxious to do well."

"Does she still keep her diary? I hope so."

"Regularly, every night. Some of it is quite lengthy," Gabriella said, then she laughed. "She says she wants to have a complete record of her getting to America and of her life there so she can give it to her children."

"I am keeping one too, but maybe not for the same reason." He looked at her with a different look as he finished.

"I know what you are thinking, Herwald," she said.

He quickly looked away, then said, In Anna's last letter ... I got it a few weeks ago, she ... said ... you ... now have ..."

"A child," Gabriella finished for him.

His face reddened. "Please, I'm so sorry, I ..."

She squeezed his hand again. "It is a long story, Herwald. Even Anna does not know it all. Some day you will know."

"I shouldn't be prying."

"Things happen to people, Herwald. Things that take time to sort out and become clarified. And to learn to live with."

He smiled, inspecting her. "Now you are in the American Army!"

"Believe me, I'm as shocked as anyone about all that has happened. The Lord moves in mysterious ways."

Herwald's expression changed. "You still believe in God?"

"Of course, don't you? Anna does."

His eyes fell. "It ... is hard," he muttered.

"Why should it be easy?" she asked. "Anything worth having should never be easy."

"Maybe it's not worth having."

She gave him a hard look. "All God asks is that you give Him a chance. I can tell you from experience He will not abandon you; He will keep chasing you as any caring friend would."

Herwald laughed. "You have a way of saying things," he said. "I'm so happy to know you. You have helped me and Anna and you helped our poor mother when things looked so bad for us. I only wish I knew what happened to her. I ... guess she's dead."

"It's a likely possibility. She was very sick when she came to the convent. And there was so little in the way of medicines."

He hung his head briefly. "She was a good mother."

"Anyone could see that," Gabriella said.

Herwald perked up and his expression changed. "How long will you be in England?" he asked.

She shrugged. "I don't know. They don't tell us. We just follow orders." She laughed

"Maybe the war will end soon."

"From what I can tell, Herwald, I believe the war is far from over. It's hardly begun," she offered.

"What is this unit you belong to?"

"It's an airborne unit."

He frowned.

"Paratroopers," she said. "They jump from airplanes," she explained.

"You! Jump!"

"No, no. As far as I know women and not permitted to jump," she clarified. "We travel mostly by truck although some of us fly and land in gliders, wooden planes that have no propellers. They are pulled by another plane and then cut loose to land by gliding down to the ground."

"Sounds dangerous."

"It can be, yes," she replied.

His eyes dropped. "You believe the war will not end soon?"

Her face hardened. "It does appear that way," she muttered.

"It is so hard to stay happy."

She took his hand. "Listen, Herwald, a person can only live one day at a time. Some things are simply beyond our reach. They are occurring in another place, and, if they are bad things, we can only pray for the people to whom they are happening."

"And work to help them."

"That's what this war seems to be all about, maybe," she said.

"That's what I keep telling myself," he replied. "That I am helping."

She grinned. "I hope you get to America soon, Herwald, so you can work to help this war end. It would also give you a good chance to see Anna."

"I wish I was going like my friend Klaus Fuchs. He's already there with some of the other scientists who worked here in England."

"Making new kinds of weapons, I suppose?"

"It's all secret work. I've taken an oath."

She smiled. "Knowing you, Herwald, no one could drag a word out of you if you have taken an oath."

"Would you like to walk the campus? Everything is quite peaceful," he said.

"Let's. One day I'll get to see Cambridge and Oxford as well," she smiled, pulling him. "It'll be like our old time at Gottingen."

They spent the next two hours walking, talking, expressing their worries about the war and their hopes for the future. That evening Gabriella returned by train to her unit west of London.

49

OCTOBER 2, 1943
BREMEN, GERMANY

General Reinard was standing in Colonel Fritz Eichenstat's office looking at the photographs on the wall.

"Mussolini is safe in Germany," he said, his back still to Eichenstat. "Skorzeny and his team got him out of Italy."

"So I've heard," Eichenstat replied. "They used gliders, it seems."

Reinard laughed. "Skorzeny is a hero. He put those gliders right down in top that mountain, surprised the Italian guards keeping El Duce prisoner, and flew him back to a grateful Hitler who presented Skorzeny with the Knight's Cross and a promotion to Major for the operation."

"It might have failed," Eichenstat said.

Reinard turned around and walked toward Eichenstat. "By the way, has Skorzeny ever contacted you?"

"No," Eichenstat shook his head.

"I believe he will."

Eichenstat remained silent.

"I hear he's planning other operations," Reinard said.

Again Eichenstat did not reply.

Reinard fixed his eyes on him. "Think of it, Colonel; your dead father would be pleased that you would be using your talents working with Skorzeny."

The remark made Eichenstat's head come up sharply. "I'd be upholding the family tradition, is that it, General?"

"Of course, what else?"

"My father gave his life for Germany. It killed my mother," he said harshly.

Reinard hesitated, then said, "Going into business after the war with a Jew did not help him," Reinard commented. "The Jew cheated your father."

Eichenstat wanted to defend his father, but he was well aware of Reinard's sentiments about such things and wondered if it would mean anything.

"My father was a good man."

"Yes, but he had a naive streak, especially when it came to the Jew."

"I can't accuse my father of having been naive," Eichenstat replied.

"Are you implying that it was *Germany* that betrayed your father?" Reinard's eyes showed their suspicion.

Eichenstat replied indirectly. He shook his head. "I have thought about this for a long time, General. All I can say is that maybe my father was a man whose heart and mind were conditioned in a way that made him vulnerable in the politics that grew up around him."

Reinard grunted agreement. "That's a good way to look at it, Colonel."

"It helps me whenever I think of my father, General."

"Well," Reinard said, straightening himself. "You will never fall into that trap of siding with Jews, I'm sure, having seen what happened to your father."

"You could say that my father taught me a great deal."

"A hard way to learn a lesson, Colonel."

Eichenstat wanted Reinard out of his office but he had to be careful. He said, "I'll be waiting to meet Skorzeny."

Reinard grinned as he headed for the door. "You can't miss the scar," he stopped briefly to tell Eichenstat. "A superb symbol for a man who does what *he* does."

"Good day, Colonel."

50

NOVEMBER 12, 1943
BREMEN, GERMANY

Otto Skorzeny was a tall man, approaching six and a half feet, and from his appearance a man in top physical condition. General Reinard had been right, the scar on his face was the first thing most eyes were drawn to. He wore his SS insignia on his right collar; the Knight's Cross sat high up on his uniform collar just below his neck. His hair was black and combed straight back. His eyes were brown and he wore a small mustache.

"Heil Hitler," he said with a stiff, robust salute.

"Heil Hitler," Eichenstat replied with less enthusiasm. He watched Skorzeny for any sign of condemnation of his weak salute. He saw none.

In the weeks following his last visit with General Reinard Eichenstat had taken the time to make inquiries about Otto Skorzeny. He was 35 years old, Austrian born, graduated as an engineer from Vienna University where he was a member of the dueling society, the source of his scar. He joined the Nazis Party early. By 1938 he was a member of the SS and the Gestapo.

As a military fighter he first gained recognition in 1941 when his SS unit was sent to stamp out a revolt led by Yugoslavian officers. Two months later he and his unit were part of Germany's invasion of Russia where he was wounded. In April 1943 he was assigned to oversee and develop the training for a new school for special agents whose purpose was to operate as saboteurs and to work in espionage and as paramilitary units. He formulated the attributes for the ideal agent: one skilled in the use of firearms and grenades, abilities and knowledge of automobiles, motorcycles, even locomotives; good swimmers, and a special talent - be able to parachute from an airplane. He also wanted men who could speak one or more languages other than German, especially English, Italian, Russian, or Persian.

"Congratulations, Major," Eichenstat said. "A daring display of courage."

"You speak of El Duce?" Skorzeny replied knowingly, smiling.

Eichenstat wanted to get right to the matter at hand. He changed his tone, saying, "Now you see me as ... possibly joining your unit?"

Skorzeny nodded. "You have some skills; some you don't have. But all my agents don't have all the same skills. That may be asking too much, but each has the basics and is exceptional in some."

"Which do you see me possessing?"

"Language mostly. That's the hardest to acquire in an agent. The physical attributes center around being well conditioned and you seem to me to satisfy that attribute."

"I do?"

"Yes. And you have excellent ability with a weapon, especially the pistol. Almost selected to Germany's Olympic team in '36."

"You formed your opinions from reading my dossier?"

"That and the things General Reinard and others have told me."

"I see."

"A good skier, and a respectable swimmer. You showed considerable stamina and dexterity in officer training. You have the family breeding to function authentically as a cultured individual as well; that could be important to me in some future operation. You come from a family that is sophisticated and urbane according to General Reinard. He has been kind enough to tell me about your family, Colonel. Fact is, he is the one who first brought you to my attention."

"Would you like to sit down, Major?" Eichenstat asked.

As Skorzeny sat down he said, "How do you feel about your present assignment, Colonel?"

"I like it well enough."

"Really?"

"Does that surprise you?" Eichenstat asked.

Skorzeny eyed him for a moment. "You seem to be a man who might like a more challenging way to serve Germany."

"What makes you think that?"

Skorzeny smiled. "Some of the things I have learned about you, Colonel, that's all."

"General Reinard does not know everything about me, Major."

"Of course he doesn't, but there are others beside Reinard; as I said, I have inquired with others."

Eichenstat hesitated. Who could Skorzeny have talked to, he wondered? He then said in his own defense, "I believe I am performing a valuable service in my present position."

"Come, Colonel, you can't really be all that satisfied with rounding up Jews to be shipped off to ... other places. It is rather depressing, is it not?"

Eichenstat had to agree with the analysis, but, as he had convinced himself, he had to engage in allocating unknown individuals to an unhappy fate if he was to have any chance of making his deceptions at the convent in Köln possible. It was for Gabriella that he did this; that's what he had always told himself. Did it make it right? He was beyond trying to answer that question. He knew that turning his command over to some replacement would do two things: one, it would put the convent in danger and, two, it would most likely expose what he had been doing and open him up to a charge of treason. He could be shot. He had to stay out of Skorzeny's clutches, no matter what, and remain in his present position.

"I've got some important operations in the works, Colonel. You might like to be involved."

"I am not all that interested in any more excitement, Major."

"You haven't heard me out," Skorzeny replied.

"I'm sorry, of course."

"How would you like to be in on the assassination of Eisenhower, and Churchill even?"

Eichenstat was dumfounded. "Major?" he said, narrowing his eyes. "Are you serious, or are you testing me?"

Skorzeny smiled wildly. "One has to plan boldly, Colonel. One has to consider all the possibilities; it is wise to consider what possible actions might change the status of the war for Germany."

"Kill Eisenhower! Just like that!"

"Well, my plan, still is in the formative stages, of course. It works along a time line developed *after* the Americans and British come ashore, most likely somewhere in France. They are honor bound to attempt an invasion, give it one try. If they succeed and get a foothold sufficient to advance aggressively toward Germany itself, Eisenhower, as Commander in Chief of all forces will set up his command somewhere close by the action, surely. That's when we'll strike."

Eichenstat's heart was now pounding. The man seemed serious in his thinking.

"What do you think?" Skorzeny asked. "Sound ... reasonable?"

"Suppose the Americans and British fail at their invasion?"

Skorzeny grinned. "Then they will have to seek a truce. The American and British people will insist on it. They will not tolerate a second attempt and see more of their young men killed."

"You are sure?"

"They have the Japanese, remember. They have not made much headway so far against them."

"Pearl Harbor will make the Americans fight to the end. They will likely succeed. That's my opinion for what it's worth," Eichenstat said.

"One with which I agree. That's why a failed invasion of Europe by the Americans will mean a truce with Germany. The American people will want their leaders to concentrate on Japan and leave the Germans and Russians to fight it out."

Eichenstat knew that this made sense. But could the Americans and British be stopped on the shores of France? He wasn't so sure. "There is some legitimacy to your thinking," he told Skorzeny.

"Of course," Skorzeny said, "The Fuhrer will have other operations for me, I'm sure."

"One thing concerns me in this matter, Major. My rank. I outrank you."

"Rank is flexible in my unit, Colonel. The Fuhrer gives me complete jurisdiction in deciding just how to handle that."

"And how would you handle my situation?"

Skorzeny hesitated, then smiled. "You know, I haven't considered it. I first wanted to see what kind of person you are."

"And?"

"I'll have to think about that. If I have a mission that could really use your capabilities I might call on you."

"Fair enough, I suppose, seeing as I have little say in the matter."

Skorzeny's stare was questioning. "I prefer to have volunteers, Colonel. I don't need reluctant comrades slowing down my operation. But, if I believe someone has an exceptional qualification for a special mission I'll take him. It's as simple as that."

"I see your point, Major."

Skorzeny smiled, "Now tell me honestly, wouldn't you like to be in on the assassination of Eisenhower? We'd all be national heroes. Your father would be proud."

Eichenstat knew that his father would *not* be proud. As it was, his father, Eichenstat had long decided, would be dishonored knowing what he was now doing. For Eichenstat, what was worse was that he could see no way he could ever remedy his condition.

51

NOVEMBER 30, 1943
AACHEN, GERMANY

Colonel Fritz Eichenstat had scheduled his trip to Aachen to visit Father Konrad Schroeder in order to have enough time to return to Bremen the same day. His aide and driver, Sergeant Stut Uber, had been informed by Eichenstat that Father Schroeder was a friend of the Reich who had something sensitive to tell him and that the priest always preferred to meet alone. Uber had been told to occupy his time and be back at the Church at three o'clock to pick up Eichenstat so they could then drive back to Bremen before dark.

"Maybe there's a beer hall, Sergeant," Eichenstat said.

"Yes, Sir. Maybe the library as well."

"I can't help you there, Sergeant. Be back here at three."

LEN ALBERSTADT

"I'll locate it, Sir. Three o'clock. I'll be here."

As Uber swung the car around and stopped, the door to the priest's residence opened and Father Schroeder came out. Eichenstat got out and headed toward Schroeder. Uber drove back out the main road and turned right.

Eichenstat and Schroeder shook hands at the top of the steps. "It's been nearly a year," Schroeder said.

"Hello, Father."

They went inside. Father Schroeder offered Eichenstat a drink, which he politely declined.

"I instructed my cook to have a lunch prepared. We shall eat shortly. Let's sit down. How have you been?"

"I don't sleep well."

"Have you lost weight?" Schroeder asked worriedly.

"A few pounds, maybe," he replied. "Tell me, have you heard anything?" he asked the priest.

Schroeder nodded. "You may get something soon."

Eichenstat straightened up. "How soon?"

"It will require some traveling on your part. To Rome."

"Rome!"

"The city is still in German hands. You could travel there provided you have the authorization. Could you get it?"

"Of course. What would I find in Rome?"

"In the Vatican there is a man who might have information."

"Me, in the Vatican!"

Schroeder laughed. "It has received German officials before. Some say too enthusiastically. But you don't have to go inside the walls."

"Can you get this information? Pass it along to me?" Eichenstat asked Schroeder.

"It's too risky. Besides you might like to see first-hand what he has," Schroeder told him. "And, you look to be a man who needs a vacation. Relax a little."

Eichenstat shrugged. "What is the man's name? How would I get in touch with him once I am in Rome?"

"He'll find you," Schroeder said.

"How will he know I have arrived?"

"He goes to the same place every day. A hotel lobby. He has coffee there, a special blend."

"What Hotel?"

"Hotel Nardizzi. It's located on Via Firenze, 38."

"He goes there every day? What time of day?"

"Morning. Eight o'clock."

"How will he know me?"

"He'll recognize you by your actions. You go to the desk, ask if a man named Rothmann is staying there. Then ask if you might take a room on the top floor. You will be politely denied. Then walk away and go sit down in the lobby by the main entrance."

"How long will this man be in Rome?"

"He's taken up residence in the Vatican. He's there for the duration of the war, I suppose."

"Do you know him?"

"I do."

"But you, yourself have no information for me?"

"None, except what I've told you."

"I'm disappointed. When I received your message I was hoping for more."

"Rome may bring you some relief. I'm sure it is good news."

Eichenstat sat silently, then said, "What has your life been like here?"

"Bombs and more bombs."

"The damage could not be hidden. It is like Köln," Eichenstat said.

"What are the generals saying? Can they stop it?"

Eichenstat looked down. "They are hoping for some kind of truce with the Americans. Some believe that if the Americans fail in their attempted landings on the continent they will seek a truce and Germany will be spared. I'm not sure how the Russians feel about that. If there is a truce the Russians will have to take us on all alone. They will not be so successful in battle if we are freed from defending the West."

"The Americans and the British have already done massive damage. The people have suffered great losses," Schroeder said.

Eichenstat hung his head. "I fear there will be more, much more. Tell me, what have you heard about the Jews in this area?"

"They are almost all gone now. Some are still hiding. I hear whispers."

Eichenstat got up and began walking. "What else could I have done? What ... chance ... I had to do it. Gabriella ..." His voice cracked.

Schroeder remained seated, knowing what Eichenstat was thinking, and the predicament he was facing. A more classic dilemma he could not imagine.

"You have saved lives, Colonel," Schroeder finally said.

Eichenstat turned toward him. There was anger on his face.

"Am I fooling myself? Should I have walked away? Volunteered for duty on the Russian Front! Anything but what I am doing now?"

"Then what would have happened to the convent in Köln, and the people there?"

"They might not survive anyway," Eichenstat said. "The sisters are trying to fool the authorities with false records and papers. They are only getting by with it because of my help. That woman, Mother Superior, is ingenious," he said, displaying his true admiration for her efforts. "I wish I could be as calm about it as she seems to be."

"She prays for calmness, Colonel, I'm sure."

"Like you, Father? What do you pray for?"

"You don't believe in prayer, do you Colonel?"

Eichenstat did not reply.

"Colonel?" Schroeder persisted.

"No."

Schroeder smiled. "Gabriella told me of your beliefs, or lack of them. You and she used to argue about it all the time."

"Yes," he said, barely audible. "We did. It was a wonderful time."

"Maybe, if things turn out, you will have that opportunity again," Schroeder said.

It was then that Eichenstat reached into his jacket and took out his wallet. He pulled out a photograph and stared at it. "It is the only one I have." He then showed it to Schroeder.

"Younger days," Schroeder said."

"Better days. That was taken on the campus of Gottingen University."

"Who is the young man with you and Gabriella?"

"Herwald Burkitz, Anna's brother."

"He the one who went to Britain?"

Eichenstat nodded, taking back the photograph.

During their meal Eichenstat said, "I have failed at being a human being, Father. I should have seen what I was being drawn into. I should have gotten out. I remained, believing I could work around it, change it maybe. I waited too long."

"You helped Gabriella get out. You saved one life at least, and you, yourself, know you have saved others. What would have been the outcome if someone other then yourself had been in charge?"

"I have said that very thing to myself countless times, Father," Eichenstat spoke in a matter-of-fact manner. "That seems the only thing I can make myself believe if I want to maintain some degree of sanity and make sense of this. If General Reinard, or one of his staff, looked hard at my records, or asked around, he would surely have me up before a court martial. I would be shot. The Americans will execute me when the war is over, if I survive."

It was a statement that Father Schroeder had no way to refute, but he said nothing.

The two men talked for another hour. Eichenstat looked at his watch. "My driver should be here." He went to the door. "Right on time," he muttered.

Eichenstat turned and looked at Father Schroeder. "I wonder how many more there are like me? Trapped."

Schroeder came over to him. "God is with you, my friend."

Eichenstat hesitated. "I'd like to really believe that," he replied. "If only it were true."

52

DECEMBER 7, 1943
ROME, ITALY

It took Colonel Fritz Eichenstat a week to get his orders for leave to Rome. General Reinard had no objections and wished him a good time.

"You need a rest," Reinard had told him. "Relax. And remember, there are some Italian women who appreciate the Germans."

Eichanstat knew why Reinard had said it.

He arrived in Rome late in the afternoon. He went directly to the quarters reserved for officers and unpacked. Later he had supper in the first small café he saw. It was a chilly night but the change in scenery of the street made for a pleasant walk. The streets were busy; soldiers not in abundance, but plenty enough to know that the Germans were running things here. At the café there were all German officers, a few enlisted men, but no Italian military. There were about an equal number of civilians, mainly young women in the company of German soldiers. Eichenstat sat alone, watching them, wondering what they were thinking about regarding their present situation, about the war in general, maybe about life after the war. The women might pay a price for their familiarity and friendliness. He knew many soldiers who relished being a part of this war. Eichenstat wondered if they really knew what they were probably in for later. He, himself, was losing faith. Hitler had taken them too far down a path of destruction. Even if the Americans and British did seek a separate peace with Germany and she was not defeated in the usual sense there would be much more death and destruction before it was all over. Then there were the Russians. They had unmistakably demonstrated their capability for intense madness and ruthless killing. One could not count on rational behavior when it came to what Hitler had unleashed in the East. As Eichenstat sat at his table he thought of himself: *you will not survive this.*

He ate little of his meal but had more than his usual evening drink and left slightly inebriated. He found his way back to his quarters with no difficulty. He arranged for a driver to meet him the following morning to take him to the hotel. As usual, he spent a restless night. He dreamt awful dreams which were coming more and more frequently.

The following morning the driver took him to the Hotel Nardizzi. Once inside the hotel lobby he did exactly what Father Schroeder had said. The desk clerk smiled when he asked for a room on the top floor.

"All occupied," the clerk told him.

Eichenstat then turned and looked around quickly at the other parts of the lobby and the room with the wide opening where many people were sitting at breakfast. He went and sat near the main entrance as Schroeder had instructed. He felt awkward, out of place. From his vantage point he could see about two-thirds of the dining room. He guessed the man he was suppose to meet was somewhere inside probably watching him that very moment, but he saw no one looking his way. Then he spotted the man. He knew instantly who it was. The man was sitting alone sipping a drink from a cup. There was a black hat and umbrella resting on the chair beside him. He was dressed in a suit. The description fit perfectly the one he remembered reading from the file his intelligence agents had assembled several years ago. It was Sabastian Arceneau. He glanced up at Eichenstat, then, with a subtle gesture, motioned him over.

"Colonel," the man said, "My name is Sabastian Arceneau from the Gregory Foundation. Please sit down."

Eichenstat pulled out one of the chairs. "I know of you, Mr. Arceneau."

"And I of you, Colonel."

"I have a file on you."

Arceneau smiled. "A thick one," he grinned.

"Not thick enough."

"I have some information for you," Arceneau said.

"You know Father Schroeder?"

"A friend, yes."

"He has told you about me?"

"I know a great deal about you, Colonel," Arceneau said. "It is part of my job. I have to if I want to remain healthy."

Eichenstat was slightly puzzled. "What is it that you do, Mr. Arceneau?"

Arceneau smiled. "Arrange things for people."

Eichenstat rolled his eyes slightly and grinned. "For people like Gabriella Sommers?"

"For people like Sister Katherine."

"Tell me, please. How is she? Where is she? Please." Eichenstat could not hold back his emotions. "Please, I must know!"

Arceneau reached down and pulled up a briefcase from beside his chair. He took out a small envelope and slid it over to Eichenstat. "Open it."

Eichenstat hurriedly flipped open the flap and slid out a photograph. He stared at it.

"Your son, Colonel," Arceneau said. "William Steffan."

Eichenstat suddenly felt a lump in his throat; he tried to swallow, his breathing heaved heavy. He picked up the photograph and brought it up closer. "Wi ... lliam Steffan?"

"William Steffan Eichenstat to be precise."

"She did that?"

"She did."

"How ... is she, Gabriella? Is she all right? What is she doing? Where? Tell me, please."

"Slow down, Colonel."

"Tell me everything, everything from when she left Aachen to ..."

"I cannot tell you everything. All I can tell you is what I have learned from my contacts in America."

"She is in America then. I suspected but had no real evidence. Where is she? What is she doing? Which convent?"

"She has left the sisterhood," Arceneau told him.

He frowned, then dropped his eyes. "Because of the baby? Because of what I did to her?"

"She could not remain a nun after the baby was born."

"So ... what is she doing? How is she getting along?"

"My foundation is helping to support her and the baby, Anna Burkitz, too."

"Anna, she is all right?"

Arceneau smiled. "I have been told she is a university student and doing very well in her studies."

"She is so young," Eichenstat said. "University. Does her brother know of this?"

"Herwald knows. He is in England."

"Yes, I know, working for the British."

"He has recently received his doctorate. More than that I cannot say."

"Cannot, or will not?"

"Cannot," Arceneau replied.

Eichenstat did not pursue the matter.

"Tell me more about Gabriella. Is she ..."

"There's not much I can say except to tell you that she studied at one of the universities close by the convent at which she was living and she is now a member of the American military. She is a nurse."

Eichenstat's mind raced. He found one unclear sensation rolling over another. He wanted to put things in their right order and connect everything so it told a single story. It was as if he had not heard it all correctly. "American military?" he finally asked with marked obfuscation. "Can that be?"

"A nurse. She volunteered for a medical unit."

Eichenstat sat thinking, still his thoughts raced. He was imagining all manner of things. He felt relieved but still there was much he wanted to know. He had to bring his thinking into order.

Arceneau told him, "She found a way to make it happen."

Eichenstat smiled. "She could do that."

"I'm sorry I have no more information than this," Arceneau said. "It is a long way to come for just ... well, it is good news, isn't it?"

"Very good news. Tell me, is there any way you can get a letter to Gabriella for me?"

"You have it?"

"Can you?"

"Maybe. Through a friend. You have the letter?"

"I'll ... can we meet again. I'll give it to you then."

"I'm here every morning."

Eichenstat smiled. "I'll be here," he said. "Tomorrow. Same time?"

53

DECEMBER 20, 1943
LONDON, ENGLAND

Gabriella was standing in the crowded train car as it made its way toward Cambridge and the university. Herwald Burkitz had told her to get off at the Hills Road station where he would meet her. Their plan was to go to a nearby small eatery and pub that he recently had discovered. Afterward, if the weather was mildly good, they would take a walk through the grounds of the university before she had to return to her unit that evening.

Herwald had been assigned to a laboratory at the university where he was now working with several other young scientists. These days he was holding out hope that he would be sent to America to continue his work with the Americans. Several of the more prominent scientists in Britain had already departed and were now in America. His friend Klaus Fuchs was among them. Herwald wanted desperately to be included.

The train was crowded, military personnel and civilian alike, jammed in their seats, many holding packages, some gripping their bags to make sure they did not slip from their laps. There was not much overt talking but, nevertheless, there was a dull undercurrent of noise throughout. Some passengers dozed, or tried to. Those people standing rocked with the motions of the car, first bumping one neighbor then another. Two soldiers on each side of Gabriella squeezed her in. One was a ruddy faced red-head American Sergeant, the other a skinny Corporal. Rosy cheeked young boys in British uniforms were enjoying their leave time by joking and laughing with their companions. Some of the older British soldiers showed more subdued demeanor, a few with sour faces. The civilians were mostly women and old men; there were few children. There was a hard staleness of an odor inside as well, tobacco smells mixed with the human essences that float in the air when people are so confined.

Soon the train began to slow, and eventually stop. When Gabriella emerged and stepped onto the platform she looked around; she saw Herwald almost immediately. He was smiling as he approached.

"Thanks for coming," he said. "I hope you like this place I have found. I am not fully accustomed to British cooking. It may not be to your liking."

She laughed. "Mess hall food is not so good either."

The meal they had was modest and had little flavor and the beer was not what they remembered it being in Germany. They both laughed about it but did not complain. For them, such complaints seemed too grotesque at this time. So many people had little food and little of much else and were barely hanging on to life. Both knew they were fortunate.

Near the end of their meal and after they had downed several beers Herwald ask her, "Can the Americans defeat the Germans?"

"Are you worried that they cannot?" she asked.

"They seem ... kind of ragged, undisciplined from what I've seen. They are not like the German soldiers. What have you seen? You have been with them close up."

She hesitated. "Truthfully, I'm not sure how they will fare against the Germans, especially if they begin to have success closer to Germany itself. They are being asked to do a great deal, and they are not a warlike group of people. It will be touch and go, as some of my new friends say."

He laughed. "You have picked up some of the ways they speak."

"I hope I have, yes."

"You like them, don't you?"

"Very much. Very much. Something else," she said. "I find it comforting doing something worthwhile. Since I've been in America and since I have come to know them, working with them, and living with them, I have come to greatly respect what they stand for. I think the Americans are a different, new breed of people, Herwald."

He laughed. "I've heard some Brits say the Americans are a mongrel people."

She smiled. "They are. Maybe that's what makes them strong. I don't believe they'll break."

"Let's hope not."

They talked a little longer before they headed for the Cambridge campus. It was dreary and cold but it did not dampen their happiness at seeing each other again.

54

DECEMBER 22, 1943
WAJHINGTON, D.C, U.J.A.

Michael Duncan was not expecting the phone call that was waiting when he got to his office.

"Merry Christmas, Michael," Bishop Cicognani said when Duncan picked up the receiver.

"Merry Christmas, Bishop. What can I do for you?"

"I received a letter yesterday in the pouch from the Vatican. There is no return address on the envelope so I can't say who it is from, but it is addressed to Gabriella Sommers. I have no way of getting it to her with any dispatch. I don't even know where she is. Since she left Nashville I have lost track of her; she's in the Army, sure, but where. Can you help?"

Duncan thought for a brief moment. "Well, I think I can help. You called at an opportune time."

"I knew you'd know."

"In a matter of speaking, I do. Her unit is somewhere in England, but I'm sure I can pinpoint her exact location after some checking."

"You'll send it on then?"

"Better than that. I'll take it personally. I'm heading to England shortly after the first of the year on a fact-finding trip. I'll send someone over to your residence and pick up the letter. When I go to England I'll do my best to get it to her."

"Have a safe trip," Cicognani said. "And have a happy and holy feast day."

"Thank you, Bishop. Merry Christmas."

JANUARY 4, 1944
WAJHINGTON D.C., U.J.A.

The C-47 lifted off the runway in Washington at 5:35 in the morning, heading for St. Johns, Newfoundland where it would refuel. From Newfoundland it would head on to Glasgow, Scotland and then proceed to London. In addition to its fourteen passengers the plane carried a partial load of various kinds of material. In these times no plane ever went to England without a full load.

Duncan was the only one not in uniform. There were two officers and twelve enlisted men on board as passengers. From the insignias on their uniforms they all seemed to be members of the same unit. He overheard the words *echo sweep* several times during their conversations and he guessed they were discussing a new weapon he already knew something about. A year earlier he had received a lecture by an engineer at the University of Maryland, describing the workings of what this new gadget was and how the theory worked. It sounded as though these men were going to England to put theory to practice.

Duncan sat in the front seat immediately behind the pilot. He had on a leather flying jacket given to him by General James Doolittle almost a year ago when Doolittle was at the White House as part of a publicity tour. Duncan knew the jacket would serve him well in England. The damp chill of the British winters could be most uncomfortable.

When the plane reached its cruising altitude Duncan took out a folder from his briefcase. The letter he was planning to deliver to Gabriella Sommers was clipped to the inside flap. He wondered who had written it, what it said. He guessed he'd never know.

At their stop in Newfoundland, Duncan got up to stretch his legs; the others did likewise. Two men boarded, one was a Colonel, the other a Sergeant. Both men had forty-five pistols fastened to their sides. The Colonel had a briefcase locked to his wrist. Everyone knew what that meant - the contents of that briefcase were secret. The two men moved directly to two vacant seats in the far back of the plane and sat down.

The pilot announced their eminent departure and everyone found their seats again. Moments later the plane was heading down the runway, gaining speed.

Almost immediately Duncan began thinking of the things ahead of him in London. He had a lot on his mind; he had much to accomplish on this mission and he had to decide how he should handle each assignment. His boss, Harry Hopkins, wanted information and he was being sent over to get it. He pulled out a sheet of paper; on it were the names of the people he had to see. He began reviewing some of the particulars of each person's responsibilities, recalling the kinds of information Hopkins had told him he was seeking.

After running through this list of duties he fell asleep. He did not awake until his body felt the plane's descent. They were coming into Glasgow, Scotland. The stop in Glasgow was a short one and they were soon on their way again, heading to London. He watched the countryside passing below. It appeared so peaceful and serene; the greenish blue of the vegetation and the rusty brown of the soil and rock created a picture of a patchwork tapestry of highlights and shadows, all shaped by the low angle of the sun's rays streaming in from the west. Duncan's mind drifted as he watched the ever-changing configurations pass below him. It was hard to believe he was part of this war.

In London he went directly to the hotel. Tomorrow, his first meeting was at eight o'clock in the morning. For now, he needed a good night's sleep.

JANUARY 6, 1944
LONDON, ENGLAND

Michael Duncan had made all the necessary inquiries before he left Washington and he knew that Gabriella's unit as well as much of the entire 101st Division were training in the vicinity of Berkshire and Wiltshire counties, just one hundred or so miles west of London. Early that morning he contacted the commander of the 326th Medical Company, Major William E. Barfield, and asked about Gabriella. Duncan informed Major Barfield that he would be in London for only a few days and needed to see Private Sommers.

"Today?" Barfield asked.

"No, anytime during the next day or two but I'll need to arrange a meeting around my schedule, which is tight at the moment. Evening would be best. Is it possible she might get away one evening? It'll probably have to be late evening, sorry."

"Her unit is in the field at the moment," he told Duncan.

"Not jumping I hope."

"The rudiments of glider landing," he said.

"Sounds dangerous."

"It can be, quite." Barfield said.

"Can she get away for an evening?"

"Consider it done."

"Thank you. Oh, by the way, I had some small part helping get her to the U.S. and later helping get her through the process of becoming a U.S. citizen. Tell me, how is she doing as a soldier?"

He laughed. "She's a superb troop, a real bulldog. Do you know she wanted approval to try jumping from a plane!"

"Isn't that against regulations? Being a woman, that is?"

"It is, yes indeed it is. But she sure wanted to have a go at it."

"You disallowed, of course."

"I had no choice, but I have no doubt she could have handled it."

"I think I know what you mean."

Duncan then gave Barfield his hotel address and phone number. "Have her contact this number. She can leave a message at the desk about when she will get here. The desk will know how to get the information to me."

JANUARY 7, 1944
LONDON, ENGLAND

That evening Duncan made sure he had the letter before leaving the building. He met Gabriella at their prearranged location just down the street a short distance from Norfolk House on St. James Street. It was the main hub where much of the planning for the offensive against the European continent was taking place. Norfolk House was the new home of the Supreme Command Headquarters Allied Expeditionary Force know as SHAEF. Most of the people Duncan had meetings with worked inside.

Duncan and Gabriella shook hands.

"It's been a long time," Duncan said.

She was smiling. "Time," she mused, "We have so little of it, I feel. It's so nice to see you again. You have done so much for me, and for Anna."

"There's a popular restaurant a few blocks away," he said. "Dinner?"

"You said you had something for me?"

"It looks like some bad weather is coming," he said. "Let's get settled first."

The establishment they entered was crowded, and rather noisy.

"The food is passable," Duncan said. "As much as British food can be."

She acknowledged the comment with a smile.

Duncan asked the steward who greeted them, "A table where it is quiet, please. Off to the side."

They waited. Most of the people inside were in military uniform. Those who were not were mostly women. It was clearly populated by Americans.

After they were seated Gabriella said, "I was surprised when Major Barfield informed me that you had called. He said you must be an important person." She grinned, peering at him through narrowed eyes.

"Barfield said that?" Duncan smiled.

"He also made some comment wondering why you were not in the military."

Duncan grinned. "I'm needed in Washington," he said. "And besides, who says I'm not?"

She eyed him. "He thinks you have friends in high places," she said.

"High enough," Duncan replied, raising his eyebrows and laughing. "I'm in England for conferences. My boss needs info," he told her. "He wants me to make some evaluations for him."

"Oh? Your boss? You mean the man in the White House?"

"You're looking fit, very fit," he said, brushing aside her question. "Army life hasn't worn you down, I can see."

"Seems not," she replied. "I have no complaints whatsoever, and I have you to thank for my present happy status."

He nodded. "Seems then that I made the correct decision by assisting you getting into this outfit. Major Barfield sounded as if he's well satisfied by your performance and happy you are on his team."

"My Vanderbilt unit is my real team, but I know what you mean."

"How was the glider exercise?"

"We unloaded and loaded three times. Made improvements each time."

"Barfield said you want to jump. You enjoy the danger?"

"No, just want to be prepared. Can't tell when it might be necessary," she said resolutely.

He smiled. "I have to tell you that you look and act far differently than the last time I saw you," he commented. "On the *Washington*, and at Bishop Cicognani's that evening, at dinner."

She lowered her eyes. "Much has happened since then."

"Indeed it has. For both of us. To most of us."

"The war," she said. Which reminds me, you did say you had something for me, yes?"

He had almost forgotten. "Oh, sure. A letter." He reached into his coat pocket and took out the envelope. He pushed it across the table.

She did not pick it up. She was staring at it.

"What's the matter?" he asked.

She reached out slowly, almost warily, then picked it up. She opened the envelope and took out a smaller envelope. She stared at the handwriting but did not move to open it. She just sat staring at it.

"Something the matter?"

Her eyes jumped. "No, no."

"Good. You looked ..."

"How did you come by it?" she asked him.

"Bishop Cicognani. It arrived in the Vatican's mail pouch. He didn't say anything about how it might have gotten in the pouch but we both believe it was Arceneau's doing."

"My friend Arceneau," she said softly, her eyes showing her remembrances of the man with the umbrella. "I pray he's well."

Duncan nodded.

She manipulated the envelope between her fingers, as if trying to read it without opening it.

"You know who it's from?"

"Yes," she said, some emotion surfacing. "I do."

Still she fidgeted with it.

"Would you like some privacy while you read it?" he asked.

She looked around. "In this place?"

"I could go to the bar and have a drink while you ..."

"No, no, please. I have been enough trouble for you already."

"No trouble. Would you like for me to bring you something? A ... glass of wine, maybe?"

"Yes, I would appreciate that, thank you."

He got up and moved off.

She slit open the envelope with her fingernail, thinking of all manner of unhappy news she might find inside. Her hands shook. The noise of the room seemed to fade. Her fingers unfolded the paper and she began to read.

From across the room at the bar Duncan watched her, wondering. She was an intriguing woman, he thought. How much of her life did he not know, he wondered. What little he did know was enough to make him admire her grit and dedication, and the way she seemed to face life. She seemed to know who she was and what her life was to be about. He could not help but still wonder what she must have gone through to leave the sisterhood. From what he could tell, tonight she seemed to have put that behind her. But had she? Even from this distance he could see she was crying. The paper she held drooped as her grip loosened. Suddenly she got up and headed across the room. He moved toward her.

"Here are your drinks, old chap," the bartender said to his back.

"Hold 'em. I'll be back real soon," he said as he watched Gabriella disappearing across the room.

He jostled through the many tables and people to intercept her. She disappeared into the ladies restroom before he could get there. He went back to the bar and got the drinks and took them to the table.

"Dinner, Sir?" a waiter asked.

"I'm waiting for a friend. Might you come back later when she returns?"

"Very good, Sir."

She returned, looking refreshed. She was smiling.

"Good news?" he asked.

"Good news," she replied. "As good as one might expect," she then said.

He remained silent, giving her time to collect her thoughts. It was clear she had been shaken by the letter.

He said, "I am guessing but it was not from Arceneau."

She shook her head but said nothing.

"I'll shut up," he said, smiling. "Just trying to help, not being nosy."

A smile worked its way across her face. "Thank you for everything. You are a good man, Michael Duncan."

The waiter returned. "Dinner, Sir?"

He looked at Gabriella. "What would you like?"

"Would ... could we ... just sit for a while. I'm not very hungry. Sorry. You ... please, you have something."

Duncan looked at the waiter. "We'll pass for now."

"Very good, Sir."

She took the glass of wine he had brought over for her and sipped it. He took a large swallow of his whiskey. They did not speak. A very short time later she said, "Could I have one of those?" She nodded toward the drink in his hand.

He looked around and motioned to the waiter. "We'll have two more of these," he said, holding up the glass. "Doubles."

"Very good, Sir."

While they waited she began to talk. "Have you completed all your business?"

"No, one more day, maybe two."

"We are training hard. The boys are ..."

Their drinks came. She immediately took two large swallows. He watched her, stirring the whiskey in his glass but not drinking any of it.

"Gabriella," he said. "Would you like to talk a bit about the letter? It's obvious that ..."

She grinned through slightly reddening eyes.

"It's from my son's father," she managed.

"Where is he now? Is he all right? Safe?"

She grinned but it was a hapless grin. She took another swallow of the whiskey and breathed deeply.

At that moment a man in uniform approached.

"Mike," the man called out before he reached the table.

Duncan looked to his side. "Mac," he replied.

The man looked at Gabriella.

Duncan introduced the man. "This is Major General Robert McClure," he told Gabriella.

"A pleasure," he said.

She smiled and nodded. "Sir."

"Say, Mike," McClure turned to Duncan. "One of General Smith's favorite staff members is getting married and there's a small in-house celebration taking place just around the corner. Why don't you and the young lady come along? They've arranged for a little band and everything. Good time to get in some relaxation. God knows, we could use it! How about it?"

"Thanks, Mac, but we'd better not," Duncan said.

"I bet the lady would like to," he said, looking at Gabriella. "I bet she'd enjoy a little relaxation. What do you say? The evening is young. There's no telling how often we'll get any opportunities to really enjoy ourselves, and forget for a brief moment what it is we're all about over here."

Duncan looked over at Gabriella. "It's up to you."

"I'd like that," she said. "Sounds like fun."

Duncan paid the tab and McClure led them to St. James Place and into the ground floor of a three story house.

"They'll be lots of brass here," McClure said.

"Like yourself, huh, Mac?"

Duncan looked at Gabriella. "Are you uncomfortable?" he asked, thinking she might be. This, he guessed, was an unusual situation for her - a female private in uniform surrounded by so many high ranking officers.

She smiled. "No."

Duncan knew she was not telling the truth and that the letter had unnerved her more than she was letting on.

General McClure secured chairs at a table with two other people seated already. Drinks were poured. There were several bottles on the table. Of the two people already there one was a Colonel, the other a female Lieutenant. They looked at Gabriella. The Lieutenant smiled.

"Hi," she said.

"Ma'am," Gabriella replied.

The Lieutenant laughed. "Not necessary here, Private. My name is Katherine."

Gabriella stiffened instantly on hearing the name.

Instinctively Duncan reached for her hand as a gesture of support. He held it briefly, then let go.

Gabriella forced a smile. "That's a fine name," she said, surprising Duncan at her calmness. It was as if she hadn't noticed that he had even momentarily taken her hand.

The small band began playing.

"Who's the bride?" Gabriella asked the Lieutenant.

"A local girl," she said. "The daughter of a British bureaucrat here in London. A nice woman. She's thirty. I think she's been married before."

Gabriella looked around, so did Duncan. "Would you like a drink?" he asked her.

"Any of that whiskey we were drinking?"

"Scotch?"

"Please."

The band began playing the British favorite *I'll Be Seeing You*. A moment later a Sergeant approached and said to Gabriella, "Would you like to dance?"

Duncan stepped in. "Sorry, Sergeant, we were about to." Duncan got up and looked down at Gabriella. He reached for her hand.

The Sergeant backed away. "Sorry, Sir."

Gabriella got up and she and Duncan made their way to the dance floor.

"I hope I'm not making trouble for you," Duncan said, waiting for her to accept his offer to dance.

She moved in close to him. She reached up. "I have not done this for over ten years," she said. "Since university."

"With?"

"A boy," she replied.

"A boy, or *the* boy?"

She looked up at him.

"You mean the one in the letter?"

As soon as he held her he felt a different sensation than any he had felt when dancing or holding a woman. He told himself maybe it was a feeling brought on by the fact that this woman he now held in his arms was once a nun. A nun who had already given birth to a child.

She leaned against him. Her head slowly fell to his shoulder and she rested there. The movement of her body in unison with his seemed effortless, as if they were one. The sudden new emotions that began to surface in him could not be easily ignored.

The band finished playing. Duncan looked at his watch. "You know, the only reason I called you was to deliver that letter. It's getting late and you must get back to your unit or Major Barfield will regret that he honored my request and gave you the pass to come to London for the evening."

Her reply sounded weary and distant. "He gave me a pass for tonight and all day tomorrow. He told me that I'd have trouble finding transportation this late at night, so to come back the following day."

Duncan stared at her. "Where are you staying? You ... found a place in London? How?"

She reached into the side pocket of her jacket. "Here's the address he gave me. Major Barfield said it is a private house. A room there. I'll have to locate it."

Duncan looked at it. "Means nothing to me," he laughed. "What do I know about London? This is only my third time here and it's always been business. But we can find it."

They headed back to the table.

"The dance was nice, Michael," she told him.

He smiled. "Very nice, but I think we should go now."

"Having a good time, Mike?" he heard Major McClure say as they reached the table. "I hope so."

"A nice party. Lots of happy people."

"And you," McClure said to Gabriella. "A good time?"

She laughed. "I'd have to say it's probably almost as much excitement as jumping out of an airplane, General."

McClure gave her a surprised look. "You?"

"It's an ambition of mine," she replied.

"What unit are you with?"

"101st," she told him.

"Paratroopers."

"Correct. I'm medical. The 326th Company."

"You speak English with an accent," McClure said. "Sounds ... a little German."

"Correct, Sir," Gabriella told him.

McClure frowned. "When did you come to the States?"

"Several years ago." She then looked at Duncan. "Michael was a big help in getting me there. He also helped get me into the Army."

McClure looked at Duncan. "Good work, Mike."

Duncan looked at Gabriella. "She's a good troop, General."

The three of them laughed.

"I've got a full day tomorrow, Mac," Duncan said to McClure. "It's time we pulled out. Thanks for inviting us."

"Yes," Gabriella said. "I had a good time."

McClure stood up from the table. So did the Colonel who was seated beside the female Lieutenant. McClure shook hands with Duncan. "See you tomorrow, Mike."

"Good luck, Private," the female Lieutenant said from her seated position.

"God bless you," Gabriella said instinctively. "And good luck."

The Lieutenant looked surprised and laughed. "A curious expression, but thank you,"

Gabriella smiled. "A old habit, but I'm sincere in saying it."

When Gabriella and Duncan got outside there was a heavy mist in the air. The chill went right through them.

"Glad I have my Doolittle jacket," Duncan said.

"Is that what they call it?"

"Unofficially. General Jimmy Doolittle gave it to me. I'll never give it up."

Gabriella hunched herself down as they stood there, no cars in sight.

"Let's go back inside," he said.

"Wait here a moment. I'll see what I can do."

It was General McClure who solved their problem. He assigned a Sergeant to drive them.

"Brass transportation," the Sergeant said. "We have two Fords. Where are we going?" he asked.

Duncan looked at Gabriella. She reached into her pocket and got out the paper with the address. She handed it to the Sergeant. He looked at it.

"Baywater Road."

"You know it?" Duncan asked.

"Yes, Sir. Out to Piccadilly to Park Lane then a short hop down Baywater Road."

They had no trouble finding it. When they pulled up Duncan peered out through the mist, so did Gabriella.

"Wait here, Sergeant, I want to make sure the lady gets settled."

"Yes, Sir."

They went up to the house and rang the bell. A man opened the door and squinted at them suspiciously.

Gabriella spoke to him. "I have been given permission from Major Barfield to have the apartment for the night."

The man looked at Duncan. "Him too? He staying too?"

"No, just me," she replied quickly.

"It's a nasty night," the man said. "He could stay if he likes. I get paid the same. But I don't allow any more than two."

"I'll not be staying," Duncan said. "But I will be coming in for a very short time. The lady and I have something to discuss. I have an Army car waiting."

"Very good." He moved aside and led them to the small room upstairs.

The mist from the night hung on them and they brushed at it. Gabriella took off her hat and jacket, Duncan did likewise. Gabriella jostled her hair in an attempt to dry it some. They each looked around. It was not a well lit room; electricity was a luxury. Duncan shook his jacket.

"Seems cozy," she said.

"It ought to work."

"Now," she said. "What was it you said to the man; you and I have something to discuss?"

"The letter you received seemed to upset you. Oh, you tried to hide it but it did upset you," he said confidently. "Am I right?"

Her eyes fell. "Mr. Duncan, my life has been ... an unusual one so far. You could never guess." She sat down on the bed. The bedframe readjusted and let out a noisy squeak. Duncan remained standing.

"I know more about you than you might suspect," he said.

She smiled. "I suspected you did," she said.

"It's a thing I learned on the job, over the years."

"Yes, of course."

"For example, you gave your child the name Willian Steffan Eichenstat, you gave the child the father's surname."

"I considered it a matter of honor to do so."

"Colonel Eichenstat, head of an important unit in the German Army."

She sat and stared up at him. "He ... is," she said softly. "Or, was. His letter said he thought he would be relieved soon. He had ... taken things too ... far." She knew what that meant. She wiped at her eyes. Her voice broke slightly. Then she looked up defiantly. "I will never see him again, but he at least now knows he has a son who carries his name. It is a proud name, His family ..." she stopped.

Duncan spoke softly. "Gabriella, I felt I had to tell you that I know something about Colonel Eichenstat. As soon as I learned that you had given that name to your child I made some inquiries."

"Yes, you are good at such things," she said with a tinge of irritation in her voice.

"I am, yes. Colonel Eichenstat has been in the Army's records file for some time now. We know of him from several points. For one thing we know of him from Father Konrad Schroeder through Sabastian Arceneau through the Gregory Foundation."

"Father Schroeder!" she said.

"And some others, but that is no matter here. I wanted you to know that you have my sympathy. I will help you whenever I can, and, if the time ever comes, I'll consider helping Colonel Eichenstat. But he is in a rather untenable position, doing what he is doing."

She sat silently, thinking. "He now has the picture of his son that I sent to Sabastian."

"That's good," Duncan commented.

"You have no children, do you, Duncan?"

"No. Not married. Never have been. Too busy, I guess."

"Will you one day?"

"Maybe."

A smile came to her face. "Did I ever think I'd ever have a ... child?" she said to herself more than to him. A tear worked its way slowly down her cheek. She did not wipe at it. She sniffled. "You'd better get out of here. You have important work to do tomorrow. Thanks again for bringing me the letter," she said haltingly.

He started to leave. "Will you be all right?" he asked.

She grinned, the reddish wetness still encompassing her face. "Thanks for your friendship, Duncan."

He frowned.

"What is it?" she said.

"Nothing," he shrugged. "It was a crazy thought."

"Well, let's have it."

He shook his head. "Wild," he said, shaking his head as he turned and headed for the door.

"You cannot leave without telling me," she demanded. "I insist."

He stopped and turned back around. She rose and came over to him. "Let's have it. I believe in honesty, Duncan."

He faced her squarely. "All right! I was wondering what you are going to sleep in tonight. I see you brought nothing with you and it's cold in here."

She gave him a questioning look, then she tilted her head and the look quickly turned to one of speculation.

"I have a toothbrush in by bag," she said, one eyebrow lower than the other.

He laughed. "Goodbye, Gabriella." He then turned and let himself out the door.

55

JANUARY 9, 1944
HEADQUARTERS, SUPREME ALLIED
COMMANDER
NORFOLK HOUSE, LONDON, ENGLAND

In a little less than a week General Dwight Eisenhower was scheduled to assume command of SHAEF, the newly formed command that had evolved from the original assortment of planning operations known as COSSAC (Chief of Staff to Supreme Allied Commander) headed by British Lieutenant General F. E. Morgan with an American Brigadier General R. W. Baker serving as his Deputy. Together, they had assembled the first planning staff and it was that staff that began the work that would eventually lead up to the big one - the invasion of the European continent - the second front that the Russians had been demanding. Now, in a week or so, Eisenhower, the

American General, would assume command of the greatly expanded cadre of planners consisting mostly of British and American military men and women with smatterings of individuals from the other allied nations. It was an accumulation of versatile and adroit people. By now the assembly had become so large and intertwined that making it all function adequately was a job for only the most gifted of leaders. Eisenhower was suppose to be that leader; it was his job to pull it off by selecting those people who could effectively oversee the various branches and accomplish the mission - the defeat of Germany.

Michael Duncan's schedule for the day was full. He arrived at Norfolk House early. To get to his first appointment he had to pass through a series of check points. As he moved along there was no mistaking the bustle. He knew the reason - Norfolk House would soon be abandoned as SHAEF's main headquarters; it would be moving farther from the center of London to its outskirts, to a place called Bushy Park. It was Eisenhower's decision. Bushy Park was the large open-spaced piece of land lying several miles to the west of Norfolk House which was almost in the center of London. The park and its new buildings would provide more space for this growing business of preparation for Europe's invasion, now known by its code name *Overlord*. Bushy Park was farther from the heart of the city but yet still close enough to the many government functions and well-established operations already going on throughout London's center. Many operational facilities were too complex to be moved and had to remain where they were. Communication and security issues had to be considered and some would be degraded by a move elsewhere. So, everyone had to make do and compromises had to be made. It was far from a perfect arrangement yet things had to be.

It was all so daunting, yet progress was expected no matter what problems cropped up, and problems cropped up hourly. So much was at stake. A failed invasion of the continent would be catastrophic. Everyone who worked close to the nerve center which was SHAEF knew this. It was a nerve center chocked full of people who lost sleep routinely contemplating the coming events.

Several floors up from the entrance Duncan was announced and walked into General McClure's office. When he saw McClure he thought he looked no worse for wear considering the previous night's activities. His uniform was crisply pressed and his shoes were brightly shined and he was freshly shaven; his hair combed neatly. His tie fit snugly against his neck.

Duncan had first met the General a year earlier when McClure was about to leave the States to assume his new post as military attache to the American Embassy in London. At that time Harry Hopkins had asked Duncan to arrange a meeting with McClure before the General left for that new assignment. Duncan had asked the reason and Hopkins only told him that McClure would be in position to possibly make insightful evaluations regarding certain British military behavior and pick up on the shortcomings. It was typical Hopkins. When it came to advising Roosevelt this man wanted eyes and ears in as many places as he could find. He never knew when he might need them.

Duncan and McClure had crossed paths again when Duncan had accompanied Hopkins to the conference between Roosevelt and Winston Churchill in Casablanca. By the time of the Casablanca meetings McClure was on Eisenhower's staff and stationed in North Africa where he was responsible for intelligence for the European theater. It was several days into the meetings before Duncan and McClure had a chance to talk privately, and at length. The two men had spent the night drinking in McClure's quarters and discussing a long list of issues, some business, some personal. Duncan liked McClure. He thought he had a clear head on his shoulders and was willing to hear all sides of an issue. Duncan saw him as a man who rarely committed himself to a firm position too quickly, although he had his fundamental first principles, and those he would not alter. Duncan found that several of these principles he, himself held. Duncan had come to see McClure as a man like himself, cautious, but not a rigid ideologue incapable of adapting to changing conditions; he seemed to assimilate new information with a meticulous scrutiny. Duncan judged that he admitted his mistakes but didn't create burdens for himself by dwelling inordinately on some failure in the past, but rather learned from them and moved on.

Duncan had just seated himself when McClure asked him, smiling, "How did you and the young lady finish off the evening, Mike? She seemed very nice."

"Extremely nice," Duncan said.

"What's with the comment that you helped her get to the States?"

"A friend asked me to help. I was able, and I did."

"What's her story? She seemed a little preoccupied."

"I didn't come here to discuss the previous life of a private in the U.S. Army, Mac," Duncan said. "How about let's get down to business?"

"I apologize," McClure said. "I shouldn't probe into someone else's private life."

Duncan waved his hand and smiled. "You're in intelligence, it's part of your nature."

"It's convenient to think that."

The two spent the next hour going over the things Duncan had come for. When they had finished Duncan asked, "How well are you up on the German officer corps, Mac?"

"We have the most information on the ones we know about who operate mostly in the western sectors of Europe. Of course, we could always use more." McClure looked at Duncan quizzically. "You have someone in particular in mind?"

"A Colonel Fritz Eichenstat."

"I'll have to make some inquiries on that one," McClure said. "Is he someone you think might be important?" McClure asked Duncan.

"This is personal."

"The private? The woman you were with last night?"

Duncan nodded.

McClure got up from the chair and began pacing. He rubbed his chin and pursed his lips. "Not sure what I can tell you but I'll have a look." Ten minutes later he was back. He was holding a folder. "Pretty sketchy," he told Duncan.

"Whatever you can give me," Duncan said.

McClure put the open folder on the table and studied it. He gave Duncan a quick rundown. Fritz Eichenstat, Colonel, single, never married, heads an intelligence section in charge of Jewish affairs and registration headquartered in Bremen. His family has been prominent, beginning with his grandfather. A brother, older, killed in the Great War, one sister, younger, both deceased. Father committed suicide 1939; reason questionable but there may have been some connection with a plot to kill Hitler back in 1938 or '39. Mother died shortly thereafter 1940, unusual circumstances, possibly also suicide. Eichenstat is well educated, Gottingen University, speaks several languages including English; good athlete, almost made the German Olympic team in 1936, marksman, pistol. Enlisted German army 1933; rose through the ranks quickly."

McClure paused.

"What is it, Mac?"

"A recent addition. Says he may be involved in helping Jews avoid the Nazis, maybe even some smuggling Jews out of Germany. That's a new one."

"How do you get such information? You think that's reliable?"

McClure tilted his head and smiled. He glanced back at the open folder. "All it says is from Gregory by way of Santa Clause."

"A code name no doubt."

"What do you think it is?"

"Anything in there about a fellow named Arceneau?"

"Someone you know?"

"Just curious," Duncan said.

McClure closed the folder. "That's all we have."

Duncan checked his watch and then grabbed his hat. "I've got to head to G-5. Meet with a Colonel Karl Bendetsen. Any chance we could have lunch?"

McClure laughed, then huffed, shaking his head, "I'm afraid not. I've got briefings and meetings all day."

"Good luck, Mac," Duncan said.

As he reached the door McClure stopped him. "Mike, one more thing in here. Eichenstat is flagged as someone who will surely be charged after the war with war crimes."

"He's helping Jews get out of the country," Duncan said.

"He's also helping to round them up. The entire unit may be charged."

"Think Eichenstat is aware of that possibility?"

"He probably thinks the Germans will win the war, so why worry about it."

"A stalemate is about the best he can hope for." Duncan said.

56

INVAƒION
JUNE, 1944
NORMANDY, FRANCE

They would be jumping in darkness into a landing zone they had studied but still knew very little about. For the paratroopers of the 101st Airborne Division the invasion of the western part of the European continent would begin at a place on the French coast called Normandy, and it would be their first exposure to actual combat.

On paper, the mission of the 101st was straightforward: to jump and land several miles behind a section of coastal beach, code named *Utah,* and secure the area by knocking out or capturing certain designated installations, thus preventing the enemy from moving in reinforcements to thwart or disrupt the subsequent beach landings that would take place several hours later two miles to their rear.

Elements of the 326th Medical Company would arrive in three waves: first, a few would jump with the combat troops and establish aid stations in the immediate landing zones; second some medical personnel would come in on gliders along with some of the heavier components needed to set up operations, items such as trailers and jeeps and the large, bulky containers of medical supplies; finally other medical personnel might arrive in a second wave of gliders, but most of the company would come by sea after the beach had been secured. Gabriella would be on a glider in the second wave.

Watching it all she could sense the tension in those around her; she herself was not immune. From her vantage point she had no doubts about the anxieties and the frayed nerves; she could see the stolid looks on the faces of some of the officers privy to carrying out orders, many being altered on the spot. At times it was if there were no plans, but, of course, there were. At this time innovation and quick thinking had to be paramount, and someone had to come up with quick solutions. She was thankful it wasn't her. Much was at stake.

There were rumors that many of the landings were in trouble. Some of the drops were hideously off target. Glider landings were always hazardous and really nothing but crash landings of a sort where nearly everyone involved came away with some kind of injury; back, neck, ribs, facial lacerations, ankles, or worse, death. It was always the hope that the injuries would not be too debilitating and that the mission would not be a failure because of them.

Just as the plan called for, the advanced members of the division's surgical team attached to the 326th had jumped with the opening assault and managed to set up shop in the Chateau Columbieres near the town of Hiesville. In the afternoon on D-Day Major Barfield and a large number of the company's personnel departed by glider. Gabriella was with them. The remainder of the unit would come that night by sea.

Gabriella's first glider landing was near perfect. She was back on the European continent. She disembarked with the rest of the troops out the front of the wooden aircraft while in the back a jeep pulling a small trailer packed with supplies rolled out. Gabriella jumped in beside the driver, two others from the unit got in the back seat. Gabriella and the two in the back were loaded down with packages of supplies draped over their shoulders in specially designed carrying bags. The driver of the jeep stopped and waited for instructions.

"Down that road," a lieutenant said, pointing.

The driver gunned the motor and the jeep lunged forward, everyone pitching forward with the sudden move. The area was heavily wooded and the road was narrow. Branches of trees and large shrubs hung over the road in places, making their progress turn to a crawl. Gabriella brushed at the branches as they slid over her. One low-hanging branch brushed over the driver's helmet as he hunched down to avoid it. She helped to hold it away from his face. Ahead of them several members of the unit were walking, tugging their loads of medical supplies. They moved to the side, making room for the passing jeep which moved cautiously.

One of soldiers walking, a slightly built young man, was struggling with his two heavy sacks of supplies.

"Stop," she told the driver.

He hit the brakes.

She jumped out.

"Get in soldier," she told the young man.

He stared at Gabriella. "I can make it," he stammered.

She grabbed his shirt and tugged him toward the empty seat. "I insist!"

"Come on, Private!" the driver yelled. "We're in the middle of a war! Get the fuck in here!"

The soldier quickly climbed in and the jeep headed off. Gabriella began walking.

There was sudden shooting up ahead, close. Everyone flattened themselves against the ground, their eyes peering out, checking. They heard more firing. They could tell it was rifle fire, not automatic. She knew it was German fire; the sound was unmistakable. Then came a long series of shots that sounded different, American for sure. Then more German. The exchange went on for several more minutes, then it stopped. She and the others on the ground began to rise, one after the other. A soldier up in front made his way forward, slowly, to take a look. He had no weapon. He disappeared around the bend. She heard yelling.

"Damn Krauts!"

She had a bad feeling. She was the second person to reach the bend in the road. When she went around it she saw the jeep stopped. Several soldiers huddled around. There was a German on the ground and another sitting against a tree, looking lost. The German soldier on the ground appeared to be dead. No one was paying any attention to him. There was plenty of attention being paid to a second German soldier propped against the nearby tree. An American soldier was screaming at him. "White Cross, you fucker! White Cross! Hospital!" He aimed his M1 rifle at the German as if to fire it. There was fear all over the German's face; he began crying. "Yellow fuckin' bastard!" The American screamed at him.

"Soldier!" Gabriella yelled with a voice that carried command qualities.

The soldier turned.

"We don't shoot prisoners! I'm a witness!"

"Who the hell are you, a German sympathizer? Look what this fucker done!"

She walked closer and saw the soldier she had let ride in her place. He was slumped over, blood splattered all over the seat and the dash. His lower face looked like a limp, red rag. She started to retch and thought sure she could not contain it. She fought to regain some composure. She looked back at the soldier.

"Is the German hurt?" she managed to ask.

"What!"

She went over to where the German was sitting. She spoke to him in German.

"Christ!" the American soldier yelped. "What the fuck is this!"

Gabriella examined the German for wounds. She touched him and he winced. She opened his tunic. There was blood. The German's eyes began to glaze over. She told him in German to hold on. By now the other members who had been behind her on the road had reached them and some of them crowded around her.

"Gabriella, what are you doing?" a nurse asked.

She opened the bag she was carrying and took out some heavy bandages and some gauze. She pressed them against the German's blood-soaked chest.

"Can someone help me?" she asked.

"Ahh, fuck!" the American soldier fussed again, then walked away in disgust. "Fuck! Fuck!" he said.

"What are we going to do?" another soldier asked her.

Gabriella looked up at those standing around her. She sensed what they were thinking; some of them knew her background and history.

A lieutenant came up. "Let's get this show on the road," he said. We have to get to the station up ahead."

"The German prisoner, Sir?" Gabriella said, eyeing the lieutenant.

He looked down at the German, then over at the jeep where several soldiers were removing the body of the American and placing it in a body bag.

"He do that?" the lieutenant asked.

"Maybe," she said. "Does it matter? This man is hurt. He needs . . .

"What he needs, soldier, is a bullet in his head. He fired on defenseless medical personnel; we carry no weapons. Good thing those paratroopers were nearby."

"Sir, he . . ."

"Get the bastard on a stretcher. Take him with us," he ordered angrily. "This war is going to be pure hell. God help us!" He walked away.

Gabriella looked around. "Any stretchers?"

Several male personnel came over. "Put him on the top of the trailer. That's all we have."

"Okay," she said. "Can you help carry him?"

Two soldiers lifted the German, now barely conscious.

"He's lost much blood," Gabriella said.

"If we get fired on again we're using this guy as a shield," one soldier promised.

The dead American in the body bag was already lying on top the trailer. They put the German beside the dead American.

"Shit, this is obscene!" one soldier said, seeing it. "Christ!"

The German was not secure on top. The jeep started to move and he began to slip.

"Wait," Gabriella yelled.

She climbed on top the trailer and held him in place.

"Look at that shit," a soldier said to his buddy as they looked on.

It was a short trip to the medical hospital station. There were wounded lying on the large bricked entrance to the Chateau Columbieres where the unit had set up. The wounded were being attended to and having their wounds assessed to determine priority and treatment.

Sporadic gunfire sounded in the distance in several different locations. American and German soldiers were fighting it out in small groups, sometimes as isolated warriors. The Chateau seemed out of danger, for the moment. But that could change.

Doctor Daniel Gordon came out on the porch to take a look at how many wounded awaited to be treated, and what their status looked like. He had a cigarette in his hand. He spotted Gabriella as she tended the German who was being taken from the jeep trailer. He saw the body bag being lifted from the top of the trailer. Gabriella went along with the German as he was placed on the stone flooring of the entranceway along with the injured American soldiers. Gordon watched as the German grabbed Gabriella's uniform and pulled her closer. She nodded strenuously with her face close to his. Gordon sensed the

German was badly wounded and, moments later, there was no mistaking when he died. She tried to undo the grip he had on her uniform.

"Captain Gordon," a nurse said from the doorway. "We need you in here."

He turned and went back inside, throwing his cigarette away.

"Get Private Sommers in here, please," he ordered a nurse. She's just outside tending to the wounded. I need her in here."

Over the next three days the remainder of the 326th stragglers found their way to the Chateau and hurriedly jumped into their assigned tasks. The surgeons now worked three tables, operating on the most seriously wounded. By June ninth, the injured began to be taken back to the beaches for evacuation to England.

For the first several days the Germans were all around them. The hospital was bombed several times and, because of the severe damage, had to move its location. No one was killed, but the medical staff did suffer some injuries. Fortunately, many of the injured soldiers had been moved shortly before the bombs fell and, as a result, casualties were slight among the few fighting troops still confined with them.

Several days later the company moved to the nearby town of Carentan after it had been captured following some hard fighting. It remained there for three weeks before moving to the coastal city of Cherbourg along with the entire division. A week later they were all back in England.

Relieved of the stress of constant work, Gabriella took the opportunity to compose a letter to Anna and one to the sisters at St. Bernard in Nashville. She then wrote a short one to Michael Duncan. She wasn't exactly sure why she felt she should, or wanted to but after reading it over she decided to wait before sending it out.

That day the tent-like living quarters which she shared with three other nurses was quiet. She was alone. It was hot for a July day in England and both ends of the tent were flipped back and wide open for whatever ventilation breeze might come through. She heard footsteps. A soldier stuck his head inside.

"Yes?" Gabriella said.

"I have a message for Private Sommers," he said.

"I'm Sommers," she replied.

"Major Barfield wants to see you."

She got up and followed the corporal. He was a thin, lanky boy of about twenty with blond hair that was beginning to show curl from under his cap. Acne covered his face. They went into the building where Major Barfield had his office. Two soldiers were at their desks typing, another stood at a filing cabinet holding a bundle of papers which seemed too much for him to keep control of and she thought they were about to slip from his hand. The blond-haired corporal went into the Major's office. He came out and told her to go inside.

Gabriella went in and saluted.

"At ease, Sommers," Barfield said. "Have a seat."

She sat in the straight-back chair.

Barfield smiled. "Relax, please."

She grinned. "I'm relaxed. Major, really."

"General Gold has inquired about you," he then said.

It surprised Gabriella. "What about?" she asked.

"He wanted to know how you handled yourself."

She looked away for a moment. "Well, I hope I did my duty."

"And then some, I'd say. I'm promoting you, Private," he said. "For outstanding service and quick thinking."

"Oh, that," she replied.

"Seems the soldier surely would have shot the prisoner," Barfield stated.

"It did look bad."

"Captain Gordon is lucky to have you on his team."

"No, Sir, *I* am the lucky one when it comes to that."

"Well, of course, I understand. But you and your colleagues did some excellent work under some trying circumstances."

"We all did, Sir. You, yourself."

He laughed. "It was some experience, wasn't it?"

"We made it out of there alive. We're luckier than some."

He dropped his eyes. "You know, Sommers, I wanted to request that you be transferred to my immediate team."

"Sir?" she frowned.

"Don't worry, I changed my mind. That would be a disservice to your commanding officer. After all, he has a lot invested in you and you seem to like working for him."

"I'm well satisfied with my present assignment, Sir."

He smiled. "Well, no matter, you are at least in the immediate vicinity if I feel I need your services, and talents. You are a most remarkable individual. I hope you don't mind my saying that."

"No ... Sir."

"I'm sure Gordon won't object to your promotion. Get yourself some Corporal stripes."

She smiled. "Very well, Sir. Is that all, Sir?"

"That's all."

She stood up. "Sir, any word on when our next mission will be?"

He shook his head. "Nothing."

"How are things going ... over there?" she asked.

"The hedgerows have been awful. A perfect defensive environment, it seems. Inch by inch, yard by yard, day by day," he described. "Something had better be done soon. We're losing steam, and troops."

"I didn't know it was so bad."

"In a way it's beginning to look much like the last war, minus the trenches."

Gabriella remembered hearing about those trenches from her father and family's friends. "Oh."

Barfield looked at her. "I can't imagine the effect this war must be having on you, Sommers. Your background, your nationality, your family and friends who must be still in Germany; it must ..." He shook his head. "I'm sorry, I shouldn't put that burden on you."

"I pray a lot, Major," she said quietly.

He stood looking at her. "Admirable," he said.

She smiled. "I have a feeling you do too."

A quick frown appeared, then disappeared. "At times," he muttered.

She smiled. "I'm glad."

"That's all, Pri ... Sorry, Corporal."

"Thank you, Sir." She saluted and left.

The breakout from the hedgerow country, code name *Cobra*, came about ten days later. It was aimed at a weak spot in the German lines resulting because the Germans were now concentrating their troops around the battle against Field Marshall Montgomery going on for the city of Caen. Operation *Cobra* began with a thunderous concentrated air assault. Right off there were mishaps. American troops were killed accidently by bombs falling short of their targets. A week later the breakout was complete and General Omar Bradley's forces were streaming through and beginning to crawl all over the low lying countryside on the other side - ideal terrain for fast moving tanks and other motorized vehicles. Large portions of the German army were captured or killed. The war in Europe took on a new dimension now, with potentially breathtaking results.

Airborne units were not used in Operation *Cobra*. Back in England the 101st spent its time training, repairing its equipment, and readying for the next mission. Eventually it came. However, it was a mission that was not designed or planned by the division's American officers; it was a British affair, an offensive largely planned and led by British Field Marshall Bernard Law Montgomery. Its code name was *Market Garden* and it was designed as a massive, single strike through the Netherlands right at the heart of German war production - the Ruhr Valley.

MARKET GARDEN
AUTUMN, 1944

Operation *Market Garden* began on September 17, 1944 as a line of paratroop drops by the American 101st, the 82nd Divisions, and the British 1st Airborne Division, along a corridor marked by a single, narrow road across the Dutch countryside linking the towns of Eindhoven on the western end, Nijmegen in the middle, and Arnhem in the east, on the Lower Rhine River. The overall mission was to capture key bridges along this corridor and open a gateway into the German Ruhr Valley at Arnhem. The ultimate prize was the bridge over the Rhine River at Arnhem.

Gabriella got the word in the late afternoon hours of September thirteenth. She would be in the second glider wave leaving on September eighteenth along with most of the other nurses a day after the first wave.

Unlike the drop into Normandy the drops in Operation *Market Garden* took place in daylight, September 17, 1944. The 101st was dropped near the town of Son in Holland not far from Eindhoven. Son was also the destination for Gabriella and the rest of the 326th Medical Company.

Major Barfield and fifty-two others were the first to go. They left from Ramsbury Airport in the morning on September seventeenth. The trip was uneventful except for some distant flack. There were no injuries or damage to any of the equipment and the landings were not severe. They unloaded as they had been trained and immediately began tending to wounded soldiers. Soon the tents were up and surgeries began. The whole thing went according to the book. Later that day they moved into an abandoned hospital in the town of Son.

Gabriella and two hundred and eighteen others of the company left the next day from Wilford Airdrome by glider. This time their landing was bumpy, one wing cracked off as the glider struck a tree. There were several broken bones and many bruises inside, but no fatalities, although other planes suffered more damage. By that evening everyone who had made it in were all in place.

The airborne infantry's landing zone was several miles north and west of Eindhoven in the vicinity of four smaller towns: Son, Best, St. Oedenrode, and Veghel. In each town there were objectives to be reached. One regiment landed ten miles from Veghel but managed to get to the two bridges it was ordered to capture. A second regiment landed near St. Oedenrode and took the bridge over the Dommel River, its main objective. It then sent a company to the town of Best, believing the town was not heavily defended, to try and capture the bridge over the Wilhelmina Canal there. They met stiff German resistance and, by nightfall, the Americans withdrew, leaving the bridge in tact. A third regiment landed closest to the town of Son. The principal objective there was the swing bridge, the most important bridge assigned to the 101st in the Eindhoven area. German resistance delayed them just long enough to allow the bridge to be blown.

That left the bridge back at Best. It was still standing, but defended. One battalion went after it again; then a second joined them, but the Germans held. Shortly thereafter, the Germans destroyed it.

As the struggle for the Best bridge was going on another regiment moved into Eindhoven, the largest town in the region and the direct link to Nijmegen farther down the road. Soon several bridges across the Dommel River were taken. Not long after, they began to see the first trickles of troops of the British armor units coming up the road from the west.

Capturing the bridges would keep the corridor open for the movement of British armor all the way along to Arnhem where they would link up with British paratroopers who had worked their way into the town, and were holding for now. Once linked, paratroopers and British armor would then complete the mission and capture the bridge across the Rhine. That done, Arnhem would become the gateway into the German Ruhr Valley. In theory it was sound, even brilliant, but too much could go wrong, and did.

Although the initial drops appeared to come off with reasonably good order too many things went badly too quickly all up and down the narrow road, especially for the British around Arnhem. For one thing, radio communications among British units were nearly non-existent, a result of faulty equipment. As a result, coordinating movements of different units that were coming into Arnhem from different directions were seriously hampered. It was nearly impossible to call for changes in plans or inform others of a unit's changing condition. But the British suffered other misfortunes. The single most damaging one was to find the German 2nd SS Panzer Corps sitting in Arnhem on the other side of the bridge. The Germans had been sent there for rest and refitting. British planners had been either unaware of this situation, or had ignored intelligence that warned of this near certain possibility. Either way, the lightly armed British paratroopers could not prevail for long against such a force and were soon worn down. Although they fought valiantly, in the end, they could not hold, and the bridge was never wrestled from German hands.

Operation *Market Garden* was a disappointing failure leading to the loss of many men, most of whom were members of the British 1st Airborne Division. The operation's failure to succeed at Arnhem meant that, in effect, the new front in Holland was now located at Nijmegen.

Gabriella saw her share of wounded and damaged soldiers during her time at the hospital at Son. Many were walking wounded, others were more serious. Movement of the wounded back to the rear was hampered by the massive traffic of British troops moving east toward Arnhem. As a result the wounded began to crowd the hospital. The roads between Veghel and St. Oedenrode and between Best and St. Oedenrode were cut several times by the Germans only to be reopened again by the Americans. It was back and forth.

A few days after taking up her position at the hospital Gabriella learned that Major Barfield was asking for volunteers. He needed a surgical team to go to Veghel to assist a platoon of the 50th Field Hospital that had recently been attached to the company and she wanted to be included. When she finally reached Major Barfield she learned that Lieutenant Gordon had already volunteered his small unit for the job.

"So I'm going," she said to Barfield.

"Gordon volunteered you."

"Then I'm going."

"I suppose you are," he muttered. "I'm not happy about it but he insisted. He said he needs you if he is going to perform any surgery."

The team sent to Veghel remained there for nearly three weeks until the platoon of the 50th moved on to set up shop in Nijmegen. At that time Gabriella and Gordon and the small surgical team also moved. They joined another part of the company in Nijmegen which had already begun operating a hospital there.

Soldiers began coming in who had terrible injuries to their lower extremities from stepping on German mines. Several died of shock and almost all had to undergo amputations at the knee.

One night, one of the soldiers lying in bed, was despondent about his amputated leg. He was trying not to cry. She comforted him. She managed to get him to calm down some but he was still angry with his condition. How could anyone blame him, she thought.

"Might as well let the Germans have me now. Let them put me in one of their gas contraptions I've heard about. I'm Jewish. They'd like that!"

"How will they get to you? You're buddies won't let that happen." she said.

"Honey," he said. "I know more about the Germans than you do. We're operating on a thin string out there. Any moment they could bust in here and cart us all off."

"Oh," she said. "That would not be good for me."

"They'd leave the girls alone, I think."

"Even the Jewish ones."

He looked at her and frowned. He looked around. "Where?"

"Right here," she said. "Me. I'm Jewish."

"Yeah ... you ... are you ..."

"A German Jew," she said, nodding. "Honest. And I don't want to be carted off to Germany, even though I have friends and family there."

"I'll be damned," the soldier said.

"No you aren't. God loves you. Christ loves you."

"What kind of Jew are you anyway?" he asked, almost recoiling.

"A good one, I hope."

He shook his head, then grinned. She was holding his hand.

"You're going home now, soldier."

He laughed. "Down that road!"

"Soon, yes, down that road. You are a member of a fine fighting outfit and your buddies will get that road open, and keep it open."

She got up to leave. He reached to make her come back. "Tell me, how was it you got into this outfit? An American outfit."

"It's a long story, soldier."

The following day she was working in the supply room when she heard the high pitch screech.

"Incoming!" someone yelled. Then the explosions, then another hiss and another explosion. Rockets! The roar of airplane engines screamed overhead, and then faded. Everyone was scrambling, yelling. Dust and pieces of brick and mortar tumbled about. She ran toward the door and into the room where the patients were in their beds or chairs. Many were already on the floor, waiting for the next blows, but no more blows came. It was over.

There were casualties. Inside the building two of the officers were killed instantly along with one enlisted man. Outside, a Quartermaster truck was delivering rations when it was hit by a bomb, killing three of its men. In the company there were several injured, two seriously. She knew one of the officers who had been killed. He was a Lieutenant and he had a wife. He and Gabriella had shared a few leisurely talks during times of calm and she immediately began thinking of what he had said to her. He could hear his voice. He was not a medical man; his duties were strictly in administration, in supply. That evening Major Barfield was looking at a photograph from the man's wallet as he was putting his personal effects in a large envelope readying them for movement with the unit to another location farther to the rear of the division. The hospital had been damaged too severely to continue at its present location.

"I haven't had to write one of these letters before," he told her as she stood at the door where he had seen her watching him. She told him that the orderly she had sent to check on a suitcase full of medical supplies told her he could not locate it. She wondered if it was here in his office.

"Forget it," he said. "It'll turn up."

She left and sat outside. She needed some air. Sitting on the fender of one of the vehicles that was loading up for the move she began thinking of the thing she had not thought about in a long time - coming to terms with the quick, sudden death of people like the young Lieutenant. Could she convince herself that in war people have to die? Could she accommodate the reality of all this? There was no time, she told herself. Other more important things always pushed that kind of thinking out of the way. Maybe to save lives, other lives had to be sacrificed. That was the only answer she had at the moment; it was the only one she always had. She had not moved beyond that. Not yet.

She slid off the fender and went back inside. As she walked she couldn't help but whisper a silent prayer for the widow who would be soon receiving the awful news of her husband's fate.

57

LATE FALL, 1944
MOURMELON, FRANCE

Operation Market Garden lasted seventy one days. When it was over the 326th Medical Company was ordered out of Holland and sent to Camp Mourmelon, in France, along with almost all of the elements of the 101st Division. It left behind only four members to tend to the division's rear detachment. By December 1, 1944 everyone from the medical unit was out of Holland and back in France.

Even though Gabriella was back at Camp Mourmelon she had a hard time forgetting. The scenes of her giving her seat in the jeep to that young soldier, and his almost immediate death because of it, and the death of the lieutenant in Nijmegen during the rocket attack on the hospital kept flashing before her when she tried to sleep, or tried to write a letter. The pictures were always just below the surface and they popped up routinely. She had always found refuge in thinking that such unhappy things were God's will, but that was a belief that was becoming harder for her to hold on to. It was her nature to struggle with such things. Her training in philosophy had a tight hold on her and she easily fell into the mode of examining all the parameters of a situation on her way to a satisfying answer. She had not found that satisfying answer yet and she feared she never would.

She put her best efforts forward as she tried to tend to the business of nursing and being a member of the 326th. News about the war was everywhere, mostly hearsay, but some reliable.

The most unnerving news was what she heard about Aachen. She learned that the battle for the city had been deadly and there had been much destruction. Bombs and artillery had smashed its buildings; there was much rubble. Aachen was the first major city on German soil to have been invaded by ground troops and it was a city that marked a powerful symbol for the Germans, and for Hitler. It was the birthplace of Charlemagne and the site of his tomb in the great Cathedral. Aachen was more than just another German city. Hitler referred to the coronation of Charlemagne as the beginning of the *First* Reich and he ordered Aachen defended to the last. The costs were high. It was a murderous, dirty battle, street-to-street, house-to-house, room-to-room. Both sides suffered terribly. The end had come on October twenty-first when the German defenders surrendered after suffering five thousand casualties and having fifty six hundred prisoners taken. The American's losses were being reported at five thousand killed, wounded, or missing.

Hearing of Aachen brought thoughts of Father Schroeder to Gabriella's mind. Had he survived? Where was he now? By any chance, she thought, had Fritz Eichenstat been involved? It all made her so sad and added to her depressed spirits.

When she had first arrived back at Camp Mourmelon she had found several letters waiting. Several were from Anna, who was doing well, working hard, gaining on the world. She was studying still at Vanderbilt; history and math mostly. She had even gone to a football game and been on several picnics in a large park outside the city.

One letter was from Sister Mary Ursula telling her how much little William was growing and changing and how much she enjoyed taking care of him. The other nuns helped some, she told Gabriella. Her last part of her letter touched Gabriella deeply. The nun wrote how much she admired and respected Gabriella for the way she was living her life and the way she seemed to possess an inner peace after all the things that had happened to her. Sister Mary Ursula wanted to be like Gabriella. There was a picture included. Gabriella held it, thinking of her child, and of Sister Mary Ursula, young and excited to be a nun, still able to see things with some idealism. Maybe, Gabriella too had once been that way.

There was one other letter. She turned it over, seeking a return address. There was none. It looked official, but not military. She slipped her fingernail under the flap and sliced it open. The letter heading read: White House, Washington D.C. It was from Michael Duncan. All it said was that he hoped she was doing all right. He knew she had been in Normandy and guessed she had been, for some of the time anyway, in Holland, only because he knew the 101st was playing an integral part in the operation. The letter was dated October twentieth. He signed off as *Your Friend.*

What the letter didn't say was that Michael Duncan had been making inquiries about Colonel Fritz Eichenstat based on some of the things he had learned from General McClure. These inquiries had led him almost immediately to Sabastian Arceneau and the Gregory Foundation. At the Gregory he ran up against some rather stiff resistence; even his usual ploy of trying to bluff his way around these obstacles didn't work at first. However, his persisted attempts did manage to dislodge some valuable information from one of the staff members who knew more about Eichenstat because she knew of the Gregory's relationship with Sabastian Arceneau, and Father Schroeder. Besides, as she stated to Duncan, she liked the manner in which he asked his questions and felt he deserved some honest answers. From all he had learned from these limited sources Duncan had concluded that Eichenstat was more than a mere German soldier who happened to be a Colonel in the German Army. The man was playing a dangerous game. He was not a traitor in the strictest sense, but he would surely be seen as one by the Nazis, and as a war criminal by any tribunal after the war. Duncan had worked this information over in his mind many times and he always came up with the same conclusion: The odds were against Eichenstat coming out of this war with much of a future, no future at all really. But the man had a conscience and he was acting on it the best he could. Duncan was certain Eichenstat was a tortured man.

NOVEMBER 30, 1944
BREMEN, GERMANY

Colonel Fritz Eichenstat was packing his belongings. He had been away for the past week, trying to get ready for his next assignment. He would be part of Major Otto Skorzeny's team of infiltrators who were ordered to move behind the American lines in the big German offensive planned for the Ardennes Forest in Belgium. Preparations were still moving forward but the attack would begin in three weeks. Eichenstat had fought his transfer for as long as he could but Skorzeny had gotten what he wanted.

Eichenstat stood in his office and looked at the boxes he had assembled. There was only one small box that he really cared about, the one that contained a few personal possessions; the other boxes contained military material all belonging to the Reich. There was no box for his immediate family; there was no immediate family any longer.

He was not officially relieved of his duties just yet, however. His replacement had not been assigned according to General Reinard. Until then he was to remain in his headquarters unless Skorzeny needed him to be away for training, or something else; then Eichenstat should name a temporary replacement from one of the lower ranking officers, preferable Major Hans Brauer. General Reinard had a fondness for Brauer, and Eichenstat knew the reason.

He placed the boxes to the side of the room.

His aide, Sergeant Stuts Uber, surprised him with the announcement that Major Otto Skorzeny was arriving shortly.

"Did he say why he was coming?" Eichenstat asked.

"No, Sir."

"Very well."

Uber left and Eichenstat sat down to wait. For some reason he was calm. He had resigned himself to his fate but he did want to have time to arrange for the one small box of his personal possessions to be taken to the convent in Köln, however. He hoped Skorzeny would give him that time before he took him off to their unstated destination. He still had the thought that after all this was over that, somehow, Gabriella would find the box at the convent, broken and destroyed as it was. He called for Seargent Uber.

"Seargent I want this box delivered to the convent in Köln."

"Immediately, Sir?"

"After I leave."

"Yes, Sir."

Five minutes later Skorzeny arrived and was shown in.

He was smiling. "Now you will see what real war is all about, Colonel. You will play a big part in a very important operation. No more silly inglorious moving around of people and keeping track of insignificant peasants who just get in the way of the Reich's destiny, huh? We will be decorated by the Fuhrer."

This is a madman, Eichenstat thought. He talked like a man who saw all this as some great adventure in which he got to play a hero's part. Maybe he had a death wish. Maybe it was because Skorzeny was a man who was fortunate not to have had to live with the things Eichenstat had been living with. Eichenstat had already determined that Skorzeny saw himself as a pure Aryan warrior. In return, Eichenstat suspected that Skorzeny saw him as something much less, but he had skills that the Reich needed now, and it seemed clear he was about to get to try them out.

Eichenstat showed no emotion; he was beyond that.

"Listen, I believe you have already resigned yourself to not coming back. I can tell when a man has reached that point," Skorseny told him.

"Maybe I shouldn't participate then if I see myself that way?"

Skorzeny narrowed his eyes. "No, Colonel, I cannot afford not to have you along. You speak English too well. And, besides, after the training you received, you will serve my purposes better then any other man I have. You put on an American uniform and you could fool General Eisenhower himself." Skorzeny laughed.

"Oh, yes, the man we are going to assassinate?" Eichenstat said dismally.

Skorzeny's face brightened. He said excitedly. "Yes, yes, we could get that far. Yes indeed."

"Is that our objective?" Eichenstat asked blandly.

"No, we are being sent to disrupt the initial communications and create confusion behind their lines. We alter signposts, we create panic in the rear by getting the enemy to think they cannot trust anyone, not even their own people. That's why the uniforms and the language. They will believe we are Americans."

"And if we are captured?"

Skorzeny shrugged. "They will stand us against a tree and shoot us. So what of it? Are you afraid to die for the Fuhrer?"

"I'd rather live for the ... Fuhrer," Eichenstat said. "Dead I am no good to him. Neither are you. There are not many of us left. I've seen the figures. We're not staffing divisions at full strength. We now send them out at only ten to eleven thousand men, Major. That's not even two-thirds normal size. Raw, inexperienced kids with little or no training. They are divisions in name only."

Skorzeny lowered his gaze, and shrugged. "That is why we must succeed. When Colonel Peiper punches through and gets to Antwerp we will have the Americans and British in a bad way. They will have little means to supply their troops. They will surely seek a truce then. When that is done we can take on the Russians with full force."

Eichenstat thought it best to cease this conversation. He could not stand to hear such talk any longer. He had heard too much of it in the past and look what it had brought them. "Any further advice, Major?"

"Remain light on your feet, Colonel, and ready to move quickly."

"I get the picture."

Skorzeny reached the door and turned. "This offensive will get Aachen back in German hands, and it will remain there."

The mention of Aachen brought Father Schroeder's face to Eichenstat's mind. He thought: should he try to contact him? What use would it be, he wondered. He had thought of the priest all the while Aachen had been under attack. Now, once again, he would be directly in the line of fire as the Germans moved back through the area to recapture the city.

Eichenstat said with dry emotion, "I'm sure the Fuhrer will be pleased."

Skorseny slapped his gloves together and smiled broadly as he left.

Eichenstat thought: the man can't wait to get back in the fight, as hopeless as it seemed.

58

MID-DECEMBER, 1944
CAMP MOURMELON, FRANCE

The ranks were buzzing: *Home by Christmas.* The Germans were finished and everyone had it figured: collapse could not be far off. For the previous two weeks the number of German prisoners had risen daily, and was still on the rise; they came in weary, depressed, demoralized, hungry, sick, and injured. Gabriella saw some of them in the hospital set aside for POWs. She had helped treat a few of the more seriously wounded. They were her own countrymen, Germans; it gave her a peculiar feeling. She felt that some of the other members of the company were watching her to see how she might react to this circumstance. To her, the German soldiers were injured and needed attention, that's all she saw; that's all she could afford to see.

Home by Christmas. The sentiment had gained momentum and now it was mid-December; everyone was preparing for the traditional celebrations. They were gathering up materials and food items for parties where feelings long repressed could be let loose. It was good therapy just to be able to anticipate it all. The war in Europe was almost over.

Gabriella had just fallen asleep on her small, flimsy canvas cot when the yelling woke her. She heard hurried footsteps outside. She sat up, then threw her legs over the edge and shuffled with her shoes; she stood and threw on her robe.

"Everyone up! Out!" came the cry.

It was Sergeant Pickens. He was Major Barfield's chief organizer and unofficial watchman of the headquarters office.

He stuck his head inside. "Move, move! Get your gear! We have been ordered out!"

"Where to, Sarge?" she asked.

"Somewhere in Belgium," he yelled. "Don't know where exactly but they say we're needed." He darted back out the tent and on to the next one. She could hear him yelling again. "Up and out! We got business!"

Only a few people knew exactly where they were headed; it was a place called Bastogne. The entire division would be on the move. She gathered up the equipment she was expected to have with her; every member had such a package of materials. Everyone was scrambling. In addition, she was responsible for certain other medical supplies and she rushed to the supply room where men were already packing and moving boxes around. She stood for a while checking their progress and making sure they included everything. As soon as there was a carton or crate fully ready there were men waiting to lift it up and move it to the trucks and jeeps now forming up on the roads a short distance away. Eventually orders came down the line and the last of the soldiers still on the ground began climbing aboard.

They departed on the evening of December eighteenth and arrived in the vicinity of Bastogne at ten in the morning on the following day. They had ridden all night. The weather was the worst it had been in a long time, icy cold, windy at times, blowing snow, foggy, just miserable. They could hear guns in the distance. There was a steady shouting as they disembarked. On the ground they waited for orders. Major Barfield assembled his company. Lieutenant Colonel Gold, the division surgeon, and Barfield conferred. They then took off together in a jeep with Sergeant Pickens driving.

Gabriella made her way to a patch of trees a short distance away where some of the members of her small surgical team were standing, shivering, beating their hands together and stomping their feet to augment the warmth of their bodies. Trucks moved past them in a constant stream, heading east.

"They're moving into Bastogne," one of the men said.

"How far away?" Gabriella asked him.

The soldier shrugged. "Ten, fifteen miles, they say."

"I wonder if we'll go there too?" she said.

Someone nearby said, "Major Barfield and Colonel Gold went off to find a suitable location for our clearing station somewhere outside of Bastogne proper."

Soon Barfield and Gold were back.

"Listen up, Gold ordered. "We're going to set up the clearing station just down the road a few miles." He pointed.

"Where the hell is this Bastogne?" someone yelled.

Gold replied, pointing, "Ten miles down this road. We'll set up about seven miles back from the town."

"Where the hell are the Germans?" another asked.

Gold and Barfield looked at each other. Barfield pointed. "Out there," he said. "Listen, men, this is a nasty counterattack the Germans have unleashed. That's the word I received. This won't be an easy time for any of us. Everything is still very fluid and no one knows what to expect. But we must hurry; we have little time to get ready. Improvise. The guys in the division are counting on us. Let's get moving."

Everyone scrambled back into the vehicles. Their motors had not stopped running. Now the scratching and grinding of gears rumbled through the night air. They began to move. A short while later they stopped again.

"This is it," Barfield yelled from up front. He began directing things. Tents went up, crates and trunks were unpacked and the place began taking on the look of a clearing station and field medical facility.

More and more soldiers began hurrying past them, heading in the direction from which they had just come, back away from Bastogne. Their faces were drawn with looks of considerable anxiety; an inner panic had set in. Many were empty handed, no weapons, a sure sign of a hasty retreat.

It soon became apparent that these were the troops who had first faced the Germans as they came out of the Ardennes.

"What's happening?" Gabriella asked one of them as he hurried past her on the open road.

He stared at her with red, wide eyes. "Germans everywhere," he managed to tell her. His voice trembled slightly. "Lots of em.' Tanks too." He shook his head, then pointed over his shoulder. "They came out of nowhere."

"Good luck, soldier," she said to his back.

The last of the trucks carrying the men of the division moved into Bastogne. Wounded soldiers were already coming into the station and both Barfield and Gold knew that something would have to be done to lessen the burden on the station.

Major Barfield bagan checking his map. "The 107th Evacuation Hospital. It's not far," he said to Gold. "Word is they have set up in Libin," he pointed. "Ten, twelve miles to the south from where we are here. I'll take several trucks of injured there and see if I can requisition some additional ambulances from them and bring them back."

Gold told him, "I've got to dispatch some of our jeep ambulances to our regimental and battalion surgeons around Bastogne. Four or five vehicles to each unit should do it."

"Sounds right," Barfield agreed. "Let's hope it's enough to get their wounded back to us."

Just before five o'clock that evening Major Barfield took off with five ambulances full of patients, headed for Libin and the 107th Evacuation Station.

Gabriella and the others worked at getting ready to handle whatever came at them. They had been trained well and they felt they were ready. But planning was never all inclusive or took care of every contingency; things could unravel. This time things did unravel in a bad way.

At about ten thirty that evening they heard the unmistakable rumblings and clanking of armored vehicles coming down the road. Within minutes the entire station was being sprayed with machine gun fire. Staff and patients fell to the ground and began crawling for cover. Several trucks outside were riddled with bullets; soon they were ablaze from the shells. The machine gun fire continued for fifteen minutes. No one in the unit had fired back.

A German officer came forward.

"This is a medical station!" Gold yelled, throwing his arms in the air. "Didn't you see the white cross!" Again he pointed.

From his demeanor it appeared the German was not moved by Gold's outburst. He spoke German to Gold. Gold shook his head.

"Sommers," he yelled. "Get Sommers up here. I can't make sense of this guy."

Everyone looked around.

"Sommers," someone yelled loudly. Gabriella soon appeared inside at the other end of the tent.

Outside, sitting in an American jeep, dressed in the uniform of an American Captain, Colonel Fritz Eichenstat heard the yell for Sommers. He turned toward the yell. He jumped out of the jeep.

"We have to move on, Colonel," his driver said. "Up this road."

Eichenstat ignored him. He headed for the tent and peered through the opening in the flaps. He saw the German officer. He went in further and positioned himself off to the side between two German soldiers who were watching for any sign of trouble from the Americans. There was little light in the tent. The mayhem of the shooting had thrown everything into disarray. There were only two small lamps with flickering lights. Shadows floated heavily through the place.

The German officer spoke to Gold. Gold turned to Gabriella. "What did he say?"

Gabriella grimaced. "He said we are all prisoners of war and will be taken into Germany."

From the corner of the tent Eichenstat maneuvered to get a better look. His mind screamed at him. Gabriella! He was in near shock. His heart pounded. He inched to the side to get a better look. "Gabriella," he said to himself again. "Oh, Gabriella. How the hell could it be you?"

"What about my wounded?" Gold was saying to the German. "Ask him," he said to Gabriella.

She spoke in German. The officer raised his chin stiffly and spoke.

Gabriella listened and then told Gold, "He says the wounded must come too. Everyone must come. We are all prisoners."

"I need some time," Gold said. "Thirty minutes at least, maybe a little more. Tell him. I need time to prepare the wounded for movement."

Again Gabriella spoke in German. The officer saluted Gold and said something.

Gold turned to Gabriella.

"What?" he asked.

"He says to hurry. The trucks are outside. He has no time to waste. The town is being surrounded."

"Bastogne?" Gold asked her. "Bastogne is being surrounded?"

"I suppose, Sir."

"Prepare the wounded for the trucks," Gold ordered loudly to those around. "Pass the word. There is to be no resistance. We are a medical unit protected by the Geneva Convention. Any resistance will mean ... well you all know what it could mean. Get moving. They're not giving us much time."

Everyone jumped as they followed Gold's orders, getting ready. There was constant mumbling and some cursing as they worked; patients grimaced in pain when moved.

Colonel Fritz Eichenstat was so disoriented at seeing Gabriella he had no immediate notion of what he could do. All he knew was that he had to get to her. But what then? His brain burned hotly inside his head. His temples ached. He was nearly delirious. He watched her. She turned and went out the other side of the tent. Instinctively he followed her. German soldiers were everywhere now, watching. Within a few minutes wounded American soldiers began being carried out of the tents on stretchers; some were walking unsteadily, medical staff helping them.

Eichenstat knew that he could not let Gabriella once again fall into the hands of the Nazis. He would have to help her escape. Easier said than done. The soldier whom Skorzeny had assigned to him as his driver and who would accompany him on their mission to disrupt things behind enemy lines waited in the jeep. The man was a dedicated Nazi, Eichenstat could not forget that; if he did he would likely be dead. But he was going to be dead no matter. This sudden new conflict was going to lead to his demise, maybe Gabriella's as well. He desperately needed to come up with some kind of scheme to get her to safety.

"Captain," he heard the German commander say. "Shouldn't you be on your way west?"

"Where will you take these people?" he asked the man.

"Back down that road we just came in on."

"Prisoners slow us down," Eichenstat said.

"Would you have me shoot them all?"

"Of course not," Eichenstat replied.

"What else can I do? I have my orders to circle this end of the town and remove any enemy I find. These are not combatants. I have no choice, slow us down or not. Finding them here in our way was not my idea of a favorable circumstance." He turned away and left. "Good luck on your mission," he said to Eichenstat.

Eichenstat knew his time to do something was running out. He began to look for Gabriella, he poked his head in the closest tents, then moved to the next ones. He turned to see her coming out of a tent some distance away; she was carrying a suitcase and seemed to be having a hard time of it. She was headed straight toward him, her head down, shoulders hunched, lugging the suitcase.

When she got close enough he said, "Gabriella."

Her head popped up and she nearly stumbled. He caught her. The suitcase fell to the ground. "It's Fritz, Gabriella."

"Good Lord! Good Lord!" she cried. "No, it can't be! It *can't* be!

Two German soldiers nearby were watching this event unfold. When Gabriella fell and Eichenstat caught her they laughed.

He pushed her away. "Don't cry all over me, woman!" he said loudly. "Pick up your suitcase," he continued, sounding authoritative. "Here, I'll help you." He leaned down and retrieved the suitcase.

The two soldiers walked off. An American soldier came out of tent nearby. He paused, standing with one crutch and a bandaged foot. He hunched himself against the cold.

Instinctively Gabriella said to him in a stammering voice, "Can ... I ... help ... you, soldier?" There was a near rage running through her body now. She had never felt so confused and bewildered. She made a motion to go to the soldier, then stopped awkwardly, looking back at Fritz. Her legs wobbled, then she fell to the ground. He bent to pick her up. The soldier hobbled over. He peered down. Fritz put his hand beneath Gabriella's head and lifted it slightly. She opened her eyes.

"Oh!" she cried, moving as if to regain her feet. "Oh! This can't be!"

"She's exhausted," the soldier said. "Maybe she's frightened by what these huns might do to her."

Eichenstat said in English, "Move on! Get in the truck!"

"Sorry, Sir," the soldier said.

From behind them another soldier said in German, "We have to get out of here, Sir." It was the jeep driver.

The American soldier who was just walking off turned back and stared at the two of them. "What the hell ... is going on?"

Eichenstat spoke in English. "Get moving soldier. Get in the trucks."

"You're ... not Americans. You sneaky bastards! Why the hell do you have on American uniforms? Bastards! Sneaky fuckin' bastards."

Gabriella struggled to her feet. Fritz helped her. She had heard the outcry of the soldier with the crutch. She inspected Fritz and the other soldier who had spoken in German to him. She looked into Eichenstat's face. "Fritz?" she said.

"Sir," the jeep driver said once again in German. "We must move along. We will miss our deadline. Commander Peiper is counting on our deceptions. His tanks could be already ahead of us. We must confuse the enemy. That is our plan. Bastogne is nearly surrounded now."

Colonel Fritz Eichenstat had made his decision.

"Let's go, Sergeant. I'm taking the American woman and this wounded soldier with us."

"Why? They ..."

"They could help us make our deception better don't you see. We are taking this soldier to get medical care. The nurse here is assisting us. That's our story. That's our deception if we run into any American units."

The Sergeant smiled. "Excellent, Sir," he said in German.

They all headed toward the jeep.

They passed the German officer who commanded this unit, the one who had spoken with Gold.

Eichenstat told him, "Taking two of them with us. Help fool the enemy if we are stopped."

"Innovative," the officer replied.

Fritz took Gabriella by the arm. "Not a word from you," he told her. "Help the soldier, Sergeant," he said to the jeep driver.

After they had all arranged themselves in the jeep and were ready to pull out, Colonel Gold yelled at Gabriella. "What ... where are you going with these men? Who are you?" he asked Eichenstat, not recognizing him from the unit and seeing his rank.

Eichenstat drew his .45 pistol and pointed it at Gold. "I decide where the prisoners go, Sir!"

"It's ... all right, Sir," Gabriella said. "I am helping this soldier and we will be joining the convoy when it leaves."

"Move out, Sergeant," Eichenstat ordered. The jeep jumped forward and disappeared into the fog.

"What the hell is going on?" Gold mumbled as he stared after them. "An American Captain points a .45 pistol at an

American Colonel and ... Shit!" he cried. He was still unsure. Someone called for him. His mind switched into another gear.

After Eichenstat's jeep had driven for about a mile they reached a sharp right-angle turn in the road.

"Stop, Sergeant," he said.

The Sergeant hit the brakes.

"Get out," Eichenstat ordered him.

The Sergeant looked over at Eichenstat. Eichenstat had his .45 aimed at him. The expression on the Sergeant's face showed his bewilderment and surprise.

"Sir?"

"You'll meet up with one of our other units. They'll be coming by soon."

"Sir?"

"Do as I order, Sergeant! I have no time to waste!"

The Sergeant began to obey the order but he did so with a motion that kept the right side of his body toward Eichenstat. When his foot hit the ground he made a quick reach with his hand and wrapped his fingers around the barrel of the gun. He pulled it upward while twisting it away from him. Eichenstat yanked backward. The Sergeant wrapped his arm around Eichenstat's upper body and the two men fell out of the jeep. The gun went off. The two kept rolling and grunting, breathing heavily, snow covering their uniforms, each trying to get the pistol. Gabriella jumped out of the jeep and was now on her knees beside the struggling men. The suddenness of the Sergeant's action and what she was witnessing made her mind go fuzzy. Time itself seemed to stop; she couldn't move. As she watched she kept telling herself to do something. She tried to think, but there was nothing. There came another shot, this one muffled by the two bodies and the snow. She jumped, hearing the subdued pop. One of the men grunted.

"Uhhh."

Eichenstat stopped fighting, he went limp. The Sergeant rolled over, pushing Eichenstat away, the gun resting in his open hand. In one quick motion Gabriella grabbed it a split second before the Sergeant's hand came down where the pistol once sat. He started to get up, keeping his angry eyes on her face.

"Shoot the fucker!" The American soldier in the jeep yelled.

Gabriella pointed the pistol at the German. He was laboring to catch his breath. Hunched on one knee the German's face told her he was about to lunge. He seemed almost daring her to shoot.

"Pull the fuckin' trigger, girl!" the American soldier screamed again. "He'll kill us!"

She squeezed the trigger. She saw the dreaded look in the German's eyes. The bullet struck his throat, hitting his artery. Blood splattered her and made hissing noises as droplets landed on the snow. Still on one knee, the Sergeant went limp and slumped next to Eichenstat. The two lay side-by-side, motionless in the disturbed and red splatter snow.

Gabriella stared at the dead German. She was shaking, the pistol still held tightly in her trembling hands. Then she dropped it. Her heart was pounding.

"Good job! Good job!" the American soldier cried.

She looked up at him, then back at the motionless body of Fritz Eichenstat. She crawled over and touched him. Fearing the worst. He lay on his side. She pushed him on his back.

"Gabri . . .ella," he said, his eyes barely open.

She tried to move him but it was too much. He was a big man, dead weight now.

"I ... can't ... move, Gabriella." He partially raised himself with his arms. "I'm hit, I believe. Yes, I know I am."

She glanced at the dead German. His eyes were open, staring at her.

"Can you help, soldier?" she asked the soldier in the jeep.

The American soldier was weak and hobbled from the wounds to his leg. The morphine was beginning to wear off. He grimaced as he worked his way to her. He stared into Gabriella's face. She knew what he was thinking.

"It's all right, soldier. This man and I are old friends from Germany. We went to school together." Then she thought enough to say, "Now, because of the fates of war, he is our prisoner."

"He's wearing an American uniform," he said bewilderingly.

She didn't know what to say.

"He'll be shot!"

She was slowly regaining a clear head. "Only if he recovers from his wounds. We don't shoot wounded prisoners." It was a thought that sickened her.

The soldier shook his head. "Let's just leave him."

"If we run into any Germans he could save us."

He nodded, flinching slightly in pain. "You're right. Didn't think of that."

"Help me."

Together they managed to get Eichenstat into the back seat of the jeep.

"Can you drive this thing?" she asked. "I'm afraid I would have a tough time."

"What choice do we have." He twisted his body and got behind the wheel.

She climbed in the back with Eichenstat.

"Which way?" the soldier asked.

"Bastogne is behind us."

"So are the Germans, remember. Our station was overrun and everyone captured."

She thought.

The soldier fussed. "Shit! We're fucked!"

"At least we know what's behind us. Up there in front we don't know . . .in the dark we could be fired upon by either side! Our best chance is back toward Bastogne," she said.

The soldier started the engine and worked the jeep into a position to turn around. "Bastogne here we come."

As the jeep rolled past the dead German dressed in the American uniform she looked down. His wide, once fearful eyes were directed toward the sky. She thought they were condemning her. The jeep's wheels began to spin.

"Easy does it!" the soldier said to himself.

Gabriella held Eichenstat's head in her lap. "Where are you hit?"

He grimaced. "I think ... I can't move my legs."

The night around them was pitch dark and misty with icy cold fog. The going was slow. She expected to be fired upon at any moment.

Gabriella held Eichenstat tight. "Fritz, why are you here? Why the American uniforms? Do you know . . ."

He coughed as he tried to speak. "Diversions," he managed to say. "Pretending to be American officer."

"Bastard!" the soldier said.

"Hush, dear Fritz," she said.

"Jesus Christ! We're going to get our asses blown off out here in the middle of this fuckin' snow covered piece of foreign shit soil and ... you two ... Christ!" He banged the steering wheel with his two fists.

It was so surreal, Gabriella thought. Was this another of those God-given moments; an opportunity to complete some journey, to finish something. It was too convoluted to have come about by coincidence. Mere chance could never have produced this end. She looked at Fritz.

"Are you in pain?" she asked.

"Screw him!" the soldier said.

When they drew near to where the clearing station hospital had been set up they crept ahead carefully. They listened, but there was only the still silence of the night. They entered the area, then stopped, checking. Everyone was gone. They picked up the faint noises of motors fading in the distance.

"That must be the Germans going back to ..."

"To Houffalize," Eichenstat said almost inaudibly. "They'll be sending sentries back very soon. Keep going."

The several American trucks that had been set ablaze during the German attack were now only sending up light smoke from their bullet riddled, unworkable remains. Much material from the company was strewn about. Gabriella and the soldier looked into the darkness down the road toward Bastogne. Soon they could no longer hear any motor noises and it was deathly quiet again. The snow was falling more heavily now. All was quiet. Their breathing caused an added fogginess around them.

Eichenstat was breathing hard, deep breaths. He hurt badly now.

"Gabriella, hold my hand, please."

"Christ!" the soldier mumbled disgustedly.

Gabriella reached over and held Fritz's gloved hand. Her other hand touched his face. This was the father of her son, William, she thought. He was trying to save my life, the life of the mother of his son. The life of the one he wanted to be his wife. It was far more than that. God would not allow this to end here. Something else waited for her.

"Let's move forward, Soldier," she said.

The jeep inched along steadily. The cracking of the snow and ice beneath the wheels was the only sound they heard. Then came the sudden distant boom of heavy guns; a moment later the shrill whining of shells flying overhead.

"HALT!" A voice in the darkness cried.

The soldier jammed the brakes hard; the jeep slid forward and stopped. Two American soldiers emerged from the side of the woods, rifles pointed. They came closer, warily observing them. "Don't make any sudden moves," one said. "What unit you from?"

"The 326th Medical Company," Gabriella replied. "We ... escaped. The company was captured by the Germans just moments ago, back there a mile or so."

The soldier came over and looked at Fritz. "He badly hurt?"

"He's a fuckin' German!" the soldier behind the wheel said angrily.

The other sentry shifted the bolt on his M-1 rifle. "Maybe all of you are," he said.

"What!" the soldier behind the wheel said. "If I were a German would I ..."

"Yeah, yeah. We have been warned about such infiltrators. What's the password?"

"How the hell should we know!" the soldier replied. "Look, ..."

"Tell me, what's a Tom Mix?"

Gabriella hear the soldier's words but they meant nothing to her. She had been trained in password and recognition but ... this question was ..."

"A Tom Mix is nothing, but Tom Mix is a cowboy movie star, you asshole," the soldier driver replied.

The two sentries looked at each other.

"Who's Costello and Abbott?"

"Abbott and Costello," the soldier answered again. "We're Americans, except for that guy lying there," the soldier added.

"The Corporal here, is she American?" one of the soldiers asked. "Looks to be."

"She's okay," the soldier replied. "She's a nurse in the 326th. She was helping me and some other guys when ... the Germans busted in on us. Shot up the place pretty bad."

"They wouldn't send a woman to do ..." one soldier remarked, looking at Gabriella.

"Seems right," the soldier said. "Okay, get goin'. Tell the commander about the 326th being captured. That's what probably happened to that truck that was headed there with some wounded. We never saw the truck return this way. They probably got captured too. Poor bastards."

The soldier shifted the jeep into gear but held his foot on the brake.

"Hey," one of the soldiers said. "If this guy is a German, he's in American garb. He will likely be shot as a spy."

"No shit!" the soldier said.

"No," Gabriella cried.

The two sentries eyed her, unable to make sense of her objection.

"That's usually the way it is," one of them remarked, shrugging; he then came over and inspected Eichenstat more closely. He looked up at Gabriella. "Is he hit bad?"

"Seems bad, but we're gettin' out of here," the soldier driving the jeep said. The jeep began rolling. The two sentries were left stomping their feet in the snow.

The jeep crossed into the perimeter of the town of Bastogne and soon found what appeared to be the main street. It was a mass of activity. They asked for the closest medical station. When they arrived at the station on one of the side streets Gabriella

"Watch this man," she said. "I'll get some help."

She jumped out and ran into the building. There were injured soldiers sitting and lying in different places and positions. She looked for the commanding officer. Then she saw a Lieutenant. She went to him.

"I'm Corporal Sommers," she said. "I must report that the 326th Medical Company has been captured. I escaped ... and"

"We had some hint that the 326th was captured. You are sure?" the Lieutenant asked.

"I was there. I escaped. There's ... a Captain ... outside. He's wounded."

"Well, get him in," he told her. He looked around then ordered two men to go with Gabriella.

They brought Fritz Eichenstat inside and stretched him out on a table. The Lieutenant began examining him. Gabriella stood beside the table and helped take off some of his clothes.

"He was ..." she did not finish.

Fritz Eichenstat was not conscious. Gabriella took off his gloves and rubbed his hands continuously, trying to make them warm. He was pale.

"I believe there's internal bleeding," the Lieutenant said.

"Are you a surgeon?" Gabriella asked.

"No."

"Is there one nearby?"

"There are several but they have their hands full with other casualties."

"Yes, of course," she muttered. "He can't move his legs."

"Spinal wound, maybe," the Lieutenant said.

They pulled off his overcoat, then a jacket. Now the bloody clothes underneath showed.

"Oh, God," Gabriella whispered.

"May have severed an artery," the Lieutenant said, looking more closely. "There's been a lot of blood lost."

"Oh, Fritz," Gabriella said. "Dear Fritz."

The Lieutenant looked at her.

She replied weakly, "An ... old friend."

"Sorry."

Gabriella knew it was bad. There were not many such injuries amid this kind of mayhem and confusion that had favorable outcomes. She wanted so much to cry but knew she could not.

Suddenly there was a screech of an incoming German artillery shell, then a gigantic explosion that shook the building, caving in a portion of the front wall, knocking bricks and chunks of mortar down on the soldiers. Dust swirled upward, choking everyone in the room. Then there was another explosion farther down the street. The vibration rolled through the building a split second later, shaking it for a second time.

Gabriella held on to keep from falling. She looked up at the ceiling, waiting for the roof to give way. It was holding. She was all right, she realized, but there was mayhem all around her. She looked at Fritz on the table. Dust covered him. Soon, those still standing and away from the front wall began running to those near the front. All she heard was crying and moaning from soldiers underneath the rubble of brick, wood, and chunks of mortar. She inspected one soldier; he was dead, a large piece of mortar on his head. The dust was floating downward now. There were still soldiers lying motionless. The open spaces in the front wall gave Gabriella a good view of the outside street. As she worked at moving debris she got closer. She looked out. She had never seen a shell crater up close right after it had landed. The jeep in which had brought her to Bastogne was upside down and bent in half. Bodies of dead and injured soldiers were scattered about. She counted at least four who appeared dead; many more were wounded. She then looked at the dead soldier closest to her and recognized him as the young man who had been in the jeep with her. His legs were gone.

"Oh, my God!" she whispered, then turned away, unable to look.

With that soldier's death she knew that the fact that Fritz was a German soldier masquerading as an American soldier would not be immediately revealed, but it had taken the violent death of this young man whose disfigured, torn body was now draped across a pile of stones to seal her secret. She knew she was responsible. She leaned against the wall, feeling she was about to lose control. Moments later she struggled back to the central part of the room, stumbling on the pieces of the building that now covered the floor. The Lieutenant was back standing at the table, Fritz's body still in place, his face totally unrecognizable because of the dust. She went to him.

"He's dead," the Lieutenant said.

She did not hear another word he said after that.

"I'm sorry. He may have been dead when you brought him in."

All she could do was stand there and look down at Fritz Eichenstat, the father of her child. She brushed the dust off his face as best she could. His pale face looked nothing like what she remembered of him from their school days. Now she would never know what he had been doing for the past few years. They would never talk again, never argue, never discuss philosophical things, never fight the good fight together, never ... discuss St. Augustine, or Aquinas, or St. John of the Cross, or that horrible Nietzsche. They would never travel together to see America. They would never ... For them, together, it was over.

"We need the table, Corporal," she heard the Lieutenant saying.

Before she knew it two soldiers were taking the body of Fritz Eichenstat away. They carried it to another room.

As she watched them the Lieutenant said, "Grave Registration will have to take it from here."

It jolted her mind. She quickly followed the two soldiers into a room in the back. As they placed Eichenstat's body on the floor she asked them, "Are there any grave registration personnel here now?"

"Over there," one nodded.

She saw a man bending over one of the bodies and taking down information on a pad. He then fastened a tag on the toe of the dead soldier and checked the man's dog tag. She approached. He was not an officer.

"I'm with the division's medical unit," she began.

He looked up, then got to his feet. "Your problem?"

He addressed her in a tone she did not expect.

"That man ... that body over there," she pointed. "May I talk to you about that individual."

"Sure, but make it quick."

They walked to Eichenstat's body on the floor.

"Yeah?" the soldier said.

"He is not an American soldier," she told him.

His eyes widened, then he looked down at Eichenstat.

"He's got on American uniform, insignias. What do ..."

"Let me explain," Gabriella said.

"Maybe you'd better."

"I only want to make sure that his body is correctly identified. You see he and I were friends in school years ago in Germany."

The soldier's brow went up.

"You tellin' me the truth?"

"His name is ... Please write this down. Make sure your records show that I was the one who told you this so that afterward the proper authorities can contact me for verification. Here is my serial number. I am Corporal Gabriella Sommers and I am a member of Major William Barfield's Medical Company attached to the 101st Airborne Division. We ..."

"Hey, slow down," he said. He had not written down a thing she had said. "Begin again, please.

She then spent the next few minutes making sure that the body of her friend was properly identified. When she had finished she asked, "Can you think of anything else that might be needed? I know this is an unusual situation."

He frowned again. "Yeah, it is. I can't think of anything else. I'll make sure it is done."

"Thank you."

She looked at Fritz once again, for the last time.

"Tell you," the soldier said. "They probably would have shot your friend if he had not died. American uniform? What was he doing?"

She said weakly, "Struggling to be a descent human being, I believe."

She knew the soldier could not understand.

Bastogne was now surrounded and for the next five days those inside defended their positions heroically. She found Major Barfield who had managed to find his way back into the town after taking that ambulance convoy to the 107th Evacuation Hospital at Libin, escaping the capture by the Germans of the clearing station. For the next several days he and Gabriella worked with other stragglers of the 326th and a mixture of other medical personnel from other medical units to put together a formidable cadre of people who provided as much medical care as they could. Supplies were short at times, especially morphine and plasma, and at times, penicillin. Surgeons were particularly in short supply. To counter this deficiency several surgeons from other units outside the besieged Bastogne volunteered to make risky trips into the town by glider and Piper Cub. On December 27th a road into the town was opened. The wounded now had a way out to a clearing station, then to an evacuation station.

The next day Major Barfield relinquished his command to a new commanding officer who then accompanied the unit to Camp Mourmelon, France to train replacements and re-equip the 326th. Gabriella was not part of this new deployment. She volunteered to join with another medical unit and stayed with the 101st in Belgium.

The German's counteroffensive in the Ardennes had failed in its objective. The Americans were close to moving full force into Germany now. By January twentieth, according to the stories circulating, Germany was on the verge of total collapse. There were more and more incidences of Germans retreating, forming weaker and weaker defensive positions, being pushed aside and retreating even more. British Field Marshall Bernard Montgomery was preparing to move into the Ruhr Valley and strike at the heart of Germany's heavy industries. The city of Aachen was immediately in front of him. In Late January the 101st was ordered to leave Bastogne and was trucked to the Alsace-Lorraine region where they were position in the town of Haguenau on the Moder River. There they faced the Germans who were in position on the far side of the river. The air was full of the feeling that the war was winding down. Still, casualties occurred. Deaths were modest in comparison to Bastogne, but the feelings of anger and sadness still struck Gabriella when she witnessed them. The same thoughts went through her head each time she witnessed a soldier's death in the hospital bed, or on the operating table, or one who was brought in already dead. She thought of those in the poor man's family who would never see their son, or father, or husband alive again.

She and Lieutenant Gordon, now a Captain, worked in the same sections much of the time. Finally, on February twenty third the division was relieved and they spent the next few days packing and moving back to Mourmelon, a truck trip of some one hundred and sixty miles. Mourmelon, a camp about one hundred miles from Paris, provided the rest she needed. It offered the rest everyone needed, none more than the troops who had been under the daily stress of combat, fearing much of that time that maybe they would not get home. The thought was universal: maybe I'll get this close to coming out of this war alive and then fate will step in and I'll be killed in some freakish way. That kind of thinking only added to a soldier's stress.

MARCH 15, 1945
CAMP MOURMELON, FRANCE

A big surprise came on March fifteenth when General Dwight Eisenhower came to decorate the 101st with the Presidential Unit Citation for its heroic defense of Bastogne. It was the first time in American history that a unit as large as a division had been presented with this particular citation. She was proud to be a witness to the ceremony, knowing, as she did, a number of the men present who had lived through those awful frigid days at Bastogne. Life has a strange way of unfolding, she thought, watching Eisenhower make the presentation to the division's commander, General Maxwell Taylor. She was fortunate in having a good view of the main event. In a quick turn she thought of Fritz Eichenstat and she wondered where his body was now. Then she frowned, shaking the cobwebs out of her mind. She would have to find out, one day.

A week before Eisenhower's visit the word had spread fast that the Americans had captured the Ludendorff Bridge over the Rhine River at a town called Remagen and had poured across large bodies of troops and vehicles. It was a stroke of good fortune. Two weeks later the Americans made another crossing of the Rhine, this time at Oppenheim, a small town seventy miles to the south of Remagen. It was there that troops of the Fifth Infantry Division, part of General George Patton's Third U.S. Army, had pushed across and established a bridgehead. It was another good break for the Americans.

But it was the bridge at Remagen that was the true prize. It was a city Gabriella had visited several times, mostly to see the great cathedral. It was a beautiful city. She had even stood on the banks overlooking the bridge that was now the prized possession of the Americans. Finding the bridge still standing was a gift from God. Surely many lives and much valuable time was saved in being able to make a bridge crossing rather than making the dangerous assault over water to get to the other side. She imagined that it would not be long before the Americans would be moving into Köln. After all, it was only twenty miles to the north of Remegan. In her mind's eye she could see GIs entering the city and working their way through the remains around the great cathedral and eventually through the neighborhoods. In time, some would make it to her convent. What would they find? Would Mother Superior be there to greet them? How about the other sisters? How many were still alive?

Suddenly she felt a sadness. Her life was far from what she had envisioned it would be on that day when she had taken her final vows. How did it all happen, she wondered? How did it come to this? Was God truly behind this? Many could not believe that a loving God could allow such horror to engulf so many. She grew sadder thinking of it all. Then she realized that such questions were all part of her ongoing search. She was always searching. She was still trying to put things together, to make sense. God gave her a brain, she would use it, she had always said. Her training had been burned into her bones. She knew no other way. But it was a search that could cause more than a few aches. For on many occasions she could not find the totally satisfying answer, the perfect, beautiful answer she hoped for. However, not searching would be a sacrilege. It would be a denial of who she was. Like it or not, she was caught. She would have to continue and somehow learn to live with the answers she found. At times she admitted that her life could end without contentment; true understanding was always a long way off, she felt. It was a thought that only made the sadness grip her more tightly.

Being able to keep working was a blessing. It was during such times that her mind had to be focused on the business at hand; she could not afford to lapse, and when she was working the things at hand gave her brain a momentary rest from too much contemplation.

Of course, her son, William, was in her thoughts much of the time; he was always there in the back of her mind. It brought her happy, brief respites. She was now standing alone at the end of her tent. The flaps were open. She had been there for some time casually watching the activities going on across the way. Then, once again, she looked down at the photograph and thought of the reason this boy had been conceived in the first place. So many people took so many chances to make sure she and her unborn child would have a chance to survive. So many. Each of their faces flashed before her. Those faces had been with her a long time; they were with her always, as were those of her mother and father. The fates of many of them were unknown to her now. How many were still alive? She knew of only two who were not: her father, and Fritz Eichenstat. The others she could only guess about. One day she would find out.

She put the photograph back in the leather folder and placed it in her pocket. She had to get some rest; she was scheduled for duty that evening.

59

APRIL 1, 1945
CAMP MOURMELON, FRANCE

Everyone was now watching the Ruhr Valley. That was where the Germans were about to be surrounded and cut off. The military was calling it the *Ruhr Pocket*. At Camp Mourmelon the word was out that the 101st Division was moving to the west side of the Rhine near Dusseldorf to aid in this encircling effort. The division's mission would be to guard a part of the west side of the Rhine extending from Worringen on the west side of the city of Cologne up to the town of Wesel to the north where Field Marshall Montgomery was sending his troops across the river into the Ruhr Valley. Worringen, the town where part of the division would be stationed, was not Köln proper, but it was close enough for Gabriella.

This was her chance, she thought. If she could go along with the 101st she might be able to move south through the city and get to her convent and see first-hand what shape it was in. She could learn who might still be alive. She immediately hurried to see Major Moore, the officer who had replaced Major Barfield as commander of the 326th Medical Company.

"I haven't received any orders and frankly, I don't expect to," he told her. "Looks like we'll be staying here."

"I must get to Köln," she told Moore. "This may be my best chance."

From the look on Moore's face she thought that he was clueless as to why she insisted on doing this. She was wrong.

"I know something of your reasons, Corporal," he said. "Major Barfield wrote me a brief letter about you. He said you are an exemplary soldier, one with a very unusual background."

"Yes, Sir."

He smiled, leaning forward over his desk.

She persisted. "Isn't there *some* way for me to go with the division?"

He was silent for a moment, then shrugged, sitting up now ramrod straight. "Have you considered the fact that there is still fighting inside Cologne. It's sporadic, but still there's an element of danger."

She pondered, peering into the distance. "Maybe, but ... there has to be a way."

"You are aware that much of the city has been ... totally destroyed," the Major added. "Almost nothing left standing. I know that's something you don't want to hear but ..."

She looked away. "I must go and see."

Moore shook his head. "You'll get there eventually. Besides, I've heard that most of the people left the city long ago for the rural areas and smaller towns. The place is probably abandoned, except for a few German soldiers."

"The sisters would not have left," she replied.

"I wish I could help you, Corporal. I can't assign you to some outfit and then have ... if something happened ..."

"Thank you, Sir." She saluted.

She spent the next several days wracking her brain as she watched the division move out. A week went by, then two. She spent those weeks in a state of mild desperation, thinking the opportunity was slipping away. No matter what she did, she could find no solution. She remained in Mourmelon.

In the middle of April the division along the Rhine received orders to leave and head to Bavaria. When she heard this she knew her best chance to reach Köln had evaporated. As had happened two weeks earlier, her medical unit was ordered to remain in Mourmelon. There was plenty to do in camp. Wounded soldiers were still arriving from the front.

Once in Bavaria the division's mission was to secure Hitler's famous retreat at Berchtesgaden which it did with little difficulty. Almost immediately Berchtsgaden proved to be the next thing to heaven on earth. It gave the men relief from the constant weariness of having to live in the field and sleep on the ground or in shabby, torn-up buildings. For once they had the best accommodations and, to the pleasant surprise of many, alcoholic drink of all kinds which they found in the wine cellars. For the men of the 101st it was a fitting end to their ordeals.

On May 7, 1945, the Germans surrendered to General Eisenhower at Rheims, France. The war in Europe was officially over. In Camp Mourmelon celebrations were jubilant and often

a little rowdy. There was too much pent-up emotion that had to
be unleashed. When Gabriella heard the news she went inside
her tent and knelt beside her bunk and began to pray. She had
much to be thankful for. She prayed for her son, she prayed for
her mother and father, she prayed for Fritz Eichenstat, she
prayed for Father Konrad Schroeder, she prayed for Sabastian
Arceneau, she prayed for all the men and women of the 101st
Airborne Division, she prayed for all those who did not survive
this war, she prayed for Bishop Micara, and Bishop Cicognani.
She prayed for Colonel David Gold, the chief surgeon of the
101st and Lieutenant Daniel Gordon and all the members of the
326th captured at Bastogne and still not heard from; she asked
God for their safe return home. She prayed for Sister Marie
Magdelene, Mother Superior of her convent in Köln; she prayed
for the sisters at St. Bernard in Nashville, she prayed for Anna
and Herwald. There were so many. She began to cry, sobbing so
heavily that she shook. She collapsed onto her flimsy bed
weeping uncontrollably. There was so much to unburden, she
thought.

Gradually the noisy celebrations taking place outside came
drifting to her. There was laughing, and crying; everyone was
overjoyed and emotions rushed out in all forms. Celebrations
and feelings that people were now having were coming from
such depths and were those that a person might experience only
once in a lifetime, if ever. A war like this had never happened
before - it had affected nearly everyone on earth in some way.
For so many people, the effects had been profound. Life had
changed; everyone could feel it.

Eventually she walked to the end of the tent and looked out,
wiping her eyes with the back of her hand.

"Gabriella! Gabriella!" yelled one of the nurses with whom
she worked regularly. The woman was in a ring with other men

and women holding hands and moving wildly in a large circle, singing joyously.

"Come on, Gabriella. The war is over! It's over!" she yelled.

Gabriella offered a smile and waved, appearing happy. She had the feeling that many of the people she was watching would never again celebrate with this much utter joy in their hearts. That alone was a sad thought.

MAY 15, 1945
CAMP MOURMELON, FRANCE

Gabriella had spent the week following the surrender of Germany caring for the wounded and working with all the new people now assigned to the 326th. During all that time she did what she could to find some way to get to Köln. She saw only failure. One afternoon that suddenly and unexpectedly changed when she was called to the office of Major Moore. She entered and quickly walked over. She saluted Moore at his desk. Out of the corner of her eye she saw a man standing by the window. She turned her head; it was Michael Duncan.

"Hello, Corporal," he said with a slight grin.

Her face brightened. "Hello, indeed," she replied.

He nodded and came forward and shook her hand. "It's nice to see you again."

"It ... is, yes," she said haltingly, trying to regain her composure. "Why ..."

He shrugged. "Another mission for the man," he said. "Preparations for a big conference. He wants me to ... well I'll tell you later." He looked at Major Moore.

Moore already knew what Duncan had come for. He said to Gabriella, "Corporal Sommers, I'm granting you a week's leave. You need rest."

Gabriella looked at Moore. "Sir?"

He grinned. "A pass, Corporal. You have a week off."

"I ... a week?" she flustered. "Thank you, *Sir!*"

She then looked at Duncan with narrowed eyes. "Is this your doing?"

He nodded sheepishly. "You might say that."

She returned her inquisitive stare to Moore.

"He's a persuasive man," Moore said to her.

"Why?" she asked, looking at Duncan.

"I understand you want to go and see your convent in Cologne," Duncan said.

She was dumbfounded. "I do indeed. I've been ..."

"Well, we'll try and arrange it," Duncan told her.

"How?"

"We'll discuss that later. Let's get out of here. Would you like to have dinner?"

"I ... well, most certainly," she managed to say.

"Major, we'll be leaving," Duncan said, moving toward the door.

Moore now had a broad smile on his face.

As Gabriella and Duncan reached the door, Moore said, "Corporal, I told you that Major Barfield had written me about you."

"I remember."

"He failed to mention some of the people you know." He gave Duncan a look.

Duncan was grinning.

After leaving Major Moore's office Gabriella and Duncan walked to her tent. Inside she stood near her small bed, thinking, waiting.

"I'm not sure what to do," she said.

"Pack some things," he told her. "Civilian things if you have them."

"No, I have only military uniforms."

He laughed. "We'll have to get some in Paris," he told her.

"Paris!"

"The best place."

"We're going ... to Paris?"

"For now, yes, then we'll head to my meetings, then off to Cologne."

The mention of Köln made her perk up. "How did you know?"

"Major Moore told me," he told her.

"Why are you here?"

"Gathering information, like I said."

"As you were before when you were in London."

"That's correct."

"After Paris I go to Ike's headquarters in Versailles; see some people, and then off to Cologne."

"You'll come back here to get me after your meetings?"

"No," he grinned. "No, you'll be coming with me if that's all right. No use making a long trip back here after my business is done."

"This is all happening so ... quickly," she said.

"Well, it's simpler this way. Can't keep driving all over. We'll go to Paris, get you some civilian clothes, then ... I believe I can arrange accommodations in Paris for the night. Tomorrow we'll head to Versailles. Then, when I'm finished there we'll head off to Cologne. I'll see if I can arrange to have some troops assigned to us and get proper transportation to help us get to your convent. How's that sound?"

She was overjoyed beyond belief. God had finally answered her prayers, she thought.

Paris was a little less than one hundred miles away from Camp Mourmelon. Duncan had an army jeep and a fast driver. The road was not crowded until they reached the city, then they had to slow down. It was five o'clock. The place was alive with both soldiers and civilians. The streets were bright with lights; cafes were crowded, shops were numerous and they sped past their fronts.

"Is there merchandise in all these stores?" she asked.

"Enough, I suppose. They'll be more very soon, I imagine."

Her hair was blowing. It felt good. She hunched down to gain a little protection.

He laughed.

She did, too. The new surroundings, the freedom, the brightness of the streets, everything presented a new, more cheerful atmosphere. She felt her spirits being lifted.

"Let's see what's available in the shops," he said, tapping the driver on the shoulder as an indication to pull over.

They climbed out.

"We could be a while," Duncan told the driver. "Keep an eye on our belongings, please."

The driver nodded. "Yes, Sir."

Gabriella was observing the people up and down the street.

"Let's try this way," Duncan said. They headed off, weaving back and forth as they passed people. They came to several clothing stores with garments in the window. He pointed. "How about it?"

She stared at the display.

"Go inside and try some of the things on," he said.

She did; he waited. She came back out. "They're too expensive."

He laughed. "I'll cover it."

She shook her head. "I can make do with what I have."

"Wouldn't you like to dress in civilian clothes after all these years?" he asked. "I'll cover the cost."

"Please, no."

"How about if I give you a present. Do me the favor and make me feel good. I'd really like to have dinner in Paris with the only charming woman I know of in this lovely city. You need to celebrate, I need to celebrate. Please, for me."

She laughed. "You do have a way with words."

"My bread and butter," he replied.

He followed her back into the shop. An hour later they came out. He was carrying a large bag, she had a small one.

"Thank you for the dresses and the pair of shoes and the accessories," she said.

"Don't mention it."

They reached the jeep and climbed in.

"I have to find you some accommodations," he said as they sat there.

"Where are you staying?" she asked him.

He laughed. "Don't know yet."

The driver turned around. "Want a suggestion?"

"Lead the way," Duncan said.

Within fifteen minutes they pulled up in front of a quaintly decorated three-story building that looked to have been built by a committee many decades ago, maybe several centuries. One could not always be sure in a city with so much history.

Duncan addressed the driver. "Corporal, you know of this place? Is it ..."

"Respectable?" he asked. "Oh, yes. You'll be pleased."

"You believe they will have accommodations available?"

"The officers in my outfit have been using it," he said. "Would you like for me to go inside and arrange for a room for you and the Corporal?"

He laughed.

"Two rooms, Sergeant. Two rooms."

The soldier recoiled. "Jesus," he said under his breath. "I'm ... sorry Ma'am; sorry, Sir. I ... well ... ahh hell."

Gabriella laughed, relieving his embarrassment.

"I'll handle this, Corporal," he said to the driver as he got out.

A little while later he came out. "We're all set," he said. He turned to the driver and said. "The owner at the desk saw you through the window. She told me that any friend of Corporal Bull Norris deserves the best accommodations in the place. Seems you're well known is these parts, Bull," Duncan said, laughingly."

"Glad to be of help, Sir," the driver replied, half sheepishly.

"Pick us up tomorrow morning here at eight o'clock. We'll be heading to Versailles," Duncan told him.

"I'm yours for the duration, Sir."

60

MID-MAY, 1945
VERSAILLES, FRANCE

Corporal Bull Norris had been accompanying Gabriella around the grounds of Versailles Palace for the past hour, ever since they had dropped off Michael Duncan and watched him head off to his meetings. Gabriella had seen photographs of Versailles but none of them presented the same feelings of beauty and majesty as seeing it in person. They were out of the jeep and walking. The weather was ideal.

The Corporal finally worked up enough courage to say, "About yesterday, Ma'am," he began.

"No apology is necessary, Corporal," she replied, sensing what was on his mind.

"Thank you, Ma'am. It's okay if you want to call be Bull, Ma'am," he said. "My real name is Jimmy."

"I'm Gabriella," she replied.

"Word around is that Mr. Duncan is a big shot."

"Big shot?" she said. "Oh, yes, I see what you mean."

"From Washington. That's the word. Some of the guys are saying he's from the White House direct."

"Yes, I have heard that too."

"You believe it?"

"Makes no difference does it? He's a nice fellow."

"Seems to be. He must be a big shot being able to go inside that building where all the brass hang out. They seemed to be expecting him."

"I'm certain of it."

My Captain said to give Mr. Duncan whatever he wants."

"Did he?" she said, smiling.

"This is a big place," he said.

"Magnificent."

"Are you and Mr. Duncan old friends?"

She smiled. "You ask a lot of questions don't you Jimmy?"

"Sorry, Ma'am. So sorry. I ... I'm sorry," he stammered

She laughed. "Mr. Duncan helped me out once way back when."

"Oh, I see."

"Without Mr. Duncan's help things in my life would have been much different probably. For one thing, I would not be in the American military. I would not be here in this place right now."

"How so, Ma'am?"

She turned and looked at him.

"Sorry, Ma'am. I ask too many questions."

"It's a very long story, Jimmy."

"Mr. Duncan says you want to go to Cologne after he's finished here. That right?"

"That's correct, I do. I guess you'll be goping along."

"If Mr. Duncan says."

They continued walking. Eventually after several turns they got back to where the jeep was parked.

"I better check in," he said. "I'll be right back. You'll be okay here?"

"I'll ride with you."

As they drove up they saw Duncan talking to a man whom Gabriella thought she remembered having seen before. She saluted as she walked up to them.

"Corporal, you do remember General Robert McClure," Duncan said.

McClure returned her salute.

"That night in London, yes," she replied. How are you, General?"

"About to depart for home," he said. "Stateside."

"It's been a long war," she said.

"Too damn long. Duncan says you want to go to Cologne."

She looked at Duncan. "I do, very much."

"The General has provided some help for us,"Duncan said. "He's providing a small plane; we can fly to Cologne. We'll have some company when we get there and they will look after us and help us get to where you want to go."

"Thank you, General," she told him. "This means a great deal to me."

"Duncan has told me a little about you, Corporal. I hope you find things as well as can be in Cologne."

Her eyes dropped. "I have heard some of the things about what has happened there. I'm ... bracing for the worst, I suppose."

"I've seen some of the aerial photographs," McClure said. "It's pretty bad."

Again she lowered her eyes. "I know," she said dispiritedly.

"If I can help in any other way let me know," he said. "But I'll be leaving soon, so ... well Duncan knows who to call on here if you need help. I've given him some names. I wish you all the best, Corporal."

"Thank you, Sir," she said, then saluted.

After General McClure had disappeared back into the building, Duncan called over to Corporal Norris who was babysitting the jeep.

"Norris, I'd like for you to come with us to Cologne for a few days?"

"My orders are to remain with you as long as you need me, Sir."

The plane touched the ground in a small grass-covered field ten miles from Cologne and rolled bumpily to a stop near a tree. It was clear the passengers were glad they would be able to walk around again.

Two jeeps were approaching. "Must be our escort," Duncan said.

The jeeps arrived just as the plane's passengers climbed down to the ground. The lieutenant in the lead jeep jumped out. Gabriella and Corporal Norris saluted. He saluted and introduced himself as Dominic Torribelli.

"You with General McClure's unit?" Duncan asked.

"My orders are to give you any help you might need. We'll be staying in Kerpen. It's a small town right over in that direction. Easy trip into Cologne tomorrow morning. I know the main roads in. They've been checked for mines."

"We'll follow you then," Duncan said.

The houses in Kerpen came into view after a short drive and they had made it to the top of a small rise. The town seemed almost untouched by the war. Their accommodations were more than Gabriella expected to see. At this stage she would have gladly slept on the ground in weather like she had experienced in Bastogne if she had to. She was finally going to make it to Cologne, finally. Before she fell off to sleep she said a prayer.

The following day Duncan told her that they would fly over the city and get some bearings as to just where they would be headed. They used the great Cathedral as their reference. It was not difficult to locate the general area using the large Aachener Pond as her guide. From there she could pick out the wide Aachenerstrasse immediately north of the pond.

She directed the pilot. "That way."

He banked the plane and headed west, following Aachenerstrasse.

She spotted the convent grounds right away. Her heart sank.

"Can we get lower?" she asked.

"Treetop if you like," the pilot said.

"Not quite that low," Duncan replied.

They went down. The pilot banked once and they were right above it. Everyone's eyes searched the scene below. Duncan watched Gabriella's face.

"My God," she whispered. "My ... God." She began to cry.

The pilot took the plane in a tight circle several times around. They saw no people at first, then someone appeared from behind the debris of a partially crumbled down wall. The figure was dressed in a nun's habit. She looked up as they passed over and held her hand to her eyes, shading them from the glare. Gabriella could not tell which of the sisters it might be.

"I'm sorry," she said. "Forgive me."

Duncan took her hand. She did not react, she squeezed it very tight as they flew around for another pass. She relaxed and Duncan released his hold on her hand.

"Seems we could make it there rather easily," he finally said after they had completed another pass over the remains of the convent. The nun was now gone.

When they got back on the ground at Kerpen they drank some coffee and then assembled some equipment and loaded the two jeeps. They drove straight for Cologne, arriving from the west.

An hour later they were on Aachenerstrasse inside the city proper. Now that she could reach out and touch the rubble she thought the devastation seemed far worse than she had seen from the air. The road was passable requiring only minor twists and turns but there was debris cluttering every street she saw. She saw no buildings still in anything like their original condition; almost all had their roofs caved in, along with much of their walls. There were huge holes in the ground. Where once entire buildings had stood only heaps of wood and brick and stone where present. Here and there dazed and dreary looking people stumbled around in the rubble, searching through the debris. American military personnel were stationed on the corners, sometimes in jeeps, sometimes in trucks; a few tanks were on station. More often than not the soldiers stood smoking, smiling, relieved. Now that the shooting had stopped they could look forward to a longer life and get the chance to see their families again.

As they continued driving she tried to remember the names and locations of the side streets, the ones that crossed Aachenerstrasse. She knew they were getting close when they passed Stadtwald-Gurtel on her right. Klosterstrasse would be just two blocks ahead, and the main entrance to the convent.

Corporal Norris continued maneuvering the jeep around all the debris from bombed out buildings whenever they impeded their passage.

She scanned the street ahead, anticipating the mess she would see at Klosterstrasse.

"Easy, Bull," she said. "Here it is."

Bull stopped the jeep.

"Down this street," she instructed.

Corporal Norris turned right and inched the vehicle forward.

She looked ahead and saw the entrance only fifty feet away, or what used to be the entrance. She wasn't sure she wanted to see what was behind the jumble that was once the wall. The jeep went forward and stopped. They were now directly in front of the convent. No one spoke; they only looked in the direction of the convent buildings.

"No one," Gabriella said after a brief inspection

"We saw one person for sure when we flew over," Duncan reminded her. "There could be more. Only one way to find out."

Gabriella looked at him. He nodded. She nodded.

"Let's go, Bull," Duncan said.

Norris and the other jeep rolled ahead, then stopped.

The main buildings were right in front of them, or what was left of them.

The main building had no roof at all and nearly all of its walls were in ruin. Gabriella thought she saw a collapsed desk mixed in with bricks and stones in the location where Mother Superior's office had been. The pages of torn and ripped books fluttered here and there among the rocks. The several smaller buildings that encompassed thr main structure showed a similar state of destruction. There was one exception. The building had a good portion of its roof still in place and its walls were in pretty good shape. Its roof did have several small holes most likely made by falling blocks of stone thrown from the exploding buildings nearby. Not a single standing wall had any windows left intact, just open spaces where wood and glass once stood.

Gabriella began to choke up. Her mouth was suddenly dry and she could not swallow.

"Does anyone have some water?" she asked.

"They guys in the back jeep must have," Corporal Norris said. He stopped and jumped out. He was back quickly with a canteen. Lieutenant Torribelli was with him.

"Anything we can do?" he asked.

Duncan shook his head.

Gabriella twisted the top of the canteen off and took several large swallows. She got out of the jeep and began walking slowly toward the entrance of what was left of the main building. The massive front doors and their frame were still upright; the walls on either side had been reduced to half their normal height; their once organized stones were now piled in a line marking the former presence of the wall itself. A good number of their stones had been thrown out and were now sitting isolated in the open ground. The small bell with the leather handle still hung in its place by the main entrance, just as she remembered it. Habit and tradition told her to ring it. She did. The sound it made seemed almost ghostly, for in its new surroundings its vibrations traveled back and forth against the now collage of rubble all around it whereas before, in the days when she was living here and the walls were still up and the roof still on, this tiny bell was snug in its housing and gave out a pleasant tone. No more. The bombs had changed all that. The bell's tone had recorded the structure's recent torture.

She heard movement in the back, around the far, partially destroyed wall. A nun appeared. She was young; her habit was dirty, ragged and worn. She moved slowly, cautiously as she stepped through the debris, trying not to stumble. She came closer and Gabriella walked toward her, doing her best to avoid the loose rocks and stumps of broken wood as she moved.

"Hello," Gabriella greeted her with a gentle voice when the two were close.

The nun gave her a slight bow. "How may I be of service," the nun asked.

"What is your name?" Gabriella asked.

"Christina," she said.

"What name have you taken as a sister?" Gabriella asked.

"I am a novice," the girl replied. "I have taken no name."

"I'm Gabriella Sommers. I was once a sister at this convent."

The girl blinked, not quite sure what to say.

"Sister Katherine," she told the girl. "That's the name I chose."

"Oh!" the girl said. "You … oh."

"Are there any other sisters here?"

The girl's head went down, her eyes looked away from Gabriella. "They … we have been … some left … they are not here any longer," she managed to say.

"No one is here but you?"

"Mother Superior … is …she's ill though."

Gabriella jumped toward the girl and grabbed her arm. "She is here! Take me to her, please! Please!" She began dragging tugging as she tried to walk. "Where is she?"

The girl's feet got tangled and she nearly fell. Duncan was behind her and grabbed her with two hands.

"What's the story?" he asked Gabriella after restoring the young girl to a state of stability.

"There are some people inside, I believe," Gabriella said.

"Let's take a look," he said. He turned to the others and told them to remain outside for now.

Duncan, Gabriella, and the nun walked around the fallen walls and went into a small structure, the one that had most of its roof still in place except for a few holes. Gabriella remembered it well; she remembered all the buildings as they once were. The side walls were not as complete as they appeared from a distance; small sections were open but there was more to these walls than any of the other buildings. As was true of the other buildings this one too had no windows in place, only open spaces where once the wood frames of glass sat. There was only one door. The girl led the way. Gabriella knew the layout of the rooms inside. She remembered how the room was always bright with the light from the large four-lamp chandelier and the many lamps positioned around the room. That was no longer. Things were different now. It was a dreary looking room with lurking shadows and too many darkened places formed by the flickering of the three candles. There was a small pot hanging above a tiny fire over near the side wall. The aroma of cooking food floated in the air. Her eyes darted, searching for Mother Superior. Her step quickened as she moved to the second room. She saw the woman on the bed. She rushed forward.

"She is weak," the girl said from behind her.

Gabriella knelt down beside the low bed.

"Oh, Mother Superior. It's Sister Katherine. It's Gabriella," she said close to the woman. She reached for her hand and took it. The woman opened her eyes and smiled instantly.

"Dear Sister Katherine. You ... Oh how much I have prayed to see you once again. You are alive."

Gabriella broke into tears. Her head fell over the woman's breast. Mother Superior caressed her.

"Sweet Gabriella, sweet Gabriella. We have missed you," she whispered. "God has watched over you."

Duncan came over and stood beside the young girl.

"My friends have brought me to you, Mother Superior," Gabriella said.

Mother Superior's eyes looked past Gabriella to Michael Duncan, standing to the side. Gabriella got to her feet.

"Why are you dressed like that, Sister Katherine?" Mother Superior asked.

"I am a member of the United States Army, Mother, but I am on leave. These are regular civilian clothes I purchased in

Paris while I am not on duty. I'll tell you all about it later after you gain your strength."

Mother Superior said bitterly. "A soldier. A soldier like Colonel Eichenstat," she said. "So many soldiers, so many, so much destruction, killing. Our sisters and the people we had living here. All dead, gone," she said. "Colonel Eichenstat left us stranded here. He never returned. We ..." her voice faded. "They came after he left us. He shouldn't have left us."

Gabriella's heart sank. What could she say. She fought to say something. "Don't blame the Colonel, Mother Superior. He didn't want to leave. He was taken away."

"You loved him, Katherine?"

"In a very special way, yes, Mother."

Mother Superior smiled. "I could see the signs. It's no sin. I do know now he was a good man. I always didn't think so."

Gabriella looked at the young girl standing beside her and asked, "Has there been a doctor here?"

The girl shook her head. "No doctors around," she explained.

"We can change that," she said, looking at Duncan for approval.

"I'll get the others," he said.

Mother Superior did not want to leave the convent. Gabriella knew what the place meant to her and did not fight her resistence. Gabriella performed several simple tests and asked her some questions and determined that the only things the woman needed were a steady intake of nutritious food, and rest.

"Is there any running water here?" she asked the young nun.

"No, Ma'am."

"Where are you getting your water?"

"The well in the cemetery."

"It could be contaminated," Gabriella said. "Bad water."

"I boil it all."

"Still, we might be able to improve that."

"We could bring in fresh water," Duncan said. "I'm sure the boys outside will have little trouble with that."

"I'll remain here. Have them return with water and food supplies and ... any chance of getting a generator and ..."

"I think I know what you will need here, Gabriella," Duncan said. "Let's see what the guys can do. I am not privy to what's immediately available."

After Duncan and the others left Gabriella went about seeing what she might do to make things better. She had not lost sight of the fact that she had to return to Camp Mourmelon in four days. There was not much time.

Late that afternoon, a truck pulled up outside the crumbled walls of the convent. The two enlisted soldiers under Torribelli's command began unloading the supplies they had brought. Corporal Bull Norris gave them a hand. Several minutes later a jeep drove up. The officer next to the driver got out and came over to Gabriella and Duncan.

"Word is you need a doctor here," he said.

"Not a serious case, Captain" Gabriella said.

"Captain Roger Ball," he said. "The town of Kerpen is one of my stations."

"We have two patients inside, Captain."

An hour later, after examining Mother Superior and the young nun he was ready to depart and return to Kerpen. Before leaving he gave Gabriella and Duncan his diagnosis.

"The older nun is just malnourished and worn down. She's pretty healthy otherwise, I think. The young nun is the same. Nutritious food is what they need. If they get it they will be back to normal in a week or two."

"I'll arrange for them to get some good food."

The soldiers had long ago finished unloading materials.

"What's the plan?" Lieutenant Torribelli asked Duncan. "We staying, or going back to Kerpen?"

"I'm remaining here," Gabriella said, checking with a look at Duncan.

"I'll remain here as well," he told Torribelli.

"That means me too," Norris added.

"No, Bull, you go back to Kerpen. There's no reason to stay. Just check back tomorrow. We'll take things from there. Tomorrow, maybe the day after, I will have to head back. My schedule is getting tight and I have reports to present to my boss."

Gabriella tried to persuade Duncan that he did not have to remain at the convent, but had no success.

"I've still got time," he told her. They spent the remainder of the day getting things in place.

"I informed the Lieutenant that after we leave here I would appreciate it if he would check in here regularly," Duncan told her after they ate the evening meal.

"They are going to require a lot of help," she said. "All these poor people are going to need help, lots of it. The whole city is in ruins."

"The aftermath of a gruesome war."

"Will they survive? How will they survive?"

"For now all we can do is try to help the two who are here. Uncle Sam has plans to begin caring for the immediate needs of the others."

"You have been a good friend," she said. "I could not have done this without you, just like I could not have gotten into the Army without your help."

"We do what we can," he replied.

"You are so modest," she smiled.

They were sitting alone at the one small table in the other room from where Mother Superior and the young nun now slept.

"We've been so busy we have not found sleeping arrangements for ourselves. I suppose there are no beds around," Duncan said. "Are there?"

"I doubt it."

"Well, at least we have some blankets the boys brought."

"Before I leave I'll try to see if I can get some better mattresses and bedding for Mother Superior and Christina. The linen and blankets are a help but they could use more," Gabriella said.

That night they both slept on the floor, each using several blankets folded over to act as mattresses. Gabriella was the first up in the morning. It was barely daylight. She checked on Mother Superior and Christiana. She prepared breakfast and Mother Superior and Christina devoured the eggs and bacon and fruit that she put before them. The two glasses of powdered milk went down eagerly as well. Gabriella and Duncan ate the same, but less of it.

Mother Superior's complexion improved quickly, yet, her energy returned more slowly. She was a strong woman and Gabriella knew she would rebound in time.

"Much to do," she kept saying.

"You must rest," Gabriella told her, but the woman was insistent.

"I must show you something before you leave." She got up slowly and began walking toward the wide open area on the other side of the building. It was clear she was still weak and unsteady on her feet and their walk took extra time. Gabriella held her arm. Duncan hung back.

"Come along, Michael," Gabriella said.

The three of them were soon in the grounds of the convent cemetery. There were quite a number of bomb craters and down trees. The cemetery had been struck numerous times. They maneuvered around the craters and the dislodged chunks of earth and stone that now littering the grounds. Mother Superior pointed. "It's over there," she said to Gabriella. "Your mother's grave."

"I know, Mother Superior," she replied.

Mother Superior halted her slow shuffling walk.

"I have a small map showing the exact location," Gabriella told her.

Mother Superior took up her walk again. "Colonel Eichenstat," she then said.

"I received a single letter from him."

"Where is he?" Mother Superior asked with a caring tone. "Do you know?"

The question brought a lump to her throat. "He's dead, Mother," she said sadly. "I was with him. It's a long story."

"I so sorry, Gabriella. He seemed such a tortured man."

"Yes, I believe he was," Gabriella replied. "He was caught up in a ... foul circumstance and ... couldn't find an honorable way out. I didn't help him much either."

They walked some more. Duncan walked behind them as Gabriella and Mother Superior moved side-by-side.

"He brought your mother here, you know."

"Yes he said in his letter."

"Your mother told me the story. Would you like to hear it?"

Gabriella stopped walking. "I think I need to hear it."

"Your mother was proud of you, Gabriella."

"I made her so unhappy," Gabriella said.

"She was content when she died. I told her all about your work for the convent and what you were doing for so many people. She hadn't known. I also told her what Colonel Eichenstat was doing too. He saved many lives."

"But at a terrible price to his tormented soul. He was playing one set of people off against another; to save one he had to condemn another. How does one rationalize that! Or, live with it? I'm sure he felt like he was playing God."

"God will be kind to him," Mother Superior said.

"I pray for him every day."

Gabriella stared down at the grassy spot and the small flat plaque that was partially covered by dirt and debris. She bent down and brushed it all aside to see it better. She looked up at Mother Superior in bewilderment.

"Everyone in this cemetery has a plaque just like it," she told Gabriella. "The Gestapo paid us several visits after Colonel Eichenstat stopped coming around looking at them."

"Colonel Eichenstat worried that such a thing would happen if he were no longer around," Gabriella said.

Mother Superior picked up a broken piece of a tree branch and leaned on it, holding it like a cane. "They emptied our convent. Women, children, and a few men. That was all. We never received any more people after that. But by that time ... well, we had no more buildings and no supplies. But I have a book that has all the proper recordings showing all the correct personal data about everyone who had been here during that time. It's buried under the rubble of my old room."

"Tell me, Mother Superior, do you know anything about Father Schroeder? The priest from Aachen?"

The woman drew a deep breath. "They finally caught up with him," she said. "That's what I heard."

"The Gestapo?"

"We heard about it from a messenger from the Bishop's office. After Aachen was taken over by the Americans in September Father Schroeder and twenty or thirty others still in the town volunteered to act as city officials and help keep the place running. Well, during that big battle around Christmastime over around the Ardennes Forest the German Army returned and occupied the city again. They executed everyone who had worked with the Americans. Father Schroeder was included. That's what we heard. I could be wrong. Maybe it's not true."

"It's true," Duncan said from behind them.

Gabriella and Mother Superior both turned to face him with surprise.

"How ... why would you know such a thing?" Gabriella asked.

"Because Father Konrad Schroeder had a loose connection with the Gregory Foundation and Sabastian Arceneau. General McClure, the man you've met, Gabriella, has been running American intelligence in Europe for some time and he learned of the deaths from American soldiers who recaptured Aachen from the Germans. Father Schroeder was executed by a Gestapo firing squad."

Gabriella put her hand over her mouth and closed her eyes. She shook her head and walked away a few steps. "Everyone of good faith, all the good ones die," she moaned.

Duncan came closer and put his arm around her.

"He is in heaven, Gabriella," Mother Superior said. "Along with your mother and father and Colonel Fritz Eichenstat."

"She's right," Duncan whispered.

She leaned against him. "What will my life be now?" she said. "After all this?"

That night Gabriella had a hard time falling asleep, burdened by thoughts of all the things she had learned that day and knowing that tomorrow they would be leaving the convent. Whenever she did sleep it was not a deep sleep. Sometime during the night as sleep once again began to creep up on her there came a noise, breaking the silence. She listened. Someone was walking around. Then she heard scraping sounds, rocks being moved, and then some heavy breathing. She sat up and got to her feet. In the corner Duncan remained sleeping. She quietly walked to the doorway and listened. The sounds were more distinctive. Then she heard someone mumbling, almost a fussing at something. She made her way quietly toward the sounds, squinting to try and see better in the dark and to remain quiet. The sounds were coming from outside the building. That was when she thought maybe it was someone scavenging. She moved cautiously. Maybe she should wake Michael, she thought.

Then she heard the person say, "Here it is."

Gabriella knew the voice. It was Mother Superior. She also realized she was standing not far from the pile of rubble that once was Mother Superior's room.

"Mother Superior?" Gabriella whispered.

"I found it Gabriella! I found it!"

Gabriella walked closer and the figure of Mother Superior came into view more clearly. "Found what, Mother? What is it?"

"Your box," she said. "The one the German soldier brought from Colonel Eichenstat. It is here. I had forgotten all about it."

Gabriella looked at Mother Superior. "A box? Where?"

Mother Superior pointed to the ground. "There. It was not destroyed."

Gabriella knelt down and moved the box. It was not large, or heavy as she lifted it. It was made of wood and had several German seals stamped on it in black. She stood up with the box in her hands.

"Open it, Sister," Mother Superior said.

"Not here," Gabriella replied. "I must have more light, and a table."

"Do you know what is inside?"

"No, Mother."

"It must be something very special for Colonel Eichenstat to have it brought here for you."

"Yes, it most likely is special, very special I have a feeling."

They both moved carefully through the rubble and darkness and went into the room where Mother Superior had been sleeping and closed the door. Gabriella put the box on the table and lit one of the candles.

"Sit here, Mother. You must be tired," Gabriella said.

"Open the box, Dear."

"Yes."

Mother Superior sat down.

Gabriella looked at the box. "It is sealed tight," she said. "Maybe we should wait until morning and we can find something to open it with."

Gabriella spent the remainder of the night back in her makeshift bed thinking of the box which she kept beside her. She imagined all kinds of things. It was frightening and exciting all at the same time. Her anticipation was almost like what she remembered feeling as she waited to open a birthday present from her parents. Slowly the early morning sky turned brighter as daylight approached.

Michael Duncan rolled over. She was looking at him.

"Sleep well?" she asked.

"Well enough. And you?"

"Not all that well," she said. "I couldn't stop the turmoil in my mind from yesterday. And then last night I learned a most unsuspecting thing. It seems Colonel Fritz Eichenstat left some things for me here at the convent. Mother Superior remembered it in the middle of the night and began stumbling around trying to find it under all the debris. She was fussing and pushing rocks around, making all kinds of noise. But she found it. That's it right there," she said, pointing. "That's the box the Colonel left me."

He looked over at the box.

"It's tightly fastened with metal brads," Gabriella said. "And I could not find anything to open it."

Duncan got to his feet and made a slurping noise with his mouth. "I need to brush my teeth," he said as he came over and looked at the box. "We should have no trouble opening it."

He excused himself and turned away.

"Coffee is brewing. You want a cup?" she said.

"No sugar in mine," he said, leaving the room..

When he came back he found Gabriella and Mother Superior sitting at the table. Gabriella handed him a cup of coffee.

"Let's get at that box," he said.

"Open it, Sister," Mother Superior said.

"Maybe I should be alone when I open it."

"Would you rather?" Duncan asked.

Gabriella could see the disappointment on Mother Superior's face.

"No," Gabriella replied. "It's probably just some incidental keepsakes Fritz wanted me to have. Can you find something to open it, Michael?"

"This should work," he said and took out a Swiss Army knife and pulled out one of the blades. "Here you go."

The metal brads came out without much trouble. When the last one was out Gabriella lifted the top off. It was filled with sawdust packing. She brushed some of it aside. On top was a fat brown paper envelope. Beneath that was a smaller letter-size envelope with the words *Sister Katherine* written on it. Beneath that was a package wrapped in brown paper and tied with a string. There was nothing else. She laid each of the items on the table. She lifted the larger envelope and unfastened the metal clasp and turned it so that the contents slid out. There was a folder of papers and some photographs. One set of papers was bound in a heavy red cardboard and tied up with a red string twisted around a metal clamp. She unwrapped the string and the folder opened.

"Looks like legal papers," Duncan said.

Gabriella began reading. "Oh," she said. "Oh, Fritz."

"What is it, Sister?" Mother Superior asked.

Gabriella whispered. "It's Colonel Eichenstat's will," She said. "He . . ." She frowned at the papers as she flipped from one to the second and last page, reading quickly. "Oh, Fritz."

Duncan looked at them over her shoulder and read what he could.

"My guess is that Colonel Eichenstat left his entire estate to you Gabriella, and his son, William Staffan."

"How can that be?" she asked.

"Well, in the new Germany you will have to file a claim based on this document." He shrugged. "See what happens, but it looks legal enough. It says here," he pointed. "that the particular papers are in a bank in Berlin. There's a deed to a house and a bank account. When things settle down you'll have to hire an attorney in Germany and file the necessary documents. A probate of sorts."

"Oh," she said. "Oh, Fritz," she repeated.

She put the papers down.

She then lifted the letter-sized envelope. "I'll wait to open this," she said. "I'll open this last. Maybe it will explain things."

She then reached and took the package wrapped in brown paper and unwrapped the string that was around it. She unwrapped the paper. It was a book with a worn brown leather cover. "Oh, Fritz," she mumbled. "Dear Fritz."

"What is it, Sister? The book?" Mother Superior asked.

Gabriella shook her head and turned the front of the book so they could see the title - *Of the City of God.*

"What's it mean," Duncan asked..

"It's a special book, an important Catholic book," Mother Superior said.

"Why did he send it to you, Gabriella?" Duncan asked. "Do you know?"

She managed a smile. "We often fought over the ideas in this book. It's written by St. Agustine. We also fought over Augustine's other book, *Confessions.* The Colonel was not a big believer in such things," she said. "But I believe he was a good man, given what he had to face."

"I'm sure," Duncan said.

Gabriella then began going through the photographs. "His family," she said. "His mother, father," she said, holding each one. "His brother and sister, I believe," she continued. The last one was a small photograph. "The Gottingen campus," she said, staring at the photograph. "Fritz, Herwald Burkitz, and me." she informed them.

"You were such a pretty girl, Gabriella," Mother Superior said.

"Yes, Mother. Fritz thought so too."

Open the other envelope," Mother Superior urged..

Gabriella fumbled with the envelope.

"Would you rather do it alone?" Duncan asked.

She hesitated. "No. I am comfortable."

She used her fingernail and broke the sealed flap. There was only one page inside. She read silently. Tears formed in her eyes as she read. She sobbed lightly. "Oh . . . Fritz."

Mother Superior put her arm around her. "Can you tell us, Dear?"

Gabriella read the letter aloud. "Dear Gabriella, I borrowed this book from the Gottingen Library years ago and never returned it. I guess that makes me a thief unless, maybe, you could one day return it. I tried, Gabriella, to find and understand the strong pull this man Augustine had on you. I tried his Confessions and then went to this City of God in hopes of understanding this man who took you from me. I failed. I guess I didn't want to admit to myself that he was a far better human being than I could be and that you were better off with him then with me. Take care of yourself, and William. I hope you will have a fulfilling and happy life. All my love."

She began to cry more heavily.

Mother Superior hugged her tightly.

Duncan could only watch.

61

EARLY JUNE, 1945
CASTILLO STREET BRIDGE
SANTE FE, NEW MEXICO, U.S.A.

A worn and slightly dented automobile slowly moved over the bridge on Castillo Street in Sante Fe, New Mexico and came to a stop. On the other side of the street a short, chubby man with a round face got up from a bench, walked toward the vehicle, and got in. As he did, he lifted the large envelope that lay on the seat and placed it in his lap. The car moved off again, and for the next ten minutes Klaus Fuchs and his passenger did not speak. They drove back and forth across part of the city, the driver repeatedly checking the rearview mirror with an anxiety he tried to mask, suspiciously eyeing every automobile in their vicinity. Finally he parked at the end of a dead-end street. The passenger patted the envelope on his lap.

"A sizable delivery," he said.

Fuchs looked at him with a placid yet pleased expression. "There are those who will appreciate what's inside, I'm sure of it. It could be the final piece."

The passenger nodded approval. "There is someone else on the inside who has been helpful as well with such things."

"I am not surprised," Fuchs said.

The chubby man gave a shrug, "Who knows? Others could be there, too."

Fuchs shook his head. "So, my work is being checked?"

"I could not tell you," the chubby man shrugged.

"Of course."

The passenger asked, "Is there any other news?"

"The device will be tested soon, probably within the month."

"Where? A place in the desert; codename *Trinity*. I am scheduled to be there," Fuchs told him.

"Very convenient for us. I don't believe any of our other friends will be attending."

"Too bad, it could be a grand show."

"Only if it comes off as planned," the passenger replied.

Fuchs grinned. "Some of the notables are placing bets. Even Oppenheimer himself."

"For success, or failure?"

Fuchs frowned. "Success, I assume, but there is a tension about one point. Bethe and Kistiakowsky are anxious about something, I believe."

"What?"

"Don't know for sure. You know Los Alamos. The compartmentalization of the work makes it difficult for any one person to see what another is doing, especially if they are working in another division."

"I thought you said Oppenheimer eliminated compartmentalization as being too restrictive on the flow of ideas."

"He tried, but General Groves insisted it be kept in place."

The chubby man shrugged. "Too bad."

"It makes it more difficult putting together a firm package of all the critical ingredients. Of course, that's the whole purpose of compartmentalization, to enhance security, after all. Only when we have one of our large, joint sessions can you get an idea of some of the other kinds of work being done and how one piece might fit with another."

The passenger thought, then said as he put his hand on the door handle. "Until our next meeting then."

He then got out, taking the envelope.

AUGUST 6, 1945
HIROSHIMA, JAPAN

A single bomb, codename *Little Boy*, was dropped on the city of Hiroshima. Estimates were that approximately 70,000 people were killed in the original blast. News stories said that the bomb was a nuclear device that had been developed at a secret laboratory in the small town of Los Alamos in the mountains outside Sante Fe, New Mexico.

AUGUST 9, 1945
NAGASAKI, JAPAN

While the Japanese military and civilian authorities debated their situation after the Hiroshima bombing another bomb, codename *Fat Man*, was dropped by the United States Army Air Corps on the city of Nagasaki, killing approximately 40,000 people. This bomb, like *Little Boy*, was a nuclear device and was also built primarily at Los Alamos.

AUGUST 15, 1945
WHITE HOUSE
WASHINGTON D.C., U.S.A.

Word came to President Harry S. Truman that representatives of the Empire of Japan had announced their country's surrender.

It meant that an invasion by ground troops would not be necessary! Military officials in Washington had been in the late stages of planning for just such an invasion. Everyone had been expecting a long and bloody engagement, and estimates of American casualties had been put as high as one million. The American's experiences on Okinawa had shown that the Japanese soldier would fight to the death with no inclination to surrender. As a result, American casualties had been high. Planners feared the same, or worse, would occur on the Japanese main islands and Washington had doubts the American people would support such losses among their fighting forces. The country was weary and worn out with war. As it was, even after the bombs had been dropped and everyone could see the destruction, there were still plenty of Japanese military who wanted to fight on and defend the homeland. There was even a coup in the works to overthrow the Emperor and have the military rule the country totally.

For those American GIs who were unlucky enough to have been selected for the invasion force, *Fat Man* and *Little Boy* most likely saved their lives.

SEPTEMBER 2, 1945
THE BATTLESHIP U.S.S. MISSOURI
TOKYO BAY, JAPAN

Representatives of the Showa Emperor, *Hirohito*, the self-acclaimed quasi-divine leader of the Japanese people, climbed aboard the *U.S.S. Missouri* and one by one signed the instruments of surrender under the watching eyes of General Douglas MacArthur and thousands of servicemen from all the Allied countries. When all the dignitaries and representatives had signed, World War II was declared officially over.

SEPTEMBER 19, 1945
SANTE FE, NEW MEXICO

Klaus Fuchs had new information from Los Alamos to pass on. Once again he met with his contact in Sante Fe, this time near a small church. Fuchs then drove his old Buick into the hills. The envelope that Fuchs handed over had a statement regarding his impressions of the explosive test at Trinity along with data about the rates of production of plutonium and Uranium 235. He included the fact that sintered nickel was the material used within the barriers for separating Uranium 235 from 238.

His contact held the envelope. "I suppose Kistakowsky's and Bethe's concerns were unfounded after all," he said.

Fuchs exhaled heavily. "No, they apparently were real. Few knew about it but they had discovered a serious miscalculation regarding lens configuration using the material they were using. Seems no one thought to take into account the atomic nature of the material being used for the lenses. They had ignored that in their calculations of shape. It's a delicate calculation, it turns out."

"They must have worked it out quickly. After all, the thing went off," the man sitting beside Fuchs said. "Hell, you saw it. The Japanese witnessed it; twice!"

Fuchs raised his eyebrows, then smiled with resignation. "Bethe called a meeting afterward. I forget the exact date, about two weeks afterward. It was there that he announced the solution, and how they had come by it." As Fuchs finished this statement he laughed.

"What's so funny?"

Fuchs shook his head. "The fellow who made the correct calculations and worked out the mathematical relationship between the atomic nature of the material being used and the shape of the lens was a guy who joined Los Alamos at the last minute. They brought him over special from England. His name is Herwald Burkitz. According to Bethe it was Burkitz who saved the day."

"Had you ever heard of Burkitz?" Raymond asked. "Did you get to meet him?"

Again Fuchs laughed. "Years ago, in Germany. Later, about 1939, he got out of Germany and came to England to study and we had some contact there as well." As Fuchs spoke he continued to laugh periodically.

"What do you think will happen to this fellow Burkitz now?"

"They should give him a medal."

"Will they?"

"Probably not, but they will use him. Already I have heard they are making advances to convince him to work with Edward Teller on his dream weapon, *the super.*"

"Could this Burkitz be recruited to our side?

"Little chance, I think."

"You seem certain."

"You asked me."

"If he is with Teller they will surely try again."

Fuchs shrugged. "Not my worry now."

THREE YEARJ LATER
APRIL, 1948
WAJHINGTON D.C.

Herwald Burkitz walked into the old stone building that was part of the Smithsonian Institution known as The Castle. He did not know who it was he was to meet there. He had been told only that there was a man who requested to meet him and that it had to do with his work with Dr. Edward Teller and the Atomic Energy Commission. Burkitz went to the room, as instructed.

Two men were already there. One he knew, the other he did not.

"Hello, Herwald," one said.

"Hello Michael. How's Gabriella?"

"Doing fine. She's staying busy. Thanks for coming."

"What's this about?"

Michael Duncan gave the other man a look but did not introduce him to Herwald.

"Dr. Burkitz," the man began in a deep voice. He was not a very impressive looking man. He was nothing like Michael Duncan, but he had a seriousness about him, especially in his eyes. "We have followed your work with Dr. Teller," he said to Burkitz.

"Challenging work," Herwald said. "But mentally invigorating."

"And damn important," the man said.

"Yes, very."

"I'll get to the nitty-gritty, Dr. Burkitz. You are now a citizen of this country I understand."

Herwald was not sure where this was going. "As of last year, Sir."

"Well, Dr. Burkitz I assume you love this country. You swore to defend it."

"I did, Sir. I'm honored to do so."

"Well, your new country has a job for you that is a bit unusual, but vitally important to its security. We have been watching the way things have been going and we want you to accept the Russian's offer to spy for them."

Herwald went blank.

"A double agent, Herwald," Michael Duncan said.

"We know they have approached you" the unidentified man said.

Duncan broke in. "You have the temperament, the brains, and the security position the Russians want to exploit desperately."

The man behind the desk asked Burkitz, "What is the code name used by the individual who approached you? What name did he give you when he first contacted you?"

"That was back in 1946, Sir. He said his name is John, I believe."

The man opened a folder revealing a photograph.

"That's him," Burkitz said.

"He's now back in Moscow," the man said. "But someone else will replace him and probably contact you. When he does, we are requesting that you accept his offer."

"I know nothing of such business, Sir."

Duncan smiled. "We'll give you all the material to hand over to them. You'll continue in your position with Teller, of course, working on legitimate matters which the Soviets will not know about."

"May I think this over, Sir?"

"Naturally. But remember, your contact with us and this meeting is top secret," the man told him. "Mr. Duncan assures me that you know what that all means."

Burkitz and Duncan looked at each other.

THE SAME DAY
EVENING

Gabriella heard Michael come in the front door. She knew he would immediately head to the baby's bedroom upstairs and wake her up in order to play. She heard him take the stairs almost two at a time. She could not hear him but she imagined him talking to the infant in his playful gibberish as she had seen him do so often. She went to the bottom of the stairs just to have a better chance to hear the happiness in his voice. It was a sound that always made her heart fill with joy and contentment. She never got tired of hearing it. Duncan loved his new daughter so much and Gabriella could see it in her husband every time he was around the child. It was a special love a father has for his daughter. In Gabriella's mind a daughter had a different hold on her father, she knew. She couldn't explain it. It was the same way with her father, she thought.

The baby's half-brother, William Steffan, was next door playing with his friend.

Gabriella listened for a while longer and then went back to the kitchen. Dinner was about ready.

Michael came down the stairs holding the baby.

"She was awake," he said, following Gabriella into the dining room where she began putting out the silverware. "Must have been waiting for her dad," he grinned, raising the child in the air and putting his nose to hers.

Gabriella smiled to herself. "Of course she was."

He laughed.

"Anything happen in your world today, Michael?"

"Routine," he said in a matter-of-fact way, keeping his eyes on the baby.

"I got a call from Herwald," she said.

"Oh. How is he?"

"He said he is in Washington on business."

"Probably meeting with one of those scientists he works with."

"Would you go next door and get William." she asked, continuing to lay out the silverware. "And then you can come home and try and get your darling daughter to go back to sleep."

Michael again pressed his nose against his daughter's and grinned.

"My little Katherine," he said.

EPILOGUE

History records that a meeting in Sante Fe, New Mexico, as described in the last chapter, did indeed take place, although some of the dialogue is fictitious. The driver of the automobile was Klaus Fuchs, a German-born physicist and a spy for the Soviet Union, working within the confines of the large and secret laboratories at Los Alamos, New Mexico. The passenger who sat beside him was known to the Soviets by his codename: Raymond; his real name was Harry Gold. He was a chemist from New York, and the man responsible for seeing that top U.S. military secrets found their way into the hands of officials of the Soviet Union. Inside the envelopes which he took with him from that automobile was information of historic consequences.

LaVergne, TN USA
16 July 2010
189799LV00004B/51/P